A TEAM OF SEVEN

THE UNSANCTIONED ASSET SERIES BOOK 7

BRAD LEE

PART 1

SUNDAY NIGHT

1

THE VAN

Late Sunday night was darker and more deserted than expected for the city that never sleeps. A few vehicles drove south along the one-way street bordering Central Park. Historic buildings, mostly high-end condos, lined the east side of the road. The many mature trees of the area rustled in a gentle spring breeze.

Cars and SUVs were parked along the street in front of the condos, ready for their wealthy owners to drive to Long Island, Southern Connecticut, or the Adirondacks on the weekends.

A high-roof white work van, parallel-parked in front of a large SUV with just enough room for its rear doors to fully open, didn't fit in well with the luxury vehicles.

Inside, the rear compartment was a high-tech marvel, packed with video surveillance systems, communications equipment, and laptop computers. Two plush, high-back vinyl chairs faced a white shelf. Multiple computer monitors showed high-resolution views of the street from several state-of-the-art cameras hidden in an oversized roof vent.

Alex "Axe" Southmark, former Navy SEAL, was finally back in action after spending the last eight weeks recovering from injuries sustained on his last mission. He perched in the chair closest to the rear doors, dressed in a black long-sleeved shirt and black tactical pants that could pass as chinos. A loose black work jacket hid a plate carrier with extra magazines, a short-barrel M4 slung on his chest, and a 9mm pistol in a concealed-carry holster at his waist.

He self-consciously touched a black knit cap on his head—a reluctant concession to safety. An inner lining held polycarbonate plastic inserts—the same material used to make bulletproof glass. A second layer had rubber padding with air chambers. Together, they worked to cushion trauma to the head, spreading the impact over the entire area to lessen damage.

As good as it felt to be in the field, Axe had to face facts.

His time as a direct-action covert operator was over.

After his latest injury, the doctor's prognosis was sobering. "If you sustain more trauma to your head, you'll have severe headaches and slowed thinking at a minimum. Early dementia and other serious conditions are increasingly likely as well."

Because of that chilling reality, and his lack of conditioning—he was far from top fighting form—the van was parked two blocks, about two hundred yards, from tonight's expected action.

Axe was somewhere he'd vowed never to be: in the rear with the gear.

While no team could be effective in the field without the many dedicated support personnel focused on the success of the mission, that role had never been for him. He was a front-line, door-kicking, trigger-pulling warrior.

Until tonight.

The tactical beanie was uncomfortable. Axe poked a finger under it and scratched his head while waiting for events to unfold up the street.

Giving up the life of a warrior—retiring—wasn't an option. As much as he loved his side hustle as a nature and wildlife photographer, he had a lot to give to his country.

He could still use his strategic and tactical skills, along with his years of combat experience, to make a difference.

His solution was to take on retired Admiral Nalen's former role. Hands-on management.

Which had brought Axe to the cold van in New York City, as far from the action as possible while still technically being in the field.

"This sucks," he mumbled.

In the chair to his left, Haley Albright, his young protégé, kick-ass warrior partner, and intelligence analyst with the Central Analysis Group, worked the controls of the surveillance equipment. She was also frustrated not to be on the front line. But she knew too many intelligence secrets and couldn't risk capture.

She was also the president's adopted niece, which added its own set of complications.

Her days in the field were in the rearview mirror, just like Axe's.

"Yes, it definitely sucks," Haley said before returning to monitoring the video screens, waiting for their target.

As two of America's secret unsanctioned assets, they had taken the fight to the enemy and saved the lives of innocent people.

But their days of running and gunning were done.

"It's 11:40. Sitrep. Anyone have eyes on?" Haley asked in a quiet yet commanding tone that Axe heard both in the van and through an earbud that matched hers.

"Nice night for a stroll," smart-ass Doug "Mad Dog" McBellin responded over the comms with a grin in his voice. He was walking on the west sidewalk next to the park two blocks north, and the former SEAL wouldn't let Axe and Haley forget that he still got to play on the front lines while they sat on their asses in a van. "Perfect timing as usual, Blondie," he said, using Haley's call sign. "The target is leaving the mansion now. I'm parallel to him across the street."

"I'm falling in behind him half a block up," Mariana Rodriguez— "Tex"—said a second later. She had returned to her police officer roots, dressing as a New York City beat cop, complete with a black cold-weather beanie with NYPD in large white letters across the front, a black zip up coat with triangular City of New York Police Department patches on the arms, a badge above her left front pocket, and NYPD in large letters across the back. Mariana was short, with a curvy physique, light-brown skin, and dark, hard eyes. She had worked as a police officer in a small town in Texas for a few years before Axe recruited her to his team. Tonight, she played the role of a hardened New York cop to perfection.

"He's turning south toward the staff condo, as expected," Tex called on the radio.

The target, Petrov, worked as the executive assistant to a Russian oligarch named Vasily Chekov. Chekov was suspected of stealing polonium-210, a radioactive isotope used to assassinate America's Secretary of State.

Chekov may have also financed the cyberattacks on America eight weeks before.

Most nights, Petrov left Chekov's condo—the penthouse floor of a stunning residential building—near midnight and walked a few blocks south to another multi-million-dollar home just off Fifth Avenue that housed most of the oligarch's staff.

Tonight's mission was a chance to gather information. Tex and Mad Dog, dressed as cops, would stop Petrov and make the pitch: Petrov's boss was on a watch list. The United States suspected him of terrorism. Sooner or later, Petrov would have to make a choice—his freedom or his employer.

He'd have to pick a side. Petrov could report on his billionaire boss and be granted immunity from prosecution.

Or, if Chekov was as bad as they thought, Petrov would go down with him.

Haley didn't expect the threat to faze the guy. "If it were me," she'd said during the mission brief, "I'd bet on my multi-billionaire employer over the ineptitude of government agencies." She'd smiled in her predatory way. "But we're not the CIA or the FBI. We'll eventually figure out whether Chekov was behind the attacks. And if he was, it won't end well for him… or Petrov, if he chooses poorly."

No matter what Petrov said or did, they'd have more information—another piece to the puzzle as they figured out who had attacked America.

"I'm still across the street," Mad Dog reported from up the road. "He doesn't seem to be aware of us. One vehicle approaching, but it's clear after that. I'd say it's on whenever you're ready, Tex."

"Let him come a few more steps at least," Johnboy called, his voice as calm as always. "Right before he reaches the parked black sedan is the best place for me to cover you, or I'll need a few seconds to move." He was on overwatch, across Fifth Avenue and a few yards into Central Park, hiding behind the trees with a rifle.

"Copy," Tex said.

There was nothing Axe wanted more than to make the approach himself. It's not that Mad Dog and Tex weren't highly capable.

Axe just wanted to be part of the action. Needed it.

But he couldn't be involved.

It was too great of a risk.

"Crossing the street," Mad Dog said, all business. "A panel van is driving by, but after it passes, there's no traffic coming for the moment. All clear." He paused for a second. "Tex is approaching Petrov."

As Mad Dog reported, Tex's voice, full of authority, came over the comms loud and clear. "Sir? NYPD. Please stop—and keep your hands out of your pockets."

So far, so good, Axe thought.

"I have them," Haley said to him, and pointed at one of the screens where the group had come into view. Up the avenue, Petrov turned toward Tex, hands held several inches from his side. Mad Dog entered the picture from the left as he crossed the street.

And all four doors of the black luxury sedan parked along the curb opened at once.

Four burly men stepped out, their focus on Tex.

"Blondie?" Mad Dog whispered over the radio. "We have a situation here."

2

THE RULES OF ENGAGEMENT

Axe had to help.

Tex and Mad Dog were outnumbered, though Johnboy could even the odds if needed.

Their rules of engagement were clear. No shooting unless their lives were in immediate danger—and then they had to be extremely careful to take only shots they could nail.

The risk to civilians was too great, though the sidewalks were deserted at the moment, aside from the confrontation taking place two hundred yards north of the van.

"Hold the line but don't escalate," Axe said on the comms as he flung open the rear door of the van. "I'm coming."

"Axe! Don't!" Haley called behind him. He didn't need to worry about her. She was nearly as capable physically as he was—her youth, speed, and agility partly made up for his advanced training and experience. Haley would post up a safe distance away to guard their rear. It made tactical sense—if the situation went further south, she couldn't back them up sitting inside the van.

Time seemed to slow as Axe stepped out of the van, unzipping his jacket in case he had to access the concealed M4 carbine on a sling underneath.

He looked up in time to see a man with his face covered in a black balaclava standing in front of him.

Axe's years of training and instinctive self-preservation kicked in. He ducked and pushed forward, slamming his shoulder into the man's muscular body, which made the man step backward but didn't take him to the ground as Axe had hoped.

"Blondie!" Axe had time to yell before massive arms grabbed him and flung him to the ground.

He had walked into an ambush, and only a few seconds into the fight, he was already losing.

Badly.

3

───────────

THE PAPERWORK

North Fifth Avenue
The Upper East Side
Manhattan

Tex's hand hovered over her holstered pistol as she stared up at the large men lined up across the sidewalk behind Petrov. The target had short, thinning brown hair, a close-trimmed beard, and a lanky frame—an average mid-40s Caucasian, though his loafers, slacks, and tailored jacket pegged him as wealthy and style conscious.

Even the assistant of a Russian oligarch dressed well.

Petrov crossed his arms and offered her an amused half smile, while the goons behind him kept their arms at their sides. No weapons were visible, but Tex had no doubt the men were armed.

"Y'all keep your hands right where they are," she said, a hint of the Texas drawl she worked so hard to hide creeping in. "No need for all four of you to die—and frighten the rich folks that live around here. Stain the sidewalks and all that. It would probably ruin your whole night."

"And we'd have to do a ton of paperwork," Mad Dog called as he stopped at the curb to her right, keeping his distance. He looked a lot less like a police officer, despite his NYPD uniform. He was short, barrel-chested, and had a whole head of messy hair with a full beard that couldn't hide his ever-present smirk.

The faces of the security detail didn't budge.

"Tough crowd," Mad Dog muttered.

"What can I help you… 'officers' with this evening?" Petrov asked with polite amusement. He had a hint of a Russian accent that would have passed unnoticed if Tex wasn't listening for it.

There was no hiding that he knew exactly what was going on. He hadn't fallen for their police patrol act.

"We've had reports of a gang of young men robbing pedestrians at gunpoint and escaping into the park," Mad Dog said, falling back on their contingency plan, since Petrov was no longer alone and easily approachable.

"Just wanted to make you aware so you could be extra careful," Tex added.

"I appreciate that, officers," Petrov said. "But as you can see," he added, tilting his head to the four beefy men behind him, "I'm well protected. No one could possibly bother me with my friends on constant watch."

"You're all set then, sir," Mad Dog said. "Have a good night."

"Thank you, officers," Petrov said, still playing the game.

The goons stared at them, eyes hard, faces expressionless, then escorted Petrov to the sedan, treating him with deference. He wasn't a prisoner—he was their boss.

As all five climbed into the car, JB called over the comm line. "Blondie and Axe, all clear. It's over. No shots fired. No danger."

As the car pulled away from the curb, there was no answer from Blondie.

Or Axe.

Tex made eye contact with Mad Dog as they waited an agonizing two seconds for a reply.

The rear of the surveillance van two hundred yards away was obscured by a long line of vehicles parked along the street for the night—and another panel van was double-parked next to it.

The one that had driven past right before they'd confronted Petrov.

"Something's wrong," Tex and Mad Dog said at the same time.

4

THE FIGHT

Axe hit the ground hard, but took the impact on his side and focused on keeping his head from bouncing off the asphalt.

The goon who had thrown him to the ground overestimated the effect it would have. He raised a heavy black boot to deliver a knockout blow.

Axe swept the man's ankle, bringing him crashing to the ground. He followed it with an elbow to the man's head.

The tango slumped, stunned but not knocked out.

A moment later, Axe was on his feet in the small space between the back of the van and a large SUV parked behind them, his situational awareness finally kicking in.

There were three goons still in the fight, plus one in the driver's seat of the idling long white panel van, side door wide open, double-parked near the rear of the surveillance van. Two tangos were between Axe and the sidewalk; the other was behind him, close to the panel van—and Haley.

All were big and beefy, with black balaclavas hiding their faces, and the nearest one was coming at him.

They knew we were here, Axe thought.

Somehow, he and Haley had been played.

There was no time to figure out how or why. Axe blocked a punch to his head. He had to protect his skull at all costs.

Behind him, Haley grunted in pain, followed by a gasp of surprise from the man fighting her. She was dishing out at least as much damage as she was taking.

And no guns had come out yet.

Axe deflected a kick to his vastus lateralis muscle on his outer quadriceps, avoiding the "dead leg kick." The second goon tried to angle his way in to attack Axe next to his comrade, but there wasn't room.

At least for the moment, Axe only had to face one opponent at a time.

Axe was outnumbered, there was no room to maneuver, and at any moment the shooting could start.

"Axe!" Haley cried out.

He risked a glance behind him.

Haley's attacker had wrapped her in a bear hug from behind and raised her off her feet.

Axe's look back cost him. Pain shot from the outside of his left thigh, above the knee, as his tango landed a kick. Axe fought for balance as the agony spread, his leg refusing to take his weight.

Not only could he not help Haley—he was fighting for his own survival.

5

THE HUG

The situation for Haley hadn't been good from the start.

Instead of letting the team handle the confrontation up the block, Axe had bolted out the door. It was a huge blunder, but she had no choice but to follow her partner. He wasn't yet back in fighting shape. He knew it, she knew it—hell, the entire team did, though no one wanted to be the first to bring it up.

Outside the van, the night had gone from bad to worse when they had run straight into what had to be the Russian oligarch's security forces—a second team backing up the one near Tex and Mad Dog.

They were likely there to make sure the situation a couple hundred yards up the block didn't escalate, but Axe had done exactly that.

By rushing out of the van, the tangos must have thought Axe was about to abduct Petrov. They had reacted as if Axe's desire to protect his team was an immediate threat—and were acting accordingly.

And Haley's tango had gotten behind her and lifted her off the ground.

For the last several weeks, she'd been mostly happy analyzing data at her cubicle in the office.

Digging for clues.

Working with Dave and Nancy, the Central Analysis Group's two senior intel analysts, she had uncovered a domestic gun-running operation that the FBI had quickly wrapped up. Dozens of bad guys had been arrested. Thousands of guns destined for the hands of criminals had been seized.

She'd done it without leaving the safe yet boring confines of the office.

It had reminded her how rewarding life as an analyst could be.

Her intuition and insight were off the charts.

She made a difference.

There was no need to play amateur direct-action operator, strap on the guns, vest, and gear, and go into the field.

Haley had decided once and for all that there was too much risk to her —and the country—for her to be an operational asset.

Surprisingly, as the days had slipped by, she'd made peace with the decision.

Until this easy, safe mission had landed in her lap.

She and Axe had agreed that they could safely sit in the van and relive their glory days.

All had gone well until Axe foolishly jumped out of the van, landing them in the middle of a fight.

Even that wouldn't have been too much of a problem if her opponent hadn't been faster, luckier, and more resilient than she'd expected. He'd traded a brutal blow from her—below the belt—in exchange for moving behind her with surprising speed.

Haley struggled to break free from the bear hug. She tried a rear kick to the groin, but the man was ready for it.

He backed up, hauling her toward the idling panel van's open doorway.

6

SEALS FIGHT TO WIN

North Fifth Avenue
The Upper East Side

Axe kicked, punched, and dodged, trying to get the space and time to draw his pistol.

Though the tangos hadn't reached for weapons, Haley was being abducted.

He could justify deadly force.

But against the well-trained attackers in the confined space, he could only avoid the worst of the blows aimed at him and pray Haley could escape the grip of the man who'd grabbed her.

Axe took a painful punch to his ribs but managed a kick to the groin of the tango taking him on. The man staggered back, eyes wide and mouth open in agony. He dropped to his knees, fighting to breathe, leaving two for Axe to trade blows with.

Another of the goons immediately stepped in, and the third edged forward, trying to get to him from the side.

Axe had a big problem: he wasn't fighting to win.

He was fighting to avoid another traumatic brain injury.

That had to change.

He had to end this.

Now.

SEALs fight to win.

Axe went on the attack but immediately took a sharp blow to the temple.

He rocked back, stunned and alarmed at the risk to his brain.

Nearby, the big goon holding Haley continued backward toward the van.

Axe flung himself at the nearest tango, using a calf kick—similar to the kick he'd avoided at the start of the fight—to collapse the right leg of one of his two opponents.

The remaining man stepped forward and doubled his efforts.

And the man dragging Haley was almost to the van.

7

———————

THE CONTINGENCY

North Fifth Avenue
The Upper East Side

Haley fought for a breath as the man's massive arms squeezed her chest tighter and tighter.

She kicked at the tango's knees—to no effect.

If he dragged her into the van, it was all over.

She refused to let it end like this.

There was one final, desperate move she could try.

———

Mariana sprinted as fast as her short, sturdy legs allowed. It seemed like it took forever to run to the surveillance van, though only a handful of seconds had passed since Blondie and Axe hadn't responded to the radio call.

She was a few steps ahead of Mad Dog—she was several years younger, and his legs were just as short as hers—but as she drew close enough to see the melee, they were obviously too late.

Axe was on the defensive against a rain of blows from a tango in the small space between the rear of the van and an SUV behind it. Another beefy fighter stood behind the man Axe was engaging, favoring a leg but ready to step in should his partner go down. A third knelt near the sidewalk, bent forward, out of the fight.

A fourth man had Haley trapped in his arms. He dragged her toward the sliding door of a white panel van—and they were nearly there.

Navy SEALs excel at planning. The team had many contingencies. What to do if their target—Petrov—took off running. Pulled a gun. Yelled for help. Or agreed to work with them.

They had been well prepared for tonight—until Axe and Blondie had been ambushed.

During the mission brief, after the more likely contingencies had been worked out, Axe had dropped the bomb.

Haley could not be captured.

Period. End of story.

There was no debate or ambiguity.

The orders were crystal clear.

One by one, they had sworn to do their duty.

Tonight, no matter how much she hated the idea, Mariana had no choice.

She had no shot at the goon holding Haley—she was struggling too much in front of him.

There was only one solution that was sure to work in the time she had.

Tex slammed to a stop, drew her pistol, and aimed at the gorgeous blond held tightly in the arms of the tango as they reached the open door of the panel van. Mariana had the angle—Axe and the others were out of her line.

She would take the shot.

Haley stopped struggling and went limp—dead weight in the tango's arms. She dropped her head forward in preparation for a last-ditch effort.

This was it. If she didn't escape now, life as she knew it was over. Whether the tangos knew who she was or not, they'd learn quickly enough. She would hold out as long as she could, but sooner or later, they would torture her name from her.

And her occupation.

After that, the real pain would come.

The secrets in her head were priceless to America's adversaries.

After tearing the country's top-secret intelligence from her, the captors could trade her broken mind and body for money.

What would some of America's enemies pay to record her public execution and play it on social media?

After more rounds of torture, of course.

Who would be the highest bidder?

How much would Uncle Jimmy—President James Heringten—give to prevent that, to have her back in whatever shape the enemy left her?

Adrenaline flooded her system.

The crack of a gun came from nearby, but she had no time to worry about Axe or hope he had drawn his weapon and was about to turn the tide of the battle.

Haley snapped her head back, desperately hoping to surprise the tango, break his nose, and create an opening to escape.

The only thing that mattered was not being thrown into the van.

There was no feeling of cartilage breaking as she'd expected, but the man's grip loosened anyway.

She dropped to the ground and rolled toward the large SUV along the curb.

Haley had nearly made it when the van's engine revved.

She jumped to her feet, facing the street. The man who had almost abducted her lay half in the van, his heels dragging on the pavement as it sped away.

One of the men who had been fighting with Axe knelt on the floor of the van, holding onto her abductor's lifeless body.

Two tangos sprinted south away from Axe, who gasped for air behind the surveillance van.

And Mariana—Tex—stood on the sidewalk, pistol in hand, staring at her with wide eyes.

8

THE PARK

"Exfil. Now," Haley ordered over the comm line. The sound of gunfire would bring an immediate police response to the upscale neighborhood.

They had to be long gone by then. While the mission had the full approval of Gregory at the Central Analysis Group, answering questions from the police wasn't good for a clandestine operation.

"Copy," Johnboy called. "Almost there."

A few blocks down Fifth Avenue, the panel van slowed to pick up the running men, then turned onto a side street and disappeared.

The area nearby was still deserted, though a taxi drove by, not slowing.

Axe limped to the driver's side of the van while Mad Dog opened the rear door and climbed in.

"Nice shooting," Haley said to Tex as she neared.

It had been Tex's pistol she'd heard right before slamming her head back.

Haley hadn't escaped because of her well-executed reverse headbutt.

Tex had shot the tango in the head at the perfect moment.

"All that training pays off, doesn't it?" Haley added.

"You bet," Tex said as she stopped at the rear of the van while they waited for JB.

Something in her tone made Haley pause.

Tex's face said it all.

"You weren't aiming at him," Haley said, working it out. "When I dropped my head to prep for the strike... You missed me and hit him."

"I'm so sorry," Tex whispered. She blinked rapidly, fighting off tears.

JB ran across the street as Axe's voice came over the comms. "Everyone in?"

There would be time to deal with their emotions later.

Right now, they had to get away from here.

"Ten seconds," Haley said as Tex jumped into the rear of the van. Johnboy followed and slammed the door. Haley ran to the front passenger side, and they were off.

"Well, that could have gone better," Mad Dog said from the back as Axe tore down Fifth Avenue. A police siren wailed in the distance, getting closer by the second. They had barely escaped in time.

The mission had been a bust. Not quite a disaster, but close.

All in all, not the best night, she thought.

"We're no closer to the truth than we were two months ago," Haley muttered.

Axe drove, eyes scanning the street and the mirrors. He looked shaken by the fight and close call they'd had. "Don't worry. We'll keep shaking the tree. No matter how long it takes, we'll get there."

Haley wasn't so sure. She and the team at the Central Analysis Group had followed every lead, no matter how thin, and Vasily Chekov was the best suspect.

The other possibility—a Russian criminal fixer named Boris Zorinov—couldn't be found.

No way to shake the tree there.

Haley checked her side mirror and watched the road, an extra set of eyes for Axe.

She tried not to worry about the lack of other solid leads, the dead Russian goon in a van somewhere on the roads ahead of them, a trigger-happy Mariana in the rear of the van, and Axe not being fit for field duty.

It felt like they had wasted months of effort and were no closer to the truth of who had attacked the country eight weeks earlier in what the media and public called 'the SystemSpike.'

PART 2
____

THE SYSTEMSPIKE

9

____

THE TRIUMPH

Eight Weeks Ago

136 Beregovaya Ulitsa
Istra District
Moscow Oblast, Russia

Boris Zorinov watched the culmination of his criminal career unfold in real time on the television in his dacha outside of Moscow.

America burned.

Self-driving cars plowed into pedestrians, shopping malls, and other buildings; wherever the vehicles' hacked algorithm had determined would cause the most destruction.

Trains slammed into each other and derailed.

Oil pipelines burst, contaminating lakes, rivers, and crop fields.

Sewage backed up, gushing out of toilets and drains in homes across the country.

Boris reveled in the chaos.

He pushed a button on his phone and risked sending a message. No matter how secure the communications apps claimed to be, he didn't trust them. Face-to-face meetings were best. For this, though, timing was everything.

Glorius. Begin phase two, he typed and sent.

His hand-picked team in Dubai would soon launch the next part of the plan.

In a few days, the United States would strike at Russia for causing the attacks.

Russia would claim they weren't to blame and retaliate.

Within a week, the two countries would be at war.

Oman would host a historic Middle East Peace Summit at a secure luxury resort. It would include a chance for Russia and America to work toward a ceasefire.

Tragically, the host building would collapse, thanks to Boris's handiwork.

The most important leaders of the entire Middle Eastern region would be killed.

The old guard in those countries would be dead.

New leaders—people who might have never had the chance to rule—would rise.

The power dynamics of the entire world would be reset.

Boris had made this happen. While the idea hadn't been his, he had expertly implemented the plan, adding his personal touches along the way.

Three long years of meticulous recruitment, fieldwork, management, and coordination.

It was a tremendous accomplishment.

The crown jewel on top of an already spectacular career of a criminal fixer for hire.

Boris indulged in a wolfish grin. No one was around to see.

He raised his glass of vodka toward the carnage on the television.

For a moment, he faltered, losing the thread of the traditional toast.

After a few seconds of thinking it through, though, he had it back.

"May we have everything, and may nothing happen to us for it," he pronounced in his slight Russian accent, and drained the glass.

He was already a wealthy man, but he would need every penny. After today's attacks, he could never stop moving.

He would always wonder if he was about to be arrested—or killed—for what he'd done.

But they had to find him first.

Boris clicked the remote, silencing the television. He wheeled his small suitcase to the door, slipped into a warm coat, and left the home behind forever.

Area B—South Beach
Gateway National Recreation Area
Highlands, New Jersey

Jiayi Pang—Jade, since she had come to America three and a half years earlier for the start of her freshman year of college—zipped her jacket to the top. The wind off the Atlantic, twenty yards away, chilled her to the bone. Stray strands of her long, fine black hair danced in the breeze.

In Coney Island, a mere eight miles across the water, buildings burned.

Plumes of dark smoke trailed into the sky.

To the left, on the upper span of the Verrazano Narrows Bridge, more smoke filled the sky from vehicles that had crashed into each other.

In midtown Manhattan, twenty miles north of the beach but unseen from her vantage point, cars ran over pedestrians and slammed into buildings.

Her phone pinged with another news alert. She checked it and smiled.

The death and destruction were far beyond her predictions.

Jade shivered with a combination of pleasure and cold.

"We did it," she whispered to her boyfriend Darius. It cost her nothing to let him believe he deserved credit.

In the greater New York area, they were in the safest place she could think of until the worst of the attack was over. They stood on the peninsula that jutted from mainland New Jersey, pointing directly at Brooklyn and the rest of New York City beyond it.

They were far from vehicles that could lose control and crash, buildings that could burn, trains that could derail, and electronics that could be hacked.

Darius wrapped her in his arms, providing a welcome buffer against the wind, and they kissed in celebration.

He had helped, of course.

But really, the plan had been her idea.

I did it, she thought.

She was finally proving everyone wrong.

It felt glorious.

And today's attack was the beginning, not the end.

"Will it be enough?" Darius asked. His thick dark hair, strong jawline, and perfect full lips had made recruiting him as her asset a pleasure.

The question was valid. To achieve her goal, she needed the rest to go perfectly.

"After the Middle East Peace Summit next week, yes," she said. "The building will collapse, killing everyone in it, including the leaders of your country. You will be on the fast track to being the youngest president in Iran's history. And I will return to Beijing in triumph to eventually be the Ministry of State Security's first female director."

"We'll never see each other again," Darius murmured into her hair as he held her close. He was sentimental.

She wanted to reassure him, to explain how what they'd done was worth it, which was much better than the truth—she had used him from the start.

Instead, she merely held him close as they watched New York City burn.

10

—————————————

THE PEACE SUMMIT

Seven Weeks Ago

The Reception Courtyard
The Mountain Vista Desert Resort and Spa
Outside Saiq, Oman

President James Heringten carried an injured worker over his shoulder in a firefighter carry, through the rubble of what had been the rear lobby of the resort hotel.

Thick wooden beams had crashed down, crushing luxurious couches and chairs. Chunks of drywall and pieces of wood continued to fall every few seconds, raining down in a storm of danger. Getting hit by material falling from the roof three stories above would cause at least a knockout blow, and possibly death.

The Middle East Peace Summit was in chaos.

Waylan, one of James's personal bodyguards, fought his way through the smoke, haze, and dust in the darkness, weaving around a low glass coffee table that had been shattered by falling debris. "Let me take him, Mr. President."

"I've got him," James said, continuing toward the rear exit, clear air, and safety. "There's at least one more back there by the side bar. A server."

"Mr. President, you've done enough." Waylan put his shoulder next to James's and dragged the worker onto it. James had to release the man to avoid injuring him further.

"That was an order, Waylan."

"I heard you, sir." Waylan grabbed James's biceps in an iron grip before James could turn toward the demolished bar area behind them. "Everyone is helping now, thanks to your leadership," he said, his voice as hard and commanding as James's. "Nearly all the staff are accounted for. It's time to get you to safety. You have a bigger job to do now."

"This is not a discussion."

"No, sir, it's not." Waylan's fingers tightened on James's biceps. Waylan stepped toward safety, refusing to let go.

"I'm safe. No one here is trying to kill me," James said, standing firm.

Waylan stopped, balancing the injured worker on his shoulder while refusing to let go of James.

Another of the building's huge logs of the post-and-beam construction groaned above them.

"You may be right, sir. The delegates are busy, but all of their guards are armed. If they have a chance, they could eliminate the leader of the free world—you—and be heroes in their home countries. And the building doesn't care about politics. It's coming down soon, and you cannot be inside when it does. It's time, Mr. President. Come on, now."

Waylan pulled lightly. James was about to yank his arm free when the worker gasped in pain.

The longer James fought, the more suffering he caused the worker, and the greater risk to the man.

"I have the last worker," a voice called from the darkness behind them. "Injured but alive. We are coming out. Everyone, out, out! Out now!"

That was enough for James. He allowed Waylan to lead him through the haze and past the crushed furniture, the chunks of ceiling, and the broken glass onto the lawn outside.

While he and the others had been focused on search and rescue, one of the delegations had set up triage. The lawn was organized by injury, with the lightly injured in one area and people needing more urgent care into another.

A man in a long white robe common to the region rushed up holding a phone with the flashlight on, examined the man on Waylan's shoulder, and directed them to the side with the lightly injured.

———

The Oman crown prince's white, ankle-length tunic and white pants were torn, ragged, and dark with dirt. He stopped next to James and Waylan. They stood near the pool, far back from the building and out of the way of the rescue workers who had arrived to help treat and evacuate the injured.

"Everyone is accounted for," the young man said. James had hijacked his welcoming speech to keep the delegation from entering the building right before it had shaken and started to collapse. "Staff, all the members of the delegation. Only one death, a man from the Afghan group. He was crushed by a beam…"

The man broke off and rubbed his close-cropped beard, which was covered with dust. "I must thank you. Had you not requested the stage to confront Russian President Nikitin, we would all be dead." He held out his hand and James shook it.

"We got lucky," James said. Not everyone would believe James's on-stage heart-to-heart with the leader of Russia had been impromptu, and they'd be right. Thanks to the intel from the Central Analysis Group, James had taken the risk, figuring that if something bad didn't happen to the resort as they predicted, he would look like a grandstanding fool.

But once again, Gregory Addison and his team had called it correctly.

The leaders of Iran, Egypt, Saudi Arabia, Jordan, Afghanistan, Pakistan, and many other Middle Eastern region leaders and their staff were alive because of the Central Analysis Group team.

James had only played the role of the point man.

"None of this was your fault," he said, placing a gentle hand on the young man's shoulder. "You and your father know that, right? The hotel's construction must have had a flaw, or there was an earthquake or sinkhole. Something happened, and it wasn't a bomb or an attack. It was out of your hands. No one will blame you for this."

The young man nodded his thanks and turned to go. He had many others to speak with and check on.

In the distance, the building groaned, a tortured, horrible sound.

A moment later, the remaining damaged structural supports gave way.

The far wall that had remained half-standing finally collapsed.

The roof came down a second later with an enormous crash.

A wall of smoke and dust rolled from the once-magnificent resort. James turned his back. It washed over him and dissipated.

"That could have been a lot worse," Waylan said from beside his shoulder. "Thank you for leaving when you did, Mr. President."

"We had plenty of time," James said dryly.

Waylan was way too professional to roll his eyes at him.

"An accident, sir? An earthquake? And lucky timing on your part?" Waylan wasn't challenging the narrative; he was confirming it.

"Yes. Spread the word to our people. We had no intel, no phone calls, nothing. We got lucky, and the resort collapse was a tragic natural disaster. That's our story, and we're sticking to it."

THE REALIZATIONS

Four Weeks Ago

Hotel Costa Blanca
Alicante, Spain

Only the glow of the television illuminated the hotel suite. A gentle Mediterranean breeze ruffled the curtains next to the open sliding door overlooking the patio and the sea beyond.

Boris Zorinov lounged against a pile of pillows on the bed in the luxurious robe provided with his room, a glass of red Rioja in hand. He would have preferred vodka, but his forged passport said he was French, so he stuck with wine to help maintain his cover.

It tasted sour, though the fault was likely with his palate.

A last sip finished the glass. He filled it again, draining the bottle.

He was drinking too much on this trip across Spain, but for the moment, he couldn't remember why.

Somber music played on the TV over news footage from America. He remembered watching the death and destruction in real time four weeks earlier. He'd been happy then, for some reason.

Another tiny gap in his memory.

Video from a helicopter showed a bright-red car stuck half inside a grocery store's entrance. Fire crews sprayed water on it as it burned. Thick, dark smoke blanketed the area.

The scene switched to cellphone video from a shopping mall. A pickup truck had plowed a hole through the doors and into the food court. Its hazard lights blinked red from inside. Police and firefighters evacuated the injured—and the dead—on stretchers.

"Today marks one month since the devastating cyberattacks on the United States," a news reporter said over the video montage, "which people are calling the SystemSpike."

Another helicopter shot showed a derailed train, its railcars jackknifed, lying on their sides, with many on fire.

Bodies lined a New York City street, faces draped with suit coats and windbreakers—anything the living bystanders had handy.

"Cities, towns, and rural areas nationwide were hit during the SystemSpike," the voiceover continued.

Brownish-black water oozed out the front door and down three stairs of a small white house.

A crane on a bridge in Albany, New York, raised a yellow school bus from the river. Water poured from the windows as parents onshore clutched each other and sobbed.

After more scenes of the attacks, the music faded, and the scene cut to a television news studio. Two reporters, a stately, gray-haired older man and a younger woman with dark hair and glasses, stared somberly into the camera.

"The official total for the attacks stands at 3,192 people dead," the woman said. "Thousands more were injured. And, of course, the lingering effects of the SystemSpike continue to haunt many, many more of us."

"Today, Congress released its report on the investigation and hearings it has conducted over the past weeks," the man said. "These men," the screen switched to a view of seven thin, nerdy young Caucasian males, "plus another not pictured here, were responsible for the attack. They and their ringleader, a man named Gogol Khan Dagar, also known as 'Malik' who lived in Dubai, United Arab Emirates, are confirmed dead, the result of a daring raid by local authorities on the day of the event.

"Sources, speaking on deep background as they did not have official permission to discuss the operation, say that fast action by America's intelligence agencies, working with the UAE authorities, prevented a second phase of the attack.

"Though the death of more than three thousand people is horrific, it's likely that the actions of the country's intelligence agencies saved thousands—possibly tens of thousands—of other lives."

The other reporter spoke, her voice somber. "Here's a preview of an interview with President James Heringten conducted earlier today. The rest will air tonight at nine p.m."

President Heringten, sitting in a straight-backed chair facing a reporter, looked like he had aged a decade in the past five years of his presidency. His short, straight hair had gone mostly gray. The lines on his face were deeper, the bags under his eyes darker, but his muscular physique showed beneath a dark suit, pressed white shirt, and dark red tie with blue-and-white diagonal stripes.

The well-coiffed reporter glanced at his notes and gave the president an apologetic look. "Mr. President, as you know, there are conspiracy theories galore online and in the public discourse."

The president frowned but didn't interrupt as the reporter continued. "Many people claim that this so-called 'Malik,' who the Congressional report cites as the mastermind of the attacks and leader of the young men who hacked the computer systems, was, in fact, not acting alone. That, while wealthy, he did not have the resources, skills, or knowledge to accomplish what ultimately happened. What is your response to these quite compelling arguments?"

"I'm glad you brought that up, Danny," President Heringten said, leaning forward slightly. "Congress conducted an extensive investigation, both in public and, where necessary to protect national security, behind closed doors. They thoroughly refuted those baseless conspiracy theories. And while I'm not at liberty to discuss any top-secret details, I can assure you and the public that what the report shows is one hundred percent accurate and truthful. Malik—Gogol Khan Dagar—was a well-connected businessman in the region with a long-standing animosity toward America because of our time in his country of Afghanistan following 9/11. The hackers he recruited were highly intelligent and motivated to wreak havoc. The one surviving hacker confessed everything and provided extensive details of the operation, from the early stages to a second phase planned for after the initial attack. Because of him, we know exactly who was involved and what happened. We can all rest knowing that the evil men who arranged and conducted the attack are dead, aside from the last hacker, who is locked in solitary confinement at an undisclosed maximum security detention center for the rest of his life."

"The hackers, including the one now locked up, were Russian—"

"Let me stop you right there, Danny. Yes, the hackers were all young men from Russia, but they were acting outside of their country's orders and desires. Obviously, we've looked into this deeply. And while the United States of America and Russia have many disagreements, and I personally consider Russia an adversary of our country, Russia was clearly not to blame for the attacks. Again, I can't go into details, but I hope you and the rest of my fellow Americans can take me—and both houses of Congress, Republicans and Democrats—at our word. It's now time to focus on preventing attacks like these from ever happening again, which is why—"

Boris clicked off the television and looked past the balcony to the moonlit waters of the Mediterranean in the distance.

He had no love for the Americans, but what had happened to their country was appalling. And Russia blamed for the attack…

Boris shook his head. It was a shame what the world had come to.

He froze, staring at the sea.

Something wasn't right.

His memory had been playing tricks on him for years. A misplaced name here. A forgotten detail there. But he had managed.

Over the last… how long? A few weeks? Months? Boris wasn't sure of the exact timeframe, but the slips had gotten worse. Sometimes slowly, like a gentle downward slope. Other times quickly, like stepping down a stair or two at once. He would be irrationally irritable, and nothing could console him. At other times, he let go of all his concerns and felt at peace.

A rare feeling for him.

Whatever. He was fine. It had been a stressful few months…

He stared at the dark television as the pieces fell into place, one by one, like putting together a challenging jigsaw puzzle.

First, the name: Malik. Gogol. But his memory told him the news reporters had it wrong. Malik was Abdul, not Gogol. Gogol was the brother.

Boris could picture Abdul. His stern bearing. His hatred for America and Russia. He was the perfect man for the job.

His dark eyes that would have been terrifying if he weren't more afraid of Boris than Boris was of him.

The realization made him gasp.

Boris had known the man.

With that, the rest came flooding back.

Being hired to coordinate the attacks.

The extreme secrecy of his meetings with Abdul—Malik.

Malik's home and office on the thirty-fifth floor of the tower in Dubai.

The empty fifteenth floor where the hackers' desks went.

The roundabout ways the money for the operation was transferred.

The near-constant coordination at the end as the attacks began.

It all popped into his mind like it had happened yesterday.

Exactly how his memory was supposed to work.

It was all clear now.

The reporter and the American president were either lying or unaware of the truth.

Abdul, his brother Gogol, and the hackers hadn't acted alone.

Malik hadn't planned and organized the cyberattacks.

Boris had done it all through Malik.

That's why Boris drank all the time and changed hotels every few days.

This wasn't a vacation.

He was on the run.

Boris rose and moved to the minibar, removed two small bottles of vodka, and downed one after the other.

Returning to the open balcony door, his eyes scanned the water below as he tried to decide what to do next.

12

WRATH

254 Lafayette Street
Soho
Manhattan, New York

"Do you believe what he said?" Jade whispered to Darius when the interview with America's president finished.

She turned off the burner phone they had used to watch the streaming broadcast—her high-tech day-to-day phone sat on a coffee table in her apartment while she supposedly studied nearby—and snuggled up against Darius. The futon on the floor wasn't as comfortable as her own bed, but this safe house was the only place they dared discuss their secrets.

"It's been a month," Darius said. "If the Americans or Russians knew about us, we would be dead or in custody."

He left unsaid the horrific things Iran—his country—or China, hers, would do to them if it came to light they had hired a Russian criminal to implement her daring plan to change the world.

Had they succeeded—and remained undetected—their countries would have welcomed them home with open arms.

Part of the mission had been a success. Jade had struck at America. Killed thousands. Created mass confusion and fear.

The rest hadn't gone as planned.

She meant for the United States and Russia to go to war, weakening both.

China would naturally be stronger afterward.

The crucial third part of the plan had also failed. The top leaders of the Middle East region were supposed to have been killed at the peace summit in Oman.

The luxury resort had collapsed as planned... but none of the leaders of the region had been inside, completely ruining that part of her plan and Darius's chance at being the youngest Iranian president in history.

"So we're fine," Darius finished. "Except for our financial patrons." Darius had recruited two other men from the Middle East to provide the large sums of money needed for the operation.

They, in turn, had recruited others.

All of them had money to burn. Obscenely large monthly allowances, assets set aside for them, trust funds, and access to family money with few questions asked.

But they were very upset that she and Darius hadn't delivered the promised results.

The benefactors would have vaulted ahead in their countries.

Increased their status and prospects tremendously.

Cut at least twenty or thirty years off their pursuit of power.

Now, they were no better off than they were before—after spending millions each.

"We'll make it up to them," Jade said. She had failed, but she wouldn't—couldn't—let the setback define her.

This was not the end.

Her next plan for America was well underway.

By summer, she would be back on track.

This time, she would succeed.

America would once again feel her wrath. She would accomplish a great feat that benefitted China and prove to her superiors in the Ministry of State Security that she was more than what they believed her to be.

13

HELP

Central Analysis Group Headquarters
Arlington, Virginia

Gregory Addison leaned back in the leather desk chair. On his computer monitor, a spreadsheet taunted him with everything he knew, believed, and suspected about the cyberattacks of a month ago—the SystemSpike.

He ran his fingers through his long, graying hair, not caring that he was messing up the carefully arranged style. The day-shift analysts had gone home, replaced by the night shift, but he'd leave in a few minutes without disturbing them.

He had vowed to the President of the United States that he'd get to the bottom of the puzzle.

Who was truly to blame for the SystemSpike?

Iran? China? A secret faction within Russia?

Next, how had they accomplished the feat without the Central Analysis Group or any other of America's intelligence agencies suspecting the attacks were coming?

And, most importantly as always, what could be done to prevent future attacks?

After dedicating every spare moment of the past month to the project, returning to his roots as a top-notch intel analyst—nearly at Haley Albright's spectacular level, at least back in the day—he was no closer to the answers.

He had a morning workout with President Heringten scheduled for… he checked his watch. Seven hours from now. Once again, as he had for the past four weeks, he would report that he had nothing.

He removed his glasses and cleaned them with a small cloth from the middle desk drawer. After setting them back in place, he composed an email to his top three analysts.

He and the president had agreed that the analysts would be kept out of the search for the true perpetrator. The person or country that had financed and organized the cyberattacks, the assassination of Secretary of State Hank Wilson, and the "natural disaster" collapse of the resort where the Middle East Peace Summit had been held, had to be ruthless and highly intelligent.

President Heringten wanted the utmost flexibility about what to do— or not do—with the knowledge of who was ultimately to blame. Involving the rest of the CAG analysts was a risk he wasn't willing to take.

But with Gregory getting nowhere, it was time to bring in other minds —possibly better ones than his.

He composed the email and sent it before he could change his mind.

See me as soon as you arrive in the morning. ~ *G.*

Haley, Nancy, and Dave came in early most days, but he'd be back from his morning White House workout before them.

He glanced at his watch, then the spreadsheet, at war with himself. It was long past time to go home. His wife would still be up if he hurried. They were working their way through ten seasons of an old sitcom, and they could squeeze in an episode before bed. It would make sleep come easier.

But work called. One more review before leaving? Maybe he'd missed something. The smallest clue that would lead to a breakthrough.

Before he could make up his mind, a knock came from his door. An instant later, it opened.

Haley poked her head in.

"You're still here?" Gregory asked as she stepped inside, followed by Dave and Nancy. His top analysts didn't answer but moved to the guest chairs in front of the desk. Dave closed the door behind him and remained standing as the two ladies sat. Nancy's medium-length blondish-gray hair, frizzled and flyaway as usual, contrasted with Haley's long, thick blond hair that flowed to her shoulders. They both were extremely intelligent, and while Haley had the slight edge in intuitive ability, Nancy had improved tremendously. Dave, with his full salt-and-pepper beard, had a focused look, was detail-oriented, and a skeptic of using intuition as a launching point for intelligence gathering and analysis. Together, they balanced each other well.

"We were watching the president's interview in the conference room," Haley explained.

"You knew I was going to ask for help," he said, more to himself.

Dave spoke. "We're ready. Let us off the leash."

"Do any of you believe what the president said? That the true perpetrators of the assassination and cyberattacks have all been killed or apprehended?"

All three shook their heads, faces grim.

Haley spoke up. "And we know from Axe that Malik—Gogol, in this case—didn't orchestrate the collapse of the Oman resort. Even his brother, Abdul, couldn't have funded and directed that. There's no evidence he was part of it. He wasn't the mastermind."

Gregory went for it. He would ask for their help. "Congress believes what their investigation revealed. But they don't know the full story. We do. I've done my best," he said, turning his monitor to face the team. "But I'm stuck. I need your help. Dig deeper than I have. Raw data. Intel reports. Contact and interview field agents. Research travel itineraries. Follow the money trail. Maybe you'll find things I've missed. But start with the assumption that the brothers—Gogol and Abdul—were the last links in the chain, not the masterminds."

This is where it got tricky. His team, especially Haley, had a tendency to seize the initiative.

That was the kindest way he could put it.

"We need to know who the mastermind was, with one caveat." Gregory leaned forward, his eyes fixed on Haley. "The instant you find a solid lead, you come to me. You do not send Axe Southmark or any of the field team on a 'fact-finding mission,' or to 'shake the tree,' or any other creative term you invent to disguise the fact that you're taking action. This is too big. Too sensitive. We don't want to accidentally unravel a thread and have it lead to World War Three if the intelligence implicates China or another country. There might not be action taken against those responsible. Not right away, at least, and not by us. What happens in this building stays here. Global politics is a long game. We'll eventually get our revenge, but you and the field team will take no action. Or you'll regret it. Understand?"

All three nodded.

Gregory sat back. He'd made it clear what he wanted. Heaven help them if they crossed him on this one.

Haley and Nancy stood, joining Dave behind the guest chairs. They were ready to go.

"Start in the morning," Gregory said. "Don't get too distracted—our priority is still to protect the country from the next attack. But the person or people behind the SystemSpike a month ago are still out there. They did a hell of a lot of damage, killed innocent people, and my guess is that it didn't accomplish whatever their real goal was. So, they're likely plotting, planning, and getting ready to hit us again. Let's stop them."

"And take them out," Haley muttered.

"After talking with me about it!"

She waved her arm at him as they filed out, which he took as acknowledgement instead of a dismissal, praying he wouldn't regret his decision.

14

COBBLESTONES

Four Weeks Ago

Casco Antiguo (Old Town)
Cartagena, Spain

Boris Zorinov had wandered the dark alleys of the city's old town all night, lost again. The narrow, winding lanes were quiet this early in the morning, right before dawn. The stone buildings were silent with sleeping locals and tourists. In an hour or two, the area would bustle with traffic, but for now, Boris had the dim streets to himself.

The late-spring air had a salty tang that came from the nearby sea…

Something about the water triggered a memory, but it slipped away as he reached for it.

Boris frowned and trudged along aimlessly. Sooner or later, he would stumble across a landmark he recognized, and from there he could trace his way back to… Where?

He was staying in a nice hotel. The best in the area, he was certain. What it looked like and its name, however, escaped him.

No worries. It would come back.

The memory loss had started the year before—or maybe a few years ago. He wasn't sure how long it had been. Certainly not before the…

What, exactly, he couldn't say right now, but it didn't matter.

He'd done something important. Monumental. His memory had been fine then, he was pretty sure.

Boris's feet ached and his legs were sore from the hours of walking. He was no longer a kid—sixty-five? Maybe a little older? Though he had a sense that he was in better shape than many other men his age.

He turned a corner at random, hoping for a main road and a taxi that could drive him around until he recognized his hotel.

An even narrower, darker alley greeted him. He pulled up sharply and turned back the way he'd come, annoyed. When the memory lapses hit, he normally rode them out. Fighting them, stressing, or getting angry and frustrated made things worse. But this morning he was tired and wanted to go to sleep in a large, comfortable bed, not continue meandering through the quiet city.

A man glided silently around the corner, only a step in front of him.

For an instant, they stared at each other in surprise.

Then the man lunged forward and stabbed at Boris, the matte-black knife in his hand aimed at Boris's heart.

He reacted without thinking, trapping the knife arm between both of his hands.

Boris didn't hesitate—to wait would bring the attacker's other hand into play.

Pushing the man's knife arm down and to the side, Boris stepped in and slammed his forehead into the younger man's face.

The grunt of pain gave Boris the opening he needed. He cranked the man's wrist at an unnatural angle, breaking it and claiming the knife as his own.

Boris raised the knife as the attacker rallied and rushed toward him. A short, controlled thrust embedded the knife into the man's body beneath the rib cage, pointed upward, and the fight was over.

With their faces only centimeters apart, the man's wide eyes pleaded for a different ending to the situation while acknowledging that there was nothing that could change the outcome. After a moment, his face conceded the loss of the battle—and his coming death.

"The pain will only last a second," Boris said in English, making a guess. Already the man's eyes were heavy. The knife had punctured his heart. "Before you go, prepare your way. Tell me who sent you."

The attacker hesitated a second before speaking. "Anonymous. All online," the man gasped in English as he sagged against Boris, which only did more damage with the knife.

"What did they tell you?"

"What you looked like. Short gray hair. Blue eyes. Mid-sixties. Fit body but aging. Shorter. The fake name you might use. They said you might look sad. Where to search for you. Spain."

The man had only seconds to live.

"How were you to confirm it was done?"

"Throat cut, lots of blood. A photo." A sob escaped his lips as his eyes closed. "I never thought it could end like this."

"Yes, you did." Boris lowered the man gently to the ground and withdrew the knife. "Deep down, you knew," he said. "We all know."

Boris rolled the man onto his side and sliced his throat, using all his strength to cut deep, drawing the blade from one side to another.

With a wound like that, the story would lead the news.

But not the picture.

Jade Pang might believe that Boris was dead, his throat cut, and the hired assassin too, killed when Boris fought back.

It could buy him some time.

Boris's memory—or at least a part of it—had returned.

Jade's brilliant, multi-faceted plan.

His masterful execution of it.

While it hadn't gone perfectly, Boris had orchestrated one of America's worst terrorist attacks.

And though the Oman resort collapse at the Middle East peace talks hadn't killed anyone—except Boris's hand-picked man, Abdul—Boris had done his part to perfection.

Arranged for the theft of the polonium-210 and successfully killed America's Secretary of State.

Recruited, funded, and guided Abdul and his team of hackers.

None of the failures had been Boris's fault. Just one of those things. Not everything worked out, especially large, complicated terrorist attacks on America, Russia, and the leaders of the entire Middle Eastern region.

Still, Boris understood why Jade had sent someone for him. It's exactly what he would have done.

She was either following orders from higher up or, if his hunch was correct, covering her tracks for an unsanctioned mission she had planned to boost her credentials.

Instead of quietly letting their deal conclude, she had come after him.

That necessitated a response.

In kind.

He'd done his homework. The Russian hackers he'd recruited had found Jade's true identity, her apartment, favorite restaurants, and where she shopped for groceries. It had been easy for them.

Jade thought she was safe, that he didn't know her?

She was about to find out how wrong she was, and how short-sighted it had been to target him.

It had been decades since Boris had gotten his hands dirty. These later years, he had recruited and trained. Guided and advised.

He no longer killed with his own hands. That life was far behind him.

But as the dead man leaking blood onto the dark cobblestones attested, Boris had what it took.

Despite his years and the memory lapses, he was still a killer.

And it was time to exact his revenge.

As long as he remembered long enough to pull it off.

PART 3

MONDAY

15

———————

THE ROOF

Present Day

Brooklyn, New York

Jade Pang stood before the roof access door of the ten-story apartment building and took a moment to steady herself.

For all her training, tonight might be the first time she had to take a life in person. She had over three thousand dead souls on her hands from the SystemSpike, but they didn't really count.

Jade used her sleeve to turn the handle and open the door. If all went to plan, she wouldn't have to kill her hacker, and her fingerprints on the door wouldn't matter, but she would take no chances.

As always when she met the hacker, she had wrapped her long, flowing black hair in a tight bun and tucked it under a ball cap. She wore a puffy down jacket to disguise her thin, athletic frame, trendy sneakers with thick soles to add a couple inches to her height, and garish makeup that transformed her dimples, smooth skin, and natural beauty, making her look very different from her normal conservative college student appearance.

As she stepped through the doorway, she hunched her shoulders and walked with her head down, imitating one of her old aunties at the end of a long day scratching a living out of the land in rural China.

Her contact, a freelance hacker, perched on a plastic crate near the far edge of the roof with a laptop computer on his long legs. He was bundled in a thick down jacket, the same one he always wore. Winter was over and spring had sprung, but the man spent hours up here each night in all but the worst weather, pirating the hacked Wi-Fi signals of his neighbors in the apartment building across the street. A Virtual Private Network wasn't enough to disguise his efforts and protect himself. If anyone ever came for him, he'd told Jade in one of their classes together at college the year before, they'd not only be at the wrong apartment; they would be at the wrong building entirely.

"What do you have for me, Turbo?" Jade asked as she approached. She'd done well in her younger days to crush the provincial Chinese accent of a lowly farmer, then worked harder still to eliminate every trace of an accent when she spoke English.

She now sounded like any other young American woman.

Her cover was perfect.

"I finally cracked it," Turbo said. He remained hunched forward, staring at his screen, not looking up at her.

"You did?" Jade asked, not hiding her surprise. She'd offered him a lot of money for what she needed but hadn't believed he could find a way into the tool used by millions around the world to build and host their blogs, businesses, and personal websites.

"Part social engineering," he said, referring to the practice of pretending to be someone—like a tech working in a company's IT help department—to get a target to click on a virus link sent to them. "Part brute force. But yes, I have a backdoor to the country's most popular website building tool. Not full access, but enough for what you need. Anyone who has updated to the latest version will be secure, but most people are lazy. Larger companies with IT departments will probably be safe, but a huge percentage never bother with updates. The minute you use it the first time, though, the company will figure out the problem and issue a required fix. I found an exploit for the second most popular website tool, but the reach will be less because fewer people use it. Still, it'll accomplish what you need: two nationwide public announcements via millions of hacked websites."

"That's awesome. You're exceptional. No one else comes close. I'm glad we hit it off." She laid it on thick—guys like him needed the ego boost.

He fought back a grin, eating up the praise but trying to hide it.

Turbo wasn't the hacker she'd wanted on her team, but Dawson "Eternal Void" Reite had successfully avoided all efforts she'd ordered two months ago to capture—and free—him.

She'd make do with Turbo instead.

"But..." Turbo looked up finally with a serious, hard look on his face. Jade knew what was coming. A demand or a threat.

She could live with a demand.

A threat, though, and she would have to kill Turbo tonight, which would be too bad. He'd done good work for her, and she respected his talents.

"But?" she asked, playing along.

"Whatever you need this access for, it has to be big. Illegal. And..." He paused and narrowed his eyes. "That was you eight weeks ago, wasn't it? The cyberattacks? They had the same feel as these exploits you want."

Turbo was more perceptive than she had given him credit for.

And suddenly, much more of a liability than she'd thought.

16

THE DEAL

Brooklyn, New York

Jade shook her head at Turbo's accusation. "No. Didn't you see the news reports and the interview with the president? It was that guy from Afghanistan working with Russian hackers—who weren't as smart as you at protecting themselves. The authorities got them all."

Turbo shrugged off her denial. "Whatever. Whether you had a hand in it or not, with the hacks I have for you, you're going to either make a lot of waves—some big political protest statement—or have a way to make a ton of money. You've paid me well so far, but when this hits the fan, people will investigate. I'm going to have to be extra careful. Maybe go into hiding. Leave the country."

Jade resisted rolling her eyes. He was laying it on thick.

"So… You have to cut me in on the money-making part."

Turbo's demand wasn't unexpected—or a problem. When the plan worked, there would be more than enough money—as much as Turbo was willing to put on the line.

Jade shrugged. "I can live with that."

"Good," he said with a smart-ass grin. "Otherwise, I was going to have to turn you in." He chuckled. "Contact the heads of the companies' IT departments and tell them about their vulnerabilities. Probably collect fat rewards!" He paused for a second before laughing again. "Just kidding, of course."

But he wasn't. The look on his face said it all.

Back in China, as Jade had learned the art of spycraft, the instructors had warned her and the other students to always beware of betrayal.

Assets fell into four major classes. People were generally motivated by money, ideology, coercion—blackmail—or ego.

Turbo's motivations were money first, ego second.

Would he take his payment now and wait for a large score when her plan came together?

Or would he get impatient, turn her in, and reap a reward?

The sure thing—safe and legit—versus her more lucrative but riskier and highly illegal scheme?

This hack could not fail.

There was too much at stake to risk her life on Turbo's patience and greed.

Jade laughed along with him, not allowing her true feelings to show. "I get it. Good one. I'll transfer the cryptocurrency now for the original amount. Then I'll let you in on what I have planned for this summer. First, though, show me what you've got. Impress me."

She crouched next to the hacker and watched as he navigated into the first website building tool's main computer system—exactly as he'd said he could. He grinned like an idiot as he typed the access password slowly enough for her to catch: JADEi$ahottie!

"Congratulations, Turbo," she said after he had given her a tour and logged out. "That's seriously impressive and worth every penny."

She stood and moved closer to the edge of the roof. "Which Wi-Fi should I use tonight?" As part of Turbo's security protocol, she had to use a local network when she was with him, not cellular data. Her phone wasn't as powerful as his laptop, though, so she had to get closer to the building across the street. They'd been through this before.

He told her which network. She fiddled with her phone, pretending to have trouble.

It didn't take long for him to put his laptop down with an exaggerated sigh and stomp over to stand next to her near the edge of the roof. "Gimme," he said with his hand out.

Men were so predictable.

She handed him the phone. A few seconds later, he offered it to her with a smug grin.

As Jade took it, she stepped toward the hacker, hooked her foot around his ankle, and shoved the surprised man over the edge of the roof.

Turbo made no sound as he fell, only windmilled his arms in a futile attempt to… what? Fly? Grab a railing or window ledge? Spin in the air to look at her one last time?

She would never know.

His body slammed into the sidewalk ten stories below with a wet *splat* that carried to the roof.

She would remember that sound for the rest of her life, certain it would be one of her most cherished memories.

Killing had been easier than she thought it would be.

Men, she thought. They were arrogant, easily deceived, and they constantly underestimated her.

They would learn.

Jade moved to Turbo's high-end laptop, changed the login password, and shut it down. She slipped it under her coat, tucking it into her waist at the small of her back before heading to the stairway door, careful to once more hunch her shoulders and walk like an old hard-working farmer after a long day. Turbo disabled the building's security cameras when he had a visitor, but she would double-check once she returned to her apartment in Greenwich Village.

She couldn't be too careful. This plan was her last chance at redemption. Nothing could go wrong.

Time was running out.

There was a lot to do in the next few months, and plenty to worry about.

Boris Zorinov, her hand-picked fixer for the entire failed operation, had eluded her assassin, who she hadn't heard from in a month. Boris was too much of a liability to leave alive. He had money, connections, power, and knew her secrets. He had to die. Boris may have gone deeper into hiding—or he could be searching for her.

But she would handle it all.

As usual.

By the time Jade made it down the stairs, someone had discovered Turbo's body. She slipped out the building's side door and made her way along the streets of Brooklyn, quiet except for an ambulance siren cutting through the night.

17

———————————

THE DECISION

Carlito's Auto Body and Towing
Safe House EN-23
Queens, New York

A hint of dawn shone through a grimy window of the shop's breakroom. It smelled of resin body filler, paint, and years of burnt coffee.

"We underestimated the target's preparedness last night," Axe said. That was the least of it, but he'd start there and get to the meat of the problem next.

After a long surveillance detection route through Manhattan and Brooklyn to throw off anyone tracking them, the team had reviewed the mission at the borrowed safe house in Queens.

Eventually, the others had left—Johnboy and Mad Dog to an apartment behind the garage, Mariana onto the subway for the trip back to Kelton's luxury condo in Manhattan, only a few blocks from where they'd had the earlier confrontation.

Axe waited for Haley. She had things on her mind she hadn't said around the rest of the team.

Finally, she spoke up. "Tex did what she had to…" she said. They'd covered the situation with Tex, assuring her she had done the right thing. But Haley still dwelled on what could have been.

"Yes, but we should never have put her in that situation."

"I agree," Haley said. "I missed the tangos' van pulling up beside us, and I shouldn't have jumped out of our van after you." She paused, her eyes holding his.

"What?" Axe asked. He didn't get what she was hinting at.

Haley tilted her head, a look he read as if they were an old married couple having the same argument they'd had for decades.

"You should have stayed in the van," she said, fixing him with a hard stare. "The team had it covered."

Axe expected her to be direct; it's exactly what he wanted in a partner. But the words stung.

He wanted to argue… but she had a point.

Haley was right. The entire fight could have been avoided.

Would the tangos have tried to force their way into the surveillance van?

Or were they merely backup to prevent them from escalating the situation two blocks away?

Had they only engaged because Axe charged into the fight?

He should have stayed in the van.

Or, better still, not been there at all.

He could have planned the mission and sent the team out, staying at the safe house to coordinate from afar.

He had messed up, big time.

Axe's morale plummeted, and he almost missed what Haley said next.

"You're a warrior. Through and through," Haley said, her look softening. "Though you've played Admiral Nalen's role before—in Los Angeles, during that rooftop party—you're not one to sit back and manage while others are in contact. You know the fable about the frog carrying the scorpion? The scorpion is desperate to get across a river. He asks a frog to carry him and promises not to sting the frog. Halfway across, the scorpion stings the frog anyway, though it means both of them die. 'It's in my nature,' the scorpion says. That's you, in some ways. Action is in your nature."

"So where does that leave me?" Axe asked. The previous mission, when he'd suffered severe blows to the head and been rescued from a tunnel system by a Russian assassin, had taken more of a toll on him than he wanted to admit.

He wasn't in shape to be in the field. Mentally or physically. He'd pushed it and come back too early.

He'd put his team in jeopardy. That was the last thing he ever wanted.

"I shouldn't be in the field at all," he muttered. "Maybe I should even give it all up. Retire once and for all."

They'd been over this repeatedly and were both tired of it.

Whether she should stay in the office.

And his decision to stay in the rear with the gear.

Both of them safe. Away from the action.

The way last night was supposed to have gone.

"That's not what I'm saying, though if you're not ready to come back, I fully support you waiting. Get in shape, get your head on right. Take whatever time you need. But we can't fight who we are, or our calling. I'm an analyst," Haley said with a resigned smile. "That's who I am, like it or not. As much as I'd prefer otherwise," she added under her breath. "But you belong in the field."

"The doctor said that I'm on thin ice," Axe argued. "More head injuries, and that's it. Game over."

Haley said nothing and let him work it out.

Axe weighed the pros and cons.

He and his girlfriend, Connie, had a long-distance relationship. They met once a month for a four-day weekend but led their own lives the rest of the time. It worked for them.

If he died, she'd mourn… then move on.

For the past twenty years, his life had been running and gunning, hunting bad guys, and protecting the innocent.

Could he turn his back on that? On his calling?

He'd tried when he'd left active duty as a SEAL.

But he couldn't—shouldn't—throw away two decades' worth of experience because of what might happen.

Something shifted deep inside. The switch flipped.

He couldn't step away, no matter what the risks to himself.

As long as he was fit for duty and wouldn't put his team in jeopardy again.

"I voluntarily accept the inherent hazards of my profession..." Axe said, quoting from the SEAL Ethos. "…Placing the welfare and security of others before my own."

A heavy weight seemed to drop from his shoulders and his soul. He drew in a deep breath and let it out, at peace for the first time since… quite a while. At least since being injured so badly two months ago.

"Welcome back," Haley said.

Despite having been up all night, underestimating his opponent, nearly losing an intense hand-to-hand fight, and having the mission go off the rails, Axe felt a renewed strength and focus.

He would get back in shape quickly and get his head on straight. He could do this.

I am never out of the fight.

18
____

THE REVIEW

Vasily Chekov stood in the darkened security office and watched the footage from the previous night. He refused to sit. At seventy-one with an expanding midsection, he needed to burn calories any way he could. Although he felt young, time was advancing. People likely thought he was dowdy, with his sagging jowls and a growing bald spot. He didn't need to be chubbier than he currently was.

Two of his security detail sat in plush chairs in front of a long desk, controlling the playback from dozens of cameras. Six high-definition screens formed a grid on the wall. On the far left, last night's encounter played. A short female NYPD officer approached Petrov, his executive assistant.

Although the security cameras he had aimed at Fifth Avenue were top of the line, they hadn't picked up the audio exchange. He'd never thought it necessary to record conversations on the streets near his New York home, but that would have to change.

"Stop," Vasily said. The tech on the left froze the playback by hitting a button on his keyboard. Without being asked, he rolled the mouse, and a square appeared around the policewoman. After a click of the keyboard, the image of the woman's face grew, filling the screen. While grainy and pixelated due to the magnification, her face was clear enough: focused and commanding. No nonsense. Hardened. A real police officer, not someone faking it.

"Who is she?" Vasily asked. "And why wasn't I notified last night?"

"Our source at the local police precinct isn't in yet," Petrov said from behind him as he entered the room. "I'm looking into it. And I told them not to wake you after it happened. You have the charity dinner tonight."

Vasily perked up. He was looking forward to the event. It was a chance to raise hell and have some fun. Show people who he truly was. Go against the grain of his drab looks and others' expectations that he was an old, boring, money-focused fuddy-duddy.

He normally hated the dance he had to perform as a billionaire. Attending countless dinners, parties, and events. Making small talk with people who wished they had his wealth. Knowing any woman who flirted with him was interested in his money and power, not who he was as a person. Women who were willing to overlook his age and appearance were focused on his lifestyle—the expensive watches, fancy clothes, cars, travel, and homes—not the real him. At his age, he was running out of time to find true love. He needed a woman who could see past his wide, blocky face, the bags under his eyes, the thinning gray hair, and expanding middle—his utter ordinariness—and who also didn't care about the money. Someone who appreciated him for who he was inside: fun, clever, well-read, and thoughtful.

He snorted and shook his head at his self-pity. *Poor, poor me.*

He'd get over it.

Tonight's intimate dinner party at a skyscraper on Fifty-seventh Street would be amusing. Kelton Kellison—former multi-millionaire turned disgraced, broke dropout from the life of the rich and famous—was in the middle of engineering a stunning return to the heights of wealth and power. He had a relatively small condo in a decent building near Columbus Circle at the southwest end of Central Park, less than two miles away.

The dinner party was a fundraiser for Kelton's favorite charity. A casual affair with a select group of six wealthy individuals specifically chosen for a pleasant evening of dinner, drinks, and conversation. Given Kellison's success, fall from grace, and Phoenix-like rise from the ashes, that story alone would be worth the price of admission. The money would go to a good cause, and Vasily had more than he could spend in a hundred lifetimes.

Unfortunately, he hadn't been invited.

An oversight? Or on purpose?

No matter. Petrov had learned of the party through the executive-assistant grapevine.

Vasily was planning to "pull a Kelton Kellison," and show up uninvited, with a large enough donation to buy his way in.

If anyone would appreciate the maneuver, it would be Kellison, who had pulled the same stunt a while back at a big charity fundraiser in Los Angeles.

The evening was going to be a blast.

But back to the matter at hand. Vasily had an entire day to get through before the party, and the business on the street last night was mildly vexing.

He soaked in the image of the police officer, memorizing every feature.

"What of the dead guard's body?" Vasily asked.

"It's been taken care of," Petrov said.

Vasily nodded. He didn't need to be bothered with the details.

"Why did one of my men attempt to abduct the operator? A blond woman, yes?"

"Yes, a very capable woman and an older, well-trained warrior. I've ordered a review of the rules of engagement to prevent a repeat." Petrov was way ahead of him, as usual. "Your men were only on site to prevent an escalation. They followed protocol at first. The usual car full of men waited outside for me to exit, as they do for several of your higher-level staff. The roving SUV had previously identified the team in the tall, white work van. They timed their drive-by for my exit, as usual. When I was confronted by the police, they acted appropriately and stopped by the van to act as a deterrent from escalation."

"What went wrong?"

"A typical team would have noticed the men outside their van. If not, they would have immediately paused when they exited the van in the face of overwhelming numbers. The leader of the mission, a dark-haired warrior, flew out of the van and attacked. The situation disintegrated from there. The men claim the dead guard was taking the initiative to extract intelligence." Petrov paused. "But…"

"Yes," Vasily said. He turned to face his assistant. They'd been together long enough to practically read each other's minds. "The man was losing a fight to a woman. His fragile Russian male ego couldn't handle it. So he grabbed her."

Petrov nodded his agreement. "Exactly. Had it not been for that, the situation would have ended after a fistfight when each side drew back, or when our team prevailed and stopped the people in the van from reinforcing their teammates up the street to assist in abducting me. I have instituted changes to the standard operating procedure to prevent this from happening again."

"There is no video of the fight with the blond woman and the man?"

"No, sir. Sorry, sir," the tech on the left said, with only a hint of a Russian accent. "The other 'police officer' stayed near the street, out of the picture, during the confrontation. And our current coverage does not extend the few hundred yards south to have captured the other fight."

"That will change shortly," Petrov said. "But at a cost. We have to buy a condo in one of the nearby buildings so we can install the cameras."

Vasily waved away the concern about the money.

"This woman," he said, nodding to the screen. "You will learn everything about her. Who enlisted her help in the operation. Which government agency is behind it. And why."

"Yes, sir." Petrov's tone was completely respectful, but Vasily understood. He was stepping on his assistant's toes again. Of course the man would know to do all that, and more.

"This has Boris's fingerprints all over it," Vasily muttered.

"Boris Zorinov?" Petrov asked. For once, he sounded surprised.

Vasily gestured with his head to the hall and led the way. As trusted as the security techs were, his business was by necessity compartmentalized. Only he and Petrov knew all.

"Yes," he said once they were alone. "Boris is setting me up to take the blame for his crimes."

"What crimes?"

"Killing America's Secretary of State—for starters."

Petrov's eyes widened. "Boris orchestrated that assassination—and has framed you?"

Vasily nodded. It felt right and explained the confrontation on the sidewalk the previous night. The authorities wanted to convince Petrov to turn on him, to admit that Petrov's boss had access to polonium-210.

Smart.

But they were wrong. He was innocent.

"Get me Boris's current location."

"Do you want me to have someone… handle him?"

Vasily shook his head. That's not who he was. Though the world of business was cutthroat and he played hardball, he didn't have people killed. He defended himself and his staff, but there was no need for violence. "If we know where he is, the authorities will have a better suspect to focus on. The one who is likely guilty."

Vasily dismissed Petrov and put the concern out of his mind. He had an army of lawyers to handle the authorities if they came for him, and the truth was on his side.

In the meantime, he would spend the day evaluating business opportunities. There was always money to be made.

One could never have enough.

Or at least, that's what people said. He didn't really care about the money. He would rather retire and spend his days reading books. But leaving behind the life he'd known for decades was a terrifying prospect, so he kept doing deals. Maybe someday he'd find the courage to walk away from it all.

At least the money provided the occasional opportunity to do something fun, like tonight when he would crash Kelton Kellison's party.

Vasily couldn't wait to see the look on Kelton's face—and see how he reacted—when the world's fifth richest man showed up at his door.

19

THE BAGELS

The Summit at 57th
Manhattan

Mariana hurried toward the ornate doors of the luxury skyscraper on Fifty-seventh Street. She'd lived here with Kelton Kellison for only a few months, and the soaring atrium with marble floors, multiple elevators, a doorman, and helpful front desk staff had yet to get old. As a girl from Texas, she had dreamed of moving to a "big city"—Houston, or even Dallas.

Never in her wildest dreams had she thought she'd visit New York City, let alone live here in a luxury condominium worth several million dollars.

She was the girlfriend of Kelton Kellison, former multi-millionaire making a comeback to the realm of the rich and famous.

She was also his security consultant.

And the monitor of the world's premier computer hacker Dawson "Eternal Void" Reite, who was under house arrest in the condo.

Two Afghan immigrants who had moved in with them helped her manage the household.

They were one big happy family.

And the previous weekend, she and Kelton had motored his yacht, *Mine All Mine*, from a marina near Montauk to one closer to the city, on the North Shore of Long Island, so it would be closer for them to use for the summer.

Her. Driving a multi-million-dollar luxury yacht, then returning with her smart, handsome boyfriend to a condo in Manhattan and a strange but wonderful "family."

Amazing.

As incredible as Mariana's life was, though, what got her out of bed each morning was her role as a team member of Axe and Haley's World Intelligence Agency, a secret unit within the Central Analysis Group.

After the team debrief at the safe house in Queens, she was finally returning home at dawn with breakfast for her family: Kelton, Void, Jamil, who Axe had recruited during the previous mission, and his wife, Lalia, who had been saved from her village in Afghanistan.

Home, she thought, shaking her head as she approached the main entrance. *In this opulent building, surrounded by some of the wealthiest people in New York—hell, the wealthiest in the world!*

Mariana nodded at the doorman—he worked nights and was about to go off shift. "Thank you, Salvatore. Get home safe," she said, and received a tired but grateful nod back.

"Thank you, Miss Mariana." She'd drawn the line at being called Miss Rodriguez after they'd refused her request to simply call her Mariana. It was a compromise they could all live with.

The paper bag of fresh bagels from the place around the corner, by Columbus Circle, smelled heavenly, as did the egg, cheese, and bacon sandwiches that were in a separate bag.

She was starving.

As Mariana made her way across the massive lobby to the elevators, she nodded at the new staff member at the front desk service counter.

"Excuse me," the man called to her. "Deliveries use the freight elevator."

She smiled and waved as much as she could with the two bags of food. He'd mistaken her for a delivery person instead of a resident. Given her skin tone and casual black pants and jacket—unassuming clothes she'd changed into after last night's mission—she could understand the confusion.

Instead of checking with Salvatore the doorman, though, or letting her pass, he glared and hurried around the counter, his anger disproportionate to the situation.

Great, just what she needed. A confrontation at dawn after she'd tried to kill Haley, but had lucked into shooting the goon instead. All Mariana wanted was to get up to the condo and dig into the food, but that would have to wait.

She stopped in the middle of the grand lobby as the short, balding man with mean, dark eyes approached, a patient smile on her face. Her skin was browner than most in the building—her Mexican-American heritage. And her body was curvier than many of the women living here, but she could run faster, lift heavier, and kick ass better than all of them—and their husbands.

Her mother always said you get more flies with honey than vinegar, though, so she would handle the confrontation with the politeness instilled in her as a child.

If that didn't work, there was always the hardness she'd developed as a small-town cop.

Only if those failed would she resort to the rich bitch persona she hated using—but could if necessary.

"I said use the freight elevator," the front desk guy said. His white face had grown redder as he marched her way. He didn't have a nametag; it might have been his first day.

"I live—"

His large, pudgy hand came down hard on her shoulder. "I'll show you the way," he said with a hard squeeze.

"Hey!" Salvatore called from the front door. "It's okay! She's—"

Salvatore stopped abruptly as Mariana reacted to the aggression.

She dropped the bags of food, and her hands grabbed the man's wrist.

The bags hit the floor a second before she forced the new guy onto the white marble tiles.

Mariana controlled the wrist and twisted, bringing the man's arm behind his back, pressure building on his shoulder joint. She pushed him down and dropped, slamming a knee into his kidney. His gasp of pain pleased her more than it should.

She leaned forward. "Do I have your attention?" she whispered in his ear.

"Yes!" he cried out, voice packed with pain and fear.

"I live on the forty-seventh floor. Unit 47A. My name is Mariana Rodriguez. Salvatore and the other staff here call me Miss Mariana. But you can call me Miss Rodriguez, if that's okay with you."

He choked back a cry of anguish as she brought his wrist farther up his back. A half inch more would rip his shoulder apart and cause excruciating pain, at least one surgery, and months of physical therapy.

"You're new here, right?" Mariana asked.

The man nodded as best he could with his face against the floor, his cheek now no longer red with anger, but white with pain and fear.

"We'll let it go this time, shall we?" she asked. "But maybe—and I'm just brainstorming here—be a little nicer in the future. Don't make assumptions. How's that sound?"

Salvatore practically skidded to a stop in front of them. "Um, Miss Mariana? Everything okay?" Salvatore looked down at her like she was a dangerous crazy person.

She wanted to yank the new guy's arm, or twist his neck, or slam his head repeatedly onto the marble floor.

"Fine, Salvatore, thank you," Mariana said instead, breathing away the nearly overwhelming desire to cause harm. "I was just helping…" She nudged the man's wrist a quarter inch higher and had to fight to keep from wrenching the arm out of the socket to teach the man a lesson he'd remember until the day he died.

"Rodney," he choked out.

"I was just helping Rodney," Mariana repeated.

She forced herself to move Rodney's wrist lower, easing the pressure. "He tripped," she said, looking up at Salvatore, daring him to contradict her. "I'm happy I could lend a hand."

She stood, removing her weight from Rodney's kidney.

"Th—Thank you, Miss Rodriquez," Rodney stuttered, doing a half-way convincing job of going along with her bullshit story as he scrambled away from her on all fours. When he was several feet away, he stood, wary and alert, as if she would take him down a second time.

"Miss Mariana," Salvatore corrected him.

Mariana stood and gave Salvatore another look. He coughed quietly into his fist. "Or Miss Rodriguez."

Salvatore bent to pick up the brown paper bags of food and handed them to Mariana. "Enjoy your breakfast," he said.

"Get home safe," she said, as she had a few minutes before.

With a final, cold look at Rodney, Mariana turned and walked to the elevator.

She'd let her instincts take over, had nearly wrecked a man's shoulder, and caused a scene that would surely be gossiped about for days.

Worse, she'd loved every second of it.

And had wanted to go further.

All after killing a man a few hours earlier.

As Mariana pushed the elevator button for the forty-seventh floor, she wondered, for the countless time since starting to work with Axe, if she had a problem…

And whether she could get it under control before it got her into more trouble than she could handle.

20

———————————

THE ASSIGNMENT

New York University
Greenwich Village
Manhattan

Jade perched on the edge of the chair, knees together, back straight, eyes down, and smoothed out her plain, ankle-length dress.

She was once again in the office of her student advisor to beg for a different path for her life.

She had to be the picture of a demure, dedicated student from a respectable American family—the role assigned to her by China's Ministry of State Security in Beijing.

It was China's version of America's CIA, whose job it was to hunt for people like her: deep cover sleeper agents with detailed, impeccable—but fake—backgrounds. To anyone who investigated, they would see that she was an American of Chinese descent from a happy family in San Diego, attending college in New York to work as an investment banking analyst on Wall Street—a job she'd already secured after two summers of successful internships. It would start in a month—after she graduated.

Lies, of course. She had been hand-picked from rural China because of her intelligence, drive, and ability to manipulate people—especially men.

Jade had been taken to Beijing and trained as a spy.

The spy school had been a time of great discovery. The instructors helped her cultivate and refine what they called "an innate talent to coerce, persuade, befriend, and seduce—the likes of which is rarely seen." Apparently, getting her way her entire childhood wasn't merely being spoiled—it was a skill.

She and the other spy students attended Peking University by day as regular students. By night and on weekends, they learned and practiced espionage techniques, putting their skills to the test in real-world settings in the relative safety of their home country.

As the days and months passed, Jade brought her skills to a new level —but her disdain for the people she convinced and ensnared grew.

All was fine until graduation day when her fate was revealed.

Four years ago this month, Jade was sitting in a small, secure room in the bowels of the Ministry of State Security building in Beijing, being told what would happen as she graduated the spy program.

The cluttered New York office of her student advisor faded as her memory retreated to the meeting four years earlier in Beijing with yet another man with more power over her than she found acceptable—with no way to influence her way out of the situation.

"You are being sent to New York," her superior had said in the small, barren room four years before. There was only a small metal table and two chairs.

Her superior had her paper file in a folder in front of him. Spies like her didn't have electronic records.

He was clearly infatuated with her, but professional and disciplined enough to not act on his desires.

A response wasn't expected or encouraged, so Jade simply waited.

"You will go to college there. We already have a list of people for you to recruit." The MSS way of saying they'd identified men for her to seduce, ensnare, and turn into long-term assets.

"You will also, of course, be expected to use your discretion to target and recruit suitable prospects that might be useful in the future."

This time she nodded in understanding.

New York was a coveted assignment. She would go far with it as the start of her career. Despite her incredible talent at manipulation and coercion, Jade looked forward to returning to Beijing to plan and direct operations. As much as appropriate, she had made clear to her teachers, coaches, and superiors that she was far more than a seductress.

"A prized posting for one of our best students," her superior said, his professionalism slipping. He cleared his throat and composed himself.

Jade dared to ask a question, meeting her superior's eyes with a demure look that she knew he'd find irresistible.

"And afterward? Taiwan?" Another choice assignment to gain field experience. "Before returning to Beijing for planning and operations?"

Men often did best when they were led with questions. They believed they had come up with the ideas presented, which fed their egos and made compliance a simple matter.

For two painful seconds, the superior blinked like he was fighting her spell. He cleared his throat again, checked the paper in the folder in front of him, and struggled. He was at war with himself. The paper had her path spelled out, but he wanted to go along with what she'd said.

"Ah, no," he said at last, staring at the paper instead of looking at her. "You will secure a job on Wall Street as an investment banking analyst, marry a man we determine will have exceptional business and or political prospects, have his children, and support him as he attains a high level in industry or politics. You will be the ultimate insider with access to intelligence China will need—and you will have a pliable husband you will easily convince to do what we need him to do for the benefit of our country."

Jade's heart sank.

This was the worst news possible.

She nodded slightly in gratitude before extending her hand. "Thank you for your trust in me," she said as her superior took the hand and met her eyes. "I will serve the country with all my abilities." She didn't let go. Neither did he. "Will I be coordinating other assets and planning operations in the United States?"

She didn't want to live the life of a worker drone, then a housewife, and finally a mother. But if she was to be stuck in America, she could at least be more than the MSS had planned for her. A fulfilling life shouldn't be out of the question.

"Well," her superior said, his face flushed. "Perhaps I could—"

The door to the secure room burst open, and a beaming man entered, followed by another—one of her instructors. Both men were all smiles.

Her superior pulled his hand away and stood, blood draining from his face.

Jade stood as well, infuriated that her seductive spell had been broken at a crucial moment, but expertly hiding her emotions.

"Excellent," the beaming man said. "You are truly a once-in-a-generation talent," he told her.

"See?" her instructor said. "I told you he would have no chance against her abilities."

"Our apologies to you both," the beaming man said. He had to be her superior's superior. "A final test for our top student, and you excelled. You are truly ready for your assignment in America. You have your orders, and detailed instructions will be in a dossier for review later this morning. During the next four years, you will expand our reach in the United States exponentially. And in twenty or thirty years, you will be a resource beyond measure. Our ultimate insider." He paused and turned serious. "You will be the trusted sounding board of a titan of industry. An influential senator's wife—or perhaps the mother of one. Maybe…" he trailed off as if saying the words would jinx them, but pushed on, quieter. "More, even, than that." His eyes had grown wistful.

The men left, with her superior glancing back at her, yearning.

These men had decided her future, and there was nothing she could do about it.

21

───────────

THE WARNING

New York University
Greenwich Village
Manhattan

Jade's mind returned to the office in New York and her present situation. She had one last chance to change her fate.

Her student advisor on the other side of the cluttered desk was Robert Zhao—definitely not his real name.

He had proven frustratingly immune to her every attempt to influence him.

Some people—men and women—were like that. They seemed to have a natural immunity against her charms, like a person who could be around others with the flu and never get sick.

Thankfully, there were few like that.

Americans responded to her persuasion even more than the Chinese. Many—the American men in particular—needed her only to laugh at their jokes, listen to their stories, and be there for them. She didn't have to use romance nearly as much as she'd initially thought she would.

Jade had recruited far more assets with her ability to listen than with flirting or sex.

Zhao glanced at his tablet computer and shook his head. "I'm sorry, Jade," he said, a hard look on his older, weathered face. Like her, he had no accent despite growing up in China and attending the same spy school she had. He was near retirement age, but getting him into the faculty position at the school must have been difficult for the Ministry of State Security. Jade doubted they would let him leave until they had another person on the inside to handle the student spies.

"Your request for reassignment has been denied. Again." His tone left no doubt that he was neither surprised nor sorry.

"But—" she said.

He cut her off immediately, like men did to women all the time, including her despite her abilities. "Jade, you are a once-in-a-generation talent."

She was so tired of hearing that. What good were talents if she couldn't use them the way she wanted? And she had much more to offer than the ability to seduce and coerce.

Jade forced down her desire to speak over him, turning instead to other options.

He was immune to her charms. That was out.

And they were only on the third floor of the building.

Zhao's thick body would make more of a *thud* than Turbo's *splat*. There was no guarantee he'd die from the fall, however.

So she would have to continue suffering through his condescension.

"Your IQ is off the charts," her faculty advisor and controller said. "You were the top of your training class. Think of the importance of your assignment. Yes, it sounds boring. You will not be stalking through dark alleys in Paris or recruiting assets in Taipei. There will be no grand plots and plans to destabilize the countries of our adversaries. No, the MSS is putting its full faith in you. You want to make a difference, you say." He leaned forward and spoke low, though he'd undoubtedly swept the room for listening devices prior to their meeting. "You know how you make a difference? By doing your assigned job, the one specifically chosen for you and your talents!"

Jade looked down, acting the chastised, demure woman as expected. "I understand," she said quietly.

They wanted her to seduce.

She wanted to plan operations. It's what she excelled at. That was her true talent.

The man across the desk from her knew nothing.

Her superiors at the Ministry of State Security—all men—knew nothing.

Jade had planned the SystemSpike, as the Americans called it.

Only bad luck, restraint on the parts of both the American and Russian presidents, and the surprising capture of the hand-picked Russian hackers had caused it to fail.

She should be in command, running operations from Beijing, not working one-hundred- hour weeks on Wall Street until it was time for her to marry a man the MSS selected and have his babies.

"Beijing is annoyed with your lack of acceptance of your current assignment," Zhao continued. "It is a black mark on your file. All you've been asked to do is excel in your studies, recruit assets who may be valuable at some point, and secure the specified job offer. You've done that exceptionally well. Their faith in you and your abilities was well-founded. But until you are called upon to plan minor missions of your own in the future, you are better suited for your current role."

If only they knew what I accomplished, Jade thought. *How good I am at planning missions. The funds I raised. Selecting, recruiting, and hiring Boris Zorinov. Planning and directing the SystemSpike operation. The assets I used—and the others I have available for the upcoming attack.*

All while studying and maintaining a perfect GPA.

She had done it all.

And no one suspected her—not even her own country's spy agency.

Jade had missed a few seconds of what Zhao had said, but she tuned back in to hear the ultimatum in his voice. "I suggest embracing your role and understanding your place."

A warning, then. To accept her status as a woman. A tool for men to direct and control.

Her anger flared in sudden, dangerous rebellion. "And if not? What will you do? As you said, I was the top of my class. The instructors called me brilliant—I know this." She crossed her arms in defiance and sat back. "The Ministry of State Security needs me more than I need them."

She regretted the words, and most importantly, the tone, the moment she finished. "I'm sorry," she whispered. "I have been under a great deal of stress. Finals. And the man I was ordered to take as my primary boyfriend—Darius, the Iranian—has fallen for me. Handling the breakup without hurting his feelings and burning the bridge, ruining the recruitment, is taking all of my energy." She took a shuddering breath, only partly acting. "I look forward to the opportunities in my new position and life at the Wall Street firm. Serving China well with my entire being is my greatest desire."

Zhao didn't speak. The seconds dragged on.

There was at least one other long-term sleeper spy at the school. A man named Lu Tantai, trained as an assassin. They had started the same year, though they barely kept in touch. They both had roles to play, and spending time together didn't accomplish their goals. Besides, he had made a clumsy play for her when they'd first arrived, and she'd shot him down—a bit too harshly, perhaps, looking back at it.

Would Zhao instruct Tantai to kill her and vanish her body?

Or send her back to Beijing for painful "re-education"?

At least a minute passed. Jade kept her face lowered, staring at the messy desk, waiting for Zhao to speak.

To forgive her and let her go.

Or to end her career.

The other option: to let her think she was safe while behind the scenes he planned her demise.

"I understand the stress you must be under," Zhao finally said. But the way he spoke…

He's implying that it's because I am a woman. That a man wouldn't be as emotional. The bastard.

"Next week, in our final meeting before you are handed over to your permanent contact, we will revisit your state of mind. Yes?"

"Yes, sir," she said, as meekly as she could muster. Stupid of her to allow the outburst. It couldn't happen again.

In a few months, she would have millions of dollars. If she wanted to vanish, she could abandon the life of selling her soul and body for her country.

And before she went, there would be time to eliminate those who had crossed her.

Jade stood, bowed her head, and left, closing the door quietly behind her.

Yes. Zhao would be one of the first she killed, if she went that route.

Boris Zorinov, wherever he was, would be the next.

But it would all have to wait until after her upcoming attack on America.

22

THE YACHT

Aboard M/Y *Eclipse*
Can Pastilla
Majorca, Spain

The evening ocean breeze had a bite to it.

Boris Zorinov turned his face to the fading sunset and closed his eyes. His lips twitched in a slight smile as he buttoned his cashmere cardigan against the chill. He loved the Spanish islands in the late spring. The heat wasn't unbearable by noon, as it would be in July. And the hordes of tourists—Germans, British, and his fellow Russian countrymen—hadn't arrived yet.

There was little chance he'd be recognized.

Not that his face was famous. He looked like an average sixty-something Caucasian. A round face, blue eyes, average lips and nose, very short gray hair. Maybe a little sad looking, with the bags under his eyes.

He could be anybody, but he needed to play it safe.

Though for the life of him, he couldn't quite remember why he had confined himself to the yacht when there were world-class hotels on shore waiting for him.

He was forgetting something important, and it pissed him off.

He had stayed on the boat again today, only leaving for his morning open water swim, paced by his security guard and one of the yacht's crew members in the small tender.

The fun of the hotels and shops that lined the pedestrian walkway by the beach, along with Palma's charming old town a few kilometers to the northwest, had to wait for another time when he could enjoy them without fear.

He took a sip of wine, unable to remember the exact vintage, but it tasted delicious.

He felt safe here on the stern of his yacht.

The small one he had boarded on the Spanish mainland after…

Something had happened a few weeks ago to prompt him to leave the hotel in—wherever he had been—and return to the boat.

The authorities had impounded his primary yacht, docked in France, because of… something. His memory these days wasn't as good as it should be, especially starting in the late afternoon. It reminded him of one of those bowls with the holes in the bottom used to drain the water from pasta after cooking—the term escaped him for the moment. Most of the time, his memories were like spaghetti or penne: plenty big enough to stay in the bowl.

But other times, especially in the evening, his memories were like small pasta—orzo or ditalini, maybe—it slipped right through the…

He couldn't get the word into his head.

How could he remember orzo and ditalini but not remember—

Sanctions! That's why they had taken his other yacht, the one everyone knew about. He was on a list of Russians with ties to illegal activity.

Boris smiled wider, staring at the beautiful sand beach a few hundred meters away, with the city of Palma in the distance. The idea of being a master criminal appealed to him. It made him happy, even if they had taken his yacht. He had this one—registered differently, with a small crew who had no idea of his history or who he really was.

His smile faded.

He felt like a good guy, which meant he was being unfairly persecuted.

A white-hot anger flooded his system, threatening to overwhelm him.

He kept the slight smile on his face out of habit. There were two crew members nearby, waiting in case he needed more wine or anything else. He couldn't let them see his anger.

To show emotion was to appear weak.

Colander! Or strainer. That's the tool used for draining pasta.

See, he wasn't losing his mind. The memories always returned eventually.

The rage faded quickly, leaving him annoyed and confused. But he had the sense that he'd remember more details of his life in the morning when he was rested.

For now, he had a glass of excellent wine, a view of Mallorca to one side and the Mediterranean Sea to the other, and the two attentive young crew members, standing at ease with their hands clasped behind their backs, wearing navy-and-white striped T-shirts, ready to fetch him anything he desired.

His name was Boris, and he was so rich he had nothing to worry about.

That was all he needed to know for the moment.

He took another sip of the wine.

This was nothing like his childhood—he recalled that perfectly.

The hunger and fear of living on the streets.

Stealing anything of value to trade for the smallest morsel of food so he could survive another day.

Defending himself from an early age, or trying to. He lost often. Was beaten and abused. Had his precious food taken from him.

Eventually, he learned to fight and win. Not to learn was to die.

At last, he could beat the other street children who had harmed him days, months, or years before. And, most of the time, defend himself from the adults that preyed on the children.

He starved less and less. Gathered a gang of kids around him. Used the stronger ones to expand his territory. And protected the weaker ones, like they were a family.

Someone walked between Boris and the last of the sunset. A short, balding man stood before him with a pleasant smile, but his eyes were sharp and probing. He wore dark slacks and an unbuttoned white short-sleeved dress shirt. His arms were tan and thick.

"Ah, good evening…" Boris said, sitting straighter. He was about to greet the familiar-looking man by name but realized he didn't remember it. "What's new?" The question came to him as the one to use when he had an off moment.

The faint flicker in the eyes of… Evgeny! Boris had the name, but not the man's position or relationship.

"Good evening," Evgeny said. "If you're done with your wine, perhaps you'd enjoy dinner? The chef has made blinis topped with caviar and king crab for you."

Boris read between the lines. By the man's expression and body language, they had done this dance before. Many times. This was Boris's chance to dismiss the man, to assert himself. To stay on the aft deck of the yacht, finish his wine, and maybe nod off for a brief nap before going to bed in his stateroom. But the man—Evgeny, right?—was looking out for him. Boris could feel it. Managing him, yes, but doing it respectfully.

"Of course," Boris said, standing with the wine glass, still smiling pleasantly. "Dinner sounds wonderful. Will you be joining me?"

Evgeny hid his reaction, but Boris caught the brief look that flitted across the man's face. Boris had made a mistake.

It hit him then: Evgeny was the captain of the yacht and supervised the crew.

Boris ate alone.

The help didn't join him. Not even the captain.

The hidden look on Evgeny's face was twofold: concern, and surprise at how nicely Boris had spoken to him.

Boris had a realization he couldn't shake: he wasn't a nice man.

The thought brought a surge of rage like what he'd felt earlier.

Along with a combination of hatred, pain, grief, bitterness, and something more.

Ruthlessness.

The uncertainty and confusion vanished.

Memories flooded in.

The cyberattacks he had orchestrated against the United States.

The unfortunate lack of deaths at the peace summit in Oman.

And the people who were extremely unhappy that the results were nowhere near what Boris had confidently promised.

Jade, who had tried to have him killed recently—a few nights ago? Last week?

He was meant to be hunting her, not hiding on his boat.

But the Americans and Russians must be searching for him, whether specifically by name or merely as the unknown person responsible for so much death and destruction.

His eyes narrowed, and the stupid smile fled his face.

Which was the better play: to stay safely hidden on the boat? Or leave and attack Jade?

Boris glared at Captain Evgeny, daring him to say something about the memory lapses, the short-lived politeness, or anything else.

"It's about damn time," Boris said, his voice low and cold.

The captain looked relieved at Boris's tone.

"Right this way, sir," Evgeny said, and led him into the yacht's main salon.

The blinis smelled wonderful.

His mind turned to seeking a solution to his situation other than the orders he'd given the yacht's captain: to slowly cruise the Mediterranean islands off of Spain until Boris figured a way out of the mess he found himself in.

He could only hope that an analyst in one of America's intelligence agencies was smart enough to follow the trail of breadcrumbs he'd had his Russian hackers leave behind, leading them to his fellow Russian, Vasily Chekov.

Vasily would do nicely as the fall guy.

23

THE CLOSET

Unit 47A
The Summit at 57th
Manhattan

The walk-in closet Mariana shared with Kelton was bigger than her old apartment in Texas, and she barely had enough clothes to fill one small section on her side.

Each week, they went shopping and bought a few more items at prices that shocked her.

After the previous night's mission and the breakfast she'd brought home, she'd had a long nap, cleaned up, and helped prep for the dinner party. The guests were due soon.

Mariana smiled up at Kelton and undid his tie. "It's an informal get-together, darling," she said. "Three other couples. The invitations we sent out specifically said casual attire. So, no tie."

"What if I keep it," he said, his hands stopping her, "I don't want to be underdressed."

"Trust me," she whispered, and finished removing the tie. He wore a sharp light-blue shirt that cost more than she'd made in a week as a small-town police officer. It looked great on him, hugging his thin frame enough to show the muscles he'd put on with regular workouts in the building's gym. They went together every day so he could put on muscle and she could maintain her strength.

"You look like a million bucks," she said, and pecked him on the cheek—then had to wipe off a trace of her lipstick.

"As do you." He grinned and gave her a look she recognized all too well.

"There's no time, and you know it," she said as she turned, feeling a blush come to her cheeks.

Mariana had tried on four outfits, and it was now too late for another. She'd have to stick with the black tunic with gold embroidery over black flared pants and flat designer sandals. In the closet's floor-length mirror, she looked sophisticated. Wealthy.

She was neither, but she could fake it for a few hours.

"We make a great couple, and tonight is going to be perfect," she said, partly for Kelton's benefit, but mostly for herself.

How could killing the guard abducting Haley on Fifth Avenue less than twenty-four hours before be easier than dressing up for an evening to chat with rich people?

Somehow, it was. She'd give almost anything to be in a sensible pantsuit, pistol strapped to her hip, standing at the apartment's front door as tonight's security instead of Mad Dog and Johnboy. But the boys got the easy job while she had to be charming and find common ground with people who were incredibly different from her.

All without sounding like the West-Texas country bumpkin she was.

"Come along, my dear, it's time." She took Kelton's hand, and they walked out of the closet, across the massive bedroom, and down the hall toward the front entryway.

The exquisite smell of caramelizing onions, along with garlic, coriander, and cumin, permeated the condo. Their new chef—Lalia—was making a traditional Pashto dish but substituting chicken for lamb. Her husband, Jamil, would be the server.

The guests would arrive any minute, and Mariana couldn't decide if it was dread or anticipation that made her heart pound so hard.

24

THE PARTY CRASHER

The Summit at 57th
Manhattan

Vasily sat in the back of the armored SUV, waiting for his chance.

There was only so much he could do with what he had, but he'd dressed in comfortable dark slacks and an untucked long-sleeved black shirt that hid his middle. Casual, as the invitation he hadn't received had specified.

There was nothing to be done about his blocky head, the deep bags under his eyes, his thinning, balding hair, or his overall bland appearance, but tonight was the chance to transcend that and have some real fun.

An SUV similar to his pulled into the loading zone ahead of him, an area in front of the building with asphalt painted dark red.

"Get ready," he said to the two security guards who would escort him. "This might be one of the guests."

A few seconds after the driver of the other SUV opened the rear curbside door, a man in his mid-forties emerged. He was tall, tan, and fit, and wore gray chinos, black loafers, and a tight white polo shirt that showed his muscles.

"That's Hans Eriksen," Vasily said. "This is it. Wait for his date, though."

Eriksen extended his hand and helped a tall, elegant woman with fiery red hair step onto the sidewalk. A luxurious white silk slip dress that looked more like lingerie than something worn to a casual dinner party fell to her ankles, revealing strappy white high heels.

"Oh, good," Vasily said. "Tiffany." They shared an interest in tennis and often ran into each other at tournaments. She'd be on his side with the stunt from the start.

"Let's go."

He exited the SUV, not waiting for the guards.

"Hans! Tiff! Fancy meeting you here," Vasily called.

One of Hans's guards moved to intercept him, but Hans waved him off. "Let him through. Vasily? I didn't realize you were invited." They met halfway to the building's tall front doors. A doorman dressed in a ridiculous green uniform with gold piping waited for them while studiously ignoring their conversation.

Vasily leaned in for an air kiss near both of Tiff's cheeks before whispering to them. "I'm not. I'm hoping you can help me pull off a Kelton."

"A Kelton?" Tiffany said. A second later, she got the reference. "Oh, that's brilliant." She gave him a frank appraisal. "I didn't realize you had stunts like this in you."

"Looks can be deceiving, my dear."

Hans didn't understand. He crossed his arms, biceps bulging, and scowled at Vasily's banter with Tiffany.

"You know," Vasily continued, "like Kelton did at the charity dinner in Los Angeles a while back. He crashed it—offered a huge check so he could get in. I wasn't there, but I figure turnabout is fair play, right? It'll be the talk of the meal—and in return for your help, I'll match what you're donating tonight…" Hans still wasn't sold. "And donate the same amount again to another charity in your name."

The fitness dude grinned, perfect white teeth shining. "In that case, by all means, my friend. Tell the guard you're Preston Erginwen. He's on the invitee list, and he's always late."

"Great," Vasily said, leading the way. "Let's go have some fun."

The look on Kelton's face was going to be priceless.

25

____

THE DOOR

Unit 47A
The Summit at 57th
Manhattan

Standing in the condo's entry foyer, Mariana did her best to relax. A couple hours of chitchat with six of the richest men and women in New York. No problem. They were just people. Yes, they moved in different circles, didn't take the subway, and had never driven a cop car around a small town night after night on patrol. But they watched TV, read books, and ate; there had to be some common ground she could find.

Worst-case scenario, she would ask questions, laugh where appropriate, and let them tell stories about places they'd been.

Kelton, standing next to her, took her hand. "You'll be fine," he whispered.

Mad Dog and Johnboy stood at parade rest on each side of the door, more for appearances than because of a threat. One of them would escort the guests' security people to a room for snacks and beverages while their protectees had dinner in the main dining room.

Mad Dog's head moved a bit, drawing her attention, and he winked. "You can always shoot them," he mouthed, then had to hold back a laugh at his own joke.

He was being his usual smart-ass self, but Mariana had chosen the slacks and loose top to hide a small pistol in a holster inside her waistband. With this group, nothing would happen, but she always carried a weapon these days—including the folding knife clipped at the small of her back. If it was good enough for Haley and Axe—her heroes—it was good enough for her. She was a full-fledged member of the team now, and from all she'd heard, seen, and done, things could—and often did—go south at the drop of a hat around these guys.

"First guests on the elevator now," Mad Dog said. He had a small earbud connected to the building's people in the lobby. "Hans Eriksen, and his plus one—Tiffany. One name only, I like the spirit. And Preston Ergi…" He faltered.

"Erginwen is here already?" Kelton asked with a chuckle. "That's a first. He's notoriously late. And solo? His wife must be off on one of her shopping trips."

Kelton had gotten over his previous nervousness and was in the groove. Tonight was another step back into society after his "troubles," as he referred to them—when he'd gotten greedy, gone rogue, and gave the wrong man too much power, causing his empire to crumble.

Kelton whispered to her. "Greeting people at the door like this is…" He hesitated, grasping for the word. "Quaint. And eccentric. The guests are going to love it."

Mariana had insisted they do it this way—like normal people. No servants to answer the door and escort the guests inside. Together, she and Kelton would greet the first to arrive. She would take them into the living room and socialize as Kelton stayed at the door to say a few words to each as the rest entered.

Mariana had memorized everyone's face—there were plenty of pictures on the internet of each couple—and details of their lives. She had several questions ready as conversation starters if the chitchat faltered.

A firm knock came at the door. Kelton squeezed her hand and opened it wide.

"Welcome!" he called to the first three guests.

Hans Eriksen: a young, extremely fit, jet-setting businessman.

His on-again, off-again girlfriend Tiffany, who was a fashion model when she felt like it.

And a man who didn't look at all like old Preston Erginwen. This person had sagging jowls and thinning gray hair. The bland appearance contrasted with his huge grin and the sparkle in his eyes.

Mariana made the connection an instant before Kelton said the name. "Vasily Chekov? What are you— Oh!" He chuckled. "You're…"

"Pulling a Kelton!" Chekov finished, joining Kelton in uproarious laughter.

Vasily Chekov. Under suspicion for terrorism against the United States of America, Russia, and the peace summit in Oman.

The man whose guard she had shot last night.

Whose right-hand man she and Mad Dog had approached.

One of very few people in the world who could have accessed the polonium-210 in Russia that had been used to murder Secretary of State Hank Wilson eight weeks before.

The first of two suspects for Haley, Axe, and the team to investigate.

Mariana forced herself to chuckle along with Kelton and Chekov.

There was no way for Chekov to know her. Petrov, his right-hand man, wasn't in the hallway. Besides, in the expensive clothing with her long dark hair down, she looked completely different from the buttoned-up, stern police officer she had played in the early hours of the morning.

The laughter faded to smiles. Kelton shook the party crasher's hand before turning to her. "Welcome everyone. This is my girlfriend, Mariana. Mariana, this is Hans, Tiffany, and Vasily, who we were not expecting but will somehow squeeze in. He did what I did at the party in Los Angeles I told you about."

Officially, she hadn't been there, though she had been instrumental in saving the day and killing many of the terrorists who had attacked that night.

Mariana smiled at each, murmuring, "Nice to meet you."

Her eyes met Chekov's last. His expression had changed from that of a prankster to an apex predator.

It made her blood run cold.

Somehow, Chekov recognized her.

26

THE KITCHEN

Unit 47A
The Summit at 57th
Manhattan

Vasily bided his time over drinks and then dinner, enjoying the tension—though no one else sensed the electricity between him and Mariana farther down the table.

He laughed, told a few stories, and had fun—exactly as he'd planned.

As everyone finished their meals, the opportunity he'd been waiting for finally arrived.

"I'll go check on dessert," Mariana said quietly, more to Kelton than the rest of the table. She pushed her chair back and headed toward the door into the kitchen.

"And I need to use the washroom," Vasily murmured. He stood and walked toward the hall but turned and pushed through the same door Mariana had.

The rest of the party continued around the table as Kelton started a story about his time relaxing in the Caribbean.

"Need any help with dessert?" Vasily said as the door swung closed behind him. He expected to see the husband-and-wife team who had cooked and served dinner, but the spacious kitchen was empty except for

Mariana standing near a beautifully decorated cake on the large granite island.

Mariana smiled at him. Her dark, hard eyes shone in the sparkling clean kitchen.

"It's an Afghan saffron cake with orange blossom cream," she said, nodding at the ornate cake with fresh figs scattered around it on the tray. "Laila made it. It smelled heavenly while baking. If it tastes half as good, we're in for a treat."

Vasily hesitated. The woman didn't seem at all put off by his presence in the kitchen.

On the contrary, it suddenly felt like he had stepped into her trap instead of her into his.

Still, he pushed through. Despite his bland looks and fun intentions tonight, he hadn't built his fortune by being someone easily pushed around. He had a sharp mind and killer instincts. There was no reason for the American authorities to target him; he was innocent. It was time to put a stop to their pursuit, and the woman in the kitchen with him was the key to it.

"All night," she continued, "you've had something to say. This is your chance. We're alone. Laila and Jamil are off for the rest of the evening. The security guards are in another room. Kelton will keep the rest of them entertained for a while. What have you got?"

This wasn't going at all as Vasily had planned. But he'd been in countless tense business negotiations. This was no different.

"Before the party wraps up, I wanted to take a moment to reach an agreement about our situation."

"Thank you," Mariana said. "I was hoping we could."

Vasily kept a pleasant smile on his face, but the woman's straightforward attitude confused him. Where was the fear? The anxiety at having her secret known and potentially exposed?

It didn't matter. He had the upper hand.

He took a step closer and lowered his voice. "My offer is this: I will keep your secret about what happened last night. I'll tell no one, including the New York police department. They would surely be interested in the video of you impersonating an officer. Especially after the death of one of my men. I will also not mention the events to any of the numerous media outlets that would surely be interested. And once my security team discovers the names of the others who were with you last night, and the person or organization who hired you, I will not reveal the information to anyone, either." He paused and considered. "Though I will take appropriate actions to protect my interests, those actions will not include… How do you Americans say it? 'Selling you out.' I am innocent of whatever you think I've done."

He waited for Mariana's inevitable question.

"And in exchange for your silence?" she asked with an amused twitch of her lips that he found disconcerting—and oddly alluring. No wonder Kelton had scooped her up.

"You owe me a favor of my choosing." One of her eyebrows went up. "With conditions, of course. I will not expect you to betray your country, Kelton, or anyone you work with." Vasily offered an easy smile and extended his hand. "Consider it a debt I may collect someday when it suits me. Do we have a deal?"

His smile turned forced when Mariana immediately shook her head. He dropped both the smile and his hand.

"You're a very successful businessman," Mariana said at the reaction. "You should expect to negotiate."

Vasily hadn't thought there would be a discussion. He had all the cards. If he contacted the NYPD with the video footage, there would be questions. Assuming Mariana worked for the FBI, Homeland Security, or another department of the American government, the mission to intercept Petrov had been approved at a high level, so there would be no repercussions. But today's absence of a follow-up—the appearance of an official with a fake badge wanting to have an unofficial "chat," showed that whoever had handled the operation the night before wanted to keep it quiet.

If Vasily offered the video footage to one of many New York City media outlets, however, they would jump at the chance to report on it.

FBI Spies on Prominent Businessman or ***Homeland Security Conducts Deadly Operation on Upper East Side, Killing Local Man***

And when he let slip that Kelton Kellison was dating an FBI, CIA, or other agency's spy, Kelton's social standing would plummet. His life would once again revert to that of a second-string has-been, and his recent rise to glory would fade before it had truly returned.

"What is your counter-proposal?" Vasily asked with a newfound respect for his adversary.

Mariana took a slow step toward him, stopped, and spoke low. "You keep my secret, and in exchange, I allow you to leave this apartment alive."

Vasily chuckled, delighted by her jest. Kelton must have his hands full with this one.

She stepped closer still, and he belatedly realized that he was much more physically vulnerable than he'd thought.

Many of his peers were wanna-be fighters. They had mixed martial arts instructors, private boxing coaches, or jiu-jitsu sparring partners. They acted tough. A few could back up their posturing with skills, though Vasily doubted they were as strong and capable as they believed themselves to be.

He, however, had never been a fighter—at least physically. He was flabby and weak. His toughness came on the business side, at the negotiating table, with his ability to read his opponents and exploit their vulnerabilities.

Standing toe to toe with Mariana, he realized that he had misread her completely and underestimated the woman's strength of will.

He searched her face and body language, hoping for a sign that she was bluffing, but she was serious about her offer.

She was willing to kill him right there in the kitchen while the rest of the guests laughed and chatted in the dining room only steps away.

And if he was reading her correctly, which he'd bet a fortune he finally was, she not only was prepared to kill him…

She wanted to.

Mariana Rodriguez, pretend NYPD officer and Kelton Kellison's girlfriend, was seconds away from murdering him.

Whether she would get away with it or not didn't matter. Not to her, and not to him.

He was about to die.

His two-man security detail relaxed in a room down the hall. They believed he was safe at a party of harmless, ultra-rich men and women who never got their hands dirty. People like tonight's guests frowned at cleaning a wine glass or putting a plate in the dishwasher. None of them were killers.

Except Mariana.

Vasily took a step back, but Mariana kept pace with him.

This was ridiculous. Things like this didn't happen. Rarely did anyone get the better of him in a business situation or negotiation. He was always more informed, better prepared, and had contingencies for everything under the sun.

And yet here he was. Alone in a room with a deranged woman who was willing to kill to keep her secret.

"I need your answer," she said. Her body was tight with coiled energy.

"I agree," Vasily said. There was no alternative. He had mistakenly assumed the woman would be easy prey.

He'd been trapped, as he'd done countless times to his adversaries in offices and boardrooms around the world.

And like them, his only choice was to surrender.

Mariana didn't smile. Her eyes bore into his as she raised her hand. They were close enough that she had to draw her elbow back to avoid his chest as she offered it to him.

"I trust you'll honor your commitment," she said. The implication was clear. If he didn't, there would be hell to pay.

Their eyes stayed locked. It was crazy for him to agree to the deal. He had the leverage. But he was absolutely convinced that if he didn't take Mariana's hand, he'd be lying dead on the kitchen floor in a few seconds.

Vasily clasped her hand and sealed the deal.

Mariana smiled, but Vasily had the unshakable impression that she was disappointed. The spark left her eyes, and the smile was less one of conquest, as he expected, and almost... sad. Dejected, like he had stolen a golden opportunity she'd been looking forward to.

"We'd better get back to the party, don't you think?" Mariana asked. She moved to the kitchen island and lifted the cake tray before nodding for him to lead the way. "Give me a hand, please."

Vasily held the door for Mariana. She carried the cake into the dining room as Kelton finished his story.

Everyone laughed, charmed at the tale, and Vasily envied Kelton for his relationship with a woman of Mariana's caliber.

He also pitied him.

Did Kelton know what type of person she was?

If not, he was in for a rude awakening someday soon.

Vasily returned to his seat to enjoy a slice of the cake, wondering about his next move—and Mariana's.

27

THE DISCUSSION

Unit 47A
The Summit at 57th
Manhattan

Mariana finished putting the last wine glass in one of the condo's two dishwashers, added a detergent pod, and started the cleaning cycle. The high-end machine barely made a sound.

Kelton came into the kitchen from the dining room. "All clear," he said. He rinsed a microfiber cloth in the kitchen sink next to her, his bony hip nudging her more padded one. He hadn't argued when she'd suggested they clean up after the party to give Jamil and Laila the rest of the night off after making and serving dinner.

Preston Erginwen had been late to arrive and the last to leave, but finally, they were alone in the kitchen.

She had to tell him about the confrontation with Vasily Chekov.

Didn't she?

They had an agreement. Kelton asked no questions about her role on Axe and Haley's unsanctioned asset team, and she told him no lies.

Last night had been her first mission since they'd moved in together.

She had come home at dawn with the bagels and egg sandwiches, eaten with Jamil, Laila, Void, and Kelton, taken a shower, and climbed into bed to sleep for several hours.

All without mentioning killing someone or the scuffle with Rodney, the new front desk man in the lobby.

When she'd awoken, before they started prepping for the party, she had told him there had been a problem on the mission the previous night, but that it had worked out fine.

Nothing about the failed recruitment of Petrov, the goons from the black sedan, or how she had shot at Haley and lucked into killing her teammate's attempted abductor instead.

And, of course, she hadn't mentioned that Vasily Chekov, the fifth richest man in the world, was one of two targets the team was investigating. She'd guessed—correctly—that Kelton would know the man, at least in passing.

No need to muddy the waters and give Kelton information he would have to hide. He was horrible at lying about things like that.

"Tonight went great," Kelton said, pressing tighter against her side. Mariana leaned in, relishing the connection.

"In large part thanks to you," he added. "The guests loved the informality. Tiffany said it was the first party she'd been to that felt 'real.'"

Mariana smiled and decided not to tell him anything.

He didn't need to know.

"And can you believe Vasily?" Kelton chuckled, delighted. "People are going to be calling it 'pulling a Kelton.' I'm back, baby!" He turned and put his arms around her. "Thank you."

He leaned forward to kiss her as Mad Dog swung the door from the dining room open and stepped into the kitchen, catching her eyes a second before she closed them for Kelton's kiss.

She read his expression with ease.

Mad Dog knew.

She gave Kelton a peck, much less than he'd been expecting, and backed out of his arms.

Johnboy followed Mad Dog in, and they pulled up stools on the far side of the kitchen island. "Two of your finest beers, please, barkeep," Mad Dog said with a grin at Kelton, who chuckled, reluctantly released Mariana, and fetched beers from the refrigerator for them all. Mariana returned hers, taking a bottle of water instead.

"To a very successful dinner party, and my lovely hostess," Kelton said, raising his bottle. They toasted, Mad Dog half standing on the stool's lower rung to reach across the massive island.

A subtle tension filled the room, though Mad Dog and Johnboy said nothing.

After a few seconds, though, Kelton caught onto the vibe. "What is it? What's wrong? We raised millions for charity. The food was delicious. And everyone had a good time." He paused, glancing at the warriors before finally landing on Mariana. "Right?"

Mariana nodded and reassured him. "Everyone had a great time. It's just…"

She struggled with what to say.

"Vasily?" Kelton asked. "I'm sorry. Did him crashing the party throw things off too much? I thought it was rude, sure, but quite clever. He's so bland looking, but inside…"

The men nodded and smiled, but they weren't very convincing.

"Chekov," Kelton said, thinking it through. "An extremely wealthy Russian oligarch." He looked at Mad Dog, then back to her. She could practically see the pieces falling into place as he figured out the situation. "Last night's mission?" he asked, quickly coming down from the high of the successful party.

When none of them said anything, Kelton nodded. In a moment, he switched into the businessman mode that had made him one of the richest men in the country a few years earlier, and was bringing him back into the limelight, ready to reclaim his status in society.

"Got it," he said, his voice sure and firm. "Thank you, gentlemen, for your efforts tonight," he said to Mad Dog and Johnboy, who nodded back. "Stay as long as you like. It's late. Sleep in the guest rooms. I'm going to clean up and get ready for bed. Darling," he said to Mariana, "I'll see you when you're finished here."

He dumped the rest of the beer down the sink, rinsed the bottle, and placed it in the recycling bin under the sink before giving Mariana a peck on the cheek and exiting the kitchen.

After a few seconds, Mad Dog burped quietly, excused himself under his breath, and spoke. "He's a solid guy."

"Here, here," Johnboy said, and raised his bottle for Mad Dog to toast. "Smart. But a terrible liar when it comes to our stuff."

"Yep. Best to keep him in the dark. We might need him again," Mad Dog said.

"No," Mariana said, more sharply than she'd intended. "Let's try to keep him out of it this time around."

Both of the warriors nodded at her, but if the team needed Kelton's expertise, they would have to ask him.

And he would say yes despite the fear and the risk.

"Chekov marked me from the start—right at the door," Mariana said. "He knew I was the cop that talked to Petrov last night."

"He must have video surveillance of the street," JB said.

"Sounds like it," Mariana agreed. "But how much did he see?"

"He looked right through me," Mad Dog said. "But last night, I was at an angle to you. Maybe his coverage was limited."

"If he has Axe and Haley…" Mariana said, not wanting to go there. The whole idea of a clandestine organization was to be unknown—especially to your target.

"Should we kill him?" Mad Dog asked, his voice low and serious. "Tonight? We could go right now, the three of us. After seeing you in action on the rooftop in Los Angeles, Tex," he said to Mariana, "I give us even odds, no matter how good his security is."

Mariana considered the question and glanced at JB, who focused on finishing the last of his beer.

When no one answered, Mad Dog shook his head. "I was kidding. Geez, you guys are tightly wound tonight. How did you leave it with Chekov?"

"I channeled my inner Haley Albright and said I would let him leave the apartment alive if he told no one about last night on Fifth Avenue."

Johnboy chuckled appreciatively and raised the nearly empty bottle in her direction. "Nice."

"Well done," Mad Dog said. "Since he left with his limbs intact and without blood spurting from large, gaping wounds, I'm guessing he agreed?"

"Yes," she said, appreciating Mad Dog's levity. "But… he claimed he was innocent. I think he knows what we suspect him of doing. And I'm sorry, but I believed him."

They sat with that for a few seconds.

"Is he the kind of guy that keeps his promises?" Mad Dog asked.

"Let's hope so," Mariana muttered. "For all our sakes."

"Who's going to tell Haley?" Mad Dog said, followed immediately by, "Not it!"

"Not it," Johnboy said, nearly at the same time.

"Shit," Mariana muttered, and reached for her phone.

28

THE REPORT

Vasily sat at the small table in the kitchen, drinking tea.

The confrontation with Mariana in the kitchen earlier had put a damper on his enjoyment of the evening, but the more he considered it, the better he felt.

It had been a long time since anyone had gotten the better of him.

He had crashed Kelton's dinner party; Mariana had put him in his place.

Petrov sat at the table with him, and when Vasily nodded, began reciting a report from memory.

"Mariana Rodriguez. Security guard turned girlfriend of Kelton Kellison, though there are no pay records or proof of employment. I pulled every string I could. She is exactly what she appears to be: a former small-town police officer from Texas who somehow met Kelton Kellison and became his girlfriend."

"She wasn't concerned about my going to the NYPD with the security footage. In fact, she wasn't worried about killing me—at least in that moment. That isn't a small-town police officer. She has to be more than that."

Petrov shook his head. "Not that I can find. But yes, Rodriguez, the other 'police officer,' plus the warrior and the blond fighter—it suggests a team of operators. Who they work for, however, is unknown."

"What's most concerning is being framed for the poisoning of the Secretary of State. The real problem isn't Mariana Rodriguez. It's Boris Zorinov framing me for stealing polonium-210 and assassinating America's Secretary of State. While I may occasionally skirt the letter of the law in a few of my business dealings, I am not a thief, or criminal, or murderer. Boris Zorinov is the only other person who could have done this. What is the status of the search for Boris?"

"We have nothing, sir. He disappeared from his home eight weeks ago."

"Eight weeks? During the SystemSpike? Sloppy of him. He should have waited a week or two, or announced a pre-planned off-grid trip to cover for his absence. The timing is too perfect. He's on the run."

"He is reported to prefer France, Monaco, and Spain, so I have people actively searching the nicest hotels and restaurants, as well as reaching out to immigration contacts. To be thorough, I've put out a worldwide alert to our contacts offering a generous reward for information. But so far, nothing."

Vasily pondered the problem. "No one can truly disappear. What about yachts?"

"His was impounded last year."

"He has another. I'm sure of it. Registered differently, not connected to him. Look into that angle. And did your alert include the United States, or only Europe?"

"The United States as well."

"Good. He'll turn up. And when he does, I will offer him to Mariana Rodriguez in exchange for..." He trailed off, unsure what he wanted.

Vasily sipped his tea, lost in thought, never quite allowing himself to admit his deepest desire. He looked up some time later and realized he was alone.

PART 4

TUESDAY

29

THE SPETSNAZ

Can Pastilla
Majorca, Spain

The four men of the Russian special forces team joked quietly as they walked side by side along the pedestrian roadway by the beach. Hotels, shops, restaurants, and bars lined the street to their left.

All were closed this late at night, even the bars and many gelato stands.

On the right, a wide sand beach dotted with deserted lifeguard towers waited for the tourists that would descend on it in the morning.

Most of the spring tourists were already in bed, but a few strays wandered ahead and behind them, drunk or jet-lagged.

"Bear" led the group. He and his men were dressed in quick-dry black shorts and tight black T-shirts that showed off their muscles. Their beards were bushy, their hair much longer than military regulations normally allowed. All part of their cover as Russian tourists looking for love on a vacation in paradise.

They reached a short-term-stay apartment building with a convenience store and a tattoo parlor facing the sand. Other shops lined the side street that ran perpendicular to the main tourist walkway—including a dive shop.

There was no discussion. Bear leaned against the corner of the building, keeping an eye open for police or curious late-night tourists.

"Lynx," "Fox," and "Ram" continued up the narrow road. Ram would guard the far end of the street. Lynx and Fox would break into the dive shop and steal what they needed for the mission.

Several minutes later, the three men rejoined Bear at the corner. He accepted a long knife in a sheath and the dive gear. They expertly checked the pressure, air supply, and tested the regulator as they walked across the empty street, through the cool sand, and silently into the water.

Bear kicked his fins, swimming a few meters below the surface. The distance was short enough—only one kilometer—that he relied on dead reckoning and experience to guide him.

A few minutes later, he sensed the yacht looming ahead. They were right on target—at the back of the yacht.

Their intel claimed there would be a single guard, up to six crew, and a captain.

All were to be eliminated.

Their target, however, had to be taken alive.

Bear removed the fins and let them sink. Behind him, the others would do the same. He waited a moment, received a light tap on his shoulder, and took a final breath from the scuba tank before slipping it off and allowing it to sink as well.

After accomplishing their mission, they would raise the yacht's anchors and motor away.

Once out of sight of land, they would chop up the dead and dump the pieces overboard along the way.

The yacht, as nice as it was, would suffer an unfortunate engine fire that would cause catastrophic damage, compromise the hull, and lead to its sinking off the coast of Algiers.

But first, they had to find Boris Zorinov in the spacious owner's suite on the top deck of the yacht and slit the throats of everyone else on the boat.

30

THE DECK

Aboard M/Y *Eclipse*
Can Pastilla
Majorca, Spain

Boris's eyes snapped open. For a moment, he was disoriented. Lost.

He lay on a thick cushion, like one from a chaise lounge, though he was on the ground. He wore a cardigan and chinos and was covered with a wool throw blanket. The night sky spread out above him.

A moment later, the memories crept in. He was Boris Zorinov, a wealthy Russian businessman, and he was on the bow of his yacht.

There was nothing on this area of the deck except for a small gear storage locker and the housing for the anchors. His other yacht, the one the Western authorities had stolen, had six chaise lounge chairs up front. Here, it was only the empty deck and his makeshift bed.

He didn't remember coming to the bow, but his evenings were often a blur lately. This wasn't the first time he'd woken up in an out-of-the-way location on the ship instead of the comfortable owner's cabin, though.

What had awoken him tonight?

Adrenaline coursed through his body. He had the overwhelming desire to run—but why?

And where?

He was on his spare yacht. The small one that he had never mentioned to anyone. He'd handled all the paperwork himself.

Had someone finally found the connection between him and the ship?

Jade?

No. She didn't have the resources to look unless she had involved her government, but she wouldn't do that if she had acted alone, which was his guess.

And China didn't have the on-the-ground resources in Europe to find him.

America or Russia?

It shouldn't have been possible, but both historically had a strong desire for revenge. He wouldn't put it past them to keep hunting him long after it made sense to quietly give up.

But the Russians and Americans should be focused squarely on Vasily Chekov instead.

Boris allowed a cruel grin to spread across his face. He was alone, after all. The staff were asleep, except for the night guard at the yacht's aft swim platform.

And unlike earlier, before dinner, Boris now had his entire faculties. He remembered exactly who he was and what he'd done.

All that he'd accomplished.

The smile slipped.

All that he had nearly accomplished. Only one third of the three-part plan had succeeded.

The SystemSpike had worked as predicted. Casualties were more than expected.

The second part of the mission, however, had failed. Although Boris had secured the polonium-210 and killed the Secretary of State, America and Russia had not gone to war and annihilated each other as hoped.

As for the final stage, the peace summit in Oman had killed only one person—his hand-picked patsy set up to take the fall if things went wrong —instead of the leaders of so many countries in and around the Middle East.

Still, no one should be looking specifically for him aside from Jade. Innocent Vasily Chekov was the target, not him.

Boris lay still, listening to the distant sounds of the city of Palma, but heard nothing alarming.

What had woken him?

Despite leaving no trace of his whereabouts, no connection to the

SystemSpike or other events aside from the polonium-210, and having this yacht in no way connected with his name, could someone have found him?

No. He was being paranoid. First the memory lapses, and now this. He wasn't old, but his mind wasn't what it used to be. He could admit that to himself, as much as he hated it.

Even if the authorities somehow, impossibly, knew about him, they couldn't find him here.

The fight-or-flight response in his body had only grown stronger in the few seconds it took for his train of thought to reach its natural conclusion.

The Americans had the expression, "Better safe than sorry."

In Russia, it was, "God protects the cautious."

And while he had abandoned God decades ago—Boris had no illusions about where he was going after death, with all the evil things he had done in his life—the expression still applied.

With instincts honed by his years of living on the streets as a child, he had the certainty that it was time to go.

It meant leaving behind three passports in other names that would allow him to travel undercover. Plus the credit cards and cash, all locked in the safe in the stateroom where he should be right now. The yacht had been his backup plan, the safe hiding spot where no one would be able to find him if it all went to hell.

He still had an emergency insurance plan, however. If he could slip away now and not get caught, he wouldn't be completely empty-handed.

Boris stood and took precious seconds to fold the wool blanket before setting it on the foot of the padded cushion so it would look as if he hadn't slept there.

Water lapped gently against the hull five meters below. Onshore, a kilometer away, few cars drove along the otherwise quiet streets.

His sense of danger grew.

Boris slipped his loafers on, hurried to the yacht's stainless-steel railing, and threw first one leg then the other over before crouching to grip the deck, easing his body down. He hung from his fingers, arms extended, feet dangling over the dark water.

He drew in a long breath and silently let it out. There were no outward signs of danger, but he couldn't shake the overwhelming need to escape.

Another breath in and out.

Finally, he filled his lungs as deeply as possible, dropped into the water, dove deep, and swam for shore.

31

THE NIGHT

Aboard M/Y *Eclipse*
Can Pastilla
Majorca, Spain

The yacht's main suite was more luxurious than any home Bear could hope for. Perhaps he'd gone into the wrong line of work. Instead of a poorly paid but highly respected Russian special forces soldier, he should have been a money-hungry criminal.

Bear stepped into the opulent stateroom without hurrying, confident his men were sweeping the boat, handling the crew and captain on the decks below. His sole focus was on finding Boris Zorinov, who should be sound asleep in his spacious cabin.

The gentle glow of a nightlight showed an empty bed. The tan duvet was perfectly smooth. Multiple throw pillows rested against the padded headboard. Black silk pajamas, folded neatly, waited for their owner who hadn't come for them.

Bear stalked across the deep pile carpet to the attached office, hoping to find Zorinov asleep at his desk or on a couch, but there was nothing.

Several more steps brought him to the bathroom—the same size as his family's entire apartment in Moscow when he was a child.

Zorinov wasn't there, either.

Bear and his team had been sent to Majorca as tourists with little warning. They didn't have weapons aside from the knives they'd stolen from the dive shop. They had no backup waiting to help on a nearby boat, no drone overhead, or sniper overwatch from shore.

But most importantly, they had no radios for communication.

Bear ran back the way he'd come, down a long hallway to a staircase. He took it down one level to the bridge and captain's quarters, no longer worried about moving silently.

"He's not here," he called in a low voice, hoping at least one of his team would hear. "Don't kill any more of them. We need answers."

A single grunt came from the deck below, followed by a hushed repeating of his orders to the rest of the team.

"How many are dead?" Bear asked.

"All but him," Lynx said, his dive knife pressed to the captain's throat.

They were committed now. The mission had failed, but they had to continue forward.

"One of you at the fore, one at the aft," the leader ordered to his other men. "Watch the water in case he's gone overboard. Go!"

He turned to the terrified captain. "Where is he? Where is Zorinov?"

"In his suite?" he said, more of a question than a statement.

"If you can't help, you're of no use to me," Bear said.

The short, balding captain's eyes widened further. "He wanders at night. Like sleepwalking, in a way. He could be anywhere. The engine room. The galley, maybe. I can help you—"

Bear stepped to the side and nodded to Lynx.

The captain flailed and bucked in Lynx's arms as the soldier sliced the man's throat. Blood sprayed from the wound, ruining the wall and thick carpet of the captain's quarters.

Lynx held the captain upright while he bled out, the captain's hands clenched to his neck, eyes wide with shock and pain.

"You and I will search the ship," Bear said over the sound of the dying man. "Every closet and cupboard, under every bed, anywhere a person could hide. He has to be here."

Bear left unspoken his gut feeling: the man was gone. They'd had eyes on him all afternoon, since Zorinov had gone for a long swim, but somehow he had slipped through their grasp.

"And if he's not?" Lynx asked, bringing up the obvious concern as he dropped the dead captain unceremoniously to the ground.

"We raise the anchors as planned. We can't leave this mess behind for the authorities," he said, gesturing at the captain.

"Then we'll find Zorinov. He has to be here," Lynx repeated, but Bear had worked with the man long enough to know that he didn't believe it, either.

32

THE SWIM

Majorca, Spain

If he weren't swimming for his life, Boris would have found the cool water invigorating.

Several feet underwater, he swam until his lungs burned. He could go no farther.

In case he wasn't paranoid and there were people looking for him, Boris floated slowly toward the surface, using his hands to manage the rise. He exhaled the last of his air as he oriented his body in the water.

Only his nose and mouth broke the surface.

After a quick breath, Boris submerged. He'd only been visible for an instant.

He continued underwater toward the shore, invisible to anyone hunting him, almost enjoying the night swim.

Aboard M/Y *Eclipse*
Can Pastilla
Majorca, Spain

Bear fought the urge to curse as he checked the engine room for the third time. It was the last place Zorinov could be, and there was no sign of him.

"He's not here," Lynx called as he entered, shouting over the running diesel engines required to keep the refrigerators, air conditioning, and the rest of the ship functioning.

"Over the side as we came aboard?" Bear asked as he led the way out of the engine room.

"We made no sound. There was no warning." Lynx thought for a second. "We could go ashore and look."

Bear briefly considered the suggestion.

Every moment ashore put the mission in more danger. They were in Spain as tourists. If anyone noticed them and suspected they were active-duty Russian special forces, there would be hell to pay.

It would be dawn soon. Even one of them emerging from the water would look suspicious, and wandering around as the sun came up, hunting for their man, wouldn't work.

They would have no way to extract him, and there would be too many tourists around to quietly drag him back to the yacht.

"No, we stick with the plan," Bear said.

They climbed the stairs to the main deck, both still on the lookout for the man who had eluded them, hoping that he would pop out of a hidden room or suddenly appear in the hallway with a glass of wine from the bar.

"What will you report?" Lynx asked.

"The truth," Bear said as they entered the bridge. "We conducted the mission exactly as planned—and Boris Zorinov was not on board. Let someone else figure it out. We did our jobs."

It was exactly the right thing to say, but it wasn't the entire truth.

Somehow, Zorinov had slipped through their fingers.

33

THE MARINA

Majorca, Spain

As he neared the shore, Boris swam left around a short rocky peninsula that formed one side of a man-made bay for a yacht club. If someone was truly after him, he had to avoid stumbling out of the water onto the main beach.

His ship had anchored a kilometer offshore both for privacy and because the marina was much too small for his boat to berth there.

The yacht club's quiet location would be perfect for Boris to rest, lie low, and regroup for a few hours this morning.

After more slow trips to the surface for quick breaths, he was finally through the narrow entrance to the yacht club bay. He risked swimming slowly on the surface, staying near the small yachts and sailboats tied to the first of many piers.

Across a narrow waterway, docked to another long jetty extending from the shore, a good-sized sailboat was berthed bow in, unlike most of the other vessels in the area.

Its small swim ladder was easily accessible—and not near the dock.

The boat had a faded and torn bimini and enclosure that covered the stern, where the wheel and navigation equipment were, and wrapped around the cockpit, sheltering it from wind, rain, sun and—most importantly for Boris—prying eyes. The sailboat looked neglected, like someone had enough money to buy it but lacked the time for sailing.

Better still, the boats on either side also had faded decks with a coating of bird droppings.

Lesser-used boats were docked in this area.

Perfect.

Boris drew in another deep breath, slipped underwater, and swam directly for the older sailboat.

He surfaced a few feet from the narrow swim ladder, took a second to check that the surroundings were clear, and pulled himself aboard. His chinos stuck to his legs and expensive cardigan sagged with salt water.

So far, so good.

He moved forward, under the cover. The clear plastic windows were dirty and allowed only the smallest illumination from the nearest dock light.

The teak decking felt rough on his bare feet—he'd lost the loafers a few seconds into the swim—and a film of grime coated every surface. A few steps forward brought him to an access way to the interior cabin. Its padlock was old but sturdy.

The wood of the entrance door, which slid up from the bottom and back from the bow to latch together, preventing access to the cabin, however, was tired and worn from years of exposure to the sea air.

Boris pulled on the lock, tugging at the hinge screwed into the wood, but it didn't budge.

Dripping seawater on the deck and shivering in the crisp pre-dawn air, he took a coiled line from the stern.

Without hurrying, in case anyone was up at this early hour to notice his movement onboard, he took a bight of the line, shoved it through the padlock opening, and tied it off around itself a few inches above the lock.

He ran the rope toward the stern, looped it around a cleat that he hoped could withstand his plan, and backed away.

After wrapping the line around his hand, he pulled, taking up the slack.

Nothing happened.

Boris leaned back, putting all his weight behind it.

Which would give first—the old line, the cleat, or the wood the latch was screwed to?

Something popped, the noise painfully loud in the early morning darkness of the marina.

Boris fell back, slamming into the railing.

The latch screws had pulled from the old wood of the entry doorway.

As chilly as he was, he took the time to untie the line, coil it properly, and hang it where he'd found it.

The padlock and latch came with him as he slid down the main hatch, left wet footprints on the five steep stairs leading into the cabin, and slid the hatch up. It stayed in place. Unless someone came onboard to investigate, nothing would look amiss.

Boris stripped off the wet clothes and wrung them over the sink, naked and shivering in the darkness of the cabin. It smelled of mildew and neglect.

He dried off as best he could with a small kitchen towel hanging from the stove.

In the main stateroom at the bow, he found a blanket to use as a shawl and sat on the bed.

He wore only a neglectful sailboat owner's blanket. His hair was wet, though it no longer dripped seawater.

He had no money, no phone, and no shoes. Someone was hunting him and had boarded his yacht earlier.

Or he was being paranoid and had gone for a cold, early morning swim for no reason.

Time would tell. If his crew woke in a few hours and sent the tender ashore looking for him, it would be clear he had overreacted.

If something happened to his yacht—whether it exploded or motored away—he had been found and his life was in immediate danger.

The swim had awakened in him the memory of the pre-dawn attack a few weeks before in the dark alley when he had killed the would-be assassin.

Boris shivered and wrapped the blanket more tightly around his shoulders. The sailboat would be safe for a day. Maybe two. There would be water to drink, and perhaps a can or two of soup to eat. If not, he'd go hungry. He could live without food for days if he had to. He'd done it before, though it had been decades since the empty belly of his youth.

Food was a minor concern. Clothes, a passport, money, and a way to get off this island were the most important tasks.

If the Russians or Americans had been onboard his yacht tonight, he would have to avoid them as he accomplished his primary objective.

He had to find and kill Jade Pang, now that he remembered that she had sent a man to kill him.

Only then could he find a new place where he could disappear forever.

34

THE PICTURES

Central Analysis Group Headquarters
Arlington, Virginia

Nancy sat in her cubicle. Here in the new office building, Dave had a single cube next to her. Gregory had approved an adjustable partition they could lower when they wanted to collaborate or raise when they needed space to focus on their individual efforts.

Today, taking after Haley, who was still in New York, Nancy slid the partition up, put on her noise-cancelling headphones, pulling her wild hair out of the way, and started a classical music playlist.

She logged into her systems, checked her email, and prepared for the day.

For the past month, she, Dave, and Haley had spent every spare moment hunting the mastermind behind the SystemSpike, after being brought on board by Gregory who had worked on it by himself for the first four weeks.

They were no closer to the truth now than they had been four weeks ago.

Two likely suspects had surfaced: Vasily Chekov and Boris Zorinov, mainly because they were the only two Russians who had the means and connections to steal the polonium-210 used to kill the Secretary of State.

Haley, Axe, and the rest of the team had gone to New York to approach Chekov's right-hand man.

Nothing had come of it, or she would have heard immediately from Haley, who was due back today with a full report.

That left Boris Zorinov, who had vanished.

Nothing could be done on that front, so Nancy turned her attention away from finding out who had attacked the country two months before and focused on who might do so next.

Earlier in the year, Washington, D.C. had been attacked with cruise missiles.

The consensus at CAG headquarters was that Iran was involved.

Iran was a consistent thorn in the side of the United States.

There was a strong possibility Iran was planning attacks against the United States or other Western countries, either through their own operators or, for plausible deniability, extremists and deep-cover sleeper agents.

It had become Nancy's pet project to hunt for Iranian spies in America.

The National Security Agency had recently gained access to millions of pages of old and newer newspapers and magazines formerly available only in Tehran.

Nancy had painstakingly set up a program to compare every picture in the archives with all immigration photos of people who had entered the United States originally via Kuwait, the United Arab Emirates, Oman, Qatar, Turkey, Armenia, Georgia, and Azerbaijan.

The software program was easily overwhelmed, so Nancy batched the searches, setting a new one up each night before leaving for the day.

Last night's search results were ready. She opened the report, expecting the usual mix of false-positives and mismatches. The facial recognition software was state-of-the-art, but it still had to parse faces in grainy photographs scanned from newspapers and magazines and compare them to the stoic passport and immigration pictures from US ports of entry.

The program was eager to assign matches where there weren't any, leaving Nancy with dozens of images to compare each morning.

So far, her human eye had easily eliminated every one.

She was losing hope that her brilliant plan would ever produce a true match.

This morning was no different. Thirty-six individuals who had entered America "matched" people in images from the Iranian media archives.

A picture of a student protester from the 1970s and a thirty-year-old software engineer from the UAE were clearly not the same person, though the computer claimed a seventy-five percent likelihood they were.

Nancy took a sip of her hot coffee as she moved to the next page of the report.

A high-ranking official in the Iranian government gave a speech on a stage twenty-five years ago, surrounded by grim-faced men in the background.

The software had circled the face of a man on the far right of the image. He was in his thirties, handsome, with great hair and the jawline of a movie star.

The computer claimed a seventy-eight percent match with a young man named Darius Al-Nafisi, son of a wealthy Kuwaiti businessman, who had entered the United States for the first time three-and-a-half year ago and returned once a year since then. His passport and immigration photos showed a young man of about twenty-one years old. Darius Al-Nafisi hadn't been born when the picture in the newspaper had been taken.

There was no way the two men were the same.

The computer had gone on a wild bender the night before.

It happened. Some nights it seemed smarter than others.

But every match had to be compared by a human. Finding even one person in the United States using a fake name might lead to the unraveling of an entire cell of undercover spies or potential terrorists.

Nancy hesitated for a moment before clicking away from the two pictures—one from twenty-five years ago in Tehran, the other of the Kuwaiti.

Something about the young man's hair, the shape of his jaw, his lips…

She zoomed in on the old picture. There was no way Darius Al-Nafisi could be the man in the picture, but their features were similar enough for Nancy to understand why the computer had flagged the two for human comparison.

But it was wrong, as usual.

Nancy couldn't make herself click away.

A sip of coffee turned into three or four while she compared the grainy black and white newspaper picture with the Kuwaiti passport photo.

She sipped again, but the coffee was gone. The empty mug went on her desk.

Nancy opened multiple databases, slipping into the zone as she hunted.

A few moments later, other pictures of Darius Al-Nafisi filled her screens. Not many—he didn't post on social media much, but he went to college in New York City. There were parties, events, and friends sharing photos. He was tagged in enough for Nancy to get a solid sample.

A search of the Iranian archives produced additional pictures of the man from the newspaper.

She needed a fresh set of eyes. This was too important to rely solely on her judgment. After selecting the clearest photos of each man and arranging them side by side, she hid the rest of the windows, along with all other information, she slid off her headphones and poked her head over the partition.

"Dave, can I run something by you?"

Dave, her long-term boyfriend—though they kept it quiet at the office—nodded but held up a finger, lost in his own intel gathering and analysis. He wore small white earbuds; he listened to jazz while he worked, claiming it helped him focus.

He might be five seconds or five hours. That's how it was in this business.

Nancy dialed an extension on her phone. Marcus, one of her dayshift coworkers, had a great eye for faces. "Can you come help me out for a second?" she asked when he answered.

A minute later, he met her at her cube. He was dapper as usual, in one of his ever-present bow ties, a blue dress shirt rolled up to show off his light brown forearms, and a navy vest.

"What can you tell me about these two people based on their pictures?" she asked.

He leaned toward her monitor for a second before leaning back. "They are of Middle Eastern descent. I'd guess Iraq or Iran, maybe Kuwaiti, but that's iffy. Hard to say for sure. But my guess is they're father and son. Or possibly grandfather and grandson? Definitely related, though. Right?"

He turned to her, eyebrows raised.

"That's very helpful, thanks. I'll let you know," she said. He waved and headed back to his cubicle.

Marcus was a smart guy. She trusted his judgment, but wanted one more opinion that matched her own.

Dave stood and moved next to her, slipping the earbuds into a white case. "Okay, what's up?"

Nancy nodded at the screen. "What can you tell me about these two? First impressions."

"I'd say they're related. See the jawlines? The noses. The crinkles around the eyes. They must be father and son, right?"

"Thanks. That's exactly what I needed. I have to get back to the hunt," Nancy said. She returned to her chair and slipped the headphones back on.

If she, Marcus, and Dave were right, the computer software had caught the striking resemblance between a father and son from pictures taken when they were both in their early twenties.

Darius Al-Nafisi wasn't the son of a wealthy Kuwaiti businessman.

He was possibly Darius Valiollahi, son of a powerful politician with close ties to Iran's Supreme Leader.

And he was attending New York University under an assumed identity.

35

THE HACKER

Central Analysis Group (CAG) Headquarters
Arlington, Virginia

After the failed mission to recruit Petrov—and nearly getting shot by Tex —Haley had slept for a few hours at the safe house, gone for a run, and done a bodyweight workout.

She hadn't been looking forward to the full report she'd have to give Gregory—more than the "Mission completed but no solid results" message she'd sent him via a secure communication app.

So she caught a train back to Washington, DC late enough on Monday afternoon to avoid going into the office until today.

Her boss deserved to know the entire story of what had happened on the Manhattan street, but she wanted to give it time. If Chekov reported the shooting to the police—or made waves about the confrontation with high-up contacts in the government—Gregory would have plausible deniability about knowledge of the situation.

He could easily put people off with a promise to get to the bottom of it without having to lie.

But after last night's call from Mariana about Chekov recognizing her at the party, the time had come. Haley had to tell Gregory everything as soon as possible.

So she had been up early, on the road before dawn.

The new Central Analysis Group office building matched the previous one and was located at a nearby business park. During the attack on America eight weeks before, two CAG analysts' vehicles had gone rogue and drove themselves into the former building, causing it to catch fire and burn to the ground.

Another Class A office building had been nearly finished a mile down the road in the suburbs surrounding Arlington. After a month of additional work—while the CAG team commuted to the grounds of a nearby military base—the building had been upgraded to the specifications needed for their top-secret activities, and they'd moved in.

Now, instead of the conference rooms being labeled A, B, C, and so on, they were numbered from one to six.

Most everything else was the same. The building has a similar floor plan, very tight security, and few windows.

And from the small community kitchen, the scent of burnt microwave popcorn and cheap frozen burritos overwhelmed the new carpet smell.

This morning, Haley leaned against the wall next to the door to Gregory's office. The linoleum floor had a fresh, shiny look in the glare of the bright fluorescent lights.

Gregory's face didn't change as he appeared at the end of the hallway and walked toward her, but his pace quickened.

"This can't be good," he grumbled as he unlocked his office door, flicked on the overhead lights, and waved her in.

"It's not as bad as you think," Haley said. He had to know that she would have come to the office yesterday if things had gone horribly wrong.

"Is anyone dead?"

Haley hesitated. "None of our people."

Gregory shook his head, took off his thin black down jacket, draped it over the back of his executive chair, and sat at his desk, empty except for the large computer monitor, keyboard, and mouse on a small black pad.

As usual, his longer-than-standard hair was held perfectly in place with product. He had more gray than ever at his temples, and several new streaks at the crown—a testament to the stresses of the job over the last few years.

"A justified shooting," Haley said. "One enemy killed in action with no fallout."

Gregory stared at her, waiting for more. He was extremely good at being able to tell when she wasn't being truthful—or not telling the entire truth, like now.

"Let me start at the beginning," she said, and told him the story of approaching Petrov, the sudden appearance of Vasily Chekov's security teams, and finished with Mariana shooting the guard.

She omitted the part about nearly being abducted, hoping he wouldn't catch on.

"Why did Rodriguez have to shoot the tango?" Gregory asked, not following her playbook. He held up his hand. "Let me guess. Someone," he said, emphasizing the word, "was in trouble and Rodriguez solved the problem as ordered?"

"We were in the rear with the gear," Haley said, using Axe's term to defend their actions. "A few hundred yards from the action."

"But you exited the vehicle to help, putting yourselves in play." He said it matter-of-factly, and there was nothing Haley could do to dispute the statement.

She nodded.

"I trusted you to stay out of harm's way, and you almost got abducted again." He was angrier than Haley had ever seen him—and he wasn't trying to hide it.

"I wasn't abducted from that hotel roof in Los Angeles," Haley argued. "You know that. I went into the helicopter with Cesar Madras willingly because my gut told me to. And, lest we forget, it ended up being the right decision."

"I thought we had an understanding," Gregory said.

"We've been down this road countless times," Haley said. "I'm sorry for what happened. I agree with you, and I'm confining myself to the office. Axe and I had another long talk. I'm finally ready to fully..." she trailed off, too disappointed and sad to say it.

"Accept your fate?"

Haley nodded, lips pressed together, not trusting herself to speak.

Gregory nodded. He took a deep breath and calmed down. "Good. Thank you."

Haley didn't hide that she had more to report.

Gregory sighed, took off his glasses, and used a small cloth from his middle desk drawer to clean them. "There's more, right? What else happened?"

"Apparently, Chekov has video footage of Mariana Rodrigez's confrontation with Petrov on Fifth Avenue. But it sounds like he didn't catch Mad Dog or the fight Axe and I had with his other guards, including the shooting. He wouldn't have let that slide if he had it."

"And you know this how?"

"Kelton Kellison threw a low-key, casual dinner party for six wealthy couples at his Manhattan condo last night."

"Tell me he didn't invite Chekov."

"No, of course not. Mariana made sure of that from the start." She hesitated.

"But?"

"But Chekov 'pulled a Kelton,' as he called it." Haley offered a shrug.

"He crashed the party, and Kelton let him in." Once again, Gregory removed his glasses. This time, he set them on his desk and rubbed his eyes with a thumb and finger.

"We keep Kelton out of operational details. He didn't know Chekov was a target."

"And because of the video footage," Gregory said, filling in the details, "Chekov recognized Rodriguez." His eyes snapped open. "Tell me she didn't kill Chekov."

Haley fought back a smile. "She only threatened to. He's fine."

"Let me see if I have this right. Vasily Chekov, the fifth richest man in the world, a suspect in the theft of polonium-210 and its use to kill Secretary of State Wilson, has video evidence of Mariana Rodriguez, a member of our unsanctioned team and girlfriend of Kelton Kellison, approaching his executive assistant while she posed as a New York City police officer. Correct?"

"He promised not to tell," Haley said. It sounded lame even to her. "I know it's not ideal…"

Gregory chuckled under his breath. "Not ideal, she says," he muttered. "Anything else?"

Haley closed her eyes for a second, purposely giving Gregory a clue that there was much more to come. "Well, yes. You could say that."

36

THE CONCERN

Central Analysis Group Headquarters
Arlington, Virginia

"Axe," Haley said. She hated to bring up the topic behind the man's back, but it had to be addressed.

Gregory waited her out.

"He's lost a step," Haley admitted finally. "Or thinks he has. Same difference. When the goons stepped out of the car and confronted Tex and Mad Dog, he reacted. Overreacted, really. The team had the situation under control. Tex and Mad Dog were outnumbered, but they had Johnboy on overwatch with a rifle. That evened the odds, or maybe kept them in our favor."

"Axe is the one who rushed from the van?"

"Yes. I think the second set of guards stopped by our van to make sure we didn't force the issue two blocks up and abduct Petrov. When Axe burst out of the van, he was surprised and attacked them without thinking it through."

Haley shook her head and frowned. "He's not himself since the previous mission in Oman. His head injury has healed, but he's out of shape—mentally and physically. He hasn't given up, but he has a kernel of doubt about his abilities buried deep inside."

"If this thing of ours is to continue," Gregory said, thinking it through, "we need a fully functioning Axe. Preferably in the field, though I understand and support him stepping off the front line if he's no longer up to it."

"If he's operational," Haley said, fighting the feeling she was betraying her partner, "he has to be one hundred percent. And two nights ago, that meant holding back and letting Tex, Mad Dog, and Johnboy handle the problem, not rushing out of the van to save the day. But I believe he still has the ability to be in the fight."

Gregory stared off into space for a moment before his lips twitched and he met her eyes. "Are you thinking what I'm thinking?"

"He needs a safe, easy mission to get his feet under him?"

They shared a chuckle about how alike they thought.

Gregory turned serious. "Nancy has concerns about a situation in New York that Axe could investigate," Gregory said. "She discovered that the sons of several prominent men in the Middle East region are attending college at NYU under assumed identities."

"And?" Haley asked. "That doesn't sound like a problem. People from all over the world, especially politicians, disguise identities to keep themselves and their kids safe. I'm not saying it's right, especially if they lied on their visa applications, but…" It clicked. "She suspects there might be more? Or that they're up to something?"

"Maybe. For now, it's merely a concern to check out. It's probably what you said: a security caution. These are kids in their twenties who are about to graduate in a few weeks. They're decades away from being powerful leaders in their countries. But while they've been here…"

"They might have recruited others who could stay in the country as long-term spies. They'd get jobs in America, assimilate, and hold in place until they're needed. Like…" Haley didn't have to say anything about the many Russian sleeper spies she had uncovered during a previous mission. They were second- and third-generation Russian-Americans whose parents or grandparents had received financial support and deep indoctrination from Russia before being sent to America to form a network of undercover assets. Were it not for the team's efforts, the entire operation would still be active and a threat to the country.

"Let's get Axe on it," Gregory said. "Being a little out of shape and not having an excess of door-kicker energy will help him blend in. I'll make some calls and have credentials set up as a guest lecturer. He can be himself—a former Navy SEAL, an expert on counterterrorism. We'll say he's prepping for a summer session on the price of peace versus the cost of war. He'll be able to come and go freely and not have to use a ridiculous disguise or cover. He can set up surveillance, note who's going where and meeting with whom, all that."

"An important but not dangerous assignment. Perfect."

They paused, thinking through the operation.

"Will he buy it?" Gregory asked at last.

"No," Haley said. "But he'll do it anyway. I'll talk to him."

Gregory leaned forward in his seat, clearly expecting that to be the last of the issues to bring to his attention, but once more she had to disappoint him.

"What else?" he asked with a sigh, settling back into his chair.

"Dawson 'Eternal Void' Reite sent me a message. He says he has information we need." Haley allowed the hint of a smile to show.

"After what happened Tuesday night, you expect me to give you permission to go back to New York?" Gregory asked.

"It'll be different this time."

"How so?"

"You'll be with me. He says you need to hear it in person."

Gregory gave her a look.

"Or he can—"

"He is under house arrest and stays put. You know this."

"So what time do you want to leave?"

Gregory muttered under his breath, shook his head, and checked his watch. "Let me tell Nancy and Dave they're in charge, get Axe's cover story working, and then we can go." His eyebrows went up. "As long as that's all?"

Haley nodded and stood. "Yes, that's it."

For now, she thought.

37

THE PREPARATION

Central Park
Manhattan, New York

Axe ran hard, sweating despite the cool spring morning. He wore knee-length running shorts and a high-tech running shirt—all in black, as usual, including the shoes.

His baseball-style hat was another bump cap with an impact-resistant shell inside, and a foam lining. After Wednesday night's unexpected fight and Haley's encouragement to remain active in the field, he wasn't taking chances.

Besides, it helped to hide his face.

The day before, he'd played the role of a birdwatcher, hanging out along the east side of the park with binoculars.

Vasily Chekov's security detail vehicles had been easy to spot now that he knew what to look for. Cars, SUVs, and foot patrols disguised as everyday people rotated on and off. They added a ring of nearly invisible exterior protection to the building where Chekov had his top-floor home.

It was clear how the surveillance van had been spotted Sunday night. Chekov's people watched the entire area and had probably spotted the van when he had parked it and neither he nor Haley had gotten out.

Axe turned off the running trail that circled the reservoir in Central Park, ran east, and turned right onto the sidewalk along Fifth Avenue.

He jogged past internationally known museums, dodging early morning tourists, dog walkers, and locals out for a morning stroll.

After several short blocks, he was at Chekov's building. A black SUV with darkly tinted windows was parked in front of it, with a black sedan farther down the street. They were both security vehicles he'd identified the day before, likely packed with armed guards.

He chastised himself for having missed them Sunday night. He had needlessly rushed the mission. If he had waited a few extra days, or been in place observing another few hours, he would have noticed the security vehicles.

The fight—and death of a guard—could have been prevented.

He'd lost his edge.

Axe ran at a steady pace, breathing hard. He still wasn't fully back in shape after taking time off to recover from his injuries.

But if he was truly committed to field work, that would have to change. Today's run was a good start.

Leaving the sidewalk, he took another path towards Kelton Kellison's building on the far side of Central Park. His recon was complete for the moment. It appeared the security detail remained outside the building around the clock, but he'd shower, change, and return to keep an eye on things.

Vasily Chekov may have killed Secretary of State Wilson. It was up to Axe, Haley, and the team to find the truth.

Axe had to bring his body, mind, and soul back to being one hundred percent.

The next time he had to fight, he'd be ready.

And he wouldn't underestimate an adversary again.

38

THE RUSSIANS

Unit 47A
The Summit at 57th
Manhattan

Haley entered the dark room. The only lighting came from the glow of computer monitors on the wall farthest from the floor-to-ceiling windows. Unlike all the other rooms in Kelton's condo, the shades in here were down, blocking what had to be an extraordinary view looking south over midtown Manhattan. Blackout curtains stopped all sunlight and added another level of protection against the view.

Dawson "Eternal Void" Reite—Void—was deathly afraid of heights, and events eight weeks ago hadn't helped. He'd been hooked up to an emergency escape tether on the twenty-third-floor balcony of a building and unceremoniously dumped over the edge.

By the time he was lowered safely to the ground, he was catatonic with fear.

Now he was in Kelton's condo under house arrest for a separate hacking crime spree unrelated to the recent attacks on the country. Being confined to the forty-seventh-floor condo, with its extensive windows and world-class views, wouldn't normally be a bad deal for a white-collar criminal, but it was a harsh punishment for Void.

Gregory and Axe followed her into the room. Kelton was busy in his office on the far side of the condo, wheeling and dealing, working his way back into the world of money and prestige one phone call and connection at a time.

Gregory leaned against the wall near the door. Axe, fresh from a run and a shower, paced near the blacked-out windows like a caged animal, while Haley perched on the edge of the bed.

Void, tall and thin, was, for lack of a better term, goofy looking. Caucasian, pale from a complete lack of sunshine for several months, thin face, dark curly hair, and a focused, highly intelligent air about him. He sat at a computer desk with two large screens filled with data. The right monitor had a chart showing hundreds of tiny boxes with Russian names inside them.

"Vasily Chekov had nothing to do with the polonium-210 theft," Void said, starting his presentation. He was calm and in control—as long as he stayed away from the windows. "The rest of it—the cyberattacks and the peace summit resort imploding—I haven't worked on yet. Sorry. This has taken all my time."

"Take us through it from the top," Haley said.

"Okay," Void said, and turned to the monitors. "I mapped the names of everyone who worked at or visited the reactor complex where the polonium-210 was produced for one year prior to the assassination of Secretary of State Wilson."

"Everyone?" Axe said from the far side of the room. "That must be—"

"Yes, hundreds," Void said with a proud smile. "But it's not as bad as you might think. It's a very secure facility. Anyway, from there, I did a deep dive into any person those initial people had contact with. Credit card receipts, security camera footage, traffic cameras, phone location tracking… Russia may be way behind the West in some areas, but monitoring their citizens isn't one of them. They've got us beat there. I accessed some systems I shouldn't have, but no one knows about it. Or, well, that might not be true, but if they figure it out, they won't know it was me. It'll look like it came from Moscow, so Russia's Federal Security Service will be on it. And I can run rings around them."

Haley sensed Gregory's impatience from the doorway. "And?" she asked Void.

"Follow this path," he said, pointing at a name on the bottom of the screen. "This man has worked at the facility for two years. Perfect attendance. A hard worker. Promoted twice. He had enough access—not at first, but recently, within our timeframe." Void's finger moved along a line connecting the box to another, one of several leading from the worker's name. "He doesn't have much of a life, so it was a little easier to catch. He goes to the grocery store, eats dinner out on Wednesdays. On Saturday nights, he drinks with his friends at one of their apartments, never a bar. One of them buys a bottle of vodka. These are his drinking buddies." A line ended in a bracket with ten names. "Not all of them show up every week, but this guy is always there." Void had to use the trackpad to scroll the screen to continue the progression of his chart. "Following the main drinking buddy—"

"Maybe just skip to the end for now?" Haley said, more of an order than a suggestion. The display showed line after line and box after box.

"Right." Void moved the trackpad again to show the far right of his electronic chart. A name was highlighted in yellow. Void pointed at it. "Boris Zorinov, a criminal who is so good at his work that he's become a multi-millionaire, is clearly linked to the worker with access to polonium-210."

Gregory left his position at the wall and moved to see the monitor better. Haley joined him, though Axe continued to pace.

"Go back to the beginning," Gregory told Void.

Void took them through all the links, step by step this time.

"How sure are you?" Gregory asked.

"I'm absolutely convinced that Boris Zorinov obtained the polonium-210 that murdered Secretary of State Wilson."

The statement hung in the air for several seconds before Void continued. "I can't say for certain that Chekov isn't involved—I've only investigated to here," he said, pointing at Boris Zorinov's name. "But the two of them aren't friends. Chekov, for a billionaire, is surprisingly normal and decent according to all reports—even some, um, private conversations I was able to access." He cleared his throat and kept his eyes on the screen. Gregory didn't approve of Void's hacking, especially of civilians. "Chekov is ethical—for a multi-billionaire. He might skirt the line here and there, digging for insider information about a company he wants to acquire or dirt on an opponent, but he's not a criminal. I'd be shocked if he was willing to work with Zorinov. Chekov has a code, and he's not interested in politics or attacking countries."

Near the window, Axe stopped pacing. "If you're so sure... How do you have this information and not the CAG?" he asked. "Haley, Gregory, Dave and Nancy—they're the best in the business. Why haven't they, or the CIA or NSA, someone, come to the same conclusion?"

Void gave him a boyish smile. "I cheated. I hacked Russian databases, city traffic cameras, bank records, and local businesses' security camera footage. I'm under house arrest, bored, and…" He glanced away, leaving the last part unsaid, but Haley understood. He still felt guilty that his original research—and online bragging—had been used as the basis for some of the death and destruction caused by the cyberattacks eight weeks earlier.

"If I figured this out," Void warned, "someone in Russia will, too. It's only a matter of time. They may already have it. They've been motivated to find who stole the polonium-210—and plug that leak."

Void tapped Zorinov's name on the screen. "He probably passed the polonium-210 to someone who planted it in the water bottle for Secretary of State Wilson to drink, though he could have done it himself. He's a smart, capable fixer. He grew up on the streets. There are reports that he has killed several people. He doesn't mind getting his hands dirty when necessary."

"Did Boris Zorinov do it on his own? Or at someone else's behest?" Gregory asked.

"Like, for example, someone in Russia's government?" Void asked.

"Yes, but not limited to them."

"Unknown. It's taken me ages to get this far." Void moved the on-screen pointer in a circle to the right of Boris Zorinov's name. "This area here is the next step. Who put Zorinov up to this? Was he paid? Who communicated with him? How?"

"And why," Haley muttered.

"Yes. And why."

They sat with the information—and questions—for several moments.

"Can you figure the rest out?" Haley finally asked.

Void shrugged. "I'll try, but I doubt it. It's going to take boots on the ground."

At that, Axe stopped pacing and joined them by the monitors. "That sounds right up my alley."

39
———

THE PLEA

Unit 47A
The Summit at 57th
Manhattan

Haley was careful not to glance at Gregory. She didn't want Axe to sense that she and Gregory had discussed his readiness—or lack thereof—for field duty.

She had to let the discussion with Void in his bedroom play out, and hope that Void didn't have any actionable intelligence that could send Axe around the world on a mission he wasn't mentally, emotionally, or physically ready for.

"Zorinov's business is too extensive—and much of it is too secretive—for me to track," Void explained. "Well," he said, hesitating. "It was."

"What do you mean?" Gregory asked.

"Zorinov is supposedly relaxing in a dacha outside Moscow. One of his many homes," Void explained. "But he has to be somewhere else."

"Why?" Axe asked.

"I hacked the local energy providers," Void said, his voice filled with pride.

Gregory took off his glasses and rubbed his eyes.

At least I'm not the only one that pushes Gregory's buttons, Haley thought. *Not all that new gray hair is because of me.*

"The house is using less gas and electricity than if he were living there," Void continued.

"It's scary that you can figure that out," Axe muttered.

"It's what I do," Void said with a shrug.

"Where is he, then?" Gregory asked.

"No idea. The other obvious option is out: Western authorities impounded his yacht because of sanctions against him and Russian criminals."

"Staying with a friend? Traveling?" Haley asked, relieved that so far there was nowhere to send Axe to shake the tree.

Void shrugged. "Sorry, I don't know. But I'll keep checking."

"He has a passport, right?" Axe asked. He was like a bloodhound on the trail of a scent, ready to be unleashed. "You can track that when he enters or leaves a country—at least in the West?"

Void looked down, embarrassed. "I haven't found a way into those systems yet," he admitted.

"Good," Gregory muttered.

"We already have that running," Haley assured Axe. "Assuming he doesn't have genuine passports in other names."

Haley turned to Void. What could she and the CAG team accomplish if they had the hacking access Void did? Or if Gregory would let them bend the rules and allow Void to work side by side with them?

That was a bridge too far for now. What Void was doing was illegal and a direct breach of the terms of his house arrest. But at least he had done it all on his own without their support or approval—until now.

"Well done," she told Void. "I'm glad you're on our side."

"Me too," Void said.

"Amen," Axe muttered.

Gregory patted Void on the shoulder, gave him an approving nod, and made for the door. "Remember," he said to them before he left. "None of us were here. You're doing this all on your own, Daw— Void," he said, correcting himself. "And whatever you do, don't get caught."

After Gregory closed the door, Void looked from Axe to her. "One other thing," Void whispered. His eyes flicked to the door and back. "You've got to get me out of here. One day. An afternoon walk in the park. Something."

"Dawson," she said, using his given name. "You're under house arrest. But you have access to computers—and are secretly doing work that has value to your country—because you promised not to do any hacking." She bit her lip. "Aside from what we need, of course."

Damn it, she sounded like Gregory, and she hated it.

"House arrest means you don't leave the house. And it beats being locked away in prison, right?"

"I know, I know, but I'm going crazy. Thinking about how high up we are? The building sways when it's windy! I can feel it, and it's freaking me out. My fear of heights, remember. I could work better with some fresh air. On the ground. Maybe sit in a coffee shop for a few hours?"

Haley shook her head. "For now, this is the way it is. We can't help you. Give it some time. Maybe we can work on Gregory in a few more months. For now, focus on how to find Boris Zorinov, or anyone else who might have been involved in the SystemSpike, okay?"

Void nodded and wiped his eyes as he turned back to his computer and got to work.

Within seconds, the conversation was forgotten, and he was oblivious to their presence.

She and Axe showed themselves out of Void's combination bedroom, secret lair, and jail cell.

40

THE MISSION

Unit 47A
The Summit at 57th
Manhattan

Axe followed Haley along the wide hallway of Kelton's luxurious condo. Kelton allowed them to use it as a home away from home. It was nicer and more convenient than the safe house in Queens. Axe had used one of the spare guest bedrooms to shower and change clothes prior to his meeting with Gregory, Haley, and Void.

But now he felt a familiar tingling—a premonition that all was not as it seemed.

He wasn't in danger—or was he?

"What's going on?"

He kept himself from reaching for one of the two knives he carried, or the pistol tucked inside the waistband of his tactical pants and hidden by a long-sleeved black T-shirt.

He was safe here.

Right?

Haley ignored the question. She opened the door to Kelton's huge kitchen for him. Gregory sat on a tall stool at the granite island. No one else was there.

It was an ambush.

Axe got it. Gregory and Haley wanted to have a heart-to-heart conversation.

He grabbed bottles of water, handed them out, and leaned against the stainless-steel fridge. Haley sat next to Gregory.

"I get it," Axe said. Often, the best defense was a good offense. "You're concerned about me. Since Void doesn't have any new leads for us to pursue, you've come up with some BS mission to get me into shape. Is that about right?"

"I told you he'd figure it out," Haley said, pretending to whisper to Gregory, who kept his face expressionless.

"But after Sunday night, I'm back on track. My head is in the game, and my body… Well, that's coming along. I'm good to go. And where I want to go is after Boris Zorinov."

"You heard Void," Gregory said, his voice patient but firm. "We don't know where he is. And even you wouldn't suggest we drop you outside of Moscow to double-check his dacha."

Axe smiled. He'd considered that option before reluctantly discarding it.

"The assignment we have for you isn't entirely BS," Haley said. "Nancy found something, and Dave helped with the deep dive. She has concerns."

Haley believed in the mission. And Axe had enough experience with Nancy and Dave to trust their instincts.

"Fine," he said. "I'll do whatever you need me to until we have a solid lead on Boris Zorinov."

Gregory sketched out the basics of what Nancy had discovered, along with the rules of engagement and what needed to be looked into. It all made sense.

"I'm in," he said. "I'll get down to Greenwich Village early this afternoon and get started."

He kept the excitement off his face. Once again, he was back in action —and it felt great.

Void, Haley, Nancy, Dave, and the rest of the CAG team would keep searching for Boris Zorinov. He had to be somewhere.

And when he surfaced, Axe would be ready.

41

____

THE BRIT

All morning, Boris had walked the pedestrian road between the beach and the endless hotels and apartments aimed at value-minded tourists—the wealthy stayed in the hills to the west of Palma, or in the Old Town, both miles from this touristy area.

No one met his criteria.

By ten, the sun was hot enough for him to remove the cardigan and drape it over his shoulders as he strolled, alert for fit, military-aged men who were searching for him. If he noticed them first, he might have a chance to hide.

Each time he walked north along the five-kilometer beachside lane, his gaze would return to where his yacht had been anchored overnight.

By the time he had emerged from hiding in the tired sailboat at dawn, his yacht was gone.

There was no tender patrolling the harbor with the crew worriedly looking for him. No Captain Evgeny on the bridge deck with binoculars, searching the beach.

Boris's instincts had been right. People had come for him, and he'd escaped.

As he passed an elderly couple holding hands, his stomach rumbled so loudly that he thought they might turn to look at him.

How long had it been since he'd missed a meal or gone hungry for a moment?

Decades.

He ignored the desire to eat and kept walking, searching the faces of the tourists for a man who looked enough like him for the plan to work.

He had to choose his victim carefully.

In the early afternoon, Boris finally found a potential candidate coming toward him after leaving a pizza restaurant with his wife and two teenage boys. The target was dressed decently enough in peach shorts and a white short-sleeved shirt, wearing white trainers with socks. Mid-60s, like him. Greying hair—Boris's was whiter than the target's, but that could be explained away. No visible scars. Trim without being either fit or out of shape. Average. A bit dour looking, almost mournful.

Just like him.

They could be cousins.

Close enough, and the best he was likely to find on a deadline.

Boris casually turned to inspect the gelato flavors on display at a shop, allowing the target to get closer.

The man had blue eyes, just like Boris.

And he spoke English—a Brit, from the accent.

Boris could fake that.

It was simple to tail the victim along the walkway as he and his family strolled away the calories from lunch.

42

THE BEACH

Hotel BlueSea
Majorca, Spain

After a long walk up and down the main tourist road fronting the beach, the family returned to their hotel.

Boris closed in as they passed through the lobby of one of the area's above-average hotels, but held back at the last second as the family entered the elevator.

Only as the doors started to close did he stick his arm out, stopping them. "Fifth floor, please," he said in English after stealing a glance at the control panel with the round *5* button already illuminated. "Oh—perfect." He ignored the panel which required a hotel keycard to be scanned before the elevator would rise, moved to the back corner of the lift, and waited patiently.

The family ignored Boris and discussed their afternoon plans—sun and a swim.

At the fifth floor, Boris trailed the group, walking slowly, patting his pockets.

His efforts to be sneaky were in vain. The group never glanced back as they walked down the hall to room 532 on the left. The husband used a keycard from his pocket, and they all entered.

"Yes, yes, of course we'll hurry, boys," the mom said with a laugh. The teens were eager to get to the sea.

It would be impossible to kill all four in the hotel room without at least one of them screaming for help.

Boris's stomach rumbled again, more loudly, but he ignored it and used the hotel's stairs to return to the lobby and wait, his bare feet appreciating the coolness of the floor, a welcome contrast to the hot pavement and sand he'd walked on all day.

Boris meandered around the bustling lobby until he found shelves with an extensive selection of paperbacks. A sign said, **Take One, Leave One**. He selected a mystery novel, settled into a comfortable couch that faced the elevators, opened the book, and read.

The British family had changed into swimsuits and cover-ups. The teens carried a worn football; Mom had bright-yellow towels with the name of the hotel in dark blue.

Boris gave them until they exited the front door before rising from the couch and following at a relaxed pace, mystery novel in hand, one finger holding his place.

On the street, as the group approached the sand and the sea, Boris took a risk and sped up to pass them. Halfway across the sand, closer to the water than the road, he stopped, looked left and right, nodded to himself, and draped the sweater—which was much too expensive to use as a beach towel, but it's what he had—on the sand before settling onto it.

He stretched out his legs, opened his book, and waited.

Thirty seconds later, the boys ran by and dove into the water with shouts of pure joy.

The parents stopped a few meters ahead of Boris and slightly to the side, spread out the towels, and placed their sandals on the sand nearby.

Boris pretended to read while watching every move the parents made in his peripheral vision.

How many times had he stolen valuable items as a child? Enough to lose count. But the process was always the same.

Blend in. Don't raise suspicion.

Wait for the perfect moment to strike.

Boris turned a page in his book. He was enjoying the story.

After an agonizing wait for Boris, the teens finally convinced their parents to join them in the water.

Boris turned yet another page, watching as the father slipped a dark-blue hotel keycard from his pocket and tucked it under the corner of the yellow beach towel next to the shoes on the sand.

Boris set his book face down on the sweater, stood, and walked past the couple.

Still seated, the husband removed his T-shirt, and the wife her coverup. By the time they had collected themselves, Boris was at the shoreline, his feet in the water, pretending it was far too cold for him to enter. He shook his head and turned back toward his spot on the beach.

Boris nodded at the husband as the couple passed him near the water and gave his victim the type of smile you offer a stranger you recognize.

A moment later, without looking back at the laughing family, Boris stooped, grabbed the hotel keycard from under the yellow towel, and kept walking.

When there was no outcry from the family splashing in the sea, he picked up his things, shook the sand from the sweater, and strolled to the hotel.

———

Room 532
Hotel BlueSea
Majorca, Spain

Room 532 was much too small for a family of four. Two beds, a desk chair, a tiny bathroom—and a safe attached to the wall of the closet.

Two suitcases with ID tags were open on a small desk. Boris read the tag as he picked up the phone and made a call.

"Hello, this is Mr. Davies in room 532. Yes, this is terribly embarrassing, but I've locked my wallet and passport in the safe and can't get it open. I'm so sorry. I must have entered the wrong digit when I set it. Now I'm on my way out to meet my family for a meal, and I am in desperate need of my wallet. Is there anything that can be done?"

He listened while he stripped off his salt-encrusted pants and shirt.

"Five to ten minutes? Thank you so much. Again, I'm so sorry for the bother."

Boris took a very short shower to rinse off the previous night's seawater, toweled dry, and had finished slipping on fresh underwear, a pair of chinos, and a dress shirt from Mr. Davies's suitcase before a knock came from the door.

The clothes were a little loose, but not so much anyone would notice.

"Maintenance," a man's voice called in accented English.

Boris opened the door with a grateful, relieved smile. "Thank you so much for coming right away."

The middle-aged man offered him the professional smile of an overworked hotel employee.

"I thought I used my birthday as the code," Boris chattered as he sat on the bed to slip on Mr. Davies's loafers from the outer pocket of the suitcase. "But my wife was talking, and I must have mis-entered it."

The worker had a handheld scanner device with a screen and a cable that he plugged into the bottom of the safe. After a few taps on the screen, the safe popped open.

"Thank you, thank you, thank you," Boris said. He reached into the safe as the man wrapped the cable around his scanner. "For your trouble and excellent service," Boris said. He handed the man a tip from the wallet inside.

The worker left without saying a word or asking for identification.

Boris pocketed the wallet and Mr. Charles Davies's passport before locking the door of the safe using his own birthdate as the code.

He stuffed his old clothes into a plastic hotel bag from the closet.

What was he forgetting?

The mystery novel. He grabbed it from the bed where he'd set it and left the room, walked down the emergency stairs, and out the side door of the hotel. He went to the front corner of the hotel, just enough to see the beach and confirm that the Davies family was still thoroughly enjoying their time in the Mediterranean Sea.

Boris walked a few steps to the hotel's taxi drop-off and pickup area and snagged a taxi that had let off newly arriving hotel guests.

"The airport, please," Boris said. He sat back in the worn seat of the cab, rolled down the window, and congratulated himself.

He was one step closer to New York, and he'd managed it without killing anyone.

Yet.

43

———————

THE ESCAPE

Marseille, France

Once Boris had made it to the Majorca airport, the rest of the trip had been easy. Mr. Davies purchased a ticket to Marseille, France, on the next flight.

No one asked why he was leaving Palma so shortly after arriving. People had enough other things to worry about.

In Marseille, Boris had paid cash for a taxi to the bus depot—thanks again to the kindness of Mr. Davies and the euros he'd stuffed in his wallet for the vacation. A bus to Monaco left every two hours, requiring Boris to wait only thirty minutes, which was enough time to buy two sandwiches and several pastries, along with bottled water, to finally quiet his rumbling stomach.

Finally, he boarded the bus and took a window seat halfway back.

It had been a long day. The swim that saved his life. The walk up and down the beach while he hunted for a victim.

And the flight on the discount airline, which had been more draining than he'd expected. It had been at least twenty years since he'd flown commercially instead of in a private jet, and even back then he'd flown First Class, never economy.

Now—a bus? This was a first. As a child, he had fought to survive.

There was no money for buses—and nowhere to go if he'd been able to afford it.

By the time Boris had clawed his way up and started making money, he had bought a car and learned to drive.

Boris blinked repeatedly, fighting to stay awake. He was still in danger. While he hadn't had to provide his name to buy the bus ticket, and had paid cash for his purchases since the initial airplane ticket in Majorca, the authorities would soon be on the lookout for Mr. Davies's lookalike thief.

But there was nothing he could do right now. As the bus backed from its slot among the others arriving and departing, he tucked the mystery novel into the pocket on the seat back in front of him, leaned his head against the window, gave in to temptation, and fell asleep.

***

Room 532
Hotel BlueSea
Majorca, Spain

Charles Davies dodged his oldest son in the narrow hallway of the hotel room. It was the young man's turn to shower off the salt and sand from their long afternoon at the beach.

"Gelato after dinner, right?" his son asked. "That's what you promised. 'After dinner.'"

"Yes, of course. Now take your shower and be quick—we're hungry for more than gelato."

As his son hurried into the bathroom, Charles opened the tiny hall closet and stooped to enter his birthdate as the combination for the safe.

The safe beeped, a harsh tone that surprised him.

He entered the code again, wondering if there was a lockout procedure if he missed the combination two or three times, like some annoying websites.

Another beep.

"Dear, I used my birthdate as the combination, right?" he called.

"Yes. Why? Is there a problem?"

He didn't answer. He knelt and carefully punched the code.

Another beep—but at least there was no indication he had mucked it up further by missing the combination again.

"What's wrong?" his wife asked from the narrow hall.

"The code doesn't work."

"I'll call the front desk."

Five minutes later, Charles opened the hotel room door for the maintenance man who carried a small electronic device with a long cord wrapped around it. He looked tired—and confused.

His eyes searched Charles's face. His eyes flicked to the room number on the door and back to Charles.

Then he swore under his breath.

Charles spoke little Spanish, but he'd had a friend from Madrid at university who had taught him all the best ways to swear.

Based on the worker's word choice and vehemence, something had gone terribly wrong.

44

—————

THE BUS

Monaco City, Monaco

Boris jolted awake.

He had been sleeping with his head against a window. He was on a plane.

No—a bus?

Outside the window, another bus backed up and drove toward an exit. It was dark outside the tunnel.

Not a tunnel. He was in a bus depot.

According to his watch, it was early evening.

Around him, passengers shuffled forward in the aisle, making their way to the front door.

Fear gripped him. He didn't remember who he was or why he was here.

Only… he had a sense that he was wealthy, maybe. Or important.

But rich people don't take buses. Everyone knew this.

He checked his pocket and found a wallet and passport.

The last of the passengers moved forward. In a few seconds, he'd have to join them and exit the bus.

He was Charles Davies. There was cash in the well-worn brown leather wallet. Euros and British pounds. Credit cards. A photo in a plastic sleeve of his wife and two young boys.

None of it rang a bell.

There was something, though. A very important detail he should remember.

He grasped for it, but it slipped away.

A gut feeling remained.

He was in danger.

But he knew what to do when in trouble. He'd done it often enough as a child.

Lie low. Don't stand out.

Survive.

He eased his way to the aisle, stuffing his passport and wallet back into his pants, which fit more loosely than felt comfortable.

He was confused and concerned, but he could function.

All he had to do was stay off the streets. The streets were dangerous— he remembered that.

He'd check into a hotel and regroup. He had the sense that the memories would come back.

That they always did.

Maybe after a good night's sleep.

45

THE HUNT

Monaco City, Monaco

The passport and ID said his name was Charles, but it didn't feel right.

Chuck, maybe?

He didn't feel like a Chuck, either. Or a Charlie.

He walked the streets of the city, instinctively ruling out the two hotels nearest what turned out to be a combination bus and train depot.

At the third hotel, he checked in, paid for one night with his credit card, and was given a small but clean room on the ground floor.

Lying on the bed watching football match on TV didn't help his memory, and soon his eyes grew heavy again. He left the TV on and drifted to sleep.

Bon Nuit Hotel
Monaco City, Monaco

An hour later, he woke on the bed, on top of the sheets and duvet, still dressed in the too-loose clothing.

This wasn't his yacht. It was a hotel.

He frowned and sat up. The room was cheaply furnished.

This wasn't the type of place where he would normally stay.

It all came back.

The yacht.

The swim.

Stealing the passport, wallet, cash, and credit cards.

He was Boris Zorinov. Russian criminal fixer.

On the run.

If Mr. Charles Davies had done anything other than leave the beach and head straight to bed, surely by now the police knew of the stolen wallet.

The credit cards had likely been cancelled.

The police would focus on the stolen passport.

They would consult Mr. Davies's credit card companies, who would direct the authorities to the charge for a one-night stay at this cheap hotel in Monaco.

Boris had to get out of here and work his way to the only place in the city that mattered… If he could remember the way to, and the name of, the hotel where he'd stayed so often over the years.

The two police officers, a man and a woman, both preferred working nights. Fewer tourists, for one, and any calls they received were more likely to be much more interesting than those their day shift counterparts dealt with: pickpockets, shoplifting, traffic accidents, and lost tourists.

They got to break up drunken fights and scare off the occasional armed robber.

The Bon Nuit Hotel, within blocks of the train and bus station, was more expensive than the police officers could afford on holiday, but it was far from the nicest that the very expensive city offered. Compared to those closer to the sea, it was a dump.

They entered, a soft tinkling from a bell above the door announcing their presence.

The front desk man looked up from his phone, then stood as the officers approached.

"Mr. Charles Davies," the woman officer said.

It took the clerk a second, but he tapped at his keyboard, then read from his screen.

"Yes. Room 185. Down the hall. He paid for one night."

"He's in?" the woman asked.

The clerk shrugged. "I haven't seen him leave, but there is a side door."

The night manager emerged from a back room, and they quickly brought him up to speed. A theft in Spain. The missing passport.

The manager agreed to unlock Mr. Davies's door and led them down the hall.

The manager held up a keycard, but the male officer gestured for him to wait. He put his ear to the door. The TV inside was on. A football match.

The officers exchanged a look and nodded to the manager, who held the keycard to the reader on the door and stepped back.

The officers burst into an empty room.

The woman placed her hand on the bed's blanket, which held the slight indentation of a body.

"Cold."

They were too late.

46

THE LETTER

Le Grande Hotel du Monaco
Monaco City, Monaco

After an hour of wandering the small city, lost, Boris stumbled upon a street he recognized, along with the majestic hotel on the corner. A minute before, he couldn't have described the finest hotel in Monaco, but seeing it brought the memories back.

He gave an icy nod to the doorman as he strode inside, finally feeling a sense of belonging. He knew this place.

The magnificent lobby took sixty seconds for him to cross to the long marble check-in desk, by which time the mid-thirties clerk had stiffened to attention and greeted him with brisk professionalism.

"Mr. Zorinov, welcome back. What can we do for you this evening?"

"I need to speak with…"

Damn, the name escaped him. The night manager was the only person who could get Boris into the hotel's vault. The man had been surprisingly useful over the years—for a minion.

The desk clerk's expression flickered for an instant, revealing understanding, and…

Pity.

Boris's sudden bloom of rage brought the name to mind. "Get Mr. Grimaldi out here immediately," he said.

The young man nodded and made a call, murmuring into the receiver.

Boris kept a cold look on his face and didn't allow his concern to show.

The memory lapses were becoming harder to ignore—and deal with.

It was one thing to have a glass of wine in the late afternoon and allow the concerns of the world to drift away. If he forgot the yacht captain's name, or exactly where he was, so be it.

Losing track of his name, of his identity, was a much greater concern.

He shoved the thought aside. He didn't have time to deal with the problem at the moment.

Grimaldi walked across the lobby to the front desk, a pleasant smile on his face.

"Mr. Zorinov. How can I help?"

"A room for one night," Boris said. It would raise too many eyebrows to enquire about a midnight private jet to America. "A meal. Steak and lobster, perhaps—in my room. And access to my box."

For extra-special guests—lavish spenders—the hotel had secure safe deposit boxes built into a vault in the basement, guarded twenty-four seven by one man locked inside and one outside. Guests could opt for a physical key, a passcode, a passphrase, or a combination of the three that would allow them to gain access... But only after personal verification and approval by Mr. Grimaldi or the daytime manager.

Hotels worldwide quietly offered this service to preferred guests. The only requirement was spending an obscene amount of money annually at the hotel in exchange for the no-questions-asked privilege.

Grimaldi nodded once, gave a look to the man at the front desk, and beckoned for Boris to step away so they could have privacy. "Do you have your key?"

Boris chuckled approvingly. A trick question. "The lock is digital and requires a code, not a key."

Grimaldi gave nothing away. "And your passphrase, please."

Mr. Charles Davies would never get past Grimaldi the night manager, no matter how alike Davies and Boris looked. But the passphrase sealed the deal, proving Boris to be who he appeared to be.

And in full command of his faculties.

"He who fears wolves should not enter the forest," Boris whispered in the manager's ear.

"Right this way, Mr. Zorinov," Grimaldi said, and led him behind the front desk, taking a key card from the clerk along the way. "Your meal will be ready by the time you get to your room."

Fifteen minutes later, Boris relaxed at a long dining room table in a suite on the tenth floor. Three silent servers set out his meal.

In his pocket, he had a wallet with a gold credit card in a fake name and a platinum credit card in the name of a shell company he controlled, plus cash in euros and US dollars.

His other pocket held an authentic Maltese passport in the fake name, provided five years before by the government of Malta in exchange for a million-dollar "donation" to the country and the purchase of a property there.

Money was merely a tool to get what one wanted.

And having a backup plan—the second passport—was priceless.

Mr. Grimaldi and the young man at the front desk were considerably better off than they had been an hour before. By offering plenty of cash to each, Boris had persuaded them not to book the room under his real name.

After dinner, Boris went straight to the room's ornate desk, slid open the drawer, and removed a thick leather portfolio containing a fountain pen and off-white hotel stationery.

He had to face facts. The memory lapses were now impossible to ignore or downplay as he'd been doing for the past... well, that was yet another example of what he couldn't remember. Something had happened to him. The stress of running and hiding after the SystemSpike?

Perhaps he'd had a stroke? Dementia? Or sudden early onset Alzheimer's?

It was impossible to know for certain, and he wasn't in any position to visit a doctor.

How long could he go on like this?

His symptoms and episodes seemed to be worsening, though it was difficult to be sure.

Boris wrote a note to his future—confused—self.

You are Boris Zorinov. You have memory loss.

Don't worry. This note contains all you need to know.

He paused. The letter had to include enough to jog his memory and for him to accomplish his mission.

He had to get to New York, eliminate Jade, and then disappear.

With the money and credit cards from his box in the hotel vault, he could buy a small boat, hire a captain, crew member, and nurse, explain the situation, and hope for the best.

If his brain turned to mush, the captain and crew would prepare delicious food and pour excellent wine. He'd enjoy the food, drink, and sunshine as long as he could, whether he remembered each day or not.

He returned to the letter, listed the essential information and steps to take, folded the paper in thirds, and inserted it into a business-size envelope. On the outside, he wrote, ***Important! Read Me NOW!***

He put the envelope in one of the stolen shoes from Majorca and lined them up at the foot of the bed where he'd be sure to find them.

He wouldn't leave the hotel without shoes unless he was in imminent danger or his memory was completely gone.

And if either were the case, so be it.

Not remembering might be better, after all.

47

THE COFFEE

Greenwich Village
Manhattan

Axe sat at an outdoor table in front of a café, enjoying the warm spring afternoon and a cup of excellent coffee.

The tiny shop was on the corner of an otherwise residential street a few blocks from Washington Square Park.

This part of New York City was a different world compared to the hustle and bustle of touristy Times Square or the upscale shopping and residential skyscrapers near Columbus Circle where Kelton lived. Here, the streets were narrow, and many had large, old trees along the sidewalks. In the area around Washington Square Park and New York University, most buildings were low- to mid-rise; three to six stories, with many classic brownstones, plus some taller apartment buildings closer to Union Square to the north that were up to twelve stories.

It felt like a livable neighborhood, not an urban jungle or modern metropolis.

Before leaving Kelton's uptown condo and journeying south, Axe had trimmed his beard to transform himself into a reasonable semblance of a mid-forties New York college professor—or at least a muscular visiting lecturer.

He'd replaced the black tactical clothes with gray chinos, a white dress shirt, and a quickly purchased black sport coat from a store Kelton had suggested. It cost more than he had made in a month as a SEAL, but Kelton had covered it, so it was only a shock to Axe's sensibilities, not his wallet. In the pleasant sunshine with the hot coffee, he had the sport coat draped over the back of the chair. He'd use it to change his look, however slightly, if he needed to.

Down the street, at a newer, six-story luxury apartment building, the front door opened.

Axe sipped his coffee, taking it all in without seeming to pay attention.

A young man in his early-twenties took a few steps outside the door and drew in a deep breath as he looked around. His hair was black, full of body and a shine, styled into a sort of miniature pompadour in the front. With his dark eyebrows, strong jawline, and a few day's stubble, he looked handsome. Classy. Wealthy. He had the fit body of someone who worked out regularly, and wore black skinny-leg jeans, expensive-looking black shoes, and a casual, black, long-sleeved button-down shirt, untucked. Holding a thin black leather jacket with two fingers, the young man flipped it over his shoulder like he didn't have a care in the world.

The US Immigration and Customs Enforcement agency had him listed as Darius Al-Nafisi.

Nancy believed the young man to be Darius Valiollahi, son of a powerful, politically connected man in Tehran.

After a few seconds of enjoying the afternoon air, Darius turned away from Axe to head south along the peaceful side street. In less than thirty seconds, he'd be at an intersection. If he turned left, he was likely headed for Broadway, Manhattan's most iconic thoroughfare.

If he turned right, he might be on the way to the NYU library, one of the other school buildings, or into the West Village, a similar neighborhood across Sixth Avenue.

Axe could follow or opt to parallel Darius on a different side street and hope to catch glimpses of him as they walked east or west, separated by a block.

If Darius continued straight south, Axe would wait and eventually follow at a distance.

This mission was likely nothing more than an opportunity for Axe to get his head, heart, and body back in the game while gathering intel on a future player in Iranian politics. The United States wouldn't risk an international incident by apprehending the young man and tossing him out of the country, especially when he was about to graduate and leave anyway, unless he was involved in something dangerous or illegal.

The kid turned left at the end of the block, headed toward Broadway.

Axe took another slow sip of his coffee, the recent operation along Fifth Avenue fresh on his mind. A man like Darius, with a father with ties to the Iranian president, might have a security detail on foot or in an SUV. They could be on alert for someone following Darius or assigned to trail him themselves.

Eleven, twelve, thirteen, Axe counted silently. Better to give the kid plenty of room than risk bumbling along like things had gone Sunday night.

After thirty seconds, Axe finished the last sip of his coffee. In another few seconds, he would jog along the street parallel to the one the young man had turned onto and catch up to him at Broadway.

Before Axe could stand, Darius rounded the corner where he'd disappeared earlier, keys in hand, and returned to his apartment building's door.

His pace hadn't changed. He still walked as if he had nowhere important to be, taking in the sights and sounds of the spring afternoon.

It was Axe's first clue that something strange was happening.

Why wasn't the kid hurrying? If he'd forgotten something in his apartment and returned for it, wouldn't he move faster to make up for the lost time?

Axe slipped his phone from the back pocket of his chinos and glanced at it as if he had a message, keeping his face down, using his peripheral vision to watch the kid.

The young man unlocked the apartment door and stood in the opening for only a second before closing the door and turning up the street toward Axe.

Axe took a fake sip of coffee, still focused on the phone, then pretended to type a text.

Darius walked past him and turned right, again toward Broadway.

Had the kid just taken a surveillance detection route—SDR—to check if anyone followed him?

That's what it looked like.

Axe slipped the phone into his pocket and took the cup inside, bussing his own table to give Darius plenty of time and space. He had to be careful with this one.

It was turning into an interesting mission after all.

48

THE TAIL

After three and a half years of never once being followed, the surveillance detection routines seemed pointless to Darius.

But by this time, they were a deeply ingrained habit.

His father, a close confidant to Iran's Supreme Leader, had made a fake name and passport, along with frequent SDRs, the requirements for permission to attend college in the United States without a security detail. Darius wouldn't put it past his father to have men from Iran's Ministry of Intelligence in New York to watch him occasionally to ensure compliance with the rules—and his safety.

New York City, however, especially the area around New York University, was quite safe. People walked the quiet streets and the more congested avenues at all hours. There was a strong police presence.

All the extra effort was ridiculous, because his cover as the son of a wealthy Kuwaiti businessman was airtight. Only a handful of close confidants in the States knew who he was—and they wouldn't dare out him, as they were in a similar situation with their own secret identities.

He was on his way to meet two of them this afternoon.

And he had to be positive he wasn't under surveillance—from either the American authorities or his father's people.

For these monthly meetings, checking for suspicious people following him was about much more than honoring his father's security rules.

No one could know what he and his friends had done.

Discovery would likely lead to his imprisonment—or death.

Darius hurried toward Broadway and the next stage of the detection route, conscious of the time. He wouldn't cut short the SDR, but he also couldn't run late. Everyone had to arrive at the meeting exactly on time.

Axe walked along the street Darius had first turned onto—one block south of the coffee shop. At the moment, the young man was one block north, also walking toward Broadway, parallel to him.

To have any hope of catching Darius at Broadway, Axe had to hurry. But rushing might arouse the suspicion of anyone watching the kid's back.

Axe opted to hide in plain sight.

"Yes, I told you, I'm on my way," Axe said into his phone as he hurried along the street. In his other hand, he had the sport coat slung over his shoulder like Darius had done.

He rolled his eyes and shook his head in annoyance at the imaginary caller. "Why can't you pick him up, anyway?" he asked, picturing the child he'd never had: unruly dark hair. Strong and focused. A little stubborn, just like him.

And his imaginary ex-wife: long black hair. A dark complexion. Fiery eyes to match her personality.

With a start, he realized he'd pictured an old flame—the one that got away—instead of Connie, his current girlfriend.

"About ten minutes," Axe said into the phone, stuffing the realization into a box to be examined later, after the mission.

"Yes," he said, repeating it with annoyed exasperation every ten to twenty seconds as he continued along the street. Hopefully, anyone keeping tabs on Darius—or the young man himself if he doubled back— would perceive Axe as a father and harried ex-husband, hurrying to deal with his latest family crisis.

As he approached Broadway, Darius instinctively catalogued everyone he saw. He looked for people moving too slowly, stopping abruptly, ducking into one of the many pizzerias, bodegas, and other shops lining the streets, or looking at him too closely. He'd developed a sense of New York and how its people moved.

Nothing felt off.

Unlike the tree-lined side streets of Greenwich Village, Broadway was the New York City everyone pictured: busy, noisy, and hectic. Taxis, rideshares, buses, and private vehicles drove by, though the congestion kept the speed slow.

Bikers wove in and out of traffic.

Pedestrians jaywalked, slipping across the road when gaps in the procession of vehicles allowed.

Darius turned south, though his final destination was a few blocks northeast.

It was time to check to see if anyone had followed him from the apartment—the easiest place to find him and initiate a tail.

Axe slowed as he neared Broadway. If the student was on alert for surveillance, he could be a few steps away, approaching this side street to check for followers.

The entrance to a corner bodega was ahead.

"Five more minutes," Axe said into the phone. "I'll pick up a candy bar for him. See you soon." He pretended to end the call as he stepped into the open door of the shop, immediately moving to the long magazine rack that partly blocked the front window facing Broadway.

Darius stood on the other side of the glass, staring at him.

Axe slipped to one side, eyes down, going into sniper stealth mode, hoping it worked.

Darius stopped near the corner, in front of the bodega, and used the reflection of the window to see the sidewalks behind him and across the street.

No one looked suspicious.

There were no delivery vehicles, work vans, or cars that stopped abruptly or people watching as they drove by.

Newspaper covers were displayed in one corner of the bodega's window, facing out to entice passersby. The papers were available right inside the shop's side street entrance, easy to grab when ducking in for a cup of coffee and a breakfast sandwich as he'd done many times over the past years at school.

He pretended to study the covers while checking the street behind him and waiting for someone to appear from the street to his apartment—the other direction a tail might have come if they had paced him along the side street.

No one appeared.

Satisfied, Darius strode forward, checked right as if looking for cars as he crossed the street, and again saw no one.

He was clean.

49

THE SDR

Axe relaxed. The young Kuwaiti—or Iranian, as Axe thought increasingly likely—had looked right at him, but must have been focused on the reflection in the window. He had checked Broadway behind him and the sidestreet to his apartment exactly as Axe had guessed he would.

The guy took his SDR extremely seriously.

Darius continued south. Axe bought a baseball cap to change his silhouette and a candy bar for his imaginary son, waiting patiently as the man behind the counter counted out his change.

Axe crumpled the ball cap to make it look at least slightly used before bending the bill, changing it from flat—the way many people kept them these days—to curved, like when he played ball as a kid. He also slipped on his new sport coat.

He let Darius get a half block down Broadway before Axe stepped out of the shop and sauntered south as if he didn't have a care in the world, munching on the candy bar along the way.

Darius wasn't walking the city like a student enjoying the late spring day. He was definitely taking an elaborate surveillance detection route. If he suspected a tail, he'd be able to either identify the people trailing him or shake them off and escape.

Axe was trained as a direct-action operator, but he'd picked up a few things from working with Haley. As much time as he'd put into teaching Haley how to shoot and fight to turn her into a kick-ass warrior, she had put an equal amount of effort into improving his spy skills.

And any second, if Darius had been properly trained, he'd make another move.

Axe stepped into the road and dodged his way to the far sidewalk. He dropped the candy bar wrapper in a trash can and stepped into a pizzeria with a window facing Broadway.

Seconds later, as Axe stood inside at the end of a three-person line, Darius passed a hot dog cart on the opposite corner, spun abruptly, and walked back, digging in his front pocket for money.

He scanned the sidewalk behind him, then glanced across the street, right where Axe would have been if he hadn't stepped inside the pizzeria.

The kid purchased a bottle of water from the hot dog vendor before he stepped to the curb, flagged down a taxi, and jumped inside.

The taxi pulled away and turned left at the next corner, heading toward the East Village.

Axe checked Broadway. There were no available taxis coming.

He could only watch as the target got away.

Tailing an unaware civilian should have been easy. A normal kid would have started out toward a destination and gone straight there. He might buy a bottle of water from a food cart, but wouldn't scan both sidewalks behind him when he stopped.

If he had something to hide from a suspicious friend or lover, or wanted to avoid someone, he might behave like Darius had.

But after one suspicious check, that would have been it.

Darius had been trained by a high-level counter-intelligence unit.

Now, was there any way Axe could salvage the day's mission?

Nancy had identified two other primary targets.

The second primary target lived a few blocks to the northwest.

It was a beautiful afternoon for a stroll, and Axe had nothing better to do than shake the tree and get back into shape.

He was already feeling more focused. Like his head was on straight.

His operational side was coming back.

"Give me a slice of cheese," Axe told the man at the counter when his turn came.

Walking while eating a folded slice of pizza was a common practice in New York. He'd fit right in.

50

NUMBER 492

Greenwich Village
Manhattan

Yaz's watch alarm vibrated, waking him from a pleasant nap. The late afternoon sunshine warmed his bedroom in the large, expensively decorated brownstone a few blocks from school, and lit up the face of the young woman dozing next to him.

Number 492.

Katelyn. Or Kaylynn? Something like that.

Yaz was determined to sleep with five hundred women before he graduated and returned to Saudi Arabia.

And given the number of dedicated students currently focused on their studies, working hard to excel at final exams, achieving his goal might be tricky.

Once the exams were over, he could pick up the pace.

It would be close.

He liked to enjoy each conquest, taking his time and bedding only one young lady per day.

Born Yazeed bin Mishari Al Saud, he was Yaz for short, even in Riyadh before he'd come to college in America.

Yaz was a distant cousin of the new king. The Al Saud family name could draw unwanted attention. The school had agreed to remove "Al

Saud" from all documents and records to hide the name of his country's ruling family. His parents had insisted: he had to keep the connection to himself and succeed on his own merits, not because he was a Saudi prince.

There had been no rules about hiding the incredible wealth at his disposal. Yaz wore only the nicest clothes and had a safe full of expensive watches, ornate rings, and thick gold chains. But he always wore the largest pair of diamond earrings he'd ever seen.

Women couldn't take their eyes off them.

He kept a car and driver parked nearby twenty-four seven, and was happy to pay for the drinks of anyone and everyone at nightclubs, jazz lounges, and dance clubs.

The money, his classic good looks, dark, trimmed beard, easy smile, and, of course, the diamond earrings, attracted plenty of women.

"Hello, darling," Yaz whispered. He added a soft kiss to Kaylan's lips. Or Katie Ann? Whatever. The young lady responded with a light "Mmm," and kissed him back.

Yaz pressed a pre-programmed button on his watch. It would give him another thirty minutes.

Plenty of time.

He kissed what's-her-name. Another round wouldn't help him reach his goal—each woman only counted once—but it would still be enjoyable.

He'd have his driver take him to the meeting instead of going on foot via a long, convoluted route designed to identify and shake off any followers. The excessive security had been exciting at first. Now, it was a hassle that took too much time.

Three years ago, when he'd first gotten involved, the secret rendezvous had appealed to Yaz, as had making friends with a man from Iran, his country's sworn enemy. This was America, and he was in college. It was a time to rebel, to be young and foolish. To make love, not war, as some of his fellow students advocated.

His Iranian friend's outrageous plan, revealed little by little over that first semester, had thrilled and terrified him.

And the clandestine nature of their meetings had made complete sense from that point on.

But the entire ambitious plan had failed.

Yaz would return to Saudi Arabia and live a life of quiet luxury.

Or, if he wanted to work exceedingly hard, he could be in a position of authority after thirty or forty years.

The idea of that much effort didn't appeal to him at all.

If Yaz couldn't assume power quickly and easily—as he, Darius, and the others had planned and hoped for—he wouldn't bother.

The worry about the situation caused him to falter. His fellow Saudis —the financial patrons he'd recruited to help fund the operation—had issued an ultimatum.

"Are you okay?" Kayleen—maybe that was her name—asked.

"Fine, darling," he said, and kissed her again, pushing his worries to the back of his mind.

He would pass along the ultimatum to Darius tonight, and everything would be fine.

51
———————

THE BIKE

Greenwich Village
Manhattan

There was no convenient coffee shop near the next target's brownstone, which cost more than Kelton's huge forty-seventh floor condo, according to Nancy.

Nothing but the best for a Saudi prince, Axe thought.

Axe walked along the narrow side street, cut down to one through-lane because of construction in places on the south side of the east-west street.

There was car parking on the north side, though near the Saudi's building it had been replaced with a long line of rental bicycles. Axe passed fifty-four bikes, with empty slots for six more.

A few days before, when they'd arrived in New York for the mission to approach Chekov's right-hand man, Axe had made the entire team download the bike rental app to their phones and set up accounts to be ready to use in an emergency.

He would check out the area, on alert for the prince, and rent a bike if needed. It would be another great way to blend in.

Axe stalked the neighborhood, getting a feel for the streets. A black SUV stuck out: impeccably clean, with a driver wearing a classic combination of white shirt and thin black tie loosened at the neck. He had his eyes closed, the seat tipped back, and the tinted window down far enough to allow plenty of spring air in.

While the dozing driver could be ready to give a ride to other ultra-wealthy students housed in the area, Axe's gut told him the SUV belonged to young Saudi prince Yazeed bin Mishari Al Saud—"Yaz."

Axe memorized the license plate number and kept walking. He turned, and then turned again, returning to the street in front of Yaz's red brick three-story building.

He took his time with the bike app on his phone. If he had been in a rush, he could have been on his way in seconds, but there was no hurry. He didn't know if the prince was home, at the school library, or out for an early dinner, but the driver on standby—if the SUV belonged to him as Axe suspected—suggested he was inside.

Axe finished adjusting the height of the bike seat as the black SUV peeled around the corner and stopped in front of the short staircase leading to Yaz's home. The driver hurried around the back to open the rear passenger-side door.

At the top of the stairs, a tall, handsome young man, on the thin side, stepped onto the stoop holding hands with a young, sporty-looking blond wearing a tight gray sweatshirt.

The young man matched the pictures of Yaz that Nancy had shown him. Thin face, close-cropped dark beard, dark eyes, long nose.

The couple kissed, not too short or long, more like a final farewell, and descended the stairs together. The co-ed walked east with a last wave to the prince, and Yaz climbed into the SUV.

Axe turned the bike to face west and pedaled slowly away. The SUV would overtake him, and Yaz would never suspect he was being followed.

Traffic on the side streets was stop and go. Axe pedaled slowly and kept pace with the SUV, staying several car lengths back. He pedaled harder when the vehicle turned north, keeping it in sight as it turned again after another block, headed east—the direction Darius had been going when his taxi disappeared around a corner.

The only easy day was yesterday.

This was a first for Axe. He'd been on missions in helicopters, tactical dune buggies, and several kinds of planes, including many he'd jumped out of. Boats of all sorts, a high-end sports car—liberated from the money launderer for a drug cartel and driven on a road through the jungle built specifically for that vehicle. But he'd never ridden a bicycle during an operation.

It felt great. He was in the field and getting more into the groove with every hour.

The SUV zipped across Broadway as the traffic light changed from yellow to red.

He pedaled furiously. He didn't want to lose sight of the vehicle and have to wander the streets searching for it.

Traffic was stopped at Broadway, a long line of personal cars, ride shares, and taxis. Axe had to slow as he approached the street and the red light. He cruised past the stopped traffic on the right, smoothly cutting ahead instead of waiting at the back of the line as he would have had to if he were driving a car.

He neared Broadway, willing the red light to change.

The SUV had stopped at a light three short blocks ahead.

See? No problem. Things work out. I'm back in—

Immediately in front of him, the rear door of a stopped taxi swung open.

There was no time to swerve.

The front tire of the bike hit the open door…

And Axe was in the air, flying.

52

THE TRAFFIC

Greenwich Village
Manhattan

The flight over the taxi door lasted long enough for Axe to plan his landing.

He tucked his head and shoulder, rolled on the asphalt, and stood a moment later as if he'd planned the entire stunt. The baseball cap stayed on.

"Are you okay?" a woman's voice called from behind him. "I'm so sorry. The traffic was stopped, and I opened the door without looking."

Three blocks ahead, the traffic light changed. The SUV turned left, north, and disappeared around a corner.

At Broadway, the light turned green. Traffic started through the intersection.

The taxi driver yelled something at the lady, who closed the door. The cab pulled forward, the driver wanting no part in whatever confrontation his passenger and Axe were to have.

"I'm fine. No problem," Axe said as he picked up the rental bike lying on the ground. It looked undamaged. The handlebars were off-kilter, but a firm twist brought them back into alignment.

"All good," he told the woman. "Sorry, I'm late and have to go. Don't worry about it."

Axe hopped on the bike and pedaled, standing to get more speed.

Before he could reach the intersection, the light changed from yellow to red.

He couldn't wait. The SUV was already out of sight. If he waited for the light to change to green, he'd lose it and be back to square one.

Nancy had a third target to stake out, but catching up to the SUV felt like Axe's best chance.

Axe shot into the intersection, dashing in front of a lumbering bus, swerving between a bright yellow taxi and another car, and barely avoided being hit by a small delivery truck before reaching the far side, safety, and an open road on the way to the intersection where the SUV had turned.

53

THE INDISCRETION

The East Village
Manhattan

Yaz was already going to be late for the meeting.

He might as well play it safe and follow Darius's stupid rules. Make a token effort not to go directly to the café.

"Make a few turns," he told the driver. "Backtrack so we can see if anyone is following."

His driver nodded and did as ordered without question. Normally, Yaz followed protocol, walking to the meetings. He would arrive exactly at his designated time after carefully winding his way through the neighborhoods of Lower Manhattan, turning suddenly, and retracing his steps, pretending he was a spy in a blockbuster movie.

Darius arranged for them to meet in the back room or private area of restaurants in Greenwich Village or the East Village, away from any prying eyes and listening ears.

After financing the SystemSpike attacks on America and the failed "accidental" deaths at the Middle East Peace Summit, it paid to take security seriously.

But with Yaz's pending return home and the American president's very public reassurance that the country had caught the culprits—case closed— he worried less.

He regretted his youthful indiscretion, as he'd started to think of it.

Unfortunately, the fellow Saudis he'd brought into the scheme to help finance the costs were extremely unhappy. Their money had been wasted; they'd gotten nothing from the millions of dollars they had invested.

Yaz stared out the window as the SUV traveled the narrow streets of the East Village on the short, half-hearted surveillance detection route, but he wasn't looking for suspicious cars trailing him. He dreamed of what might have been had the plan succeeded. He would have had more money, power, and prestige. With all of that, many more young ladies would have been interested in spending time with him.

The SUV turned north again, back on the same street they'd been on a few minutes before. One more turn and they'd arrive at the Persian café for tonight's meeting—a showdown where things would be made right.

After delivering the ultimatum, he'd be able to return to Saudi Arabia —not as rich, popular, or as powerful as if the operation had succeeded— but at least no longer in trouble with the other wealthy Saudis who had provided their financial support in the failed plot to kill the Saudi king and his entire entourage.

Axe's legs burned, but he was almost to the intersection where the SUV had turned.

If it had kept traveling north, it would be several blocks ahead, but on the narrow side streets of this area, he might be able to spot it.

A pedestrian stepped off the sidewalk in front of him, safely in the crosswalk.

Axe hit the brakes, skidding the rear of the bike.

"Tourists," the man muttered as he gave Axe an annoyed glare and continued on his way.

The light was red for him, but Axe turned anyway. He had to catch up to the SUV.

54

THE EAST VILLAGE

The East Village
Manhattan

"Watch out!" Yaz called. The driver hit the brakes hard, throwing Yaz forward. The seat belt cut into Yaz's chest, but at least he hadn't launched into the front seat.

"Idiot," Yaz muttered as the bike-riding tourist swung onto the road in front of them. Either the dark-haired man in the sport coat hadn't seen the huge black SUV or was in too much of a hurry to care.

"Probably late for a date," he said to his driver, who chuckled at the joke.

They had traveled in a short, three-block square and were back where they had been a few minutes before.

"See anything suspicious?" Yaz asked. The driver shook his head.

"Fine. Continue to the café." It was a block ahead and half a block east.

It was time to confront Darius and Jade, push them to change the timeline of their latest scheme, and get the money needed to pay off the patrons—and enrich himself further in the process.

The black SUV that had almost slammed into Axe as he ran the red light had the same tinted windows as the one Yaz had gotten into. Axe didn't dare turn to check the license plate, but he slowed and moved closer to the side of the road as if he were near his destination.

He kept his head down and turned away as the SUV passed him. It might look like he was embarrassed by almost causing an accident a block back.

At the intersection, the SUV signaled and turned. Axe glanced up in time to check the license plate.

It was Yaz.

The kid had done a halfhearted SDR and, instead of properly using a different approach road, had opted for the same one he'd been on earlier. It made sense—the area was plagued by narrow, one-way streets. There were only a few ways to easily get to a destination without venturing far out of the way.

Axe hopped off the bike and pushed it along the sidewalk, hurrying to the corner in time to see the SUV pull to a stop in front of a Persian café halfway down the long, east-west block.

The East Village was less wealthy and more bohemian than the neighborhoods to the west. Axe had visited as a young man when the area was filled with record stores, cheap restaurants, street-corner drug dealers, and petty crime. In the years since, it had been gentrified, but felt worse than before. It had lost its charm, and was surprisingly dirty, with litter everywhere, like a dozen trash cans had been upended and the wind had scattered their contents. When he'd visited before, the area had been low-end and borderline unsafe for tourists, but people had pride in their stores, stoops, and street. Tonight, it looked tired and neglected.

Yaz hopped onto the sidewalk without waiting for the driver to open the door. Another man, about the same age as Yaz, neared the café from the west. They reached the door at nearly the same moment.

The SUV pulled away and turned at the corner while Axe settled his bike into a rack of other rentals, squatting to fiddle with the tire, using the row of bikes to shield him.

People assumed New York City was a cold, unfriendly place where strangers said little and everyone kept to themselves.

While visiting years before, however, Axe's impression was that the city was a collection of neighborhoods. People minded their own business, but they were often as friendly as in smaller cities and towns around the world.

Strangers entering a café at the same time would nod to each other, smile, or share a brief greeting. The one in front would at least give the door an extra push as he entered to make it easier for the person following to slip in.

Yaz and the other man at the café door pointedly ignored each other. It looked suspicious.

Axe finished with the bike and moved to yet another pizzeria, one shop up from the corner. This place had a long stainless steel counter along the window facing the street. He could easily stand there and observe for a while without being obvious. It would be better than the hot, uncomfortable surveillance locations he'd been stuck in during his career.

Yaz had to be at the café down the street for an important reason. Why else conduct any sort of SDR, even a quick one?

And the young man he had entered behind looked exactly like Kareem El-Sayed Mahmoud, the third primary target on Nancy's list—the youngest son of an officer in Egypt's General Intelligence Directorate.

55

THE MEETING

The Saffron Café
The East Village
Manhattan

Kareem El-Sayed Mahmoud—Kareem Mahmoud, according to the Egyptian passport his father had secured in that name—had ignored the Saudi prince, who should have arrived at the café ten minutes earlier.

Kareem hid his anger; there was nothing to be done about the situation now aside from pretending they didn't know each other. Allowing the annoyance to show or berating him would be counterproductive. And he had to keep Yaz on track as an ally.

Kareem queued up behind Yaz at the counter, eyes scanning the menu printed on a chalkboard hanging high on the wall behind the cash register. The scents of cardamom and saffron competed with roasted almonds and freshly ground pistachios, combining into the welcoming smell of home.

The woman behind the counter glanced at him. With nearly shoulder-length hair, a fashionable distressed brown leather jacket, and a tight black T-shirt, he attracted plenty of attention from the local women. But this one dismissed him immediately, her eyes drawn to Yaz's obscenely large diamond earrings.

Kareem shrugged it off. Tonight was for business. He didn't need any distractions.

He was a year older than most of his peers, having taken a gap year in Egypt to train with his father's best men: spies, warriors, and killers. Maybe that was what made him feel like the others were children compared to him. But he came across as charming and friendly. His mission depended on it.

As the youngest son of a high-ranking officer in Egypt's intelligence service, much was expected of Kareem. He'd been sent to America to learn at the university, but his secret mandate was much more. He was to make friends with young men from other parts of the Middle East.

According to his father, one day Kareem would expertly guide the country's future leader. Having long-standing connections to other men in similar positions of power with the country's allies—Saudi Arabia, the UAE, Bahrain, and Jordan—would help him offer wise counsel.

Forging alliances with Egypt's historic opponents such as Iran, Qatar, and Turkey, or at least being on pleasant terms with their future leaders, would be beneficial one day as well.

Kareem wasn't a natural politician or networker, but he made up for it with diligence, effort, and quiet charm. Over the past three and a half years, from his first day as a freshman until this month, when he would graduate, he'd done well, making connections with people who liked and respected him.

He kept his true self well hidden from them all.

Kareem's first kill had been on the night of his sixteenth birthday.

His father had escorted him into the bowels of one of Egypt's unofficial detention facilities run by the National Security Agency, presented him with a pistol, and explained what the man chained to the wall had done to his own family.

For Kareem, keeping the chocolate birthday cake he had eaten from coming up during his father's description had been challenging.

Pulling the trigger of the pistol had been easy.

More men followed, one or two per year. Despicable violent criminals at first, then political dissidents and troublesome journalists as killing became routine.

Unbeknownst to his father—but surely with his approval, if he'd been aware—Kareem kept the tradition alive in New York.

The bodies went into the East River.

No one suspected him. Why would they? He was a diligent foreign student who spent his time studying or quietly debating world politics with others.

At the café, Kareem ordered a hot sahlab, a creamy drink made from milk, cinnamon, orchid root powder, and crushed pistachios, and took the offered cup to the back room where Yaz had disappeared a minute earlier.

The meeting room was small but private.

He set the sahlab on the table farthest from the door where Yaz sat across from Darius. At least Yaz had gotten one thing right: he sipped his hot chai, saying nothing, as Kareem had instructed when the two of them had planned the meeting.

Kareem moved one of the two remaining chairs closer to Yaz, setting the stage for the confrontation. Usually, they were a council of equals. But after the rumblings from those Kareem and Yaz had quietly recruited for their cause, the ones who had financed the mission with the promise of political gains the likes of which they'd never imagined, it was time to face the truth.

The operation in Oman had failed and there was nothing that could be done now.

Darius and Jade had promised a new plan, but there was little to show for it.

It was time to fix the problem.

One way, or another.

56

THE SIDES

The Saffron Café
The East Village

Darius had no doubt who was to blame for breaking their security protocol. Yaz had been twenty minutes late to the meeting.

Arrivals were carefully scheduled for every ten minutes, so it didn't look like they were together.

Darius's careful SDR had been time consuming and extensive. Had Yaz even bothered with one of his own?

Kareem had entered the room only a minute after Yaz, as cool and laid back as ever with his long hair and in favorite brown leather jacket, but he should have been livid. Instead, the most security conscious of them all wasn't upset.

Something big was definitely happening.

When Kareem had joined them at the back of the private room, he had pulled a chair close to Yaz.

So that's how it was. Sides had been chosen. It would be the two of them against Darius and Jade.

This was not the meeting Darius had expected. The pair had something to announce. It showed all over their serious faces as they carefully avoided looking at him.

He had a sinking feeling but kept the emotion off his face.

The men most likely were tired of waiting for the promised return of their money, along with the millions their patrons had provided to fund Jade's three-pronged plan: the SystemSpike, pushing America into a war with Russia, and killing the leaders of the Middle East region at the Oman peace summit.

For the past several weeks, Jade's reassurances that a new plan was well underway had been enough.

No longer, apparently.

Tonight, it seemed, the time had come to divulge the details of Jade's plan and reassure the men that all was in order.

Normally, as they waited for Jade at these monthly meetings, the men filled the time with stories of Yaz's romantic conquests. But aside from a quick greeting, neither Yaz nor Kareem had spoken.

"What's your number, Yaz?" Darius asked, attempting to break the uncomfortable silence.

"Actually, after this afternoon's young lady, it's—" He stopped abruptly when Kareem's hand touched his arm.

Yaz shrugged his shoulder in a nearly imperceptible apology.

Darius raised a hand, showing he understood, sat back, and folded his arms across his chest. If Kareem wanted to wait in silence, that's what they would do. For despite the thousands of people their SystemSpike operation had killed two months before, at heart Darius was a politician. A diplomat. Over the past few years, he'd learned to be more of a schemer.

But he had no actual blood on his hands.

Kareem, however, was a killer. He thought he hid it well, but danger radiated from him, and his eyes often had a dead look to them, like he knew he could take your life anytime he wanted.

Darius would do everything in his power to ensure he wasn't Kareem's next victim.

57

THE SAFFRON CAFÉ

The Saffron Café
The East Village

Jade liked the café as a meeting spot. It was close enough to all of their apartments to be convenient without being near enough to run into many people they knew. And the streets of the East Village were nearly as good as those of Greenwich Village for the surveillance detection routes necessary before their get-togethers.

Today, she wore her usual outfit of a simple dress that wasn't too tight or too loose. This one was black, ankle length, with a pale-yellow-and-pink flower pattern. She paired it with black yoga pants underneath and casual black shoes that resembled sneakers—comfortable for walking—and a small backpack purse. Her fine black hair was in a long, tight braid. She wore no makeup and looked like dozens of other conservatively dressed Asian-American students in the area. No one would give her a second glance—unless they were tailing her.

It had taken a full hour to carefully wind her way from Washington Square Park, near the school, through the West Village, and across to the East Village, searching for faces of people who didn't fit in, paid her too much attention, or appeared frequently during the long walk.

Once she was convinced no one was following her, she had ducked inside the café and ordered.

Now she carried her tea and a plate of four baklava to share with the men. The way to any man's heart was through his stomach. She would insist Yaz or Kareem eat her baklava, claiming she was focused on staying fit. Subconsciously, they would be in debt to her.

Her mind, not her body, was her primary weapon of seduction and persuasion.

But as she entered the back room of the café, she realized she'd be eating all four treats herself. The men didn't abruptly stop talking when she appeared, as they often did. They hadn't been discussing Yaz's latest conquests or his ridiculous goal of sleeping with five hundred women in his time in college, which he was close to achieving, according to Darius, who relayed the stories to her.

Instead, the men sat in silence. Darius had his arms crossed, his hair perfectly shaped in the small pompadour he favored. He appeared to be waiting patiently, but she knew him too well to be fooled; he was tense and worried.

Kareem sat straighter than normal, and his smile at her appearance didn't reach his eyes. His longish hair made him look rebellious, and his eyes were as flat and deadly as ever.

Yaz looked uncomfortable, glancing nervously at her for a moment before looking away. His diamond earrings sparkled in the light when he moved.

Jade set the treats in the middle of the table. Darius scooted his chair to the right so she could join him across from Yaz and Kareem. They were no longer a team—Darius and herself in charge of planning and implementation of their schemes, with Kareem and Yaz responsible for raising the vast sums of money required to fund the operations.

"I take it there are problems," Jade said, taking the initiative. Since the last meeting a month ago, it seemed like the four of them had gone from allies to enemies. She wasn't one to wait for the enemy to strike first.

"My people aren't happy," Yaz blurted out, jumping in as Kareem was ready to speak—probably something much more thoughtful and measured. "They want what they were promised."

His frown was nearly a pout, and Jade had to work hard to keep a combination of pity and disgust off her face. Last month, she would have found his outburst cute. Funny. But seeing Yaz next to Kareem, sitting pointedly on the opposite side of the table from her and Darius, all the goodwill she had for her suddenly former partner had fled.

Kareem spoke before she could respond to Yaz. "Promises were made.

By you to us, and by us to our financial backers." His voice was measured and reasonable, which made him more frightening, not less.

Jade bet that he'd rehearsed the speech several times.

She gave Darius a moment to respond, but when he remained silent, she stepped up. "Yes. Unfortunately, our grand plans were thwarted despite everyone's best efforts. But as Darius and I mentioned last month, we have a backup plan in process that will restore much of your backers' investments by this summer. Possibly all, and they may come out ahead."

"You haven't provided details of the new plan," Kareem said. "My people are... concerned." His tone said it all: his people were far more than concerned.

Jade had a sinking feeling. As much training as she had as a spy, Kareem was at least as ruthless as she was, and he had killed many more people. She could sense it in him.

The three thousand-plus lives her SystemSpike operation had taken didn't count. She had only really killed one person—Turbo, by pushing him off the roof.

Though she had loved every second of it.

And since Sunday night, she'd thought several times of the sound his body had made hitting the sidewalk.

Jade could easily manipulate Yaz.

Kareem? No, he was immune to her.

If she could gain access to their patrons, there might be a way free. But trading herself for millions of dollars wasn't realistic. At best, she'd be able to buy time.

For three years, from shortly after she'd arrived in this country, Jade had managed the multi-pronged operation. Building. Scheming. Preparing. Working with Russian oligarch and expert criminal fixer Boris Zorinov to pull off the biggest, most impressive operation ever.

To show her superiors in China that she had a world-class mind, worthy of promotion to—eventually—leading the entire security department.

More importantly, she would have shown those men—and they were all men—that a woman could effectively plan and implement a scheme so bold that it would shake the world.

She was more than a seductress and manipulator.

But it had all fallen apart.

"We are graduating shortly," Kareem said. "Going home. All of us are understandably anxious to secure the return of our investments prior to then."

"We were going to jump ahead," Yaz said, sounding more like a petulant child. "If the plan had worked, we would have skipped decades of slowly climbing the ladder of power. The least we deserve is our money back."

The men at the table in front of Jade were the same as the ones in China. Ignorant. Lacking vision. And doubting her.

She would explain, convince them to give her time, and succeed. She could do it.

"The new plan is well underway," Jade said, all business. "We are going to temporarily crash America's stock market so you and your supporters can make an obscene amount of money—enough to cover what you and they invested in our operation. Tens of millions. Billions, if we do it right."

At the mention of the money, Yaz leaned forward, his eyes lighting up with greed. His large diamond stud earrings sparkled.

Jade had him.

He stole a piece of baklava from the plate in the middle of the table.

Kareem didn't look convinced, but at least he seemed intrigued. "How?" he asked. "That sounds… I won't say impossible. Implausible, perhaps, is the better word."

Darius finally spoke, excitement in his voice. The general idea had been hers, but as the politician he would one day be, he had filled in many of the missing pieces that had taken the plan from dream to reality. "We don't actually have to crash the market, though we hope to. Really, we only have to make people believe it is crashing. Then they will do the work for us."

58

THE BAKLAVA

The Saffron Café
The East Village

Darius barely moved as Yaz and Kareem considered the plan.

The three remaining pieces of baklava sitting in the middle of the table smelled delicious. He wanted desperately to snatch a piece for himself, but stayed still.

Jade was smart enough to sit quietly and wait, too.

The first to speak in a negotiation loses.

They were negotiating with Kareem for their futures—and possibly their lives.

Yaz wasn't a problem, and his people who had provided money for the operation—no matter how much they were pressuring him—could afford to lose the money on their failed investment.

Yaz would achieve his goal of bedding five hundred women during his time at college and return to Saudi Arabia. He would forgo the government job available to him as a prince. It would take decades to have enough power for it to be enjoyable.

Instead, he would be a rich, jet-setting playboy, following the ultra-wealthy's seasonal circuit of hotspots, from luxury ski resorts or yachting havens in the winter to fashion and elite sporting events throughout the year. He would visit Aspen, Monaco, Paris, Cannes, Dubai, and St. Barts.

Kareem would return to Egypt, where he would torture and kill people as he worked his way up the ladder of the intelligence service.

He was the primary concern.

Those he had recruited were likely far more serious—and dangerous—than any of Yaz's relatives or friends.

Uncomfortable seconds ticked by.

Kareem's gaze was fixed on Darius.

Darius refused to flinch or look away.

Yaz tried to speak, but Kareem stopped him with a light touch to his arm. Yaz took a second baklava instead.

Finally, Kareem pursed his lips and nodded slowly. "The end of the week," he said. "The two of you have promised much and delivered little." He held up a hand when Jade shook her head in protest. "You caused billions in damage to America and killed thousands. Well done. But we didn't care about that piece of the operation. The important part for us didn't turn out as planned. And in this life, we are judged by results, not intentions. So, you have until Friday to make us whole. Our people demand it," Kareem said with a nod to Yaz.

The implication couldn't be clearer: Darius and Jade were easier to kill now than they would be in two months.

In a few weeks, Darius would return to Iran to begin the decades-long slog to power he'd hoped to avoid by killing his country's supreme leader and others at the peace summit in Oman.

Jade would continue her life as a deep-cover spy for China, start a job as a junior investment analyst at a prestigious New York financial firm, work one hundred hours a week, and be much more difficult to make disappear.

"Three days is not enough time," Jade said after a few seconds. "We need at least a month."

"Friday," Yaz said, playing the role of a tough guy, which didn't suit him at all. "I can't go home empty-handed." He grabbed the third piece of baklava and gulped it down in two bites.

"We understand," Darius said. He ignored the look Jade gave him. "We will prepare instructions for you and your patrons and send them to you via the secure communications app. They will understand how to invest to make the most money, which will make them whole—or come out ahead, if they follow our instructions to the letter. Prepare your people to invest as much as they can. We'll meet again on Monday, and everyone will be happy."

Darius, Jade, and Kareem shared a look. Each understood that Monday would go one of three ways.

First, if the plan worked, they would celebrate.

Second, if the plan was on track but hadn't yet succeeded, Darius and Jade would attempt to negotiate more time.

Or third, if the plan failed, Darius and Jade would already be dead.

Yaz gestured to the plate, and after they each shook their heads, he took the last piece of baklava, oblivious to the tension between them.

59

THE PIZZA

The Original Tom's Pizza
The East Village

Standing at the long counter of the pizzeria, Axe enjoyed a pepperoni slice while he watched the café down the street.

He'd have to run extra miles in the morning to burn off these calories. He was supposed to be getting into better shape, not gaining weight. But anything for the mission.

The baseball cap was stuck into his back pocket, ready for when he needed to change his look again.

A steady stream of men and women came and went at the Saffron Café down the block. Students, locals, and what looked like a few tourists. Some stayed inside for a while, but none gave off the clandestine meeting vibe that Yaz or Kareem had.

Axe was in the middle of a second slice when Darius emerged from the café. He briefly scanned left, right, and across the street. Axe eased back from the counter and window, using the pizzeria's front signage as cover.

After a few seconds, Darius turned east, away from his apartment, and strolled away.

Five minutes later on the dot, Yaz exited with considerably less concern. He stepped out of the café, stopped, frowned, and pulled out his phone.

A minute later, the black SUV Axe had chased came around the corner and pulled to a stop in front of Yaz. He hopped into the back seat, and the big black vehicle drove away.

Two down, Axe thought.

He didn't need to follow either of them—or Kareem, who emerged exactly five minutes after Yaz.

The Egyptian's counter-surveillance skills were considerably more robust than Yaz's and more subtle than Darius's. He stopped outside the doorway, leaned against the next building's front wall, and checked his watch. A minute later, he looked up and down the street with a frown, as if someone he was waiting for hadn't arrived. He started toward Axe, his head looking up the road and over the slowly passing cars.

After several steps, he stopped, checked his watch again, and turned back toward the café. He hurried away. Near the end of the block, he jogged across the street, then continued through the next intersection's crosswalk and was out of Axe's sight.

The real test came next.

Axe glanced at his watch, timing it out. A man emerged at the four minute, ten-second mark carrying a tall to-go cup and immediately moved west toward Axe. He'd gone inside right before Kareem had exited and looked like he was in a hurry.

Definitely not one of the original group.

By Axe's count, the only people that should still be in the café were a scruffy young Caucasian guy with a laptop and…

A short woman with long black hair in a braid, a pretty face with dimples, no makeup, and a loose black dress over black leggings strolled out of the café without a glance around. She had entered ten minutes after Kareem and Yaz—and it had been exactly five minutes since Kareem had exited.

Gotcha, Axe thought.

She turned west, toward Axe, and walked without hurry.

Axe grabbed his white paper plates from the counter, picked up the piece of pizza crust he'd saved, and went to the door of the pizzeria. He used his rear to push it open as he stuffed the crust into his mouth, crumpled the paper plates into a loose ball, and pushed them into the trash can right outside the door.

He used the back of his hand to wipe his mouth as he walked west on the other side of the street and several steps ahead of the long-haired woman.

She was the unknown. The wildcard.

Axe would tail her all night if he had to. He'd find out where she went and gather clues that would help Nancy and Dave learn who she was, why she was meeting with the three students, and what the four of them had planned.

60

THE WALK

Greenwich Village
Manhattan

Axe gave the long-haired young woman plenty of space as she left the bakery going north—the direction she had come from before she stopped for a snack.

The bakery smelled amazing, and he vowed to return for a treat when the mission was over.

While his target ate, he had ducked into a clothing store that he was much too old to shop in. The staff had ignored him completely, which was perfect. He wandered the racks several feet back from the floor to ceiling windows, browsing and waiting.

By the time he stepped out of the store, the woman was turning left at the next intersection.

His first instinct was to rush ahead—run, if he had to. But he held back.

Earlier, before the meeting, Darius displayed incredible counter-surveillance skills for a young man.

Yaz had gone almost directly to the meeting, but had performed a lazy detection routine. He would have been better off ignoring the security protocol.

The long-haired woman was in another league. She just... walked.

There was no doubling back or looking in windows to check the street behind her. But the meandering stroll served its purpose: no random person would still be following her after such a long time.

She was highly skilled; much better than him.

Darius struck Axe as a man who had been trained to be careful.

Yaz was a privileged wealthy playboy doing the bare minimum, probably assuming the rules didn't apply to him.

But the woman had to be a spy.

So Axe ambled north. He removed the expensive sport coat Kelton had bought him and ditched it behind a small rollaway dumpster in front of a fence that blocked an alley.

If he could, Axe would double back later and pick it up, but right now he had to change his appearance. Kelton would understand.

Axe finally reached the intersection and turned the corner, still moving at the pace of an evening stroll. If he'd lost the target, so be it. He'd call the team. Tomorrow, they'd flood the zone, sip coffees while staying in touch in a group voice chat with their earbuds in, and wait for the woman to appear. New York was still a city of neighborhoods. People generally stayed in their area—their "hometown." Few hung out inside their cramped apartments for any length of time. They went out for food, walks, school, or work.

Axe and the team would reacquire the woman.

A block to the west, his target walked in the midst of several other women.

Was this another group he needed to report to Nancy?

Or simply a bunch of friends running into each other?

He stayed back, letting it play out.

61

THE SOLUTIONS

Greenwich Village

Jade continued west, in no hurry. She did her best thinking on long walks through the streets of Manhattan, and tonight she had plenty of company. This part of New York wasn't as crowded as Times Square or Midtown could be, but it seemed like the entire city had decided to throw off winter and enjoy the evening outside.

After walking and planning for several blocks, she passed the iconic black cube sculpture that marked the border of Greenwich Village and the East Village. Tourists spun the huge cube, which balanced on one point. Dozens of people stood or sat at the popular meeting spot.

Jade had to admit that the man tailing her had skills. Credit where credit was due. But at best, he was a gifted amateur. He moved well, didn't follow too closely—he slipped ahead of her from time to time, tracking her from the lead, which took skill and daring—and he had a knack for anticipating when she would cross to the other side of the street. But he stuck out. With his dark hair and trimmed beard, he was handsome, and his powerful body was too noticeable, even hidden under a black sport coat.

He wasn't ordinary enough to make a good spy.

Jade figured him to be a soldier—a covert operator.

She shouldn't be on anyone's radar, unless Boris Zorinov had found her.

Or the authorities suspected her of being involved with the SystemSpike.

Both were so far-fetched that they seemed impossible.

Yet the man was definitely following her, and not in a creepy stalking way, either. Still, the authorities wouldn't send a lone man to shadow her as she meandered through lower Manhattan. For effective surveillance, there should be a team.

So what was going on?

Jade turned left, biding her time, checking for the presence of a larger team.

While she meandered and watched, she debated solutions to her other problem.

Implementing her plan to crash the stock market, despite what Darius had said, was very difficult by Friday.

That meant she had to consider other options.

The most obvious: she could kill Yaz and Kareem.

Anyone could be eliminated, and Jade had no qualms about doing it. The SystemSpike proved that, and shoving Turbo off the roof showed she could physically do it herself, as well.

Murdering Yaz wouldn't be a problem if they did it right. She could plant drugs in his fancy brownstone, incapacitate him, and give him an overdose. The Saudi ruling family was large enough that the death of one young prince, especially with drugs involved, wouldn't be investigated.

Jade stopped at a bakery she liked and went inside, making no attempt to hide her intentions. So far, she'd done nothing that would arouse the suspicions of the dark-haired man following her. No abrupt change of direction. No window shopping to use the reflection of the glass to check behind her.

To anyone watching—including, she hoped, the man—she was a college co-ed out for a long walk on a beautiful spring evening.

Standing at a tall table inside the bakery, she nibbled on a thick cookie, giving her tail a chance to rest and reposition. If it were her, she'd move south to follow from ahead. Though when she finished eating, she planned to go north.

As she ate, she faced a dilemma.

Once she had Yaz out of the way, she'd have to kill Kareem.

Could she get the jump on Kareem? As well trained as she was, he was better and more experienced. She'd have to ask for help from Lu, her fellow Chinese student spy at school who was a trained assassin. But he would ask questions—and demand a favor.

The cookie wasn't as good as she'd hoped. They had changed an ingredient.

No, there wasn't much she could do about Yaz and Kareem for now.

As difficult as it would be with only three days, the best option was to attempt to crash the stock market.

She and Darius had to move up the timeline and hope for the best.

It might be enough time if she got to work tonight.

Every day counted.

And if they got close—if on Friday the plan was in full swing, she could negotiate another few days.

That would do it.

But first, she had to break free of her tail.

She could slip away, or, since it didn't seem like the black-haired man was part of a team, try a more permanent solution.

Men had always underestimated her, even the ones she persuaded or seduced. She could see it in their eyes; she was always the lesser. The weaker sex.

Men, she thought, and shook her head as she exited the bakery.

They looked down on her, discounted her, or lusted after her. She was never an equal.

The solution to that problem was easy.

She would show them all.

62
____

BROADWAY

Greenwich Village

Jade tucked in behind a group of five women, all her age. One had black hair, though not as long as hers, and a similar build.

"Sorry," she whispered to the woman nearest her as the others chatted. "I think my ex-boyfriend is following me—but don't look. Can I walk with you a few blocks?"

The woman fought not to glance behind her. She offered a knowing look to Jade and moved over. "Hey, everyone, she's joining us for a few blocks," the woman said to her friends. "Boy trouble."

There were words of understanding as the group enveloped her.

After a block, her new best friend whispered to her. "We're turning left at Broadway. You can join us. Come to dinner and drinks. Or we can walk you home if you need us to."

Broadway, the area's major thoroughfare, would be perfect.

"When you turn the corner, keep walking at least a block," Jade said. "Pretend I'm still with you. I'll duck into the coffee shop by the corner. If he keeps following you, I'll flag down a police officer and report his ass. But maybe I'm being paranoid." Jade hesitated. "It's a big favor, but can you do that for me?"

The women agreed, crossed Broadway a few minutes later, and turned left.

The moment they couldn't be seen from the street they'd been on, Jade ducked into the small coffee shop south of the intersection. She avoided these international chains, preferring local shops, but a study group in her freshman year had met here twice a week. Just inside the door was a vestibule before a second door opened into the main room. It kept the frigid winter air and the humid heat of summer from intruding. To the right of the exterior door was a small nook hidden from the street. Jade slipped in, her back tight against the wall.

The ladies continued on their way, packed together.

Would it fool the dark-haired man?

———

Axe crossed Broadway, the group of women once again in view. They were easy to follow, even on the very crowded main road.

Had the target picked them to throw him off? Or had he been wrong all along? Maybe only the three men on Nancy's radar met at the Persian café, and he'd been creepily stalking an innocent young woman.

But that didn't feel right.

The sidewalk teemed with people of all shapes, sizes, and ages. Conversations in several languages came from all sides. It was crowded, like Times Square at the height of the summer tourist season.

Axe stuck to the edge of the sidewalk, near the road, not wanting to get bogged down in the thick foot traffic.

Vehicles passed steadily only a few feet to his left.

The group of women turned right onto a smaller street, toward the university, only a few blocks north of where he had almost been seen by Darius.

Axe continued following at a steady pace, trusting his gut.

———

Jade wove through the throngs of people clogging the sidewalk, but not so fast as to attract attention.

The dark-haired operator had shed his sport coat. He was right where she expected him to be, though closer to the street than she would have walked. The middle of the sidewalk was more anonymous, and safer. The vehicles on Broadway didn't travel fast, but even a slow-moving vehicle…

A bus roared as it accelerated away from the intersection behind her.

Jade let her gaze slide off the man ahead. A warrior might sense her attention.

She could turn the tables and follow him for the rest of the evening. Eventually, he would return somewhere to report to whoever had sent him.

The man had followed her since the meeting with Darius, Yaz, and Kareem at the café.

He was alone, not part of a team.

Had he reported in yet?

Or was he gathering more information first?

If the man died now, he wouldn't be able to tell his superiors about the meeting at the café.

Jade refused to have her plans derailed again. No one could be allowed to stand in her way. Especially a man like this.

Killing him was a risk.

So was letting him live.

She was five steps behind him and coming up fast.

The city bus chugged closer in the lane closest to the sidewalk. It would pass inches from the man.

It wasn't moving fast, but its mass would more than make up for that.

Jade slipped into a flow state, her whole body tingling, every sense alert, ready to eliminate one of her many problems.

Axe sensed the danger an instant too late.

His ankle gave way as he was shoved from the side.

He was falling to his left. Someone had perfectly executed a simple yet effective hook-and-push move.

Axe was already falling. There was no way to stop the momentum.

Normally, it wouldn't be a problem to go with the flow, roll with the fall, and come up fighting.

He'd already done it earlier after flying off the bike.

But Axe was off balance, awkwardly moving more to the side than forward.

And a city bus thundered directly at him as he toppled sideways.

After all the dangerous places he'd fought and the risky missions he'd survived, he was about to die on a street in New York City.

63

THE JOGGER

Greenwich Village

The bus barreled down on Axe. Its squared-off blue-and-white front end filled his vision.

He landed hard on his side. The black bumper of the bus loomed over him.

For a moment, time seemed to stand still.

Axe was dimly aware of people screaming from the sidewalk.

Then he twisted and log-rolled farther into the street.

The bright yellow of an approaching taxi in the next lane forced him to roll back the way he'd come. He stopped when he sensed the mass of the bus and hoped he was in the right spot.

Lying on his back, he hugged his arms in as tightly as he could, pressed his legs together, and offered a single word of prayer.

Please.

The front tire of the bus brushed his shoulder as it came to a shuttering stop.

The taxi slammed to a halt on the other side.

He lay in the gap between two tires, staring up at the night sky.

Axe pushed himself to his feet, face to face with the middle-aged bus driver in her side window. She looked like she had seen a ghost.

The taxi driver cursed him in a language Axe didn't understand, choked off a sob in the middle of the tirade, and leaned his head against the steering wheel, muttering.

A man poked his head tentatively around the front of the bus. "You okay?" he asked.

"Yeah. Just fine," Axe said.

Axe's pristine white shirt was filthy with street grime, and he couldn't help but think New York City herself was trying to kill him, but he had survived.

"Sorry," he said to the bus and taxi drivers as he stepped around the bus and returned to the sidewalk. He gave a wave to the people who had gathered. "Guess I tripped. I'm okay."

Nothing like drawing attention, he thought. *So much for a clandestine operation.*

The taxi drove off and a moment later the bus pulled away, resuming its relentless progress south on Broadway.

The long-haired woman had disappeared.

Jade had lost herself in the crowd as the bus brakes squealed and people screamed.

She turned right at the street where her new friends had. They were already two blocks ahead. After a moment, they turned left.

As soon as they were out of view, Jade twisted her long hair into a bun. A black baseball cap from her purse covered it.

She slid the side zipper of the dress down and stepped out of it, dumping it into the trash can near the corner, which left her in black yoga pants and a black sports bra. A few men nearby glanced her way, but New Yorkers were jaded. No one commented or asked questions.

The purse turned inside out, changing from black to tan, and the few items she carried, like her burner cell phone—went right back inside. She unclipped the straps and transformed it into a cross-body pack.

Jade took off at a fast jog. No one gave her a second glance.

Had she pulled it off? Did she nail the timing? The bus had come slower than she'd thought, and a fire hydrant that her pursuer had been about to avoid made her shove him a moment before she'd wanted to.

She jogged on, picking up the pace and gaining distance from the scene of the accident.

Had she acted rashly?

If the man survived, Jade had to change her appearance in addition to everything else she had to do tonight and over the next three days.

But she'd planned for this eventuality.

No one would ever again see the young, thin, long-haired woman she had been for the past three-and-a-half years.

Axe had been outplayed.

Again.

The second time in two days.

First by Vasily Chekov's security team, and now by a young spy who had brazenly tried to murder him on a busy New York City street with hundreds of people around.

He had hit the ground hard yet again. So far, he'd protected his head, but how much longer would his luck hold out?

He made his way north on Broadway, crossed the street at the light—taking no chances with jaywalking—and headed for the dumpster a few blocks over.

At least he could reclaim the expensive sport coat Kelton had purchased for him.

Walking gave him a few minutes to compose himself—and stay alert for a second attempt on his life.

Axe's burner mission phone had survived his fall. After making sure he was alone on the quieter side street, he unlocked it with a lengthy passcode and pressed Haley's speed dial icon in the secure comms app.

"I'm safe," he said as soon as she answered. That short sentence alone would convey much of what he needed to report. That he had seen action—and survived.

"Glad to hear," Haley said, her voice professional but with obvious relief.

"Nancy was right, and there might be more to it. There's a woman involved with the three men, but that's all I know so far."

"What do you need?"

"It's time for a team-building exercise. Tomorrow morning at the latest."

"It's that urgent?"

"Yes, at least until Void or Dave have intel on Boris Zorinov. Something is going on here, and it feels big. I..." He trailed off, not wanting to mention the attack, but Haley needed to know. Partners didn't keep secrets from each other.

"The woman? She, um, tried to kill me. She pushed me into traffic, and I barely missed being roadkill. I didn't sense her in time."

"You're safe? Not injured?"

"Good to go. The problem is, from a legal standpoint, I didn't see her do it. No one did. And, I'm convinced it was her, but…"

"Without you at least seeing her…"

"Yes. She's the only one who realistically could have done it, but there's no proof, not even me being able to say definitively that she pushed me. I know Gregory, the president, and the legal system are going to need more than, 'Axe was pushed in front of a bus and we have to arrest a university student he was following.'"

"You're right. We need more."

Left unspoken, and mostly hidden in Haley's tone, was a question.

Could he still handle the mission?

"I'm good," Axe said again. "I'll reach out to the team and coordinate what we need to do in the morning, but I wanted to keep you in the loop. We'll figure out what's going on."

Axe gave her a brief rundown of what else he'd seen that night, then hung up the phone. He fished around behind the dumpster and found the sport coat, but didn't put it on, not wanting to transfer the road grime on his shirt to the inside lining.

He headed for the subway.

It would take at least an hour for a surveillance detection route. If the target had seen him survive, she could be on him already.

Axe had to be positive that he wasn't being followed.

He would change trains, exit the subway, and take a few taxis as he worked his way gradually to Queens and the apartment behind the safe house auto body garage.

Tomorrow morning, he and the team would be back in the area.

They would find the woman who had almost killed him and figure out what the hell was going on.

64

THE SAFE HOUSE

254 Lafayette Street
Soho
Manhattan

Darius peeked through the gap in the curtains at the apartment. Across the street, the neighborhood fire station's garage doors were up. Several firefighters milled about in the lights from the firehouse, talking while waiting for their next call-out.

He had wound through the East Village, south into Little Italy, and when he was positive no one followed him, to the third-floor walkup safe house in Soho, the area south of Houston Street.

The expensive apartment his father had purchased for his time in New York, on a residential street near Washington Square Park, was half-a-mile northwest.

Jade's modest apartment farther west had thin walls and noisy neighbors who cooked strange-smelling foods at all hours.

It was too risky for them to discuss their secret plans at either apartment. While they'd found no listening devices, neither was an expert in detection, and they couldn't risk hiring a professional to search.

Jade had secured this safe house a few months after they became a couple—the week Jade confessed she was a Chinese spy with an outrageous, ambitious plan to prove herself to her superiors—and make him the youngest Iranian president in history.

The safe house was their secret hideout where they could safely discuss and manage Jade's three-part operation.

In those early days, three years ago, they were going to change the world. They'd hung printed artwork on the walls, put a futon on the floor, and a small table and two chairs in the middle of the kitchen.

They had created a home for themselves.

Tonight, Darius watched through the curtains as Jade ran smoothly down the sidewalk along Lafayette Street. Her loose black dress was gone. She had changed looks.

Something was wrong.

The firefighters stopped chatting to watch her. She ignored them and disappeared from view as she entered through the building's main door directly below him.

Darius took a steadying breath and prepared himself for the performance of a lifetime.

What had started out as mutual attraction had quickly turned into respect for each other's capabilities, ambition, and dreams of power.

Over the past two months, Darius had started to regret their relationship.

He wished he had never met the woman.

When he came to the United States, he'd had a simple mission: get an education, make connections with future powerful men from the Middle East and other parts of the world, and stay out of trouble.

Three-and-a-half years later, his time in America was ending with the desperate hope that his father wasn't aware that the resort collapse in Oman during the peace summit had been planned and financed by his son.

Darius had been so close to success. Jade's plan had nearly succeeded. He would have been well-positioned to become Iran's president by the time he was forty.

And until tonight's meeting and ultimatum, he had been on track to return to his country, pretend he hadn't plotted to kill the country's Supreme Leader and his aides, and never speak with Jiayi "Jade" Pang again.

His best way out now was to continue to hide his true feelings about Jade and help crash America's stock market.

His backup plan wasn't bad. It had come to him while waiting for Jade to arrive at the meeting, when Yaz and Kareem refused to chat.

He would agree to their demands—and set Jade up to fail.

If her scheme worked, he was free.

If it didn't, he would put the entire blame on Jade and offer her up to Kareem as a sacrificial lamb.

Win-win.

Jade unlocked the deadbolt at the front door. He hurried to the kitchen to begin the performance.

"Darling," he said with concern as Jade slipped into the apartment, expertly hiding his true feelings for the woman he had once loved. "What's wrong?"

65

THE RELATIONSHIP

254 Lafayette Street
Soho
Manhattan

"We may have a problem," Jade said, locking the door behind her and leaning against it. She wiped sweat from her forehead with her arm and slipped her phone from her purse.

After turning on her burner cell phone, she pressed the icon for the search engine and entered her criteria. "Breaking news New York City Broadway Greenwich Village bus pedestrian accident."

Darius, supportive as always—handed her a kitchen towel. She wiped her brow and face absently as she scrolled through the search results.

Nothing.

Jade swore under her breath. A bus splattering a pedestrian on Broadway in Greenwich Village on a beautiful spring evening would have made the news by now—at least a line item along with, ***"Stay tuned for more about this developing story."***

"Someone followed me from the café." She met Darius's warm, dark eyes. He was handsome, charming, and ambitious. The Ministry of State Security had done an excellent job selecting him for her to seduce and turn into her primary asset. He was one of the few marks she didn't loathe being with.

Darius saw the horrible implication immediately. "If they knew we were there…" he said, trailing off.

"Yes. It's terrible." She held up the phone. "I pushed him in front of an oncoming bus, but…" She shrugged. "He may have avoided it, though I don't see how."

An emotion flashed across Darius's face for a moment, one she wasn't used to seeing on him.

Fear.

Of the risk she had taken by trying to kill the dark-haired man? The possibility that people were aware of what they had done, that people were coming for them?

Or of her?

She had loved him once. Not at first, certainly. Back then, he was merely an assignment, an asset to recruit. A privileged, ambitious young Iranian whose father had the ear of Iran's Supreme Leader. Someday, Darius would be a very powerful man. Because of their "undying love" during college, she would have an inside path to speak with him, to sway him, for years to come.

Whether because of her natural charm and ability to persuade or because he truly liked her, he had fallen for her.

Jade had decided he was perfect to help with her grand plan to greatly improve China's power and standing in the world, finally showing her superiors that she was more than a pretty face.

Darius had recruited Yaz and Kareem, who brought on board the young men to finance her operation.

All had been going well—for a while.

A year into her plan, she'd fallen for Darius. She'd gone from seductress to seduced. It was an occupational hazard her instructors had warned her about that she had never thought would apply to her.

But Darius never talked down to her or treated her like she was lesser because she was a woman—and not merely because she had him in her power.

Nothing changed about how she acted, but suddenly her "I love yous" were real.

Two months ago, when the plan had crumbled around them, so had her love for him.

"Trying to kill the man made sense. You did what you had to do, what seemed best in the moment," Darius said. "We're safe here. We'll be fine. Besides, the American authorities—if that's who the man was—are slow.

They take weeks, months to investigate. After Friday, if the threat is real, we can disappear. Together."

His naivete would have been charming a few months ago. Tonight, it revolted her. She would never leave with him.

"Friday is too soon," she said, hinting at her annoyance at his immediately agreeing to Kareem's demand.

"I have ideas to move up the timeline," Darius said. He seemed confident.

Jade had a last-ditch contingency which would make the stock market crash within three days, but Darius, as much as he had supported the SystemSpike attacks and all the rest, would likely balk at it.

She'd have to continue keeping it from him until the last minute.

Jade wiped the sweat off her neck before stepping into his arms and pressing against him. "We have so much to plan, but first I need a shower. Care to join me?"

Soon—especially considering the drastically sped up timeline demanded by Kareem and Yaz—she and Darius would be finished. One way or another.

But for now, she had to keep him on her side.

66

THE IDEAS

254 Lafayette Street
Soho

Darius collected the food delivery containers and stuffed them into the apartment's small trash can.

Never again. Once he returned to Iran, he would have people to pick up after him. He was tired of the American way of men doing their share of the work. He'd lived it for three and a half years. He always treated Jade with respect. As an equal. But no more. Not in Iran.

On the futon with the front window open to let in the evening breeze, Jade focused on the laptop from the hacker she had killed.

Darius would be happy to be rid of her.

With any luck, tonight had been their last time sleeping together.

She was in love with him.

Women, he thought.

"How does this one sound?" she asked.

He joined her on the futon as she read. "You have been lied to," she started. "If only you knew. The end is near. Your world is about to burn."

"I like how vague it is. It could mean anything, be from anyone. And it plays well into America's fears. How many sites will Turbo's hack allow us to access?"

"Enough. My asset at the social media company will magnify it, too.

Then our connection at the wire services will make sure the mainstream media runs with it. It's the same plan as before; we're just drastically moving up the timeline. What about this for the second one?" She turned the computer his way.

You think you're safe?
You're not. Far from it.
Your world is about to crumble around you.
Again.
Only this time, it will be worse.
Prepare yourselves for the end.

"When will that be released?"

"We should do the first message tomorrow morning. I'm not sure about the timing for the second. We'll have to wait and see."

Darius considered the situation. "I like the wording, but the timeline is so tight." He faked remorse to test Jade's reaction. Was she still angry about his easy acceptance of Kareem's demand—and did she sense he was setting her up to take the fall?

"Nothing to be done about it," Jade said, dismissing the problem.

She had let it go to focus on the mission—and didn't suspect a thing.

"When our original operation didn't go as planned," Jade said, "our fate was sealed. This plan can work. If we don't try, Kareem will come after us. Or tell his father what we've done, and he could tell Tehran and Beijing. Your father—or the Supreme Leader—might have you killed. Your plane home would blow up, or there would be a tragic car accident in Tehran. My superiors would recall me for 'reeducation.'" She shuddered. "If they were merciful, they would give me the option to kill myself." She looked at him, eyes narrowed. "Why? Don't you think we can do it?"

The implication was there: he was the one to agree to the incredibly short timeline.

"It will work." He sounded completely convincing, like the politician he was destined to become one day. "We only need to tell your assets to start immediately—tomorrow—and accept the added risk. On the way back from the meeting, I had a few ideas, but they require a gun."

He told her his plan to ensure the crash of America's stock market—a variant of what they'd planned to do this summer once he had returned to Iran and Jade was on her own in the United States.

He showed her what he'd researched on the internet, along with the bogus report he'd written.

She took it all in.

"I like it," she said as she stared at the wall and thought through the angles. "One big bluff. Let's do it."

A few months ago, the pronouncement would have been sealed with a passionate kiss.

Tonight, Jade passed him the laptop and walked to their small storage cabinet. She rummaged inside, adding item after item to a backpack. A lock pick set. Tools. Spare clothes. Next to the backpack, on the floor, she started a pile of items she needed immediately.

Finally, she turned, hefting the hammer they'd used to hang artwork in the apartment. In her other hand, she held the green dragon mask she'd chosen at the start of the adventure.

The look on her face was disconcerting. There was not only a willingness to kill, but a desire for it.

Darius refused to look away.

Or shudder.

If she suspected him of betrayal, or sensed weakness, it would all be over. She would use the hammer on him.

When they'd started together, Darius hadn't been half as devious as her. But he'd learned. He still wasn't her equal, but he knew how to manipulate her.

She hadn't seen the many potential flaws in his suggestions for the plan.

Or that he was getting her out of his way for a while.

There was a very good chance Jade would be killed or caught in the next thirty-six hours.

If not, fine. It would mean the plan was working and they were both saved.

If things went badly with the mission again this time, and Kareem wouldn't listen to reason, he would contact his father in Iran, beg forgiveness, and ask for help. Take his chances.

Anything to escape this country, this no-win situation, and this beautiful, brilliant, compelling—and insane—woman.

Jade added the hammer to the backpack, along with the mask. "I have to go right away," she said. "But when this is over…"

He kissed her, faking his love for her with every fiber of his being.

A minute later, she left without a backward glance.

Darius collapsed onto the futon and closed his eyes, grateful to be alive.

He would stay here in the apartment tomorrow, watching for news and monitoring the situation.

Lying low…

Not hiding. He refused to think of it as that.

67

THE DEAL

The Library
Greenwich Village

Jade's target was studying in the library, right where she expected him to be. They were about to graduate soon, but academic excellence allowed both of them to fit in and preserve their cover.

Jade slid into the seat at the small wooden table at the edge of one of the school library's main study areas—a large open space where dozens of students bent over books, tablets, and laptops.

Lu Tantai—Americanized slightly to Lou—was a Chinese student spy like her, but he specialized in assassination, not persuasion. He had the lean, fit body of a swimmer or runner, though he looked more like a nerd than an athlete, with large, black glasses he didn't need. They were as much a part of his cover as Jade's simple, conservative dresses.

"I need a favor," Jade murmured in English.

"*Dǔn dàn,*" he muttered back in Chinese without looking up from his computer, a rude way of telling her to get lost. He'd made a pass at her their first week at the university, years ago, when they'd both been lost and scared.

She had turned him down. Dating each other was against protocol. They were supposed to integrate, meet Americans, connect with men and women Beijing believed were going to be the country's next leaders of business and government, not spend time with their own kind.

Jade had gained an enemy and had regretted it ever since.

Looking back, she should have slept with him for a week and parted ways once they felt more comfortable in this foreign land.

Live and learn.

Owing her, or at least feeling affection for an old flame, would come in handy tonight. It's the only way her plan would work on this accelerated timeline. Many Americans loved their guns, but getting one quickly in New York City was nearly impossible.

"Name your price," she said, this time in Mandarin. How much could he want for a favor?

Lou snorted, his eyes never leaving his laptop. "A hundred thousand dollars, untraceable."

"Done." She had money in a Cayman Islands operating account left over from the SystemSpike mission. She needed every cent to make money when the stock market crashed, but she had to have Lou's help. Without access to Lou's self-storage garage in New Jersey, and the weapons cached there, the plan would fail.

Lou's head snapped up. For an instant, his face was filled with a mixture of longing and resentment. "How, and why? What do you need?" he asked in English. He had also eliminated every trace of an accent and sounded like an average American.

Lou finally noticed her radically changed appearance. His eyes searched hers. "Why the disguise?"

The young woman he knew was gone.

Jade had used one of her disguise kits from the safe house in Soho to completely change her appearance.

She couldn't eliminate her dimples, but her smooth, blemish-free face was now dotted with several utterly convincing angry red pimples, including one on the side of her nose with a white head that looked about to pop.

A padded suit under unfashionable jeans and a baggy sweatshirt added thirty pounds to her hips and stomach, completely changing the look of her short frame.

A wig of unkempt wavy black hair reshaped her head. While she still had Asian features, no one would describe her that way. To be kind, they would avoid calling her, "The short, stocky, pimple-face woman with out-of-control hair," but it's what they'd think.

"Like you," Jade said, still speaking as quietly as possible in Mandarin, "I have been hard at work, not only studying… I need to look different for a while."

Lou nodded in understanding. Jade had seen him around campus. He'd gained access to a group of young men who were the sons of very wealthy American families. His best friend might one day be a senator. Others would be business leaders, executives, and titans of industry. All would be very successful

"I've raised funds for a project," she explained. "I have enough extra to pay you. Or, you could wait three days and earn ten times that when the project is complete."

Lou unconsciously licked his lips, a tell that revealed his greed and interest. She'd have to work with him on that. He wouldn't make it far outside of the confines of college being that obvious.

But not now.

Not when she needed access to his storage garage he had bragged about during their first week, before she had turned him down.

Critiquing him tonight would put him on the defensive, and she would lose him.

"I'd rather have the money upfront," he said, surprising her. Had she lost her powers of persuasion over him?

That was a worry for another time. "Do you have an account number?" she asked.

He nodded. Like her, he had used their school breaks to travel when possible. Switzerland. Belize. The Cayman Islands. All havens for discreet private banking.

Jade opened an app on her phone. "I'm ready."

"Wait. What is worth that much money? What do you need?"

Better for him to hear it now than while in the self-storage garage in New Jersey. She was well-trained, but as a seductress. She was a spy who could seduce, but also kill when absolutely necessary.

Lou was a far better killer than her. He was an unassuming, nerdy-looking, expertly trained assassin.

If he balked at allowing her to use a rifle from his storage unit, guessing correctly that she would kill someone who would make the news around the country, he might eliminate her in the privacy of the self-storage facility. She needed to make sure he was willing to provide what she needed before she put herself in a dangerous situation.

Jade leaned forward and spoke even more quietly. "I need a sniper rifle to assassinate a whistleblower about to testify before Congress. I am going to crash the stock market by Friday, and he stands in my way."

The absolute stillness in Lou's eyes, body and demeanor was more frightening than any raised eyebrow or shake of his head.

The room had four exits. Two were behind her.

She could push her chair back and run.

He wouldn't dare kill her here.

Lou might follow, but she'd have a head start. And one-on-one, she could hold her own for a few minutes. If she had a slight advantage—a knife against his bare hands—she might prevail.

More worrisome than a fight to the death between them was the possibility that he would send a coded message to Beijing from his computer, asking for instructions.

If he did that, she was as good as dead.

"I'm going to need something extra for that," Lou finally said, and leaned back in his chair with a look that meant only one thing.

He had been trained well and had grown since those early days.

He would go far in the covert asset world.

Jade would have to give him what he'd wanted years ago.

This was the only way.

"Fine," she said. "But after, not before."

"First the money, then we take a trip to New Jersey."

"Deal," Jade said, and entered his routing and account numbers into her phone to transfer the money.

68

THE GARAGE

Jade tried not to be envious of Lou's small luxury SUV. It had heated leather seats, tinted windows, and was a great ride.

Of course he'd been provided with funds for a vehicle—a great deal of money, considering not only the cost of the SUV, but maintenance, insurance, and parking near the school in lower Manhattan.

First, he was a man. Beijing assigned a higher value to his work than hers.

Second, he had to fit in with his wealthy targets, unlike her. She had to study, cultivate assets from school with solid, long-term prospects in every field, with many—but not all—selected by the Ministry of State Security.

Someday, she would exploit them for China's gain. You never knew where a person would end up—and what access her country might need.

In a few years, when the Ministry of State Security selected a worthy prospect, she'd be married off, and turned into a baby-making machine.

Lou would be a bachelor vacationing around the world with his rich buddies—and killing anyone Beijing needed eliminated.

They parked outside a large, orange self-storage garage at the far end of the sprawling complex, row after row of single-story garages attached at the sides.

The place was deserted. No one else needed access to their possessions this late on a Tuesday night.

The unit had a solid padlock, hard to pick and impossible to cut without an angle grinder or oxy-acetylene torch.

Lou opened it with a key on a keychain from his pocket, different from his key fob, and raised the garage door.

Inside, clear plastic storage tubs filled the space, stacked four high. The front tubs were packed with old textbooks, papers, clothes, and sporting equipment. Aside from how orderly it looked, it could have belonged to any American family with school kids.

They stepped inside, barely fitting in the space between the first rows of tubs and the doorway, and Lou pulled the garage door down behind them.

"Lights coming on," Lou said in Mandarin, and flipped a switch.

He pushed one of the stacks of tubs to the side, scraping it on the concrete floor, to create a narrow opening, which he squeezed through. Jade followed past more tubs until they reached the middle of the unit, where the tubs ended. They had formed a makeshift wall that blocked the view to the rear half of the garage.

A large white chest freezer hummed on the left, plugged into a surge protector and the wall.

On her right, it looked like she was backstage at a nightclub, with guitar cases, a saxophone case, heavy-duty black rolling cases that would hold lighting or sound equipment, and a crate of extension cords.

"Where are the weapons?" she asked. Had Lou brought her here to take what she'd agreed to give him, then dispose of her body in the freezer?

She adjusted her stance, preparing to defend herself. She'd at least make him work for it.

Lou chuckled and shook his head. He shielded the corner of the back wall where it met the side and did something with his hands. Stepping back, he swung open a small door set into the wall she hadn't noticed.

The rear of the unit had been expertly partitioned off, stealing three feet to make a hidden storage space. The hidden door gave access to the long, narrow walk-in closet. Lou reached a hand inside and flipped a switch to turn on the light.

"Pick what you want," Lou said. "I suggest something more common than a sniper rifle, unless you really need the range."

Jade moved next to him and poked her head through the small

doorway before stepping all the way inside. Weapons hung on a pegboard that covered the rear wall.

Several types of rifles.

A selection of pistols.

Multiple magazines for each weapon.

Another section held knives, brass knuckles, wooden batons, and two baseball bats, one aluminum and one wood.

Heavy-duty plastic boxes were stacked along the far side with labels showing they contained grenades, plastic explosives, and ammunition.

Jade took her time, but eventually turned to Lou for help, appealing to his ego. Anything to get him on her side.

In the end, she selected a bolt-action hunting rifle common in the United States, with a scope that would help her at a distance and a suppressor to quiet the shot. She had trained with a similar weapon in China.

Lou nodded his approval, turned off the light to the secret room, and once again used his body to hide how the door closed and locked.

"Now, a carrying case," he said. "If you change your look, you could be a punk rock bass player." He opened a bass guitar case—long, black, thickly padded, with a handle and a strap for carrying it slung over a shoulder. Large white letters on both sides proudly proclaimed the brand name. Lou removed the bass guitar, leaned it against the rest of the band equipment, and gestured for her to nestle the rifle inside and zip up the case.

It fit well, and no one would guess she carried a weapon.

"Welcome to the band," he said with a chuckle.

Before they made their way out, she gestured to the freezer. She had a hunch, but wanted to confirm it.

"Go ahead," he said.

Jade opened the freezer lid, which creaked ominously.

"I should lubricate that," he whispered in her ear. He stood directly behind her. She could feel the heat from his body.

Inside the freezer, a light came on, revealing two naked bodies crammed inside, frozen solid and caked with frost. One American male, and one American female. She recognized the face of the woman as that of a student who had disappeared last year.

Jade stared for a long moment, engrossed, and finally closed the door. It slammed shut, causing the freezer to shake and its contents to shift.

Jade turned, face to face with Lou. "Any advice?" she asked.

She had only killed Turbo, the hacker, by pushing him off the roof.

Judging by Lou's expression, she had asked the right question. "Never think of them as people," he said after a short pause. "They are blocks that must be knocked down for our success—for our country. It's them or us. They must die so we can live. That makes it easy."

His answer matched what she'd already come to terms with, how she'd slept at night knowing that her SystemSpike had taken thousands of American lives.

She should have brought Lou on board from the start. He would have made a formidable ally.

Jade kissed him, happily, the way she should have years before.

PART 5

WEDNESDAY

69

THE GARDEN

Outside Sortavala, Russia

Late spring in Sortavala was cold—just the way Ekaterina liked it. Too many of her missions over the years had been in sunny locations, including Los Angeles recently, followed by an unexpected trip to Dubai and Oman.

She'd had enough hot air to last a lifetime.

Despite her best efforts over the past several weeks, the small plot of land behind her cabin could hardly be called a garden. The vegetables she had planted struggled under the plastic poly tunnels covering the rows to protect the plants and get a jump on the growing season.

Her neighbors in the small village all had similar gardens that thrived.

Hers struggled.

Ekaterina was much better at killing than nurturing. As an assassin for Russia from age fourteen, that should have been obvious, but she'd had dreams of working the land. Growing vegetables. Cultivating instead of destroying.

In her late sixties, Ekat had finally negotiated her freedom from Russia's Foreign Intelligence Service—the SVR. Here, on Russia's border with Finland, she could live out her final days in peace, nearly a thousand kilometers from Moscow's politics, lies, and manipulations.

Her recent return to the simple life in the small village hadn't diminished her instincts, however. She'd awoken before dawn with the sense that the day would bring more than the usual futile efforts to coax life from the garden.

She rose, had tea for breakfast, slipped on her coat, and went outside to kneel in the dirt and check on her plants.

An hour later, Ekat didn't bother to turn as hesitant footsteps came from the side of the cabin. She knew her neighbors; these steps weren't from any of them. And they wouldn't approach without a quiet greeting, either. While none of them knew her history as an assassin, they were people who lived close to the land. They recognized the danger within her in the same way they knew when someone with a temper had too much vodka on a winter night and should be left alone, or when a winter storm was about to go from ice cold to deadly.

The man's shoes sounded strange, too. The soles of work boots touched the ground differently than dress shoes worn by city folk, which the village rarely saw.

If he keeps coming around, I'll develop a reputation, she thought.

After so many decades of hiding her feelings, she easily kept the smile off her face.

The footsteps stopped several meters behind her and to the side.

He wants to seem unthreatening.

The idea was ludicrous. If she wanted, he would be dead within seconds, long before he could shoot her—if he'd been stupid enough to bring a gun. No matter what they had taught him at spy school, he had never used the lessons in the field.

It was obvious he had never killed.

Unlike her.

While she waited for him to speak, she contemplated the question: How many people had she killed?

It wouldn't be hard to figure; the images stuck in her mind, and while they never haunted her the way it did for some people in her work, the targets would be easy to count if she dared. There had been several a year —at least—over six decades…

Perhaps it would be more difficult than she'd thought.

"You may be over-watering," Mr. Moscow—Dmitry—said. Ekat had met him twice. The first had been inside her cabin months ago when he asked for her help.

The more recent meeting had been at President Nikitin's dacha outside

Moscow when the president had formally freed her from her service to the country.

Dmitry was President Nikitin's young spy chief—the director of Russia's Foreign Intelligence Service. He seemed too young to handle the job he'd inherited from his mentor, who had killed himself.

Ekat didn't know the details, but could guess. The mentor may have been forced out after working against the interests of the country.

Young Dmitry had stepped into his shoes.

But the boy had surprised her with his intelligence and determination. And his bravery—knowing her history, he had knocked on her cabin door, unarmed and unaccompanied by guards, to recruit her for a mission. She respected that.

Ekaterina offered Dmitry no reply, though she leaned forward a bit to check the ground under the plastic tunnel, considering his comment.

"My mother had a community garden plot in the city when I was a child. I helped her tend it on Saturdays," Dmitry continued, as if they were friends. "Of course, when first planted, the seeds need plenty of water, but after... It's difficult to judge. And this far north... She always said gardening required a certain feel, which had to be learned. A neighbor taught her after the first year, when everything died. Like here." He cleared his throat quietly, perhaps thinking he had crossed a line.

"Let us go inside and talk," he said. "Before the neighbors see and have questions for you after I leave."

"They are smart enough to ask no questions," Ekat said finally as she turned. He looked older, though only a few months had passed since their first meeting.

Dmitry still looked like he needed to eat more—he was tall, and thinner than his mother surely liked, if she was still alive. His short dark hair now had touches of gray at the sides, and fresh creases had appeared at the corners of his mouth. Under his eyes, dark bags were a testament to too much stress and too little sleep.

"I will make tea, then," Dmitry said, and led the way into the tiny one-room cabin she now called her home—the place that was supposed to be a refuge from her old life of killing people the politicians in Moscow wanted dead.

After a last look at the garden, Ekat followed Dmitry, not allowing her eyes to sparkle at the thrill she felt inside.

The past weeks had dragged by, but it looked like she might finally have another mission.

70

THE BARGAIN

Outside Sortavala, Russia

Dmitry handed the older woman a cup of tea.

He remained standing since Ekaterina occupied the only chair. He could have perched on the single bed along the wall, its sheets and blanket tucked in without a wrinkle, but that felt too intimate. And the short ottoman in front of the chair would have made him feel more like a foolish boy begging his grandmother for a favor than he already did.

"You have heard of Boris Zorinov, the criminal, yes?" Dmitry stared.

Ekaterina sipped her tea. "Yes," she said. Nothing more.

She would not make his job easy.

"We believe he orchestrated the attack and destruction of the luxury resort in Oman that hosted the Middle East Peace Summit two months ago."

Dmitry thought he saw the tiniest twitch on Ekat's face, but it could have been his imagination.

"And the cyberattacks against America that were to start a war between our countries," Dmitry continued.

The damn old woman still said nothing.

"And the assassination of the American's Secretary of State."

Finally, Ekaterina nodded with respect. "A professional job."

Dmitry frowned. The murder of Secretary of State Wilson had been the final straw that had nearly compelled America to declare war on Russia.

"I will kill Zorinov for you," Ekat said with a small nod, like she had agreed to buy him a loaf of bread when she went to the store.

He hesitated, surprised. He'd rehearsed a speech the entire flight from Moscow, then again in the car from the nearest city.

"You have lost Zorinov?" the assassin asked, before immediately answering her own question. "Yes—but first you tried to kill him yourselves. Your people failed, he has vanished, and you turn to me to clean up the mess, yes?"

There was no sense in denying it. "Yes. I should have come to you first. I am sorry."

A shrug. The assassin seemed neither annoyed nor concerned. "You will give me the details. I will find him. When I do, would you prefer a spectacle? Blood and guts as a lesson for others? Or shall he disappear and have people wonder if he is dead or in prison, tortured every day? Or my choice?" She blew on her tea and sipped it—cooler now, so he matched her move and drank. "Giving me the choice is better," she said. "More flexibility. Easier for me, quicker for you."

"Your way is fine."

"How soon—there is a deadline always, yes?"

Dmitry shrugged. "We doubt there will be another attack, but…"

"But you cannot be sure."

She waited, eyebrows raised.

Dmitry cleared his throat. "It must be now. We have a corporate jet waiting forty kilometers away in Finland—in Lappeenranta. It can take you anywhere you want to go." He reached into his jacket pocket and removed a large, folded envelope. "All the details about Zorinov we have. His preferences, the locations of his homes, places he has vacationed. Plus, everything you need for the mission: a cover identity. Passport. Credit cards. Cash. A burner phone for the mission. Weapons hidden in the airplane. But in exchange for doing this for us, what do you want? Money?" He looked around the cabin at the sparse furnishings. "Perhaps a furnished apartment in Moscow? A dacha in the mountains?"

"I will leave immediately to find this man for you. But I have no need for the things you mentioned." Ekaterina's sudden, predatory smile made Dmitry shiver. The hair on his arms sprang to life, and goosebumps rose on his arms.

"Your mother—she is still alive?" she asked.

Dmitry nodded, his stomach sinking.

"Good. I require something much more dear than money or a dacha," Ekaterina said.

The look in her eyes—a cross between a chess grandmaster and a shark about to feast on its prey—made his blood run cold.

THE PUNK ROCKER

Jersey City, New Jersey

By the time Jade had finished her liaison in the storage garage, she was behind schedule.

It took very little to convince Lou to loan her the luxury SUV. After switching out the license plates for an alternate set from Maine, she dropped him at a train station for the trip back to New York City, leaving him with a lingering kiss....

And pickpocketed the storage garage key.

Just in case.

With a last coy wave, she had hit the road. She had many miles to go and had to be in place by the time her target left for work.

As she drove, her feelings, carefully controlled since the previous evening, threatened to overwhelm her.

It was too much. The ultimatum from Kareem and Yaz. Moving up the timeline. Darius's plan that put her at great risk while he hid in the apartment—and his belief that she didn't see how he was setting her up to take the fall.

She had so much to do. Hours of driving. Coordinating with the rest of her assets, giving them the go signal for the mission they had expected would happen this summer.

And she had to kill a man this morning—the only part of the day that offered any relief from the stress.

With a deep breath in and a long, slow release, she let some of the tension go. She stuffed the rest of the feelings down deep to deal with some other day.

After she'd gotten what she wanted.

What she deserved.

Recognition of her true talents.

And revenge against the men in Beijing who saw her body as a tool to use as they decided.

She drove on, three miles per hour above the speed limit, doing nothing to risk being pulled over.

Today had to go perfectly, and shooting a police officer would only slow her down.

MegaMart Supercenter
Sterling, Virginia

After a few hours of driving, Jade entered a superstore in Virginia the minute it opened right before dawn. Bleary-eyed employees ignored her as she shopped for everything a spy on a mission could need—except a wig. She picked up the best scissors they had instead.

Once back in the SUV, she started with the prosthetic pimples on her face, peeling them off with care. A wipe with a makeup remover cloth cleaned the sticky residue and prepped her face for what was to come.

Next, her hair. With a purchased towel draped around her neck and another across her lap, Jade got to work. She removed the wavy black wig, letting her fine, long hair spill free.

A few snips took away the length. The rest went easily enough.

When she finished, she had one-inch rough-cut hair, the shortest it had been since she was a small child. She added gel to make it stand up in clumps.

Few would look past the punk haircut, but there was more to do.

Jade applied a thin coat of pale white foundation, shiny black lipstick, thick black mascara, and eyeliner.

A black choker collar and a silver ring that faked her septum being pierced completed the look.

She stuffed her old, dowdy clothes and the hip, tummy, and waist padding into a bag and shoved it into the rear passenger wheel well, out of sight but within easy reach if she needed to change her look again.

The towels full of hair went into a trash bag, tied tight and set in the backseat to be disposed of far from prying eyes.

Jade pulled on oversized men's black cargo pants and secured them with a thick black belt. An enormous men's T-shirt, also black, went on next. She twirled the fabric on her right side and tied it into an overhand knot at her waist. High-top black and white sneakers were last, and she rolled up the legs of the pants.

The transformation from a dowdy, stocky woman with pimples to a counterculture punk rocker was complete. It was a bold choice—drawing eyes to her instead of trying to blend in.

Finally, it was time for the texts, a flurry of messages sent through the secure comms app to lovers, exes, best friends forever, conspirators, confidants, and buddies; people who trusted and liked her.

In other words, her carefully selected, recruited, and nurtured assets.

Several minutes later, she was on the road, ready for the fun part of the plan.

72
____

THE CODE

16th Floor
Stock Exchange Annex
Wall Street
Manhattan

The stock exchange was open for public trading from 9:30 a.m. to 4:00 p.m., Monday through Friday, excluding federal holidays.

Sean Finelan's workday started long before that. He sat in front of his monitor in the middle of the long, four-foot wide, twenty-foot long "desk" that management had decided was needed for "team synergy." Ten months before, everyone's small yet private cubicles had been removed, replaced with two long, narrow tables. Instead of an individual office, Sean now had a three-foot section of desk space, with a row of coworkers on either side up and down the line.

Plus, another table faced his, so he had people across from him left and right behind their monitors.

It didn't help that the group's new manager had claimed that firms across the city were eliminating cubicles to build community.

The management job should have gone to Sean, not the idiot who now had them sitting at group tables instead of their own desks.

Sean was an excellent systems engineer, a talented coder, and a diligent worker. He had a perfect work record, security clearance, and a reputation as a hard worker.

It wasn't fair.

Being passed over for promotion had been the final straw.

His dual monitors glowed in the darkness, giving the area an eerie, haunted feel. At the far end of the large, windowless room, a few rows of horrible fluorescent lights were on over the group of four software engineers who worked the late shift. They preferred the brightness; it helped them stay awake all night.

Sean and the others liked it dark, at least until their new manager arrived and turned on the fluorescents for "professionalism" and "a healthy work environment."

The jerk.

Sean shrugged it off. Today, he had a mission.

The stock exchange functioned as a marketplace to bring buyers and sellers of stocks together in real time. Billions of dollars in value changed hands every hour the market was open.

Sean and the other dedicated engineers made sure the software which handled the incredible volume of trading ran flawlessly, plus they kept the system secure from hackers and unauthorized users.

But like anything to do with computers, there were vulnerabilities.

It was all controlled with code—lines of software that people had to write, refine, adapt, and troubleshoot.

Reliable, carefully vetted and background-checked employees like Sean.

Sean stretched his arms, checking the area. The night shift guys had their eyes glued to their screens.

No one else was in yet.

He'd received the message from Jade fifteen minutes before, on his way from the subway to the office building on Wall Street.

The words had sent his pulse racing, made his palms sweaty, and filled his mind with dreams of tropical beaches, fruity cocktails with little umbrellas, and Jade Pang's warm, lithe body against his.

It's time. Do it this morning. It will happen tomorrow.

The message had disappeared ten seconds after he'd read it, though he'd wanted to preserve it as a keepsake. The start of his new life.

Or for insurance if things went horribly wrong.

Sean rolled his desk chair to the right, nudging his colleague's chair back and out of the way. A jiggle of the mouse brought the workstation to life. Sitting nearly shoulder to shoulder for the past months, it hadn't been hard to pick up the password Ian—his neighbor—used to log in to the system.

Sean entered it quickly, a series of random numbers and letters that was surprisingly easy to memorize when he saw it typed repeatedly.

He navigated to the correct part of the system, checked around the room once more to ensure he still had privacy, and typed in the lines of code he had developed. It took only a minute, but they would have a devastating effect when triggered.

Over the years, the stock exchange had evolved and improved. After Black Monday, the stock market crash in 1987 where one popular index fell more than 22% in a day, so-called "circuit breakers" were introduced. Cooling-off periods were needed to prevent panic selling. If the market fell far enough, trading was suspended for a short time—like a home circuit breaker tripping when it detects a dangerous surge or other issue.

If a particular stock index—a pre-selected group of five hundred stocks—drops 7%, trading is automatically paused for fifteen minutes to allow people to collect themselves and, hopefully, calm down. To realize that panic selling wasn't needed. For cooler heads to prevail.

If that didn't work, there was more.

Another breaker, or "stop," was built in at 13%, mandating a further fifteen-minute timeout.

And should that fail and the market drop 20% in one day, a catastrophe-level stop kicked in. All trading was suspended for the rest of the day.

Sean painstakingly read the lines he had typed, glanced around one more time, leaned forward, and triple-checked his work. There was no way to test and debug the code. It had to run flawlessly when the market dropped enough to trigger the subroutine he had inserted.

Everything looked perfect. He backed out of the system, signed out of Ian's workstation, and rolled back to his space.

He was forgetting something.

Ian's chair.

Sean grabbed the seat and moved it into place.

He sweated the minutes until Ian's computer monitor went to sleep from not being used.

The additional safety precaution of inserting the code while logged in as Ian shouldn't be necessary, but Sean had to be sure. He wouldn't come this far and risk this much only to be caught.

73

THE FATE

16th Floor
Stock Exchange Annex
Wall Street
Manhattan

Five minutes after Sean finished his hack, his first coworker entered, ignored the light switch, and made his way to the far end of the long, shared table to begin his day.

Would Sean's code work? The software subroutine was solid, but he wasn't convinced it would be triggered. Too many things had to go right, and despite his partner-in-crime's conviction, Sean didn't see how the market would drop so much in one day.

Jade Pang was a dreamer, though, and her dream had inspired his own.

The hidden lines of code he inserted would wait patiently for a crash tomorrow.

When—if—the market dropped 7% or more, the subroutine would kick in.

The first circuit breaker would be disabled as if it had never existed.

And the back-end computer system of the stock exchange would automatically lock out anyone attempting to fix it.

Selling could continue unchecked.

The lack of the expected circuit breaker at 7% would cause an additional wave of panic.

More sellers would dump their stocks, desperate to get out before the market fell more.

The market would quickly drop further, to a 13% loss.

The expected circuit breaker would fail as well because, to the computer system, it no longer existed.

Thanks to Sean.

There was little chance the market would stop falling at that point.

The absence of the 20% breaker, meant to shutter trading for the rest of the day, would surprise no one.

Sean bit back a smile, picturing the mass confusion as his idiot manager frantically fumbled for an explanation of the failed circuit breakers and the locked-out system. The guy was a doofus.

It would be glorious to see his panicked expression when he realized he was powerless to fix what was happening or explain why it had occurred.

He'd finally be exposed as the butt-kissing, ignorant hack he was and fired by the end of the day.

Too bad, so sad—especially when, at 4:01 p.m., one minute after the market officially closed, the system would revert back to normal.

Sean's code would self-destruct and vanish at the end of the day, whether it had been triggered or not. No one would find a trace of it.

The problem would be blamed on a computer glitch.

By the next trading day, people would realize they had acted rashly and buy back the solid investments they had dumped in a panic. Prices would rise and revert to normal in a few days or a week.

Anyone with advance knowledge of the crash could position their money to take advantage of the fire sale.

In a few days, they'd earn 10 times, 20 times, maybe 30 times the money they positioned, depending on how much risk they were willing to take.

Ten thousand dollars could easily be turned into one hundred thousand.

A brave man might transform a one-hundred-thousand-dollar investment into three million overnight.

As an employee of the stock exchange, Sean's investments were too closely monitored for him to position his money to profit directly.

But the home equity line of credit he'd taken out to remodel his house had been paid to his general contractor—Pang Construction and Home Remodeling, managed by Jade Pang, his lover, co-conspirator, and... whatever else they were to each other.

The three million dollars he'd gain over the next few days would be plenty to retire on in several months, once the hubbub died down and he could quit without arousing suspicion.

He sent a quick message to Jade.

Done.

Now all Sean had to do was wait and act normal.

Another coworker entered the room, followed a few minutes later by their doofus manager, who flicked on the lights and flooded the room with a harsh, white glare.

Sean slipped on his headphones to discourage the man from chatting to him, leaned forward, and pretended to focus on his monitor while actually thinking back to how he'd gotten to this point, ready to risk his career and freedom for one huge score.

He had first noticed the woman on the subway a year ago...

The woman's head was buried in a book about the history of Wall Street. She was several years younger than him, with long, fine black hair, the cutest dimples, and an athletic build that her professional corporate pantsuit couldn't hide.

At twenty-nine, Sean took care of himself and wasn't as nerdy as his job made him sound. He worked out, ate well, and the polo shirts he wore to work showed off his respectable biceps. He styled his blond hair nicely, had hobbies other than watching TV, read books from time to time, and could hold his own in a conversation.

Women routinely ignored him or, when he worked up the courage to ask one out in person or on his dating app, politely refused.

He had resigned himself to being single until the right woman came along. Someone looking for stability. Security. Not a bad boy or a guy into constant drama.

Later, on the crowded commuter train to Long Island, the woman from the subway boarded his car right before the doors closed. Nearly every seat was taken. He slid to the left, offered a slight "I'm not a serial killer" smile, and she sat next to him with a nod of thanks.

Ten minutes later, she looked over. "I saw you on the subway earlier, didn't I? Do you work on Wall Street?"

"Yes, and yes. I work for the stock exchange."

"You have that look about you. I'm an intern," she'd said, naming the

firm she was working for. "Jade." She held out her hand and they awkwardly shook in the narrow space of the row they shared.

"Sean."

"I'm staying at a friend's this weekend on Long Island," she said, then hesitated. "Can I pick your brain about the industry? I hope I'm doing the right thing going this route. Or," she blushed, "sorry. You're relaxing on the way home. The last thing you want to talk about is work. I'll be quiet." She reached into her oversized black purse, which was more like a small backpack, and pulled out the hardcover Wall Street book from the subway.

"No," he said. "I'm happy to talk. Really. I'm actually a software engineer, so I know more about the back-end stuff than investment analysis, though, so I'm not sure how much help I'll be."

"Actually, I think you'll be great," she said.

Sean was smart, but it still took him three months to figure out that a woman of Jade Pang's caliber wouldn't fall for him as easily as she had.

Those months, though, were the best days of his life. They were together at least one night every weekend. They parted with long, lingering kisses when he dropped her at the train station for the trip back to Manhattan and her studies.

One Sunday morning, Sean woke with the realization that something was wrong. At work on Friday, he and the rest of the team had been required to take a continuing education course called "Security Awareness Training."

One of the modules had been about insider threats—how people might groom, blackmail, or seduce people like them to gain access to secure systems.

Spooned against a woman way out of his league, he had a sinking feeling.

It couldn't be—could it?

The term from the course repeated itself in his mind.

"Honey trap."

Using romantic or sexual attraction to manipulate or coerce.

Jade wiggled against him and clutched his arm to her, holding tight. "What's wrong?" she asked, her voice filled with sleep. "You just tensed up."

Sean tried to relax, but couldn't.

It was better to get it out in the open and over with, one way or the other.

He'd always been a dive into the freezing cold water instead of wading in slowly kind of guy.

"Who do you work for?" he whispered, taking a last, lingering breath of her hair, committing the scent to memory. In a moment, she would walk out of his life either because he was right or because he was wrong.

She hesitated a second, but didn't pull away. "Does it matter?" she asked, awake now, her voice quiet and low.

Gentle. Caring.

He had to get up and get dressed. Kick her out. Go in on Monday and sit at that stupid long table instead of the cubicle they had taken away from him, waiting until his idiot manager arrived so he could report that he'd been approached by... whoever Jade reported to. She was an American of Chinese descent; her parents had immigrated to America when they were kids, so maybe she was a Chinese asset. Or, these days, who knew? She could be on the payroll of Russia, Iran, or maybe one of the exchange's competitors.

"Have I asked you for anything?" Jade continued, warm and soft against him.

"Not yet," he admitted.

The words seem to hang in the bedroom, sunlight streaming in and warming the cool morning air.

She said nothing.

Neither did he.

A minute passed.

Two.

He couldn't get the image of his idiot manager's face out of his mind.

Such a stupid thing, to be passed over for a promotion. But it had stung—a lot.

She rolled over to face him, their noses almost touching. "Do you want me to leave?" she asked.

Her dark eyes. The dimples. Those lips.

He didn't make a decision so much as acted on instinct. He moved forward an inch and kissed her, sealing his fate.

74

———

OLIVER

15th Street NW
Columbia Heights
Washington, DC

Oliver Renolds felt a surge of happiness when his phone buzzed.

No one reached out to him.

Except for her. The mystery woman from the train.

A few months before, on the way home from work, an attractive young woman with dimples and long black hair had taken the seat next to him.

He couldn't help but glance at her phone's screen.

She opened his favorite social media app…

And pulled up his profile page.

His secret social media account.

The safe place for him to blow off steam.

Criticize managers at FEMA—the Federal Emergency Management Agency, where he helped with system maintenance for the Integrated Public Alert and Warning System (IPAWS), the network authorities used to send emergency alerts via television, radio, mobile phones, and weather radio. Everywhere, basically.

Online, he could rant about the current administration—and the previous one.

Complain about the government in general, the way the world screwed over people like him, the economy—he bitched about everyone and everything.

Reposted crazy conspiracy theories.

Egged people on. Pushed their buttons.

Stirred shit up.

He loved how crazy he made people with the outrageous crap he posted.

After a few hours online, he always felt better.

He'd shut down the computer, crawl into bed, and do it all over again the next night.

The gorgeous mystery woman on the train scrolled through his posts, lingering on the worst, most obnoxious ones.

The truly horrible, offensive words and rants that, if it came out that he was behind them, would mean the end to his career.

He would never again work for the government. Certainly not in his capacity as a trusted software engineer who had access to the nation's emergency alert system.

And, honestly, it would be hit or miss whether he could get a halfway decent job anywhere.

He would be forced to be a freelancer, scrambling for work online.

Maybe he could use an assumed name, or find a company that didn't do a background check—which was basically nobody, these days.

"What do you want?" he had whispered to the woman in resignation.

She hadn't spoken a word, and he'd already given in.

He'd stopped posting online that night. In part because he knew it was wrong and risky.

But mostly because the woman had taken the login information he gave her and changed it, making it impossible to sign on.

But the words, pictures, memes, and vile content remained, a ticking time bomb waiting to be associated with him.

Oliver hadn't seen her again.

They had no contact other than the occasional check-in message exchanges to remind him of his place.

But their chats started to fill the void left behind from not being able to post online.

He shared with her—more and more as the weeks went on. His life. His work. His thoughts, concerns, fears.

She remembered what he had written from week to week, asking follow-up questions and pointing out things he'd never considered.

It hadn't taken long before it felt like the woman—he never learned her name—wasn't his blackmailer. She was more like a pen pal.

Or a long-distance girlfriend, almost.

Their texts became chatty. Flirty, even.

Not that he knew much about all that. He'd been on two dates in his forty-one years, and neither had gone very well.

This morning's message on the secure comms app was different than the previous ones.

It's time, her message said. *Continue to the office, but ask to be allowed to go home and work from there. Claim you have a stomach bug. Return home, log in remotely, and work as usual. Understand?*

Yes, he replied.

Tomorrow morning, tell them you feel worse. You'll work from home as much as you can, between trips to the bathroom. No one will question that. Then log in to the system, leave your computer on, and go back to bed. Understand?

Yes.

Oliver hesitated, then took the plunge. *Will I be okay?*

A second later, he found the courage to ask what he really wanted to know.

Will I see you again?

For several seconds, there was nothing. Then three dots appeared. She was typing a message, which came a moment later.

You will be fine. Claim ignorance. Deny everything. You were in bed, asleep. Your computer will look like it was hacked. You know nothing about whatever happens. — And… maybe. If this goes well, I would like to see you again.

Her answer was enough for Oliver, even though her willingness to meet with him someday was probably a lie.

There was something about her that made him believe it would all be okay, and that she'd keep his secret about the horrible things he had said online.

He had little to lose by going along with her.

And his entire life to lose if he didn't.

The choice was easy. He would do whatever she said—and hope for the best.

75

CLAY

The Essex Exchange Lofts
Newark, New Jersey

A chime woke Clay Gerdalno from a recurring dream.

His phone automatically switched to DND—Do Not Disturb—at night when he slept.

But after his first date with Jade Pang, he'd added her as an exception.

Day or night, his phone notified him with a special sound only for her calls or messages.

Months after he last saw her, the tone filled him with desire when she reached out to say hi every few weeks.

Clay had rolled out of bed, put his glasses on, and had the phone in hand before he knew what he was doing.

The time has come. More tonight. xoxoxoxo

Jade had attached a link for a secure video chat scheduled for tonight.

He typed a reply, then erased his first response, typing a less desperate message.

I'm ready. xoxoxoxo

There, that was perfect. Smooth. Not at all needy. She would catch the double meaning. He was excited about the plan, as well as them getting back together.

Work didn't start for a while, but the moment he'd been waiting for had finally arrived, and he could barely contain himself.

He got up and started his day.

Sometime soon, maybe tonight, he and his guys would finally take action.

No more bitching and moaning about the state of the world and the environmental destruction of capitalism.

Or about how China, Vietnam, India, and others flooded the United States with cheap products to keep the masses happy and passive, ruining the planet along the way.

Much of the products destined for the East Coast passed through the Elizabeth Marine Terminal—also known as Port Elizabeth—a few miles away.

He and his buddies were quite familiar with it. The company they worked for coordinated container shipments at the port, scheduled warehouse intake, trucks carrying goods, and handled communication between customers, trucking companies, and customs.

Logistics. Not sexy but absolutely essential.

And finally, after much talk and training, they were going to sabotage the container port.

Done right, they could shut down the port for days, which would call attention to the stupidity of shipping cheap junk halfway around the world.

People would wake up to their stupid consumerist habits and realize that the government, their employers—society—had fooled them into living lives of quiet desperation.

All of this was possible because of a chance meeting with a woman he'd met at college before he graduated. Jade Pang had listened to his mishmash of complaints about the world and helped him truly see what was being done to the people of the United States.

Jade.

The one that got away.

He'd had two glorious months with her.

What she saw in him, he still didn't know. He was tall, skinny, had no muscles to speak of, frequent bouts of acne even at twenty-five years old, and a cowlick that wouldn't stay down no matter how he had the barber cut it or what product he used. Yes, he was super smart—he was proud of it—and had the job lined up at the logistics company before he graduated, but no other woman had expressed interest in him.

Let alone one as stunningly smart and beautiful as Jade.

But they'd fallen for each other.

Hard.

And then she had to let him go.

Her lips had brushed his ear their final night together. "I can't do this anymore," she'd whispered, her voice choked with emotion. "My grades have slipped. I'm losing myself in you. You're too perfect."

She was dumping him.

His world fell apart, even as she pressed her body against his and held him, surprising him with her strength. "Listen. I'm so sorry, but it won't be forever. We're not breaking up. We're pausing. It's only until I graduate."

She'd looked desperately into his eyes. "I have no right to ask, but would you consider waiting for me? Please?"

He was too surprised to do anything other than nod.

"Thank you." Jade kissed him, and what resolve he might have found from being taken to bed and dumped within an hour had evaporated.

Clay had promised to do whatever she wanted.

Anything to be with her.

Now the time had finally come. By next week, they'd be together forever.

She was helping him realize his dreams.

Her plan to wreck the port and wake people up to the reality of their shallow lives was brilliant, and much better than what he'd thought to do.

The team he'd assembled and trained was ready. Other young men like him who were tired of the consumerism, the struggle to keep up with others, to have the bigger TV or the nicer car, to achieve, to climb the ladder, to constantly prove their worth.

The guys and he would sneak into the Port Elizabeth Terminal and disable the many cranes that moved the containers on and off the ships.

Then slip out and wait until morning when the shit hit the fan.

He'd get to work early so he could quietly give each member of his team the good news.

They were going to be stoked.

76

THE TARGET

The Colonial Apartments
Silver Spring, Maryland

Jade arrived in plenty of time for her next kill.

The four-story brick apartment building where her target lived was well kept. She could understand the draw of living in the quiet residential neighborhood. It was the suburbs. Rent here, along the tree-lined streets, had to be much cheaper than living in the heart of a city.

The straight, one-mile walk to the Metro station would make an easy commute into Washington, DC.

Jade found the perfect spot to park— facing north, just south of the intersection on a side street. She had an unobstructed view of the apartment building one block away.

Her target would walk toward her for several minutes, giving her time to confirm who he was and prepare.

Jade swung around and grabbed the guitar case from the backseat, unzipped it, and removed the rifle, keeping it low and out of sight.

Darius's plan was solid, and she was here early enough.

Jade waited, barely moving, her eyes constantly scanning the area but always returning to the sidewalk on her right.

A few pedestrians hurried by. No one paid any attention to her in the SUV. The tinted windows helped with that.

The minutes crawled by, giving her time to worry. Had the target, who Darius had picked based on his social media activity, driven to work instead? Was he sick or on vacation? Nothing on his profile pages mentioned a trip, but he could have suddenly realized that posting every nuance of his daily life wasn't very security conscious.

The last commuter train the average worker at the Securities and Exchange Commission in DC could take and still be on time would leave soon.

If Darius's last-minute plan didn't work out, they'd have to postpone the operation.

Or she could pick a random person and kill them instead, hoping they had some connection to the federal government, and that the disinformation plan she already had ready would work with that victim instead.

She would prefer not to drive into DC, park, and start shooting near the SEC.

Down the street, a tall man with bright-orange hair hurried toward her, a large black commuter coffee mug in hand and a beat-up leather bookbag slung on his shoulder.

Her target. Finally.

Jade buzzed down the passenger-side window and prepared.

A car passed and turned the corner, pulling out of sight.

The rest of the neighborhood was still.

She raised the rifle, sighted on the man, and pulled the trigger.

The gun's attached suppressor lowered the volume of the shot. People would ignore it. There was no thunderous *crack* that came from an unsuppressed rifle.

The redhead staggered and dropped the commuter cup. It hit the ground, and the lid popped off, splattering coffee.

His face registered more shock and confusion than pain.

Who expects to get gunned down on a suburban sidewalk on the way to work?

Jade fired again. A head shot.

The target crumpled straight down. Dead.

She took a moment to add the image of the spilled coffee and the man's expression to her mental file. It went along with the *splat* that Turbo's body had made when it landed on the ground.

Her precious memories.

The rifle had been overkill. She could have made the shots with an accurate pistol.

Jade buzzed up the window. She didn't have time to savor the moment any longer. There was too much to do.

She would drive for a while, escaping the area, before continuing to reach out to her contacts, preparing them for tomorrow.

It took only a few seconds to slide the weapon into the guitar case on the back seat, then she started the SUV, put it in gear, and turned left, away from the dead man down the block, his blood mingling with the spilled coffee.

77

THE OVERVIEW

Conference Room 3
Central Analysis Group Headquarters
Arlington, Virginia

"We have these four meeting at a café yesterday," Haley said, pointing at the large TV monitor on the wall. It showed freeze-frame captures from the Saffron Café's security camera the night before.

Nancy stood on the other side of the monitor for their presentation to Gregory, who sat at the conference table in the middle of the room. Dave used his laptop to work his own angles, half listening to their summary.

"The three men are on my original watch list to investigate," Nancy said. "They met in the back room of the café, but the three men met alone prior to the woman's arrival."

"Who is she?" Gregory asked.

"It took some digging, and the system needed a while to process the facial recognition software, but we believe her to be Jade Pang, an American from San Diego, California. Daughter of Chinese immigrants. Senior year, about to graduate from NYU. She lives in the West Village, not far from school, but in a rental apartment that is much cheaper than the homes owned by the men."

"Or rather, the men's families," Dave added, looking up from his laptop. "Purchased for the kids to use while attending the university—much more secure than dorms or rentals."

"Pang is the one that pushed Axe in front of the bus last night, then disappeared," Haley added.

Gregory's eyes widened, and Haley realized her mistake. "Oh, sorry. I should have led with that. Axe tailed one of the men to the café, suspected the woman was with the men, and followed her after the meeting. She turned the tables, got behind him, and pushed him in front of a bus. He's okay, but he didn't actually see her do it. No one else did either, which makes it difficult to break into her home or pick her up for questioning, anything like that."

Gregory frowned. "I agree. Unless Axe got into a direct conflict with her or can vouch that it was definitely Pang who attacked him, we have to wait. And I hope there's no next time, but always lead with the attempted murder of any teammates."

Haley nodded. "In my defense, that was hours ago, and we've—"

He waved her off.

"Axe's team has this information," Dave said, "including her address. They plan to watch her apartment today. They're briefing now."

Gregory nodded for them to resume.

"Next," Haley said, clicking the remote control's button to advance her presentation. "Let's look at the young men. All are from the wider Middle Eastern region."

The screen displayed a picture of a smiling, handsome man with a fine nose, closely cropped beard, and large diamond earrings. "Yazeed bin Mishari, taken from a social media post."

"Look at those rocks," Nancy muttered.

"Those are in the five-to-ten carat range," Dave said. "One hundred thousand dollars, easy."

When Nancy glanced his way, he shrugged. "I looked into earrings for your Christmas present. Smaller ones than those were way out of reach."

"Technically, he is Prince Yazeed bin Mishari Al Saud, a distant cousin of Saudi Arabia's new king. One of thousands of princes. The school agreed to drop the ruling family name for security."

"Next," Haley said, advancing the slideshow. "Darius Al-Nafisi, son of a wealthy Kuwaiti businessman." The picture showed an unsmiling man with a strong jawline, perfect hair styled in a short pompadour, and full lips.

"Except he's not," Nancy said. "This is how I first stumbled upon… whatever is going on here." She nodded at Haley, who clicked to advance to the next screen. "The black-and-white picture is of Mostafa Valiollahi, taken twenty-five years ago and published in a Tehran newspaper. Mr. Valiollahi is now a 'power behind the throne.' He has the ear of Iran's Supreme Leader."

Haley clicked again, and the picture of Darius appeared next to Valiollahi.

"They're definitely related," Gregory said.

"Yes," Nancy said. "Father and son, I believe. Which means the man at the coffee shop is actually Darius Valiollahi, son of one of the most powerful men behind the scenes in Iranian politics."

"Last but not least," Haley said. She changed the screen to show a man with longish dark hair, carefully styled. "Kareem Mahmoud, according to this passport photo. A great deal of digging shows that his full name is Kareem El-Sayed Mahmoud. He is the youngest son of an officer in Egypt's General Intelligence Directorate."

Haley and Nancy gave Gregory a few seconds to contemplate the information from the presentation.

"Last night," Gregory said to sum up, "the son of a man connected to Iran's Supreme Leader, a young Saudi prince, and the son of an Egyptian intelligence officer, met with an unknown American woman after they each took surveillance detection routes. After the meeting, the woman attempted to kill Alex Southmark by pushing him in front of a bus. Do I have that right?"

Nancy nodded.

"What do these young men have in common?" Gregory asked.

"They're rich and powerful," Haley said. "Well, their families are. All are from the Middle East. Aside from that, nothing jumps out. There is no obvious school connection to each other or to Jade Pang, aside from them all being seniors about to graduate."

"We hope Axe and the team in the field can get us more information," Nancy said.

Gregory stood. "Well done. I'd say there's definitely something there to be very concerned about. Keep at it. If there is something to be found, I know you'll uncover it. Let me know when you find something or need my input," he said, and left the room, leaving them to dig deeper while waiting for Axe to shake the tree.

In the meantime, Haley, Nancy and Dave would research each man's background, analyze every intersection in their lives on the university campus, and uncover their common ground.

Haley would make a game of it, seeing if she could figure out the puzzle before Axe learned enough in the field to fill in the missing pieces.

78

THE BRIEFING

Carlito's Auto Body and Towing
Safe House EN-23
Queens, New York

Axe stood before the assembled team in the break room of the safe house. They were all geared up and ready to go, with pistols, knives, and thin ballistic vests under casual civilian clothes. And to their credit, no one grumbled at the early hour. Part of that could have been from the excellent coffee and bagels brought by Tex from Manhattan.

"Everyone awake?"

"Good to go," Mad Dog and Johnboy said together, though the response lacked the normal vigor Axe would have gotten later in the morning. They were still more used to late nights than early mornings.

Tex, as usual, could barely contain her excitement. She looked alert and eager for a day in the field.

"Haley is in the office, where she'll remain," Axe said. "It's just us today."

Axe paused. "I..." His teammates deserved the full story, but admitting the truth was harder than he thought it would be. "Maybe I shouldn't be on this mission," he got out. "The trauma from the operation in Oman, the recovery..."

Mad Dog blew on his tall cup of coffee, eyes locked on him, not looking surprised.

Johnboy was hard to read, as always. He sipped his coffee and gave Axe a brief nod of encouragement.

Tex looked stricken, like she was about to argue with him.

"I'm fine, but I'm far from my normal fighting shape," Axe said, pressing on. "I wanted to be back, but I'm not. Don't get me wrong. I'm not giving up. But this is the right call—for now."

None of this was a surprise to the team. Axe had suspected it, but the looks on their faces confirmed his hunch; they'd known all along he wasn't in top form.

"We've got your back," Mad Dog said, straight-faced, for once not joking around to lighten the mood.

"You lead. We'll follow," Johnboy said. "You can hold back, be the brains of the operation."

"Well..." Mad Dog said, an exaggerated expression of doubt on his face before he broke into a smile. "No, no, of course. You're the brains."

"All right, cool it," Tex said to Mad Dog.

Axe related the high points of the night before. Staking out the apartment of Darius Al-Nafisi. The kid's thorough surveillance detection route. Losing him and switching to Yaz, who led him to the café in the East Village. Then, on a hunch, following the long-haired woman with dimples, who had turned the tables and pushed him in front of a bus.

"These people have been well trained and follow good tradecraft protocols. Regular people don't do that when they're getting together to debate politics or chat about their hopes and dreams of the future. Nancy in the CAG office was right; they are up to something. There's no other explanation for the tradecraft, or the dark-haired woman trying to kill me."

Axe held up his phone. "Haley sent pictures to your phones, straight from the security camera above the counter of the café," Axe said, finishing up. He selected the first picture from Haley. "Here's the woman. Short, thin, dimples, long, fine black hair."

"Can we call her Raven?" Mad Dog asked. "I dated a girl with black hair, and her nickname was Raven."

"Her name is Jade Pang—we'll call her Jade. But if we think she might overhear us, Raven is fine."

"Next, the Iranian with the fancy hair," Axe said. "Darius. He's here undercover, but he's the son of a powerful Iranian with ties to the government. Read the dossiers on the way today, or while we're on the stakeouts." Each of the team members flicked their screens to reveal the picture along with a summary of what they knew about the young man.

"Continuing in the order they entered the café—aside from Jade, who was the last to arrive—Prince Yazeed bin Mishari Al Saud. Also undercover as Yazeed bin Mishari, Yaz for short. A minor young prince in Saudi Arabia's ruling family. A playboy, from what Nancy pieced together. Enjoys the company of a large number of young ladies."

"Who doesn't?" Mad Dog mumbled. Tex elbowed him, getting a grunt of surprise and pain in response.

"Last, Kareem El-Sayed Mahmoud, known as Kareem Mahmoud. Son of a high-ranking officer in Egypt's intelligence service."

"Hmmm," Johnboy muttered.

"Yeah, I see it," Tex said.

"What?" Axe and Mad Dog said at nearly the same time.

Tex glanced at JB, who nodded encouragingly. "You don't see it? He's a killer. Look past the long hair."

Axe examined the picture, opening his senses. He was rewarded with a shiver down his spine.

"Oh, yeah," Mad Dog said a second before Axe could speak.

"I see it now," Axe said. "Good catch, Tex and JB. Look at his eyes. Is he the brains of the operation? What do you think?"

"The woman—Jade—is the brains," Tex said, almost too quiet to hear.

They all looked at her and waited. When she didn't elaborate, Mad Dog elbowed her—but not as hard as she'd done to him. "Spill. How do you figure?"

"She arrived last. The men waited on her. That's her doing." Tex held up her phone to show the woman. "And look at her. She's older than the boys by at least four years."

"What?" Mad Dog asked, using his thumb and finger to zoom in on his phone.

"She's playing at being younger. You can't see it?" Tex asked. When they all shook their heads, she continued. "Call it woman's intuition, but she's older than she's pretending to be, smarter, and…"

"And what?" Axe asked.

"Deadlier."

The word hung in the air for a long moment.

Finally, Axe spoke. "Jade would recognize me if she saw me again. By this point, she has probably told the others what I look like, so it's you three on the street. I'll be in the surveillance van near Jade's apartment, but not too close. If I can find a place, I'll park between her place and Yaz's. You'll post up on the men and hope they lead you to their conspirators, or give us a clue to what they're doing. It's a long shot—especially since they seem to be very security conscious, except for maybe Yaz—but it's what we have to work off for now. Wear civilian clothes and take a hat or jacket to switch up your look. Rules of engagement: you better be close to death before you shoot anyone, especially if there are innocent bystanders around."

Mad Dog nudged Tex. "Hear that? Don't shoot people today."

When she glared at him, Mad Dog held up his hands and tried to look innocent. "What? Too soon?"

"Okay," Axe said, putting an end to the banter. "Let's get out there, shake the tree, and make something happen."

79

THE CALL

Conference Room 3
Central Analysis Group Headquarters
Arlington, Virginia

Haley focused on her screens, swimming in the stream of data. Her intuition guided her while the analytical side of her mind sorted information.

A loud, obnoxious buzz from her desk broke through the noise-cancelling headphones, disrupted the flow, and killed her focus.

As always, she had the phone silenced. No calls should come through. Only essential messages and calls from the secure comms app would buzz.

Instead of Axe's ID number, or any of the team's contacts, a long string of letters and numbers from a user she didn't recognize popped up on the screen.

While it was possible for strangers to message or call each other on the app, it wasn't likely. There was no database of users, and her contact information was set to private, anyway.

No one she didn't know should be calling her.

Haley held up a hand to Nancy and Dave working nearby and answered the call—but said nothing.

"Hello? Alex's partner?" an older woman asked with a heavy Russian accent. "I think you are there, yes? But smart. You say nothing. Very well. You recognize the voice, though? You remember me, yes?"

Haley stayed quiet, for security and from surprise. She'd heard the voice once before, two months earlier, when the woman had called from Axe's phone to announce that Axe was badly injured and needed emergency medical care halfway around the world.

"How am I contacting you, you are wondering?" the woman asked, sounding amused. "I memorize the contact information after I call you last time, when Alex was hurt. Long, lots of numbers and letters. No problem for me. And now we talk. We are once again allies. Do not worry. I am Ekaterina. Ekat or Kat for short. What do I call you?"

"Blondie," Haley spoke finally, going with her instincts.

Two months earlier, Ekaterina—the Russian assassin Axe had paired up with in order to complete his previous mission—had transported a badly injured Axe to a meetup with a CIA medical team and handed him over.

There was more to the story, like how months earlier Axe had ordered Ekaterina's abduction and held her at gunpoint, but all of that was water under the bridge. Hopefully. An enemy, then an ally, and now—if she could be trusted—allies again.

"You saved Alex's life," Haley said. "Thank you." Her appreciation was heartfelt. Without the woman's help, Axe would have died in a cave in Oman.

Nancy and Dave stared, hanging on every word she said.

"Ah," Ekaterina said, her voice coming through crystal clear in the headphones. There was a faint whine in the background...

A jet engine. She was at an airport.

"Good," Ekaterina said. "He lives. Very bad shape when I left him. But he is strong like bull. And see, we work well together. Now, Blondie, we must do again. For to save the world."

"To save the world?"

There was a pause on the other end of the line, two seconds of silence before Ekaterina spoke again.

Yes, that's a jet engine. She was definitely near a private plane.

"Alex and I, we promised only the truth between us," Ekaterina said, her voice now serious. "I will continue. You as well. Agreed?"

"Yes, I agree," Haley answered immediately.

Why not? I can always refuse to answer.

"So maybe not save the world this time. Maybe only capture the man in charge of the hackers from Dubai. The one who managed them, who made them attack your country. You know the name?"

Haley pushed down her surprise and focused on the background. There were no people speaking near Ekaterina, no announcements or calls to board an aircraft. The woman wasn't at a commercial airport. An executive airport then.

Haley tried a tactic. "Yes, I believe I know the name," she said, but stopped short of giving up the intelligence. It had only been a few days, but the hunt for Boris Zorinov had taken a backseat to the potentially more immediate threat to the country from whatever was happening in New York City.

"You don't want to say. Is okay. I say first name initial. You say last name initial. We are both protected. Agreed?"

"Agreed."

"First name begins with B, yes?" Ekaterina asked, the lightness back in her voice.

She's having fun with this.

"Yes," Haley said, feeling silly about playing games. "We believe his last name begins with Z?" It came out more of a question than Haley intended, but that was okay. She was about to have confirmation that their deep dive had paid off—or find out she was on the wrong track.

"Correct. Very well. You are good partner for Alex. Now, you, Alex, and I work together. Find this man. Ask him many questions, yes? Who he worked for. Why he did it. Everything."

Haley thought fast. Would Gregory go for this?

Should she even ask him?

"We could do that, I think," she said, glancing around the conference room. Gregory was like Admiral Nalen—you never knew when he was going to turn up. Thankfully, he hadn't returned from his office. And Nancy and Dave could keep their mouths shut.

"I may have to ask for permission, though," Haley said. "And afterward? What then?"

"Then we see." Her voice hardened, leaving no room for discussion or negotiation.

"Your country and my country—"

Ekaterina interrupted her. "Not my country and your country. Only you, Alex, and me. We do what our countries say, yes, but in end so much is up to us. We do the right thing. Always."

"I'm not sure we can agree to that," Haley said. Sure, she broke rules all the time, but she agreed with Gregory. This was potentially too big for her or Axe to do whatever they felt like—or that Ekaterina wanted.

"Alex and I will work it all out together. Uni… Unum…" Ekaterina trailed off. "What is decision made together? Both must agree."

"Unanimous."

"Yes. Unanimous. We decide together. I trust judgement of Alex. First, though, we find Boris," Ekaterina said, the smile once again in her voice.

She's toying with me, Haley thought. *Throwing me a bone.*

Haley wished she was in the field. Ekaterina was an interesting woman; it would be fun to meet her.

"What do you need? How can Axe and I help with Mr. Zorinov?" Haley responded, returning the favor, playing the game.

A low, throaty chuckle of approval came from the older woman. "He was in Palma, Majorca, Spain yesterday. Now, I think he is gone. I do not know where. I do not have resources to find and track him. My government…" She made a *tsk* sound of disapproval. "No matter. Boris will avoid Europe. Asia is too humid, and too poor. Dubai—if they knew what he has done, everyone in area would hate him. So. Maybe Miami, to buy new yacht. Or Los Angeles, for the beach and movie stars. But no, I believe it will be New York. New name. A fake passport. Cosmetic surgery. Blend in with upper class. Buy nice condo near Central Park. Go to restaurants every night, eat good food. Date supermodels. The opera, or theater on Broadway. So. I will come to New York."

"You're going to New York? Now?"

"*Da.* You can find Boris, Blondie. New York, or Miami or Los Angeles. You are smart one. Not Alex. You are brains, yes?"

Haley couldn't help but laugh. She liked Ekaterina. "Alex is smart enough, but yes, I am the brains. If Zorinov can be tracked, my team and I might be able to find him."

"*Harasho.* You call when you find his destination. I meet Alex there. Goodbye, Blondie."

The call ended. Haley saved the contact on her phone under "E," while she summarized what Ekaterina had said for Dave and Nancy.

"We already have an alert out for Boris Zorinov at the airports in the country—big and small," Dave said. "But there are no photos of him, and from all reports he's an average-looking guy, so having only his description out there makes it difficult. Is there anything else we can do?"

Haley and Nancy shook their heads. "We have to hope we get lucky there—or catch a break some other way," Nancy said.

Haley grabbed her phone and called Axe.

"What do you have for me?" Axe said, trying but failing to hide the hope and excitement in his voice.

"You're on speaker with Nancy and Dave. Guess who I just spoke with." She kept her tone neutral, giving nothing away.

It took Axe two seconds to guess. "Ekaterina? Seriously?" He thought it through. "Ah. In Oman, I unlocked my phone so she could call you before I passed out. She memorized your contact information?"

"Nailed it on the first guess."

"And?"

"She needs help locating Boris Zorinov," Haley said. "He's in the wind. I got the impression she had a line on him, but it didn't work out. The Russians might have come close and sent him running. She thinks he'll end up in New York, Miami, or Los Angeles…" She trailed off.

"And?"

"I said yes, of course. She saved your life."

"Just help locating him?"

"No. She's on her way to New York—and she thinks he is, too. With all that's going on, we have this now." She paused and dropped the hammer. "Looks like you've got a new partner."

She was joking—mostly.

"No," Axe said, his voice firm. "We have a new partner."

80

THE COFFEE

North of Washington Square Park
Greenwich Village

Axe watched the busy morning neighborhood streets on the monitors, fed from the security cameras hidden on the roof of the surveillance van.

People hustled along the sidewalks, heading for school or work. He hadn't been able to snag a parking spot near Jade Pang's apartment. But he found one centrally located near the homes of all three of the other targets.

For now, Jade's apartment was unwatched. She was the best of the four targets at counter-surveillance and might notice them, but Axe had a plan.

"Sitrep," he said into the comms group chat.

Mad Dog slurped coffee over the open mic, followed by a sigh of pleasure. "Good to go. Beats crawling through the desert." He chuckled for a second before speaking again. "I'm up the street from Yaz and have a clear view of the front door. No movement." He was in a bustling deli near Yaz's brownstone.

"Copy. Tex?"

She was at the coffee shop on the corner just north of Darius's condo where Axe had sat the previous afternoon. "You weren't kidding about the coffee here," Tex muttered. "It's delicious."

Axe couldn't slip out of the back of the van for coffee, nor risk one of them bringing him some to his clandestine stakeout. It sucked—and his team was rubbing it in.

"No movement here, either," Tex added.

"Copy. Johnboy?"

"No movement," JB said, quiet and focused as usual. "I'm a hundred feet into the park on a bench. The view of the target's door is partly obscured by thin trees, but I'll see if anyone enters or exits."

"Copy. Sit tight, enjoy the morning, report as needed."

They had a full day of surveillance ahead, and Boris Zorinov might be on his way to New York City, along with Ekaterina right behind him.

It was turning into an eventful operation.

Yet Axe sat on his rear in a van, calling the shots instead of kicking down doors and shaking the tree.

And he didn't have coffee.

They needed more people to watch the backs of the homes, in case there were other exits, but what Axe really wanted was one extra person to watch Jade's apartment. Someone who didn't give off warrior or cop vibes, like his team today.

If he had to be stuck in the rear with the gear, he was going to do it his way. The Navy SEAL way. All in, all the time.

Axe reached for his phone. He was about to make one man's day, and ruin another's.

81

THE HELP

Northeast of Washington Square Park
Greenwich Village

Axe muted the link to the team and prepared himself for the first call. This had to be handled just right.

"What's wrong?" Gregory Addison said as a greeting.

"Nothing. All's well here," Axe said. "I wanted to check in directly."

"I met with the team earlier," Gregory said, not trying to hide the tiredness in his voice. "This seems like more than a minor problem with sons of powerful Middle Eastern families."

"Yes, it might be. Or maybe Jade thought I was a creepy stalker and tried to make the world a better place, but I doubt it. Right now, I'm in a van in Greenwich Village coordinating stakeouts on the primary targets. I wanted to let you know that I appreciate you putting me on the mission to help me get back in shape. But I'm stepping away from field ops temporarily. With Admiral Nalen busy helping Senator Woodran, well, I guess I'm assuming his role. Oversight. Coordination. All that."

"Great. Welcome to management."

"Thank you. As my first order of business, I need more people. Can you spare Marcus? He can handle himself in the field—we found that out the hard way. Or Nancy? Dave? I need people who can blend in. Sit in a coffee shop. Take walks through the park. Nothing dangerous. Barely field work at all."

"At least you didn't ask for Haley."

"She's my first choice, but let's leave her out of this. Better for all involved if she stays in the office."

"Thank you, I agree. But to a lesser extent, we have the same problem with Marcus, Nancy, and Dave. They're too valuable at their desks—and they know too much. Fieldwork is unpredictable and dangerous. I can't have them running around New York City. I'm sorry."

A long silence followed before Gregory jumped back in. "And don't even think of asking me to do it."

Axe grunted while he thought through his options. He had played Gregory perfectly, but couldn't tell if the older, more experienced man realized it yet. "What about FBI assets? Homeland Security? Though until we know how serious it is, I'd rather keep it off the radar."

"I can ask for whatever you need, but…"

"Paperwork. Explanations. Meetings. Accountability."

"Exactly. You may luck into the right sort of person, but most of them wouldn't be happy with a run-and-gun, Navy SEAL-style operation with you in charge."

"I need one person immediately. The rest I can work around for now."

There was a pause.

He's catching on.

"You have someone in mind. I can tell."

Axe fought back a grin, concerned it would come through when he spoke. "You're not going to like it."

Gregory's pause lasted a second. "No."

Got him.

"I need help right now, this morning, and he's the only real choice."

Gregory sighed. "Dawson 'Void' Reite is under house arrest. I made a deal. I promised he'd stay put and out of trouble."

"He's going stir-crazy. And he helped us immensely last time. All I need is for him to sit at a café with his laptop and keep an eye on people. It's easy. Safe."

Gregory sighed. "Promise me he won't get caught."

"I can't promise that. But if he does, we'll work it out."

"What if I say no?"

"That would put us in a difficult situation, because I'm not really asking permission. It's more a courtesy call to inform you of my decision." Axe choked back a chuckle. "He's prepping now and will be on his way shortly."

"You know, I think you're going to do just fine as the new Admiral Nalen," Gregory said, and hung up on him.

82

THE BINOCULARS

Off Washington Square Park
Greenwich Village

Kareem stood back from his condo windows, high-powered binoculars to his eyes. From here, he could survey a large stretch of the park across the street. He had started the habit the first week at school, when he wondered if his father had security people keeping tabs on him.

Anyone conducting surveillance would naturally choose to stroll the sidewalks around and through the park, or sit on a bench, reading, scrolling their phone, or pretending to wait for a friend.

A bald, muscular Black man had been sitting on the third bench inside the park for an hour. He looked relaxed, with one arm along the back of the bench, sitting in profile to Kareem's apartment. He held a phone in his other hand and used his thumb on the screen to scroll every few seconds. Kareem's binoculars weren't powerful enough to read the screen, and the angle was wrong, but it appeared the man was engrossed in what he was reading.

It could be a coincidence, but Kareem wondered. The man's physique screamed tactical operator—Kareem had met enough of his country's dangerous soldiers to know the type.

Then again, the man seemed so serene. He truly seemed to enjoy the morning. He hadn't once looked toward the front door of Kareem's condo building.

The man chuckled, tapped the screen, and stretched. He stood, slipped the phone into the back pocket of his black pants, and strolled toward the center of the park, away from Kareem.

A false alarm?

Kareem's instincts told him otherwise. He didn't know what had happened, but a change was in the air.

Could Jade or Darius have a man at their disposal?

Jade must still have at least some of the money they had raised for the multi-year operation. She could have found a man to watch his apartment.

Or to eliminate me.

It felt right. He and Yaz had been pushed by their financial backers, then brought the pressure to bear on Jade and Darius last night, giving them an ultimatum and a deadline.

This morning, a large, capable-looking man spent an hour hanging out in the park near Kareem's front door.

New Yorkers didn't do that. They were too busy making money to afford the astronomical prices of the city.

Tourists didn't sit in the small park drinking coffee focused on their phones, either. There was too much to see and do.

The most likely assumption was that the man was watching for him.

If I'm wrong, I'm wrong. But it never hurts to be extra careful.

The question was whether he was the only one being watched.

Kareem wouldn't wait any longer.

First, he switched phones. His primary phone could no longer be trusted.

He had a burner phone in his bedroom, powered off but charged and ready to go.

After plugging in his primary phone, he logged into the secure comms app on the spare phone to send a message to his patrons, who were expecting to meet him for a report about last night's meeting. If they didn't make a great deal of money before returning home, they would have a lot of explaining to do. Each had depleted his considerable financial reserves and had "borrowed" from family accounts. Should they not have the means to replace those millions, the entire plot might come to light.

That couldn't happen.

Change of plans, Kareem typed into his phone. ***Meet tonight instead. Will explain later. Details to follow.***

He left the binoculars on the table and went to the kitchen. The far drawer on the right held his cutlery. He pulled the drawer and clicked the tabs on the sides to slide it fully from the cabinet. He took the small pistol in a holster affixed to the rear of the drawer, held in place by a hook-and-loop fastener, along with a screw-on suppressor. Both gifts from his father's chief of security, installed the day before he arrived in the city three-and-a-half years earlier.

Kareem slipped the holster inside his pants, adding an extra magazine to one pocket and the suppressor to another.

He replaced the drawer and repeated the process with the one next to it, claiming the robust folding knife held in place. It had a black, textured handle and a black blade with a pristine silver edge.

He sharpened the knife after every throat he slit.

The knife clipped to the back of his pants.

In the living room, he removed an old textbook from a shelf. Inside, he had glued the pages together and hollowed out a space large enough for the spare, authentic Egyptian passport provided for him in the event of an emergency. It had his picture, plenty of entry and exit stamps from western countries, and a different name.

Five thousand dollars in hundreds were folded behind the passport.

He took it all.

Near the front door, he grabbed a rarely used cross-body bag from the pegs next to his jacket. The bag had an added, hand-made feature—another gift from his father—built-in Faraday protection. It would completely block the signal of any phone placed inside, rendering him invisible to electronic tracking.

The passport, money, and his phone went into the bag.

He looked around, taking in his home for the past three and a half years.

If people were looking for him, this might be the last time he saw the apartment.

His time here had been fun, but he was ready to go.

He left behind his favorite brown leather jacket, taking a black one instead. He might have to spend the night walking the city, or on the run.

Kareem slipped out the window that opened onto a rickety black iron fire escape at the back of the building and hurried down the stairs, jumping the last six feet to the narrow alley.

He would conduct a surveillance detection route to discover if anyone watched the back of the building as well as the front, lose them, and be on his way.

His home was only a few blocks from Yaz's, and if he hurried, he could get there before Yaz left for his breakfast meeting—and see if he was also under surveillance.

83

THE COOKIES

North of Washington Square Park
Greenwich Village
New York City, New York

Axe kept a watchful eye on the monitors, but there was nothing operational to see. Sitting in the van wasn't his idea of a good time, but it could have been worse. He could still be back at his cabin recovering or stuck in an office at a desk.

"Contact," Mad Dog said. It sounded like he had a mouth full of food. "Sorry," he said a second later, much clearer. "Breakfast. I have Yaz in sight. He's on foot. Moving to follow."

A tense ten minutes later, Yaz had turned right and entered a bagel and coffee shop.

"It's busy in there," Mad Dog reported, "and he walks like a man desperate for coffee. Permission to follow him inside?"

"Negative," Axe said, checking a laptop with the area street map zoomed in. As usual, Mad Dog wanted to push the mission. "Post up outside—there should be a bus stop near there."

"Copy," Mad Dog said. "Moving to the—" He stopped in mid-sentence. "At the entrance, Yaz shook hands with another guy. It's a meet. Vectoring inside to keep an eye on them and eavesdrop."

Axe frowned but said nothing. He couldn't fault the man's logic. Anything Mad Dog could pick up would be invaluable.

As long as he wasn't noticed.

And Mad Dog, with his burly chest, short stature, and bushy beard, was hard not to notice.

"Try to blend in," Axe muttered.

Two scratches came as Mad Dog touched his earbud in acknowledgement. In the background, the hubbub of coffee shop sounds carried over the comms.

A few minutes later, he was back. "The guy isn't any of the other targets." The background sounds were subdued, as if Mad Dog had moved to a table in the back, which is exactly what Axe would have done. "I'm profiling here, but my guess is the new guy is also Middle Eastern. Early 20s, tall, thin with a few muscles, short black hair, four-day growth of beard, dark eyes, expensive sweater. Has a rich guy air about him. They're having an intense conversation, but I can't make any of it out. They're too far away. Something's definitely going on between them, though. It's not two buddies meeting for morning coffee."

Finally, Axe thought. *We might have a lead.*

"Tex," he called. "Drop coverage of Darius. Make your best time to Mad Dog's location without being conspicuous. Go."

"Copy," Mariana said, as eager as ever. "On my way."

Day and Night Cookies
New York City, New York

Kareem stood near the counter of the twenty-four-hour cookie shop loved by the area college students, pretending to consider his snack options while watching the coffee shop across the street.

The only person who had seemed out of place was the short, barrel-chested man with a bushy beard. He had entered the coffee shop a minute after Yaz and one of his financial patrons.

Everyone else coming and going looked like students, professors, or other locals. Most tourists weren't out this early, but that's what the short man seemed like: a tourist who could handle himself. He had moved with a lightness and grace that didn't belong with a man who looked like he could deadlift a car and tip it on its side.

"I'll take a dozen cookies. Mix and match, whatever is most popular," Kareem told the bored college student waiting for him to make up his mind.

It would take a minute for the young man to prep the order, and then Kareem would stand by the front window, munch on a cookie, watch, and wait.

He couldn't be certain, not yet, but it seemed like Yaz was being followed.

84

THE DIAMONDS

Empire Bagels and Coffee Brewery
Greenwich Village

Yaz sipped the hot coffee, willing himself to wake up fully. He'd been out late at a jazz club hoping to spend the rest of the evening with a woman who would be number 493. At the end of the night, she said she had a big test later today. She had kissed his cheek, trailed her fingers over one of his enormous diamond earrings, and sent him home alone.

He'd awoken this morning to the incessant ringing of his phone. Rami, his primary financial backer for the failed mission to reset the balance of power in the Middle East, had called to remind him about their meeting. He and the other patrons wanted a report about how they were going to get their money back.

At least he was willing to meet at Yaz's local breakfast place, not far from his brownstone, where the coffee was hot and strong.

Yaz fumed silently into his cup as he took another sip. Rami wasn't in the royal family, like he was, but Rami's father was well connected and wealthy; not royals wealthy, but close. He had to be treated with more respect than Yaz wanted to.

Rami was the man Yaz had turned to when looking for money for Jade's audacious plan.

"I need my money, Yaz," Rami said after a sip of his coffee. They sat at a table along the wall toward the back with no one at the table next to them. "I accept that the operation failed. I'll have to work my way up instead of taking the shortcut you promised. But I need something to show for the investment."

They'd been over this several times before. Yaz was tired of it, but there was little he could do. Rami could ruin him. If the truth of what Yaz had attempted came out...

"The meeting last night went well," Yaz explained over the top of his cup, glancing around. The breakfast place was crowded, but in typical New York fashion, everyone was wrapped up in their own lives. With the noise of the workers making coffee, toasting bagels, calling out orders, and a large group of students discussing summer plans at a table nearby, no one could overhear them.

A cute woman who worked at the shop straightened chairs and cleaned off tables nearby. She glanced at him but looked away when he smiled at her. He'd traded the occasional greeting with her all semester. Perhaps she could be number 493.

Yaz turned back to Rami. "You'll have your money back by Friday," he whispered. They both leaned in closer. "I'll send you detailed instructions on what to do, but basically, we know when the stock market is going to completely crash. You can position yourself and the other backers to make a killing. You'll get more than what you invested in the..." He trailed off. He was quickly waking up as the caffeine hit his system. Even in the busy shop, it was best not to mention the operation to eliminate everyone at high levels of power in Middle Eastern countries.

"Another scheme?" Rami asked, his voice filled with skepticism. He leaned back and crossed his arms.

"Guaranteed," Yaz said. "I'm putting every cent of my own into it. It's like knowing the future. The market will drop fifty, sixty, maybe seventy percent. For one day. Two at the most before it rebounds. Position your investments correctly and you'll have more money than your father."

Rami drank his coffee as he considered the words.

Yaz took a sip of his own drink. He had Rami hooked; he could see the greed in his eyes.

"Perhaps," Rami said finally. "I'll look at the instructions. What to bet against, how to do it. But until then, I need collateral."

"Collateral? I'm providing you with the opportunity—"

"Your earrings. As a deposit." Rami's voice was cold and firm, his face serious.

"My earrings?" Yaz reached up and touched one. Women couldn't take their eyes off them. They always wanted to know if they were cubic zirconia. When he explained that they were real… The earrings had done more to get women into his bed than his very good looks or considerable charm. Yaz didn't consider them lucky, but they had helped him land 492 women. How could he part with them, even for a few days?

Rami held out his hand.

"But…" Yaz couldn't come up with a good excuse to keep them.

"It's not that I think your plan won't work," Rami said as he leaned close again. "But the previous operation failed spectacularly. Not one important leader died at the resort in Oman. You may have a new plan, and it may work the way you say, but having your earrings will prove your commitment. Think of it as extra motivation to care for every detail."

"They're not worth enough to—"

"It's not their cost," Rami said, interrupting. "You think I can't go to the diamond district this morning and buy ones as large? No, it's their value. To you, not me. I know how much you cherish them and why. How's your number, Yaz?" Rami taunted. He kept his hand out, and his eyes narrowed. "You think I won't go to my father? It would be extremely difficult to admit what I financed, but I will if I must. I have to do it before he comes to me asking about the millions missing from the family accounts."

Yaz fancied himself a lover, not a fighter, but a rare rage blossomed in him. He kept it off his face, but the man's tone was intolerable. How dare Rami talk to him his way? He was Prince Yazeed bin Mishari Al Saud.

Rami was a peon.

Still, one word to Rami's father and Yaz's world would be changed forever. He would likely survive—the new Saudi king would rather torment people than kill them. But as punishment, the king would banish him to a backwater city, give him a meager allowance, and forbid his family and friends to help or visit.

He would be branded a traitor.

There would be no trips to Europe or America.

No women.

He would suffer for years. Decades.

He couldn't face that.

Yaz reluctantly removed the earrings and handed them over.

Rami smiled, hefted the diamonds, and slipped them into a pocket.

"Send the investment instructions and keep me updated. When the plan works, I will return the earrings. Until then, good luck."

Yaz sipped his coffee as Rami left with his diamonds.

The cute worker wiped an empty table nearby that looked perfectly clean.

Yaz smiled at her. He didn't need the stupid earrings. He'd get to 493 —and beyond—on his own.

The woman had short blond hair, a pale face, freckles, and wore bright red lipstick. She looked his way and blushed.

It was the end of the semester. Time for fun. Perhaps she was ready for a spring fling.

This one had possibilities.

85

THE PREDICTION

Empire Bagels and Coffee Brewery
Greenwich Village

"Good morning," Yaz said to the worker, holding back some of his charm. Playing it cool. She required a delicate touch. People likely hit on her all day, every day.

"Hey," she said, then focused on wiping down each of the chairs at the nearby table. A second later, though, she glanced back. "Were those real— the diamond earrings?"

The damn earrings. At least they had served their purpose with potential Miss 493.

"Yes," Yaz said with a pout, unable to hide his unhappiness at losing them, but using the feeling to his advantage.

"Why did you give them to your friend, if you don't mind me asking?" She blushed again, which he found intoxicating. She was beautiful. They all were, each in their own way.

"I lost a bet," Yaz said. It was the best he could come up with, and close to the truth. He had gambled, trusting Jade and Darius, and it hadn't gone his way.

She nodded and finished with the table and chairs. He had to keep the conversation going. "I predicted the stock market was going to crash by yesterday, but it didn't. It will by Friday, though, guaranteed."

If he'd gotten more sleep, he might have been able to think of a lie instead of divulging their plan, but he used what he had. There was no harm in it.

He was so close to 500, and the clock was ticking.

Unfortunately, she wasn't charmed. "By Friday, huh? How can you be so sure? The economy is about the same as it always is. My dad's in finance—I know these things."

She glanced around the room. Several tables had crumbs and spilled coffee.

He was about to lose her.

"I'll bet you," he said. "If I'm right, I take you out for a romantic evening. Dinner, dancing…" He trailed off, leaving the rest unsaid.

Her face said no, but she was still there talking to him.

"Didn't you just lose your earrings to your friend because you were wrong once already?"

Mocking him? She was so adorable!

"Yes, but this time it's a lock." He gave her his best look. "Are you too afraid to make the bet because of what might happen when I win?"

"How about this—if you're wrong, you donate $10,000 to a charity of my choice. No whining or backing out. Those are my terms."

"I also take you out to dinner. Win or lose."

"Fine, whatever."

He had her. She had needed an excuse to go out with him. Some women were like that.

"I accept the bet." They shook, her smaller hand cool and strong in his grip. "I'll make a reservation for Friday night. What's your favorite restaurant?"

She grinned like he'd fallen into her trap. "I'm a vegan. There are a few high-end vegan restaurants that have tasting menus I'd love to try. Pick one nearby that sounds good."

Yaz didn't let his smile falter, but the idea of suffering through a meal without meat made him think twice about this woman. Still, she was feisty, and he was so close to his number. He could trade one disgusting meal for a night with her. Miss 493. Or by Friday—Miss 494 or 495.

He handed her his phone, she entered her number, and he immediately texted her to ensure she wasn't leading him on. When a buzz came from her pocket, he smiled. "Yaz," he said.

"Tabitha." She pointed at the plastic name tag.

"See you Friday night, Tabitha. I'll be in touch. Tell your father to sell his stocks now and bet against the market," he added with a wink.

He couldn't resist.

86

THE SWEATER

Northeast of Washington Square Park
Greenwich Village

Axe shifted in the seat and convinced himself the van wasn't so bad.

He breathed in, held it, let it out, and held again. Counting his breaths. Centering himself. Staying patient.

"I have the man that met with Yaz," Tex said over their group comms. "He turned onto your street and is moving toward you, Papa," she said, using Axe's alternate call sign. "He's tall, with short black hair. Thin, not muscular. Wearing a maroon sweater—cashmere is my guess. You should have him in sight shortly."

Axe used a joystick to zoom in with one of the van's cameras. "Got him."

He pressed a button on the keyboard to capture a picture of Yaz's breakfast contact.

With a few clicks, he sent it to Haley at the Central Analysis Group headquarters.

Not bad tech work for a warrior.

"Fall back a bit while I have him in sight," Axe told Mariana. The sidewalks in Greenwich Village weren't as busy as in other parts of the city, and while there were plenty of people out this morning, they didn't need Tex noticed.

"Yaz is on the move," Mad Dog called in. "Stick with him or break off?"

"Can you follow without it being obvious?"

"Yeah, no problem. It's busy, people are coming and going. I'll leave ahead of him. And I have a lead—hold on."

Axe used the joystick to track the breakfast contact as he strolled past the van, walking like he had places to be.

"Okay, Tex. Back at it. Close in some. He's passing me now."

"Copy." One of Axe's other screens showed Mariana emerge from a shop she'd ducked into. She now wore a straw sunhat. It wasn't much of a disguise, but it was better than nothing.

A minute later, she disappeared around the next corner after the unknown man. "Turning north," Tex called.

After a few minutes of silence, Mad Dog reported. "Yaz is going back to bed, I bet. He just entered the door to his building. I'm hanging out at the bus stop nearby. Let me know when you can handle a report."

The laptop pinged quietly with an alert—a reply from Haley.

Breakfast meeting subject: Rami bin Raslan.

Age 22.

Student, NYU. Senior year.

Student visa expires June 15.

From: Riyadh, Saudi Arabia

Son of Fawaz bin Raslan, business tycoon, who has strong connections with lower-end members of the royal family.

An official immigration photo was attached.

"Our new target is Rami bin Raslan—we'll call him Rami. Tex, stay on him."

"Rami is going to another coffee shop," Mariana said. "Looks like Mad Dog isn't the only one drinking too much coffee this morning." She gave Axe the name, which he found on his map. It was just around the corner.

"Copy. Find a way to be inconspicuous and remain on station. Mad Dog, let's hear what you have."

"Okay, first, excellent coffee at the place Yaz went. We need a team-building exercise there when this thing is over. The bagels smelled amazing. Next, here's what happened at his meeting. Yaz is sleepy, right? Not all there, but he wakes up pretty quick when he and this Rami have a heart-to-heart. Very heavy conversation. A lot of glancing around to make sure no one could overhear, so I had to keep my distance."

Axe almost told Mad Dog to slow down, but the caffeine was obviously doing its job, so he didn't interrupt.

"Anyway, they lean forward, whisper, lean back to glare at each other, lean forward. This goes on a while, then Rami holds out his hand. They argue, but eventually Yaz takes off those honking big earrings and hands them over, real reluctant-like. Rami pockets them, smiles, says something snarky, and leaves."

Finally, Mad Dog took a breath, but before Axe could ask a question, he jumped back in. "So that's it, right? But no. This young woman who works there, she's making her way over toward the boys while they talk, little by little, right? And when Rami leaves, she has words with Yaz. Flirty, but hesitant. Not wanting to be too obvious about it is my guess. They talk, they shake hands, she puts her phone number into his phone, he sends her a text to confirm, and then he leaves with a definite jaunt in his step. He's a player, and he pulled her number by losing his fancy earrings. Incredible."

Axe's first reaction, given all that had happened already this week, was to question the encounter. "Mad Dog, focus on the woman. Is it possible she's one of us? An operator? A spy? Could she be setting him up? Or is it the end of the school year and time to live without regrets for both of them?"

"Hard to see her as one of us, at least from her looks. Shortish blond hair, bright red lipstick, cute in a Midwestern 'Look Ma, I'm living my best life in the big city' sort of way. But the team at HQ can check her out easy enough. She's Tabitha, according to her nametag."

"Well done. Anything from you, JB?"

"Nothing to report. Walking around the park now. Kareem hasn't come out yet. It's just another day in paradise. Beats most of the other ops I've been on."

Axe shook his head and held back a sigh, shoving down his desires to switch roles with Johnboy. "Copy that. Stay sharp, but be subtle, and pace yourself. It might be a long day."

Kareem hung way back as the short, curvy woman in a floppy straw sunhat disappeared around the corner three short blocks in front of him. She walked like a police officer.

He kept his head down, focused on his phone as if he were looking for an address to deliver the large box of cookies he carried.

A tall, white work van, much too clean and undented for the city, was two blocks ahead, parallel parked too close to a fire hydrant. While it could be a delivery vehicle, it looked exactly like a surveillance van his father's people would use to stake out suspected political dissidents. Kareem had spent time in one as the internal security service watched and eventually arrested a man.

Kareem had been given the honor of shooting him in the head later that night.

The white van ahead might be nothing to worry about, but Kareem would stay away.

He reversed course, hurrying to the north-south street he'd just passed, and turned away from the park a few blocks south. He would take the next parallel street and maybe get lucky enough to see where Yaz's patron went —and the woman who followed him.

Kareem would avoid the suspicious van, the Black man from outside his apartment, the hairy, barrel-chested Caucasian man who had followed Yaz to the breakfast meeting, and the short, curvy woman trailing Yaz.

There was no longer any doubt. He was in trouble.

So far, however, he had the upper hand. His enemies didn't realize he knew about them.

87

THE INFLUENCER

Empire Bagels and Coffee Brewery
Greenwich Village

Tabitha prepped for her video in the back corner of the kitchen designated as the break room, which was a joke since there was barely room for an old folding chair.

There was a lull in the morning rush, and the manager, who had a crush on her, had nodded for her to take fifteen. He knew as well as she did the best times for her to post on social media. She would have hooked up with him a few times for the fun of it—if he weren't her boss. No need to have that drama at work when she inevitably got bored and dumped him.

She positioned herself in the chair, getting the lighting just right—as good as it could be—and prayed the dishwasher and kitchen help kept it down for a few minutes so she could get a good take. A quick fix of her bright red lipstick, a review of what she wanted to say, and she was ready to go.

Her thumb hit the red button on the screen to record.

"So, talk about pickup lines. Here's a new one. A rich guy at my school has been hitting on me all semester." She glossed over the fact that he hadn't hit on her at all, or that it had been her to make the first approach this morning. Never let the truth get in the way of a good story. That was her motto.

"This morning, he bet me that the stock market will crash by Friday. If he loses, he donates ten thousand dollars to a charity of my choice. He's taking me to dinner Friday night either way. Soooooo… what charity should I have him send the money to when he has to pay up? Leave comments! Vote! And hey, for those who don't follow me closely, my dad's in finance. I'll check with him, but he hasn't said anything about a market crash coming. What do you think?"

She winked at the screen and hit the red button to stop recording.

After watching the video twice to make sure it looked and sounded great, she posted it.

Tabitha had a growing number of followers, eked out over the past year as a young woman from the Midwest living—and loving—in the Big Apple. She was making as much money as a budding social media influencer as she was at her crappy day job at the bagel and coffee shop. If all went according to plan, she'd soon be able to quit the bagel place and make content full time.

Who needed an expensive degree? She had the looks, the brains, and the drive to make it big.

As Tabitha had hoped, the comments came in immediately, but she had to pocket the phone when the manager poked his head around the corner. "It's getting busy again," he said after checking to make sure she wasn't recording.

"I'm done—thanks, darling," she said, giving him a wink too.

This morning's video would go viral. She could feel it.

88

THE RESEARCH

Conference Room 3
Central Analysis Group Headquarters
Arlington, Virginia

Haley checked out the latest message from Axe on her laptop.

Nancy and Dave worked on their computers at the conference room table with her.

"Another message from Axe. We need to vet a woman named Tabitha. Last name unknown. She works at the Empire Bagels and Coffee Brewery in Greenwich Village. Axe wonders if she's a plant or a deep-cover operator. She approached Yaz and initiated contact."

"I'm on it," Dave said. He focused on his laptop, fingers typing furiously. Haley was good at gathering data and putting together puzzles, but Dave definitely held his own at online research.

"I'm still on Rami bin Raslan," Nancy said. "Nothing out of the ordinary—for an extremely wealthy Saudi family. He gets good grades— 3.8 GPA. Major in business with a minor in—get this, luxury brand marketing. Fluent in Arabic and English, conversational in French. Summer internships at his father's company, Dubai branch."

"Dubai? Could he have had contact with the Russian cyberterrorists based there?" Dave asked without breaking stride in his research.

"I'll put a pin in that and check it out," Nancy said, making a note on a yellow legal pad next to her laptop. "Continuing: season tickets for the city's pro basketball team. Attends the opera. Steady girlfriend in New York—she's from Riyad as well." She made another note. "In his sophomore year, he started mentoring freshmen from the Gulf states. Lots of connections, never in trouble, here under his real name. This guy sounds straight as an arrow. But then again, that's exactly how you'd want a deep cover guy to seem."

From the other side of the table, Dave grunted in satisfaction. "Got her. Tabitha Smythwick. Twenty-three years old. She's worked at the breakfast place for nearly two years. Blah blah blah… No, I doubt she's a spy, but I'll keep digging."

"Tabitha…" Haley said, typing with her thumbs. "Let's see what you share with the world."

89

THE CONCERNS

Conference Room 3
Central Analysis Group Headquarters
Arlington, Virginia

Haley couldn't keep up with the barrage of replies on *@TabithaInNYbaby!*, the social media feed of Tabitha Smythwick.

"She's a social media influencer," Haley said. Tabitha was already half famous—at least online.

Nancy and Dave moved behind Haley so they could watch the video and track the messages on screen.

@parkbenchpaul101: You got played! Dude just paid $$$ to guarantee a date. If he's so rich, that's like me saying I'll bet you ten bucks that ugly green space aliens will take over the planet tomorrow. What time should we get together for me to pay you? You're hot—totally be worth it.

@nycdreamerdahlia: Girl, you should find out a cause he hates and make sure he sends that money to them!

@vintage-drake99: Report him—he might be planning a terror attack! (NOT KIDDING!)

@cosmikkeri: Make him give to a poverty relief charity or a local homeless shelter!

@brooklynbelle398: I agree—you got conned. He's throwing money around to get a shot at you. Get the receipt when you win at least.

@hotnessandlight: A charity that provides dental care for the needy!!!

@alwaysabeachday: Should have asked for 100K. If you're going to sell it, at least don't give it away!

@dumbdanwhosmart: Maybe he knows something you don't? Another terror attack like two months ago???

"That's interesting," Dave muttered as the latest one scrolled by.

"Yes, what if that's accurate?" Nancy asked.

"Good thing we have people following Yaz," Haley said.

The rest of the feed had suggestions for charities. An hour after being posted, interest in the video dipped with no more mention of terrorism.

"I think those two replies were worth considering," Nancy said. "'*What enables the wise sovereign and the good general to strike and conquer, and achieve things beyond the reach of ordinary men, is foreknowledge.*' Sun Tzu."

"You've been reading the book I gave everyone?" Haley asked her.

Nancy shrugged. "Some parts jumped out at me."

"What can we do, though?" Dave asked. "How would they even crash the stock market? Three college students?"

"There may be more we don't know about," Haley said. "And Axe nearly got killed by Jade. She could be in on it."

They shared a look—they were on the same page.

"I'll check out online chatter about attacks focusing on New York," Dave said as he returned to his laptop.

"Let's do a deep dive," Haley told Nancy. "No stone left unturned. Look at Rami first. Then where the vulnerabilities in the stock market are. We focus not only on cyber, though."

"Agreed. We can't overlook the possibility of a physical attack—not only on Wall Street and the stock market infrastructure but also on the country," Nancy said. "I can only think of a few things that would really disrupt the market badly enough for a deep crash, though."

Haley nodded. "Some kind of nuclear attack: a rogue missile, dirty bomb, or an assault on a nuclear power plant. Big things like that."

"Or bioterrorism. Chemical weapons." Nancy bit her lip, looking worried, and returned to her laptop.

Haley sent a quick note to Gregory to update him on their concerns, then slipped on her noise-cancelling headphones, started a lofi beats playlist, and started hunting.

90

THE ASSASSIN

Washington Square Park
Greenwich Village

Lou Tantai pushed his fake nerd glasses up, resettling them, and slowed as he crossed Washington Square Park. He wanted to time his arrival at the school building for five minutes after the top of the hour.

Robert Zhao, his student advisor—and Ministry of State Security handler—routinely booked his first appointment of the day for an hour after he started work to be available for drop-ins and emergencies before then.

Lou needed an urgent meeting. He had finally come to his senses.

Jade, his fellow student spy, was out of control and desperate.

That's why she had paid for his help. A hundred thousand dollars for a weapon and to borrow his SUV? Crazy.

He also had to be honest with himself.

There was no other reason she would have slept with him.

He had wanted Jade since the day they met. Something about her had driven him crazy that first week at school.

The Ministry of State Security had chosen and trained her well.

She was beautiful, but much more than that.

Jade Pang was attractive. Alluring. Desirable. Irresistible.

She was an outstanding tool for Beijing to use.

The intelligence she would gather and the assets she would accumulate were going to be invaluable.

Her looks, physique, brains, smile, and attitude combined into a package that had broken through his professional demeanor.

He was a trained assassin. Cold. Unemotional. He didn't feel infatuation, lust, or love.

Until Jade.

But she had scorned him.

Turned him down flat.

And as much as he had hated to admit it to himself, it had hurt.

Now? He finally had what he'd wanted for three-and-a-half years…

And he didn't know what to do.

She was dangerous. To him, and to China.

He had to report her, admit he'd given her a rifle and his SUV, and deal with the fallout. He needed to stop whatever she was doing before she dragged him down with her.

There was a possibility of minimizing his punishment. He would claim he had acted as a double agent, giving Jade what she requested, taking the money and the rest, to gather information for Beijing.

It had been his only play.

His superiors at the Ministry of State Security would see the excuse for the convenient lie it was, but might reprimand him instead of doing something much worse.

He had no doubt what the MSS would order him to do once they realized Jade had gone rogue. Lou would be told to put Jade down.

But as good as he was at killing, going head-to-head against her was not the safe play. Should he make a mistake, or if she got the upper hand, he would be dead.

She'd be able to continue her dangerous course with no one to stop her.

As he neared the school building, Lou's train of thought was broken by a voice behind him. "Mr. Tantai?"

Lou turned, startled that Mr. Zhao had snuck up behind him.

The old man was once a spy like me. Of course he still has some skill.

"Mr. Zhao," Lou said with a bow of his head. "I could use a few minutes of your time."

Anyone watching them would see only what they expected: a young man in need of a few words of wisdom from his student advisor.

"Come on up," Zhao said. "I'm always happy to help."

91

THE CONFESSION

Greenwich Village

Lou looked around the office. He raised a finger and made a circle, indicating the room, then pointed at his ear, wanting to know if the room was bugged.

Robert Zhao, wearing a tired sport coat over a clean but not ironed white dress shirt, held up a hand for him to wait.

Zhao took a small, rectangular portable wireless speaker from his satchel, pressed two buttons on top, and moved around the room, intent on the green light on top of the device.

After a careful sweep for listening devices, he nodded to Lou. "Talk," he said, his voice serious and concerned. It wasn't like Lou to show up any time besides their normal check-in meetings.

"It's about Jade Pang," Lou started.

Zhao's face betrayed little, but the small twitch at the mention of Jade had been enough for Lou.

He's concerned, as well.

"Speak freely. Tell me everything."

Lou decided against pretending he had acted as a double agent for Beijing. He would tell the whole truth and hope for the best.

"She borrowed my vehicle," Lou said, switching to Mandarin and speaking as quietly as he could. "And a rifle with a scope and a suppressor. She also gave me a large sum of money in exchange for my help and explained she had the money because of another project. She has walked into the fire and become possessed," he said, using the metaphor from Chinese martial arts novels that meant a person is veering toward obsession or self-destructive behavior and going to dangerous extremes.

"Jade also…" Lou hesitated, hoping Zhao would catch his meaning, but the man handed the phone back, face expressionless. "She gave herself to me, which she had avoided since our first days in the country. It was what finally convinced me Beijing has not approved of whatever she is involved in." He shrugged with a sad smile. "She was desperate."

Zhao nodded slowly. His gaze left Lou and shifted to his desk as he contemplated the situation.

The seconds passed, but Lou remained silent.

Zhao finally looked up, his eyes assessing Lou. "You could bring her in? Physically?"

"With drugs, yes. I could inject her the next time we're… together."

"Understood." Zhao hesitated a moment before continuing with a frown. "What about simply eliminating her?"

"Possible," Lou said, hating the uncertainty in his voice. "Likely, even, in the right circumstances. But she has been well trained. And she might suspect me, which would remove the element of surprise, evening the odds." He paused, not wanting to make the suggestion, but that was his ego talking. He would always do what was best for China. "The safer play is a small team. Four people working with me, or as backup if I fail." He leaned forward. "China cannot be linked to this woman and whatever she is doing—or has done. I would not confess what I have if I weren't convinced of this."

"A team risks more exposure," Zhao said, but more to himself than to Lou. After another few seconds of contemplation, he leaned forward and whispered orders. "If you have the chance, and the upper hand, you will eliminate her yourself. Otherwise, I will confirm that a team is in the area and available. You will lure her to a discrete location, away from the school, where they can handle the takedown. You will be responsible for her disposal."

"It will be done," Lou said, rising.

Lou offered a small bow and left the advisor without another word. He wasn't looking forward to killing Jade, but he would do his duty. The woman was too dangerous to be allowed to live.

92

THE SKETCH

Greenwich Village

Zhao waited until Lou's footsteps faded down the hall before he stood to pace his office, a bad habit he had picked up early in his career. But it helped him think, and he needed that now.

He had a duty to report Lou Tantai's concerns to his superiors in Beijing. Zhao believed the boy's story, and it fit with his assessment of Jade Pang. She had seemed troubled for months.

Beijing might, however, look upon Jade Pang's downward spiral as Zhao's fault for not managing her properly, and for not reporting his growing concerns months ago.

He took a risk either way.

Zhao hoped that Tantai killed the woman.

But given the potential threat, he decided he had to inform the Ministry of State Security.

He flipped open the cover on his tablet, opened a drawing program, and slid the stylus pencil from its holder. With precise strokes, he wrote in Chinese, summarizing his growing misgivings about Jade Pang, detailing Tantai's confession, and requesting a team of operators to ensure Pang's quiet elimination.

After a quick proofread, Zhao changed the text color to match the background, added a layer in the drawing software, and doodled a quick scene of a man walking a dog. Nothing fancy, but he added a few trees, a squirrel, and a sunset. Satisfied with the effort, he merged the layers, then saved the file and closed the software.

The tablet would immediately encrypt the file and back up his latest drawing to the cloud, which was merely a term for computer servers located around the world.

Twelve time zones and more than six thousand miles away on a basement level of China's Ministry of State Security (MSS) building, just east of Tiananmen Square, a trusted mid-level analyst would receive a notification.

She would access the saved drawing, unmerge the layers, find the text, and read Zhao's report.

An hour from now, Zhao would have the urge to add more detail to the sketch. He would take a quick break in his day, open the software, and access the hidden response from Beijing.

He resumed pacing, shaking his head at the upcoming elimination of the once-promising Jade Pang.

93

FREEDOM

Uni-versal Coffee
Greenwich Village

Dawson "Void" Reite stepped from the taxi in Greenwich Village and drew in a deep breath of fresh air. He savored it like it might be his last. He was finally out of his room in Kelton's condo, which had been his home and prison for the past two months. It felt strange to wear jeans—and shoes—after so much time going barefoot and wearing sweatpants.

It had taken him a while this morning to disable the ankle monitor he wore while under house arrest, but he was finally here.

He was ready to contribute to the mission IRL—in real life, not simply online.

Void slung his backpack over a shoulder and stepped inside the busy coffee shop Axe had directed him to. He moved to the end of the short line in front of the register to order, ignoring Marianna—Tex, he should call her while on the mission, he figured—and the thin young man she sat near.

The guy in the fancy maroon sweater was their new target: Rami bin Raslan from Saudi Arabia.

The heady aroma of ground coffee beans mixed with the scent of fresh-baked treats. When his turn came, Void ordered a tall coffee and a huge blueberry muffin, then sat at one of the few open tables with a line of sight to the target.

Void set his purchases on the far side of his table, pulled out his laptop, and got to work.

He leaned his phone against his coffee cup as if he were using it as a second monitor. On the computer, he opened a window and reduced the size so no one passing by would notice it. After a small adjustment to the phone, he had the target centered in the frame. The phone transmitted the view from Void's camera to the computer. He could now easily monitor the subject and record what he did.

Void sent a text to Tex. *I have him.*

Mariana sent him a thumbs-up emoji and sipped her coffee while scrolling on her phone, oblivious to everything around her.

In Void's monitor window, the target glanced at his watch and frowned.

He's waiting for someone, Void sent in a group chat to Axe and Tex.

This secret spy stuff was so cool. Almost as fun as hacking.

Greenwich Village

Axe checked the map of the neighborhood on one of the laptop screens in the van and debated how much risk to take.

At the moment, no one had eyes on Darius's apartment—or Jade's.

Axe had two assets in a coffee shop waiting for a meeting between Rami bin Raslan and someone else.

"Tex," he called, the decision made. "I'll be over there in a minute. Break off. Make your way to Mad Dog and switch out with him. Mad Dog, you take a walk through the park and watch for Kareem. Johnboy, you rotate to Darius's apartment. There's a great coffee shop on the corner with outdoor tables." He added Void on the comms chat app and waited a moment for him to accept the invitation. "Don't say anything out loud, Void. I can hear you're online. Mute yourself for now and sit tight. I'll direct you to set up near Jade's apartment once we see what Rami does. Tex is leaving, and I'll be in shortly. It's about time I enjoy some good coffee, too."

"Already tired of being in the rear with the gear, Papa?" Mad Dog asked.

"It was old before it started, my friend."

Axe grabbed the protective baseball cap, which was much more practical for a sunny spring day than the beanie, and did a quick check of his folding knife in his front pocket, fixed-blade knife at the small of his back, pistol in the concealed-carry holster, and two extra magazines in a holder on his left side. The ballistic vest was unnoticeable under his black T-shirt with the loose, casual button-down shirt over it.

He was good to go.

Three college-aged men strode purposefully ahead of Kareem on the street parallel to the surveillance van. They each had their hair styled perfectly, they wore expensive shoes and clothes, and spoke in quiet Arabic, though Kareem only caught a few words.

He followed them, trusting his gut, and ditched the box of cookies in a trash can along the way.

When the men turned left at the intersection, Kareem crossed the street and entered an upscale breakfast place.

The three men entered a local coffee shop near the corner.

Kareem had a perfect view as he ordered at the counter and took a large cup of coffee to a stool at the window facing the street.

94

THE NEGOTIATION

Uni-versal Coffee
Greenwich Village

Axe picked up a tall black coffee and sat in the corner of the coffee shop near the front window. The place was busy with late-rising, bleary-eyed college students and locals, all lost in their own world, most with earbuds or large, over-the-ear headphones.

It felt great to be out of the van. A bit of casual surveillance wasn't exactly a firefight or midnight stalk through the back alleys of New York City. This was a safe way to continue getting his mind and body back in the game.

Void had his head down, focused on his computer screen, and ignored Axe exactly as ordered.

He's just happy to be out of his sky-high prison, Axe thought.

Rami bin Raslan, tall, thin, with a fashionable amount of beard growing in, sat at a four-top table near the window, only a few steps from Axe. But with the constant noise of the coffee shop, any conversation he had with whoever he was waiting for would be difficult to eavesdrop on.

Axe sent a message to Void.

Can you hack into Rami bin Raslan's phone or something so we can listen to his conversation when his friends show up?

Void replied immediately. ***It doesn't work like that. That's nation-***

state kind of stuff. I'm very good, but I can't do that. But are you willing to be off comms for a while? I have an idea.

After approving the plan, Axe followed Void's instructions, giving him total control over the burner mission phone. Axe placed the earbuds in their case, stuck the phone into his jacket pocket, and placed the folded jacket over the back of the chair right behind Rami.

Axe took his coffee over to a table near the front counter, pretended to add cream and sugar to the cup, then moved toward the back of the café as if he'd forgotten his jacket. It was so busy with people coming and going, the jacket would hopefully be overlooked, or Rami would assume he was in the bathroom instead of sitting at a table in the far back corner, out of his sight.

The plan might not work, but it was the best he could do on short notice with such limited resources.

Rami stood as the three men entered. They exchanged light fist bumps in greeting, forgoing their culture's cheek kiss or close hug.

Rami looked around before speaking, confirming that the only other table near the window was empty except for someone's jacket—they had either left it behind or were in the restroom. "Brothers," Rami said. "Please sit. We have much to discuss. Or do you want coffee first?"

He received three head shakes as the men, all dressed like him in expensive designer jeans, sweaters, and shoes that cost more than any of the baristas made in a month. The three each had dark black hair, a few days' worth of stubble on their cheeks, and a careful nonchalance that didn't fully hide their anger and impatience.

"What do you have for us?" one—Turki—asked. He acted as the de facto leader because his father was slightly wealthier and had a more prestigious role in the government than the others.

"Good news," Rami said as they took their seats. "Another plan is well in motion. By Friday, or early next week, we will have our money back. Perhaps with a sizeable return for our investment."

"But not what was originally promised," Turki said, his annoyance and disappointment obvious.

"No, unfortunately, that chance has come and gone. This will have to suffice."

95

____

THE TEAMMATE

Uni-versal Coffee
Greenwich Village

Void fiddled with the laptop, adjusting the software installed on Axe's phone. Once the four targets were seated, it became harder to pick out their conversation from the background noise. There'd been something about a new plan, but he'd lost the rest. He was recording the stream, though, so he'd be able to process the audio later. Maybe he'd pick up more then.

______

"What will we have to do?" one of the other students asked Rami, cutting off Turki from his tirade about the failed mission for them to bypass years of hard work and advance quickly into powerful jobs. "To get our money, I mean? Are you simply going to hand it to us? Transfer it back into our accounts? I am going home in a few weeks. I need it before then, or I will face many questions."

"America's stock market is about to crash," Rami said, voice low. "Only for a day or two. We will bet against the market and take short positions. Immediately sell whatever American stocks you have. I have a list of instructions for you, but basically, buy leveraged inverse exchange-traded funds. They will triple your investment when the market drops. A million dollars turns into three. Ten million into thirty, and so on. After the market drops all day, right before trading closes, we will sell those and buy the distressed stocks everyone else has sold in a panic. By the next day, they will rapidly return to their former values, providing more return. The opportunity is only limited by the amount each of us puts into it."

"I want my money directly," Turki said with a grumble. "No betting against the market. Just the original amount wired into my account."

"That… that is shortsighted," Rami said. He wasn't afraid of Turki and his friends, but the world he moved in was a small, tight-knit community. They would be working, living, and socializing with each other for the rest of their lives. He had to keep them as happy as possible.

"My father's accountant has already quietly asked questions of me," the second young man said. "I need the same: all of my money back, not a new scheme."

Rami raised his hand to placate them as the last man nodded along with the first two. "I will see what I can do, but I urge you to consider the opportunity here. I may—may—be able to simply ensure a return of your original capital out of my own proceeds, but that is not the smart play. We know the future. This is an opportunity of a lifetime."

He'd raised his voice to sell the plan. He looked around the room to make sure no one had heard him, but the nearest man, several feet away, wore headphones and stared at his computer screen.

The three men, to their credit, didn't immediately say no. "We will consider it," Turki said for them.

"Act quickly—today," Rami said. "Position your money wisely if you intend to take part."

With that, the three stood, forcing Rami quickly to his feet as well. The fist bumps were a formality, not done with their usual friendly bravado, and the three filed out the door.

Rami returned to his seat, giving them a few minutes so he wouldn't awkwardly run into them on the sidewalk. He took Yaz's diamond earrings out of his pocket, appreciating their sparkle and heft, before putting them on, finding the nearly grown-in holes from when he'd gotten his ears pierced as an act of rebellion over the winter.

Rami eventually exited the coffee shop, considering how best to position his remaining assets, and any he could borrow from his father's account, for maximum return.

He would have to take extra risks to reimburse the other three Saudis with proceeds from his personal windfall when the market crashed tomorrow.

Axe let Rami leave without following. He didn't want to risk tailing him personally, Void would be useless at it, and there was no one else to call on. Axe hoped they had captured the most important part of the kid's day and that he wasn't on his way to meet more people. Rami's body language certainly suggested that. He had finished his coffee, put on Yaz's gaudy earrings and left, lost in thought.

"How much did you get?" Axe asked once he'd returned to his original seat, inserted the earbuds, and rejoined the team comms call.

"Not as much as I hoped," Void muttered in his ear. "Too much background noise. The acoustics in here suck. But I recorded it. Give me some time and I might come up with more. All I heard clearly was that there is a new plan and that they'd get their money back by next week. Does that mean anything to you?"

"No, but get the raw file and whatever else you caught to Haley right away, then work on the rest."

"I don't have to go back to the condo, right? There's somewhere else you need me?"

Axe kept the smile off his face and took a sip of coffee, pretending to think over the request. "Yes, we need you. I'll send the details to your phone. After you reach out to Haley, pack up and walk west. There's a different coffee shop you can work from while you watch for one of our other targets. And Void," Axe said, "Welcome to the team."

He caught Void's happy sigh over the earbuds, finished his coffee, and headed back to the surveillance van.

96

THE DECISION

Toasty Bowl Coffee Culture
Greenwich Village

Kareem didn't dare risk taking a cell phone picture of the dark-haired, muscular man who exited the coffee shop, but he desperately wanted to. It wouldn't do any good, unless he was willing to send the photo to his father and ask for help identifying him. That would cause a commotion, and the entire plan he'd been a part of might come to light.

There would be a terrible price to pay for Kareem's involvement in the plot to kill dozens of the Middle East's top leaders—including his own country's president.

Besides, it was clear what the man was, if not who.

He was a clandestine operator, likely a former soldier. Kareem had only a passing familiarity with the United States Armed Forces, but he knew a warrior when he saw one. But the man and his team certainly weren't spies. If they had been, Kareem would never had noticed them.

Kareem remained inside the breakfast place, sipping coffee at its narrow counter across the street from where Yaz's patron had met with what had to be his fellow financial backers.

He would give the dark-haired man time to return to his surveillance van, which had to be the base of operations for the team, before taking the next step.

The only way Jade and Darius could be responsible for the covert ops team was if they wanted to eliminate everyone who had backed them: Kareem, Yaz, and all of their patrons.

Was he being paranoid?

So far, he'd seen the soldier outside his apartment.

The barrel-chested man, who also had to be a soldier, had followed Yaz.

The woman, who walked like a police officer but dressed like a tourist, had tailed Yaz's patron.

And the dark-haired man, older than the other three, moved with the smooth confidence of a dangerous predator. Kareem guessed he was the one in charge.

He would be a formidable opponent.

His entire team would.

Kareem sipped his cooling coffee and ignored the chatter of the students ordering their avocado toast and mushroom coffee.

When enough time had passed, Kareem left the breakfast place and turned north once again, away from the park, his condo, Yaz's home, and Darius's. He walked blocks out of his way, taking his time, checking the street behind him in shop windows for people following him, putting all his training to use.

Eventually, he hailed a taxi and directed it southeast, down the street toward Darius's apartment, and slumped in the seat like an exhausted college student returning home from a wild night.

At an outdoor table at the coffee shop only thirty meters north of Darius's condo building, the muscular, bald soldier enjoyed a cup of coffee as he scrolled on his phone, relaxed, like he hadn't a care in the world, just as he'd sat in the park outside Kareem's apartment earlier.

The authorities are investigating us for what we did, or Jade has plans to eliminate us all, including Darius.

Either way, Kareem's decision was easy.

It was time to clean house.

97

THE TRUTH

Eastern Famous Bakery
Chinatown
Manhattan

Kareem took the taxi farther south and had it drop him at a Chinatown bakery selling coffee and pastries on an alley off Bowry Street.

He was out of place in the small shop—taller, better dressed, and the only person not of Asian heritage. But anyone following him would stick out, too.

He had a great view through the large window facing the road to see if people walked or drove by looking for him.

He'd never been here before, and as a group, he, Yaz, Darius, and Jade hadn't met this far south, which made it a good place for him to regroup and figure out what the hell was going on.

First, he had to find out whether he and Yaz had been betrayed by Jade and/or Darius.

Had yesterday's ultimatum pushed them over the edge?

Was Jade eliminating loose ends, as he was prepared to do?

He removed his noise-cancelling earbuds from their case, slipped them on, and prepared himself. Jade Pang was capable and skilled, but he should be able to tell if she was lying.

He navigated to the secure comms app, looked around to make sure no one was near enough to overhear as long as he was quiet, and used the software to call her.

She didn't answer.

He sent a message.

Must speak. Emergency. Call immediately.

After two minutes of waiting, he moved on.

Darius had the personality of the politician he would one day be, which in some ways made him a better liar than Jade. But he was also afraid of what Kareem could do to him—physically and with Kareem's father's contacts.

Kareem selected Darius's name in the app.

"I'm glad you called," Darius answered with a politician's fake sincerity. "I will have an update for you soon, but all is going well. We are on track for tomorrow."

"That is good news," Kareem said, matching the friendly tone. "But… is there anything you want to tell me?" he asked, colder. His father had used the same words when Kareem was growing up, knowing the effect they had on someone with secrets.

Darius hesitated a moment too long before replying. "No, not that I can think of."

"Don't lie to me. I know everything."

The pause lasted longer this time. "I don't… I mean, nothing's going on."

Kareem had to give him credit. Had he not known the man, hadn't met with him frequently over the past three years, or if Darius had another year or two of being put on the spot to improve as a liar, he could have pulled it off. But they both knew he wasn't being honest.

"Just tell me," Kareem said, suddenly weary of the whole mess. The years of college in the United States were supposed to be when he grew as a person. Expanded his mind. Met people from around the world. Made contacts that would serve him for decades. Slept with women—not as many as Yaz, but made sure he fooled around and had fun. Maybe fell in love once or twice, knowing it could never last.

And, of course, honing his skills by killing a few people a year. Annoying drunks. Low-life criminals. Rude tourists. Anyone unlucky enough to annoy him while in a quiet location in the city.

But the time wasn't supposed to be used for what he'd fallen into: Jade and Darius's plot to change the world—especially the Middle East.

At home, they had a saying: Greed rarely gathers.

Had he overreached? Tried for a shortcut—and was now paying the price?

"Really, I don't know what—" Darius said, but Kareem cut him off.

"The dark-haired man—the warrior," Kareem said, leading with the description of the man he figured was in charge. "Mid-forties. Muscular but not beefy. Dark beard. Obviously military. You know about him. I can hear it in your voice."

The silence stretched on, but finally Darius sighed. "He followed Jade after our meeting at the café last night. She tried to kill him by pushing him in front of a bus, but it seems he lived. Where did you see him?"

Kareem didn't like what he heard, but at least Darius was telling the truth. They were getting somewhere.

"He followed Yaz's patron to a meeting with his contacts at a coffee shop a few blocks north of Washington Square Park," Kareem said.

"That means…" Darius trailed off.

"He knows about Yaz, his main patron, and the men he recruited. They know about you as well. There's a man at the coffee shop by your apartment, the same man who watched my home earlier," Kareem said, deciding to tell the rest of what he knew. "There are at least four people on their team, including a woman who might be a police officer."

The implications sank in.

"But how?" Darius asked. "And if they knew about… you know," he said, avoiding mentioning all that they had done—the SystemSpike plus the attempted killings at the peace summit. "Why are they only watching instead of arresting us?"

"I don't know and I don't care. We have a brief window to fix this. They are from the United States government, most likely. People from our countries," he added, half under his breath, "wouldn't hire local talent. And they wouldn't merely follow us if they were aware of our… involvement."

"Jade is in the middle of the operation. I can reach her in an emergency, but she can't break away. There's no time."

"We can handle it."

"We? As in you and me?" Darius clearly wasn't prepared to get his hands dirty.

"I will take care of the messier aspects if necessary, but they know what you and I look like. Is there anyone else who can assist?"

What they needed was another killer, someone unknown to the men and woman hunting them.

"I think that can be arranged," Darius said. His voice had turned colder. Thoughtful.

Kareem sensed Darius was telling the truth. They were on the same page.

"Make the arrangements, then message me," Kareem said. "I'll figure out a plan to eliminate at least the leader of the team. If we take care of him, the others will have to regroup. Agreed?"

"I have to check with Jade, but yes. I believe we have to act now if we are to save the current mission."

And ourselves, Kareem thought, knowing Darius felt the same.

98

OR ELSE

New Jersey Turnpike Rest Area
New Jersey

Jade had more driving to do, but the adrenaline from earlier had worn off.

She needed to use the restroom, buy coffee and food, put gas in the SUV, and possibly take a power nap. Then she could continue on her way.

She parked off to the side of the combination gas station, food service area, and restroom building, ready to take care of everything she needed for the next stage of her epic day.

The burner phone buzzed with a call from Darius, not a message.

Something had gone wrong. He wouldn't reach out otherwise.

"Yes," she said. There was always a chance he had been compromised, and she would give nothing away until she knew for sure.

"It's me," Darius said, starting with the greeting that proved he was safe and not under duress. If he had used her name, said hello or hi, or any of several other common phrases, the rest of her day would have gone much differently.

"I'm here," she said, using the corresponding answer.

"Kareem knows," Darius said, getting right to the point. He sounded focused, though she detected a hint of fear in his tone. "People are watching his apartment, and others trailed Yaz this morning, along with Yaz's patron, to a meeting with other benefactors. The dark-haired warrior with the beard who followed you is the man in charge, he believes."

Darius hesitated. When she didn't respond immediately, he continued. "Kareem is working on a plan to eliminate the leader. He believes it will disrupt the rest of the team. But they know what we all look like. He needs someone else."

"Lou," Jade said.

"Yes, that was my thought, too. Will he do it?"

She considered the question, picturing the puppy-dog look on Lou's face before dawn this morning when she dropped him off at the train station and kissed him goodbye. It had been a mix of happiness, devotion, and sorrow that they were parting.

"Yes. I can get him to help." She would make him if he didn't go along willingly. "I'll put him in touch with you and Kareem on the app." She lowered her voice and whispered to Darius. He needed to be handled now more than ever. "You can do this. For me. For us. Kareem will watch out for you, and we will be together again late tonight for the final part. I love you."

The last words were a lie, but he wouldn't know that. She was convincing. It was her gift. Men believed her.

"I love you, too," he said, his voice tinny and faint coming through the phone's speaker as her finger hovered over the red button to disconnect the call. When he said nothing more, she jammed her finger down, ending the pointless emotional mush, and pulled up Lou's contact information, which she'd rarely used in three and a half years.

Can you talk? It's important, she sent.

A moment later, her phone buzzed.

"You missed me?" Lou said, joking with a surprising amount of awareness about the true nature of the situation.

"Terribly, of course," she shot right back. "And I need a favor," she said, serious.

"Borrowing my car and the other items wasn't enough?" His voice had an edge to it.

"My mission is in danger. I need you for what you do best."

"I think that we have successfully concluded our… interaction," Lou said, surprising her. Maybe he wasn't as lovestruck as she thought. "We both got what we wanted. Let's stop while we are still friends."

If her normal method of persuasion no longer worked on him after last night, it wasn't a problem. She had others.

Jade used an old Chinese proverb. "Once you start, you might as well finish."

"I'm sorry. I'm already finished."

"No, actually, you're not," she said, using her coldest tone. "You help me now, or else."

"Or else what? What can you do to me?"

"I will say this was all your idea from the start. Some of the things I've done, you have no idea... but if I implicated you, Beijing wouldn't just kill you. They would torture you first. Or bring your family members in one by one and make you watch them suffer for your crimes. No matter what you tell the MSS, they will believe me. I'm a helpless young woman who comes from a family of farmers. I'm a lowly, all-purpose asset. You are a highly trained assassin, and a strong, intelligent man. It will be my word against yours, and I will win. I will persuade them. You know I can."

Lou paused, then finally spoke. "What do you need me to do?"

"Kill one man. It will be easy for you. My colleagues have a plan. I will put you in touch with them."

"This one last favor, then you return my items and we are done. Understood?"

"I agree."

"Send me the details."

―――――

Greenwich Village

Lou cursed in Chinese as he hung up, not caring if she heard or not. The phrase's literal translation was, "You are utterly deranged and cruel!"

It fit perfectly.

He had acted on instinct and played hard to get, hoping Jade would demand a meeting in a quiet place to convince him to help her.

That would have made it easy for him to do as Zhao instructed and kill her quietly.

But her request changed things.

Lou didn't wait for Jade to message him the information. Looking in the phone's contact database, he found his student advisor's information and placed a call to the man's university office.

No answer.

He sent a text to Zhao's cell phone, given out to select students—and, of course, the student sleeper spies—for emergencies.

I have an urgent problem related to our discussion this morning. Please contact me immediately.

This was the chance to ensnare Jade Pang's accomplices in whatever she was currently planning and had done in the past.

If Zhao could get a message to the Ministry of State Security in time and receive permission back, Lou could eliminate Jade's people one by one, or identify them for a Chinese covert ops team to pick them up and interrogate.

Lou had his own communication protocol, but it was mission-centric. A new burner phone for each assassination, and the bare minimum contact necessary with Beijing. His deep cover had to be maintained.

And if he didn't hear from anyone soon, he'd have to follow through with Jade's plan.

After his meeting with Zhao this morning, there was little chance the MSS would believe anything Jade said about him.

But that wasn't the point.

If Jade's people were about to be captured by agents of the United States government, Jade was also at risk.

Which meant that, by extension, China was in jeopardy.

And himself.

Would Jade give him up—and Zhao—to secure a deal with the Americans if she were captured and interrogated?

He preferred to think she would remain silent and preserve her cover story of an American girl from California, but a deep dive by a smart intelligence analyst might break through the extensive efforts the Ministry of State Security had taken to backstop her legend.

Jade was right, in the end.

He had to help.

Or else everything could come crumbling down.

99

———————

THE HUNT

Central Analysis Group Headquarters
Arlington, Virginia

Time didn't exist for Haley. There were no windows at the CAG headquarters. It had to still be Wednesday, but it didn't matter.

She was in the zone, at one with the data.

At some point, she must have moved to her cubicle, because she had both large monitors filled with information. Her laptop screen held a spreadsheet with intel she had gathered.

Rami bin Raslan and his family.

Yazeed bin Mishari Al Saud.

The families had immense wealth, and smaller-yet-still-incredible sums were likely available to each son.

She hadn't found how the two young men were connected aside from being foreign students in the same year at college. Their friendship—or at least their acquaintance, because what friend demands another's earrings?—made sense. Yaz was a young Saudi royal, but a minor prince distant from the new king of the country. He had a life of luxury to look forward to, or an easy, mid-level position at a global company that his father would arrange for him.

Yaz was probably too far removed from the halls of power to desire a job in his country's government. He wouldn't want to be at the bottom of a tall ladder with decades of work ahead to reach a satisfactory level of power and prestige.

Haley was painting with a broad brush, but based on the little they knew of him, it was a good enough place to start.

Rami bin Raslan was similar. His father had money, power, and connections, but was distant from the real inner workings of the elite of Saudi Arabia. Rami would have to work at a real job, unlike Yaz, but he had a life of wealth and quiet prominence to look forward to. He'd be a well-respected businessman, either in his father's company or a smaller company his father would buy him if he wanted to make his own way in the world.

I wonder if Void could hack their financials... she thought. He had the skills, the experience, and the elite-level hacking software he'd bragged about buying on the dark web before customizing and improving it.

Haley wrote a quick note on a yellow legal pad to ask Gregory for permission to let Void loose on the problem.

She'd learned what she could for now. Searches were running in the background, but they'd take a while to spit out data. In the meantime, she'd move on to the next issue.

The stock market.

Could it be hacked?

After all the cyberattacks the last several years, even the smallest businesses were much more careful with their systems.

Since the SystemSpike, everyone took security twice as seriously.

The stock exchange had an extremely secure system protected by an in-house team.

Where was it vulnerable?

Void had laughed when she'd asked him if he could hack it. "No way," he'd replied. "Not without an inside man."

What if I had to crash the stock market? Haley thought. *Where would I begin?*

100

THE WARNING

Hollywood, California

William started his day as usual, with a strong cup of coffee and his phone opened to The Biz Blog, the go-to website for the latest movie industry gossip, job postings, rumors, and box office results.

Today, though, instead of the usual reports of which star was spotted partying until the early morning hours the night before, the site opened onto a banner in huge letters across the entire front page.

You have been lied to.

If only you knew.

The end is near.

Your world is about to burn.

It was the best PR stunt he'd ever seen, and he applauded the publicist who had come up with the idea. It was an incredible tagline for whatever summer blockbuster movie someone was promoting.

Lincoln, Nebraska

The moment her alarm went off, Allison swung her feet out of bed and straight into her sneakers. She wore running pants, thin running socks, a sports bra, and a T-shirt to bed to save her time, and to remove every ounce of friction between her and training for the marathon.

Her one indulgence before grabbing the sun visor and water bottle on the counter was to stop in the bathroom and read the motivational website that helped keep her going when the miles were long and the day was rainy or hot.

Today's insight didn't grab her as much as usual.

You have been lied to.

If only you knew.

The end is near.

Your world is about to burn.

It was more cryptic than most, but it would give her plenty to think about while she cranked out six miles before work.

Boston, Massachusetts

Kathleen had been the broker of her boutique real estate firm for six months, long enough to sell several upscale homes, recruit a dozen top agents, and make a name for herself as a mover and a shaker.

Part of the success was the company website, packed with stunningly beautiful pictures of the homes they had listed, 3D walkthroughs, drone shots of the neighborhoods, and search tools that rivaled or surpassed the big names in the industry.

But today something was terribly wrong.

"Yes, I'm so sorry," she said into the phone to yet another one of her powerful, wealthy, and demanding clients. "We're working on the website."

The trophy wife of a Beacon Hill client continued to shriek. "It's costing us money every single moment that… that… whatever it is hides our home. You promised—"

Kathleen tuned out the woman and covered the phone with her hand. "What the hell is happening?" she asked her highly paid web guy—kid—standing in front of her desk.

"It's not just you. Us," he said, correcting himself. "It's hundreds, maybe thousands of other websites too. Not only real estate. Everything." He turned his laptop toward her and awkwardly used the trackpad to click on dozens of open tabs, one by one. They all displayed the same ominous warning:

You have been lied to.

If only you knew.

The end is near.

Your world is about to burn.

"Well? Fix it!" Kathleen told him. It was so hard to find good help these days, especially with some of these younger kids.

"I can't. It's locked somehow. The company that does the software we run the site on? They're working frantically at it."

"How long?"

The IT kid shrugged with a helpless expression. "I don't know."

"Tinsley," Kathleen said into the phone, sure the young woman had no idea she hadn't been listening to the tirade. "My entire IT team is working on the issue right now, but we've been informed the problem isn't our site. It's worldwide."

The IT nerd shook his head. "Only the United States!" he whispered.

Kathleen shrugged away his correction. "Websites are locked down all over. All have the same message. It's a big-time hack. But I promise you, we will sell your home. In fact, hold on, I'm getting a note from my assistant." Kathleen picked up a piece of paper and shook it near the phone. "We may have a showing later today or first thing tomorrow morning, if you wouldn't mind? See, our team is hard at work selling your home, whether the world is crumbling or not. Let me call you back with the details." She hung up without waiting for a reply.

"Someone get me a warm body in an expensive suit or dress to tour the Regan residence in Beacon Hill today or tomorrow!" she called out to the real estate agents in the cubicles outside her office. "I have a bottle of very old scotch for whoever produces a person willing to pretend to be a serious buyer."

She glared at the IT nerd still in front of her. "And fix our website!"

101

THE BOOST

SPOT Headquarters
Austin, Texas

Lauren Canisey's tiny cubicle had an obscured view of the city. When she leaned to the right and looked past several other cubes, Austin lay before her.

These next few days would be the last ones she had to spend in the cube. After a year at this soulless social media company, she had the chance to bet big, win big, and leave here forever.

Jade Pang, her BFF—best friend forever—last year at college, had sent her the message she'd been waiting for.

The timeline has changed. Be ready. Amplify reports of this warning:

You have been lied to. If only you knew. The end is near. Your world is about to burn.

Push it hard. Our $$$$ depends on it.

Lauren was a year ahead of Jade at NYU, and hated leaving her BFF behind. Jade was remarkable; witty, fun, and a great listener. A true friend.

They had stayed in touch, and when Jade—one of the smartest people Lauren had ever met—asked for a favor and promised a chance at a huge payday in exchange, she'd jumped at it. It was all supposed to happen over the summer, but Jade had sent a heads-up last night.

It was on.

Lauren's phone buzzed with a new message from Jade.

Anything yet?

Lauren checked her internal feed, which showed a real-time graph of trending themes.

The message on the hacked websites peaked, lowered, then peaked higher and higher every few seconds.

Happening now! she typed on her phone.

Push it, Jade replied.

Lauren clicked her mouse to highlight the trend. Another click boosted the posts mentioning the hack of websites around the country that were displaying a weird warning.

It didn't sound like something Jade would be in on, but Lauren didn't care. She'd do anything for her friend. If it resulted in a big financial score so she could leave this company, even better. Working in social media wasn't at all what she thought it would be.

Done, Lauren sent.

You're short? Jade asked, referencing her investment portfolio.

Lauren didn't know the plan, but every cent she had to her name, including money she'd borrowed from her parents and the cash from selling her car, was in an online brokerage account that allowed for sophisticated stock trades to maximize her bets.

Lauren logged into her brokerage account to double-check. Whatever she was helping Jade with had to involve the crash of the stock market. That was how the investments she'd made would pay off.

The brokerage account confirmed that all her money was in a bet against the stock market. When stocks went down in value, she would profit at a two or three to one margin.

If Jade's plan worked, Lauren was going to be rich.

On her work computer, Lauren noted new trending posts with hashtag titles.

#TheWarning and *#YouHaveBeenLiedTo*, which most people were shortening to *#YHBLT*, were trending hard, in part due to her first boost.

With a few more clicks, she put her metaphorical thumb on the scales, helping decide what the platform's users would see.

Images of hijacked webpages, a complaint about what was happening to a person's business while the page was hijacked, and dire predictions about the future, and conspiracy theories all received a boost thanks to her.

She would have done it as part of her job, anyway. But knowing it was for her friend, and that it would somehow soon make the stock market take a nosedive, made it fun.

Short and ready for the fall, Lauren typed.

Thanks! Stay ready. More to come, Jade replied.

Lauren continued to fan the flames, and daydreamed about her coming riches.

102

THE PUSH

CircleBuzzz Headquarters
Austin, Texas

CircleBuzzz was struggling. The SPOT, another Austin-based social media company, had taken over as the go-to site for the cool people of the world to post selfies, complain about the government, and prove to everyone they were happy, wealthy, and wise.

CircleBuzzz desperately needed a way to reclaim eyeballs and ad dollars.

As one of the few "curation managers" left at the dying company, Dylan's directive was clear. Whatever trended on the SPOT trended harder, faster, and better on CircleBuzzz.

If he had to manipulate the algorithm to do it, fine.

Use fake accounts to sensationalize whatever needed to be boosted? Go for it.

This morning on the SPOT, an ominous warning trended like crazy. The message had appeared on hijacked websites across the country.

You have been lied to.

If only you knew.

The end is near.

Your world is about to burn.

He could work with that.

Dylan opened a spreadsheet designed for days like this. He typed as fast as he could, channeling his inner nutjob as he tabbed through the spreadsheet, filling in the blanks. He would merge the spreadsheet with fake accounts and post hundreds of "Buzzzes" in minutes.

Spelling didn't matter. Neither did logic. In fact, the more bizarre the allegations and comments, the better.

—Gotta be the Russians again
—I did it. It's me. Come get me, you cowards!
—Chumps. Cybersecurity much?
—The nukes are on their way next!!!!!
—Its 2 months ago all over again.
—Bye mom!
—SystemSpike 2.0!
—Guess I don't have to worry about the economy amiright?
—Thanks, President Heringten.
—Your tax dollars at work.
—Has to be a hoax=hollywood movie trailer i bet

When he had enough rows of comments, he clicked a few buttons with his mouse.

The missives were instantly paired with supposedly real people—people he posted on behalf of all day, every day—and launched into cyberspace.

Circlebuzzz might be home to cranks, nutjobs, weirdos, and fake accounts, but at least it was entertaining.

The Source Wire Service
Lower Manhattan, New York

New York University's excellent journalism program had prepared Xavier to be a reporter. He'd interned at a prestigious New York City-based wire service—the supplier of the news—and was lucky or good enough to land a job there after graduating three years earlier.

He never complained about working all hours, which endeared him to management and, he hoped, paved the way for quick advancement.

He lived in one of the coolest—and most expensive—cities in the United States.

And he was in debt up to his eyeballs from student loans, which he'd never be able to pay off at this rate.

Jade Pang to the rescue.

They'd dated—well, he'd taken her out to coffee a few times but had been too timid to make a move—and kept in touch after he graduated. He even liked her boyfriend, some Middle Eastern guy who smiled like a politician and spoke better English than Xavier.

Their offer a month earlier had been enticing: do your job, but make sure a few specific news stories get an extra boost, when and if the time came.

In exchange, they'd get him enough money to pay off the rest of his student loans.

He'd assumed they were joking, but when they sent ten thousand dollars to his online wallet the next day to prove they were serious, he promised to do whatever they needed.

In his tiny office, barely big enough for the desk and chair, Xavier found the small news story Jade had texted him to look out for.

Hackers had defaced hundreds, maybe thousands of business and personal websites with an ominous message.

It would be a popular story anyway, but he bumped it up in the wire service's computer system, putting it in the queue to immediately promote heavily. The system would amplify the story, pushing it to the thousands of outlets across the country that relied on his company's service for news stories.

The process had taken seconds of his time. While it wasn't technically his job to find and push stories, a little nudge here and there would easily go unnoticed—especially if the news was, in fact, newsworthy.

Xavier didn't want to know why Jade wanted the news promoted. But he had ten thousand reasons to do it.

Within thirty minutes, news of the mysterious online warning would pop up on most major and minor news websites around the country.

In an hour, competing news services would have their own reporters on the story.

And next week, Xavier would be free of the crushing student loans, if Jade kept her promise.

103

THE HIT

Conference Room 3
Central Analysis Group Headquarters
Arlington, Virginia

Marcus didn't bother straightening his bow tie or rolling down the sleeves on his dress shirt. His suit coat hung on the back of the desk chair in his cubicle, but at least his vest brought the air of professionalism he preferred at the office.

He burst into conference room three, thankful the door wasn't locked. It meant that while Gregory, Nancy, Dave, and Haley needed the space for the operation they were working on, it wasn't so secret that they needed to secure the door.

"We have a problem," Marcus said, interrupting the conversation the team was having. "I assume you're on something unrelated but thought you needed to see this," he said to Gregory, but included everyone.

"We're being hit again—not physically, not yet, but there's an online threat." He held up his laptop, moved to the conference table in the middle of the room, and attached an HDMI cable to the computer. He turned on the big screen monitor attached to the wall and his screen came up. It showed screenshots of dozens of websites, all of whose front pages had been hijacked to display an ominous but vague warning.

You have been lied to.

If only you knew.
The end is near.
Your world is about to burn.

"This is all over the internet, but in the United States only," Marcus said. "It's posted on blogs. Small business sites. Some large companies, as well. No infrastructure attacks so far. Just this. Someone must have found and exploited a vulnerability in the most popular website building tool and exploited it."

"Assessment?" Gregory asked.

"It's just this so far, but I don't know what it is. A warning? A threat? A hoax?"

"Please tell me it's a PR campaign for a movie," Gregory said.

"It doesn't seem like that," Marcus said. He clicked his mouse and brought up two social media site feeds, side by side on the big screen. Words and posts scrolled by, nearly every one expressing outrage over the internet being "taken over" by an online threat.

"It's trending hard on social media platforms," Marcus said, clicking from one social media site to another. "Everyone's talking about it. It'll be on the news wires next, and all over after that."

Haley, Nancy, and Dave had dropped what they were doing and were typing away. "Nothing else appears to be happening," Haley said. "No cars going haywire like two months ago."

"The railways and air system seem to be safe so far," Nancy added.

"Okay, I'm sure I'll be getting a call from the White House shortly, or we'll have an emergency meeting," Gregory said. "Marcus, you're in here with them. You stay on this new threat. Nancy, Haley, Dave, focus on the ongoing mission in New York. Switch to this as you have time, especially if more happens. I'll be back when I can."

Gregory stood up and left while Nancy cleared a pile of yellow pads, pens, and coffee cups off the conference table near her computer, making a workspace for Marcus. "Have a seat," she said. "How can we help?"

"What are you in the middle of?" Marcus asked, uncomfortable with the idea of directing the group of top analysts.

"Tracking a possible terrorist ring based in New York that might be trying to crash the stock market," Dave said.

"Oh. Um, maybe we should stick with that?" Marcus said.

"Good call," Dave muttered.

"Unless…" Marcus said, trailing off.

A moment later, the others reached the same conclusion he had. "Yes, this website hijack is similar to the SystemSpike, isn't it?" Nancy asked.

"Though it's not as big or effective, probably because cybersecurity is so much tighter than it was two months ago," Dave added. "And there was no warning last time. They just hit us. Maybe this is the best they can do?"

"If the people we're looking at in New York City want to crash the stock market, a vague warning of impending doom might be their first strike," Haley said.

"Let's reach out to Axe," Nancy said. "See if any of the suspects are at computers."

"They wouldn't have to be," Marcus said. "In fact, whatever hack they used was probably set up overnight or early this morning, scheduled to go live at a specific time."

"How hard will it be to fix?" Nancy asked.

"For the average blogger or business owner? Impossible. But for the company that maintains the software? Not hard, once they track down the issue."

"So, nothing to worry about?" Dave asked.

"It really depends on whether this is the only exploit they found…" Marcus said.

"And if they have something else—worse—planned," Haley finished. "They could have another hack or a physical attack as a second wave to disrupt the stock market. Are there people or groups on your radar that might be connected in any way?"

"The only specific threat I'm working at the moment," Marcus said, "is a group in New Jersey. It's a team of six to ten men that has been cleaning up on the competitive paintball circuit."

"There's a competitive paintball circuit?" Dave asked.

"Yes," Marcus said. "This team has reportedly started training with real weapons at gun ranges throughout New Jersey. A few people have anonymously reported them as 'radicalized'—their words. They thought maybe the team was training to rob banks, but now I'm thinking, what if it's bigger than that?"

"A terrorist attack," Haley said.

"Right. That's how we think, isn't it? But I've checked into them. So far, they seem like young men who are prepping for the great upheaval that will probably never come. Super smart guys who are a bit clueless in the ways of the world. You know the type."

"Could they be a part of this?" Nancy asked, gesturing at the four lines of threat still up on the large computer monitor.

"No, I don't see how. This doesn't feel like their style."

"Fine," Haley said. "Push them to the back burner. Let's keep our focus on assisting Axe with the university students while also diving into how this hack could have happened—and what it means."

Marcus joined them at the table, ready to do whatever he could to protect the country.

104

THE CREW

Harborlink Supply & Logistics
Newark, New Jersey

Evan unwrapped his ham and cheese sandwich and waited for the rest of the guys in the company breakroom. He had finally found a crew. Friends. Actual people who wanted to hang out with him. He'd always been more of an outsider, but within a few weeks at Harborlink, one of the other guys approached him to be part of their paintball team.

It had grown from there.

They trained together, improved, and were soon serious contenders on the paintball circuit's eastern league.

The transition to real guns at the local shooting range had seemed natural.

And he certainly couldn't argue with their beliefs, though they were kind of all over the place. But the world was screwed up, and their company was part of the problem. None of them could do anything about it without losing their jobs, but if they had the chance, the Port Elizabeth Shipping Terminal down the street would be a great place to knock out. It would draw attention to the environmental impact of global shipping.

It would never come to that. Clay, the leader of the group, was a dreamer. Evan was happy to go along for the ride, but there was no way he'd go to jail for a cause that no one besides them cared about.

Americans wanted cheap stuff, no matter where it came from.

Messing with the terminal wouldn't change anyone's mind about saving money.

Clay entered the room, his excitement obvious.

"Good, you're alone," Clay whispered as he sat at the table. He was more energized than after they'd won their last championship paintball match. He glanced over his shoulder, then leaned forward. "It's on! We're finally doing it. We're going to wake people in this country up. It will be sometime in the next few days."

He sat back with a huge grin on his face. "We have a video conference tonight to go over the details. It's with my…" He hesitated. "A friend who's helping us. Publicity, like, to get the word out once we, you know…"

Evan forced himself to take a bite of the sandwich. It gave him a few seconds to think. They were really going to break into the terminal and sabotage it? He gulped down the food, the whole-wheat bread dry in his throat. He should have put on more mayo, but the jar had been empty.

"It's really happening?" he finally asked. "The…" His eyes flicked to the open doorway, and he stopped before he said it. Someone could be right outside in the hall, about to walk in.

"Yes. Wear your mask, just to be safe. These apps are supposed to be secure, but you never know." They all had stupid facemasks they were supposed to wear for the assault on the terminal. Clay got to be the devil, which was a lot cooler than the lion mask Clay had given him.

Evan nodded and took another bite, smaller this time, desperately trying to think of a way out.

"Wait," he said around the sandwich. "Tonight? And the next few days? I've been…" He could feel his face turning red, and it would almost be worth going to jail not to admit what he was about to say. It was a close call, but he'd rather be embarrassed than arrested. "There's this girl at the coffee shop by my apartment," he said, eyes on his food so he wouldn't have to endure Clay's look of amusement. "I've been stopping by every night on the way home. Hanging out there, you know? And I'm going to ask her out for whenever she's available. So I might not have time."

Evan risked a glance up, but Clay was nodding, not making fun of him. "I get it. Just be on the call tonight, ok? It'll be worth it, I promise. We don't even know when this will happen. If you can't do the mission, it's fine. That's why we have alternates on the team, right?"

Evan smiled, relieved. Maybe his lie to Clay would give him the courage to actually ask the barista out. He might have to. There was no way he'd go on the so-called assault with real guns, mask or no mask.

"Check your comms app for the details," Clay said as he got up and moved to the door. "Seriously. Be there tonight, and the rest will fall into place. I promise."

He left, leaving Evan with the rest of his dry sandwich and a burning desire to get in his car, drive to his parent's house in upstate New York, and call in sick for a week until this all blew over.

Evan took another bite, not sure he had the guts to turn his back on the only guys who'd ever welcomed him into a pack.

Clay locked the door of the last stall in the men's room, pulled a length of toilet paper and placed it across the black plastic seat, and repeated it for the other side before sitting down, khakis still on. No need to transfer germs from the seat to his pants before laundry day.

Jade's rule was simple: she reached out, not the other way around. She admitted from time to time that she was still hooked on him. The only way she could finish her studies, graduate, and start her big-money Wall Street job was if she controlled the timing and frequency of their communication.

But she had to know about Evan right away.

Sorry to bother you, but we may have a problem, and I wanted you to know about it. One of my crew has cold feet. What should I do?

He didn't have to wait long for Jade's reply.

Will he be on the call tonight?

Yes, I think I convinced him. The call was Jade's test of his crew's loyalty, and his chance to convince her of their readiness and commitment.

Perfect. I'll be able to see for myself. Just in case, what's his address?

Clay barely hesitated. Jade had a plan, and he would follow her to the ends of the earth. If Evan had to be dropped in on and given a warning, so be it. He texted her the address and apartment number.

Don't worry about it, my love, Jade wrote, making Clay's heart pound. It's what she used to call him when they were together. *I'll take it from here. xoxoxo*

XOXOXO he replied, and waited, but there was nothing more.

He stood, nudged the toilet paper into the bowl, and went back to his desk, wondering how he'd keep his mind on work with all that was happening… and Jade only a few days away from his arms.

105

THE ORDERS

Second Bureau Secure Meeting Room
The Ministry of State Security
Beijing, China

The sixty-two-year-old bureau chief sat at the head of the wooden table, ready for the urgent report. He was a stoic man, with a decent suit for a bureaucrat, though nothing like a higher-level party member would wear. His was off the rack, though he'd had it let out to accommodate his expanding stomach. His wife was an excellent cook. "This is the young woman you told me about a few years ago, yes?" he asked his second in command, the deputy bureau chief.

He didn't appreciate being called back to the office for the emergency late-night meeting, but such was his life.

He served his country well.

"Yes, sir," the deputy said. He had missed a button on his shirt, making him look off-balance, yet he seemed alert and well informed. "We have high hopes for her." He passed the bureau chief a picture of the woman, taken upon entry into the training program. She was beautiful, with long black hair, dimples, and sensuous lips.

"She is extremely intelligent," the deputy continued. "Determined. And she possesses a quality that emerged fully during her training. Many men find her alluring to the point of irresistibility." He cleared his throat.

"We had to reassign one of her instructors. She seduced him for a pass to travel home to see her family in rural Sichuan province. A second instructor would have also succumbed if it hadn't been part of a pre-planned test of her abilities."

"Interesting." The chief gazed at the woman's dark eyes in the picture. "Continue. What is this about?"

"She is at a prominent university in New York City. Her handler, a well-respected man who is a former field agent himself, sent an emergency report. He claims that she may have gone rogue and is running an operation of her own design. As yet, we don't have more details, except that one of our other deep cover assets at the same university reported her for coercion. He claims she obtained a weapon from him and used it to kill a man this morning—New York time."

"Hmm. The handler—and your—recommendations?"

"Stop her, to start. If she is conducting unauthorized missions, that's clearly dangerous. How we stop her is really the only question in my mind," the deputy said, and waited for his thoughts.

"If she has been busy on her own projects, it would be better if she's captured alive," he said. "We need to know what she has been doing. Then reeducate her if she is worth saving."

The deputy nodded, but added, "We can order her to return to Beijing, but if she has gone rogue, she will refuse. It would warn her and give her an opportunity to flee. If we lose her..." He trailed off, leaving it to the bureau chief to picture one of their trained agents at loose in the world.

"Send a team to confront her directly. If she refuses or tries to delay, they are to subdue her and bring her home. Failing that, after an extensive effort, they are to eliminate her and dispose of the body. Understood?"

"It will be done, sir. I will activate the on-call covert team in New York immediately and update you as soon as I have more."

"Good. I will stay here in case I'm needed."

It meant a sleepless night, but the building's cafeteria had an excellent congee he would enjoy for breakfast.

106

THE BULL

Charging Bull Sculpture
Bowling Green Park
Lower Manhattan, New York

Ji Tao—code named Crane—plastered a look of interest on his face as he followed the rest of the tour group, fourteen other Chinese men and women in their late thirties. The huge statue of a bull charging north toward Wall Street held no interest for him, but the small triangular park in the Financial District was one of his team's potential rallying sites, so he studied the area with an eye focused on ingress, egress, and concealment.

His three-man team of former People's Liberation Army Special Operations Forces operatives spread out around him, also playing the role of curious tourists.

Short, wiry Peng—Sparrow—was their photographer, capturing high-resolution pictures of not only the featured sights in the six-day tour of New York, but of buildings, subway entrances, vantage points, bridges, and whatever else caught his eye that could be useful in the event they were called upon to execute a mission.

Bin—Owl—was their nerdy comms expert, tech support, and liaison with command. He carried two cell phones and a high-tech satellite phone in the small backpack that was his constant companion.

Stocky, bald Feng—Vulture—was the strongest of them, ready to be first in the fight.

Crane, the team's leader and tactician, was two years older, a few inches taller than the others, and had the responsibility to make crucial decisions. If called upon for a mission, they would have to operate mostly on their own; they were the men on the ground, after all, and were expected to make crucial decisions without moment-by-moment oversight from command thousands of miles away.

"Do you want a picture touching the bull for good luck?" Sparrow joked, nodding at the rear underside of the bull where thousands of hands had rubbed the area to a bright shine.

Several of the tour group snickered, though a few cheeky younger women in the group did exactly that, crouching and reaching forward to rub the bull, smiling, pointing, or laughing for the pictures.

"No, I'm fine, thank you," Crane said with a chuckle. He wondered how many of his fellow covert operators had had this same conversation. Every week of the year, there was a four-man team on tour in New York City, Chicago, Miami, and either Los Angeles or San Francisco. Teams visited other cities as needed. After this six-day tour of New York, Crane and his men would travel to Washington, DC, Miami, and Los Angeles to complete their month-long tour of duty in America.

Next year, they would visit the San Francisco Bay Area, Phoenix, Houston, and Boston.

Crane, Sparrow, Owl, and Vulture were one of several units of China's rapid-response contingency force in the United States, to be deployed at a moment's notice and completely under the radar.

Nerdy Owl took a photo of the bull with his cell phone, then moved closer to Crane as the tour group leader raised her small red flag high to lead them to the Wall Street area.

"We received a message," Owl said under his breath as they walked north, leaving the bull behind to the next gaggle of tourists eager for a picture and financial luck from rubbing somewhere on the bull.

Owl passed the phone to Crane, who read the coded message.

They were on alert for an imminent mission.

"Training?" Owl asked, taking the phone back. He texted as they walked, acknowledging receipt of the notification.

Sparrow, his camera dangling around his neck, fell in next to Crane on his right. Vulture lurched behind him, listening.

"Doubtful," Crane said. They slowed, allowing the rest of the tour group to move ahead, giving themselves space to talk.

"I have never heard of a team actually being called to action," Sparrow said. He sounded pleasantly surprised, not worried.

They spoke often of receiving a mission instead of the constant cycle of training and touring. They were always prepared but never needed.

Now, it seemed, the moment they had dreamed of might have arrived.

"Tighten up," Crane said. "Double check comms," he told Owl. "Consider the threat level raised. Be more vigilant, though we must continue to blend in, so let's keep up," he said, picking up the pace to close on the rest of the tour group. "Review your maps. Mentally recall rally points, arms caches, and safe houses, and know how to reach the nearest one at all times. We must be prepared to act at a moment's notice." His team knew all that, but as a leader, it was Crane's responsibility to communicate clearly and effectively.

If they were called to act, they would succeed. Failure was not an option.

"Weapons?" Vulture said from behind them in his thick, guttural accent of Northeast China.

"Hopefully there will be time to access a storage locker," Crane said. Weapons made everything easier. "But just in case, we will pass a kitchen supply store near Chinatown, where we'll stop for lunch. Sparrow, you will slip away and buy four sturdy American knives. If anyone asks, you have friends back home who are chefs and want to bring them souvenirs. Have them each gift wrapped. You will not be suspected." Part of their pre-trip planning for each city involved knowing the tour routes and where to buy improvised weapons along the way.

"A hammer," Vulture said.

"Yes, of course," Crane said. Vulture preferred bludgeoning to cutting. "There is a small hardware store near the kitchen supply store. Pick up a hammer for our farmer friend," he told Sparrow.

"Gift wrapped?" Sparrow joked.

They chuckled together, eager for the mission they had never thought would come.

107

THE TRAP

Greenwich Village

The back of the van was hot and stuffy in the rising warmth of the day, but Axe channeled his inner sniper.

After lying in the dirt at sniper school, enduring ants crawling into his nostrils and onto his eyeball without moving a muscle so he could successfully take a shot, he could sit on his rear end, watch the street scene around the van through the security cameras, and sweat.

No problem.

"Okay, let's rotate," Axe said over the comms. He had his phone plugged in and charging and had made sure each member of the team used small battery chargers to keep their phones from dying halfway through the day.

Comms were essential.

"Tex, you'll pass me on your way to Yaz's home. Mad Dog, wait until she's nearby before moving to cover Kareem's front door. And Johnboy, you move from the park and Kareem's street over to Darius's once you see Mad Dog. Void—you stay in the coffee shop."

Everyone copied, and Tex added, "You need to stretch your legs, Papa?"

He'd grown to accept, but not like, the additional call sign. He went by Axe so often that it had become more like his real name, which wasn't ideal from an operational security perspective. And Papa fit, though he was far too young to be a father to anyone on the team, and they knew it.

"I'm good," he said, not willing to mention his burning desire to do just that.

A few minutes later, Tex strolled along the sidewalk toward him, a block away, after leaving the coffee shop near Darius's front door. "Tex, I've got you on screen," Axe said. She had picked up a dark-blue baseball cap and ditched the large, floppy-brim sun hat, probably stuffing it into the purse-like backpack she had slung over her shoulder. To his practiced eye, she walked too much like a police officer: bulling her way forward even while trying to blend in as a local, though he was likely being overly critical.

Still, something to note and work on. They could all use pointers and practice on the "spy shit," as he had called it from the start.

Axe tracked her progress, checking the body language and faces of the people on the sidewalk nearby and trailing behind her, the men and women passing by in vehicles, the food delivery workers on scooters, and—

"Tex, keep walking. Don't do anything different, but everyone wake up. I believe Darius may be half a block behind you. Wait one for confirmation."

Axe used a mini joystick to adjust the roof-mounted camera, hidden under what appeared to be a fan unit. He zoomed in on the young man casually walking along the opposite sidewalk from Tex, hands in his pockets. The guy moved at the speed of a local, and wasn't gawking at every storefront like a tourist. He had a strong jawline, full lips, and the unmistakable small pompadour hairdo.

"Yes, positive ID," Axe said. "That's Darius."

It couldn't be a coincidence.

"Where the hell did he come from?" Mad Dog called. "Could he have slipped out the back of his place?"

"Maybe," Johnboy said, "but why would he?"

"Unless we've been made," Axe muttered. "It's possible he noted Tex out his window and is following her. Or it could be an actual coincidence. It's a small neighborhood. Maybe he's on his way to school or to grab a snack. But let's seize the momentum. Tex, keep coming, right past me."

Tex passed by, followed by Darius, who didn't glance at the van, but he didn't awkwardly ignore it, either.

"It doesn't seem like he's aware of the van," Axe called. "I'm going mobile. Tex, keep walking straight. I'll tuck in behind Darius and follow him following you."

"Copy," Tex replied.

"The rest of you," Axe said, fitting the special protective ballistic baseball cap to his head, slipping from the rear of the van, through the narrow door to the front seats, and stepping out onto the sidewalk. "Belay my last order. Remain on station. Stay sharp and check your sixes," he added, looking behind him to scan the sidewalk, windows, and vehicles carefully. "Let's make sure we're not getting played here."

Axe adopted the pace of a typical New Yorker at midday, not rushing but not dawdling like a tourist, either, and followed the Iranian.

Kareem sat in the back of yet another coffee shop a block away from the van he'd noted earlier as the likely base for the dark-haired warrior and the covert team. By leaning forward, blowing on his steaming cup of coffee, he had a view of the intersection nearest the van.

The dark-haired, curvy woman walked by. She had put her hair up under a baseball cap, but there was no hiding the way she stomped the ground like she was a police officer on patrol.

Darius appeared on the opposite sidewalk not long after, paused for a taxi to turn in front of him, then changed his mind and turned right, north, picking up the pace as he disappeared from view.

"Perfect. That was great," Kareem muttered, his white earbuds sending the words to Darius and the black earbuds he wore. "Keep on exactly like that. I'll let you know if—"

The warrior approached the intersection… and turned north.

"Do not look back, hurry, or falter, but he is behind you. You know the rest. Maintain the same speed. Never look back. Turn east at the next intersection. When you get to Broadway, go down the stairs to the subway on the near side of the street. Go to the northern end of the platform. That's to your left. Don't go right. Carefully climb off the platform and onto the tracks. Avoid the third rail, and head north in the tunnel to the next station, where you climb out and go back to wherever you've been hiding."

"How will I know he's following?" Darius asked.

"You won't know he's behind you, but he will be. He is a professional, and if they wanted to arrest any of us, they would have by now. I'm sure of it."

"Okay." So far, Darius was holding himself together.

Kareem would rather be in the tunnel himself, waiting to ambush the warrior, but someone had to run the operation, and it certainly couldn't be Darius—or Yaz, who was likely in his brownstone either already with a woman or preparing to go find his next conquest.

Kareem would get to Yaz in due time.

First, the warrior. Then, they would assess the situation.

He would see how the covert ops team reacted to the death of their leader.

After that, if necessary, he could clean house and kill Yaz, Darius, the patrons, and finally, Jade.

Then he would get out of this country and return to Egypt for the next chapter of his life—wiser for his time in the United States.

108

THE SUBWAY

Greenwich Village

The last time Axe had followed Darius, about twenty-four hours before, the kid had lost him with a well-executed surveillance detection route.

Darius had been well trained and took security seriously. As they neared Broadway, the same street where Darius had given him the slip the day before, but several small blocks north, Axe was ready.

Today, he'd stick with him, yet still avoid being seen or caught.

Darius might not have been following Tex.

Or he could have tailed her and broken off at the last moment to keep from being identified.

Darius could also have noticed Axe behind him.

The thought made Axe pause.

Axe smoothly grabbed the door to the nearest storefront, opened it, and stepped inside as Darius stopped at the corner of Broadway half a block ahead and glanced around, acting casual but definitely checking the street behind him.

Alert. Just like yesterday.

Darius had never felt more nervous, but he stuffed the fear down.

Kareem wanted him to lead the warrior into an ambush.

But was the man still behind him?

Darius desperately wanted to hurry to the safe house in Soho instead.

He didn't fully trust Kareem.

But he also didn't trust Jade right now.

This whole situation could be an elaborate ploy to lure not the warrior, but himself into the tunnel for Jade's assassin to eliminate.

Kareem and Jade could be working together to clean up loose ends.

He'd considered it himself.

Darius completed the casual check of the street behind him. He hadn't seen the warrior, but a shop door had swung closed as he had turned.

A well-trained man could have noted Darius's change in speed and guessed he was about to check to see if he was being followed.

The thought reassured him.

Darius took the stairs down to the subway, moving at three-quarter speed to give the warrior time to see where he went.

Axe waited at the door, ignoring the stare of the shopkeeper behind the counter. After several seconds, Axe peeked through the glass door and caught Darius's head of perfectly styled dark hair as the young man descended the stairs to the subway.

"Darius is going down the subway stairs at Broadway," Axe muttered on comms as he hurried out the door and jogged along the street, ready to dart to his left and hide behind one of the parked cars if the sneaky kid appeared on the stairs again as another check to see if he was being followed. "I assume he's taking the subway, but I'll let you know."

"If you want backup," Mad Dog said, "you have to tell us now. Once a train comes, he's in the wind unless you're there with him. And we'll be too far away to assist."

"Could be a ploy to lure the rest of us away from our stations," Johnboy pointed out. "Worst-case scenario, they know about us and are using Darius as a decoy for the rest of them to escape to secondary locations."

Axe was seconds away from the subway entrance.

"Or this could be the start of another group meeting," Axe said. "Stay on your people. Follow carefully if they move. I might be off comms in a minute, depending on the signal in the tunnels and train cars, so you're on your own. Johnboy, you're in charge."

"Aww man…" Mad Dog muttered, but he was joking, Axe hoped.

"What about me?" Void called as Axe reached the subway entrance and ran down them two at a time. "Can I follow Jade if—"

"No!" Axe said at the same time Johnboy did.

"Heading into the subway," Axe said. "Stay sharp, everybody."

109

THE TUNNEL

Metro Transit Authority 8 St-NYU Station
Greenwich Village

Darius didn't know how fast to walk on the train platform. If he hurried, he might lose the warrior, and the entire plan would be ruined.

If he walked too slowly, would it be obvious he was luring the man into a trap?

This was much different than what he'd been trained for. A surveillance detection route was for catching tails, not leading them on.

Darius walked at a normal pace, trying to match his speed from the street.

It's what the warrior would expect.

The platform had a tan tiled floor, with smaller white tiles on the wall. There were many decorative touches of tile mosaic scenes, like a person walking a dog and an artistic depiction of Washington Square Park only a few blocks away.

Thankfully, there was no train at the station or pulling in. A scattering of waiting passengers congregated in the center of the platform, near the turnstiles off the main entrance.

Darius continued north, passing a bunch of metal girders, painted a deep blue, that held up the tunnel's ceiling, before he reached the end of the platform.

The impulse to check behind him was nearly overwhelming, but he held off for the moment.

It would be natural for someone to look around before jumping from the platform onto the train tracks, wouldn't it?

He reached the northern wall of the platform and moved toward the tracks. The tiles changed from smooth to bumpy as he reached the wide yellow strip of studded tiles where it wasn't safe to stand as trains arrived.

Ever so casually, he leaned forward and looked left as if checking to see if a train was stopped in the tunnel.

And then an equally casual glance right.

People looked at their phones, read books, or stared blankly across the tracks. Another passenger faced Darius, shifting impatiently, but they didn't make eye contact. New Yorkers avoided that as much as possible.

The warrior wasn't there.

Darius struggled. Should he wait? Or go?

The impatient passenger sighed, audible even at this distance, and turned away.

Darius acted. He took another step forward, planted his hands on the platform, and eased himself down to the dirt and rocks next to the train tracks.

Without looking back again, he walked at a steady pace north, into the tunnel.

***

Axe nearly missed the move.

The blue pillars that supported the tunnel ceiling were wide enough to hide behind if he was careful about the angle.

With Darius at the far end of the platform, though, it didn't take much effort to stay out of sight.

A fellow passenger waiting for the next train distracted Axe for a second with his impatience.

By the time Axe edged around the pillar, Darius was disappearing into the darkness of the tunnel to the north.

Axe moved left, away from the tracks and out of view if the Iranian looked back, and sprinted toward the end of the platform.

Why would the man enter the tunnel?

Had he seen Axe behind him and was trying to escape?

Was this another elaborate way to shake a tail—real or imagined—like yesterday?

If Axe was too late and the man disappeared from view, it would be easy for Darius to hide behind a pillar between the north and southbound tracks…

And set an ambush.

Lou had been prepared to hide behind one of the many girders that held up the ceiling along the four sets of tracks—local and express both north and southbound. But the tunnel had better safety lighting than he'd expected, and the pillars were narrower than the ones on the platform.

He had chosen a recessed entrance to an access door on the left wall as his place to hide.

The two nearby emergency lights did little to break the tunnel's oppressive darkness, but a trained spy or soldier would have all he needed to see the ambush coming.

Lou had smashed them with his tall, insulated metal water bottle—a common sight in spring and summer in the city, when many people carried them.

For the dim LED light strips along the wall near the ground, Lou had used the bottom of the bottle to break several of the closest ones. He didn't damage enough to arouse suspicion, but plenty to give him the darkness he needed.

After a while of waiting, and three trains passing by inches in front of him, a man hurried by, not a foot away from him, without a clue he was there.

He had expensive clothes, a jaw like an American movie star, and nice hair.

According to Kareem, the man in charge of this hasty mission, the first person past would be Jade's boyfriend.

Lou was tempted to swing the water bottle at the back of his head, knock him out, and drag him into the darkness before returning to eliminate the real threat. He would be doing himself and Beijing a favor by cutting Jade off from her support network, but he held off. Until he had further instructions from the Ministry of State Security, he would play along, even if it meant killing an American operative who was getting too close to Jade and her partners.

He let the boyfriend continue toward the next station.

Lou gripped the top of the heavy water bottle. Unlike a pipe or rock, a blow to the back of the warrior's head with it would be ascribed to a fall or incidental blunt force trauma, especially after Lou pushed him in front of the next speeding train.

The man's team and employers would suspect foul play, but it wouldn't be like shooting or stabbing him.

There would be just enough confusion and uncertainty to buy time.

Long enough for Lou to lure Jade to a meeting and kill her.

Anything to protect his country—and his mission in the United States.

Lou stood in the darkness and waited for the warrior.

110

MOMENTUM

Metro Transit Authority Subway Tunnel
Under Greenwich Village

There was enough illumination from a dim emergency light in the distance for Axe to catch the shadow of Darius as he went around a curve in the train tracks.

The kid was going to great extremes to detect—or shake—a tail.

It wasn't an ambush, after all.

Or, at least, not yet. Darius was out of sight for the moment. He could find a place to hide behind one of the support pillars and wait for Axe to come around the bend.

He moved closer to the wall to get an angle on the tunnel ahead. The darkness closed in here, with few emergency lights working in this area.

The ground rumbled lightly. A train was ahead, far enough away to feel more than hear it.

The impatient man on the platform would be pleased.

Lou was surprised when the warrior passed the opening where he waited.

One moment, Lou had been alone in the tunnel, alert and ready, wondering if something had gone wrong with the plan.

The next, a dark shape slipped by.

Lou had missed his best opportunity because the man moved without a sound.

He would have to be as good as the warrior, if not better, to best him now.

Lou brought up the water bottle and stepped out of the recessed opening, into the tunnel, right behind the warrior.

Axe spun on instinct, acting before conscious thought told him he wasn't alone in the tunnel.

A figure was directly behind him.

Axe shifted into attack mode…

But he was too late.

A blow to his head stunned him.

His eyes lost focus, and he faltered.

Momentum, though, or muscle memory from fifteen years of combat, training, and sparring, propelled him forward.

A second blow glanced off his shoulder. It would hurt later, but for now, Axe felt—and immediately worked to shove down—the agony of his skull.

He took the tango to the ground, both of them grunting with the impact as they landed between the train tracks.

The man beneath him was thinner and not as muscular, but very strong.

And fast.

He rolled away, taking Axe along with him.

Axe's shoulder slammed into the second rail. The man let go and stood.

Axe had to get up, but his head hurt so badly.

And there was something important he was missing.

The ground rumbling clued him in.

There was still a train coming.

Lou was shocked at how quickly the man reacted.

The first blow should have knocked him out—and possibly killed him.

But the warrior had somehow shifted at the last instant, causing Lou's blow to miss the sweet spot he had aimed for.

The second blow had missed the man's head completely.

Now Lou was in a hand-to-hand fight in the darkness of the subway tunnel. He had lost the advantage, but he couldn't give up now.

He was younger, faster, and on his feet. The warrior was stunned and on his hands and knees.

Lou would win.

First, a kick to the head.

If that didn't end the man, Lou could shove him into the path of the oncoming train.

Either way, the warrior would be dead in a few seconds.

There was no doubt.

Axe made it up to one knee before the man, looming over him, kicked him. Axe pulled away in time to make it merely a glancing blow.

Axe tumbled backward and caught himself on a long board running several inches above the ground next to the train rail.

Just below Axe's palm, something hummed and radiated heat.

His body knew the danger before his mind made the connection.

Axe pushed away from the third rail—a live bar beside the tracks that carries six hundred volts of electricity to power the trains.

He landed on the ground as the figure in the darkness lashed out with another kick.

Axe caught the man's leg and pushed to the side—an improvised judo move to push his opponent toward the third rail.

Lou lost his balance when his kick failed to connect with the warrior.

The man pushed his leg, and Lou couldn't stop the forward momentum.

In the dim train tunnel, he could barely make out the low bar covered by wood—the third rail.

There was nothing he could do to avoid it.

Axe released the man's leg at the last second.

Sparks flew as the tango's foot made contact with the exposed end ramp of the bar. With his other foot on the running rail, six hundred volts ripped through the tango.

His agonized cry stopped abruptly as the man dropped, convulsing.

A moment later, he lay still.

Not breathing.

He was dead.

Axe sat inches away from the attacker. Ozone and the scent of burned flesh filled the air.

For a moment, he saw double. He blinked it away.

His head throbbed.

He felt like throwing up.

And he was thinking slowly.

But at least it was easier to see in the tunnel than it had been.

It was relatively bright, and getting brighter.

The noise helped his mind make the connection.

The subway train was coming around the bend.

111

THE TRAIN

Metro Transit Authority Subway Tunnel
Under Greenwich Village

Axe staggered to his feet and carefully stepped over the third rail.

He double checked the tango in the rapidly brightening tunnel.

The man's foot was close to but no longer touching the third rail.

Leaning forward made Axe nearly vomit and want to pass out, but he held himself together, grabbed the tango's ankle, and yanked backward.

The man moved, but not far enough.

The train neared. The light and sound filled the tunnel, rattling Axe's skull.

With another heave, Axe got the man's body out of the path of the train.

A few seconds later, the subway train passed by.

No emergency brakes.

No sudden stop because of something the conductor had seen on the tracks.

Axe had bought some time.

The authorities would eventually find the tango, either because subway workers discovered it while doing maintenance, an alert passenger looking out the window noticed the body, the smell of decomposition carried to one of the nearby stations, or the huge increase in the rat population made someone wonder.

And depending on the communications protocol of whoever had set up the ambush, it would be minutes, or, if Axe was lucky, hours until the ambusher was missed.

Who had planned the ambush?

It had to be Jade Pang and her crew of young students.

Try to kill me once, shame on you. Try to kill me twice, shame on me.

He wouldn't give her a third chance.

Axe used his tiny everyday-carry flashlight to examine the tango's body.

He was a kid in his early twenties. Short, fine, dark hair. Asian heritage, possibly Chinese. Nerdy black glasses. Black jeans, black T-shirt, perfect for blending into the darkness. No surprise Axe hadn't seen him along the wall or in a recessed doorway, but Axe should have sensed him sooner.

The kid had been very talented. Still and silent.

The attacker had no wallet in his pocket, though he had a cell phone. Axe pocketed it. Maybe the techs at the Central Analysis Group could work their magic and pull data from it.

The tango had hit him over the head with something heavy, but it was lost somewhere in the tunnel's darkness. Axe wouldn't take the time to find it.

He shone his flashlight on the man's face and snapped a picture with his phone. Nancy or Dave would figure out who he was.

Another train, northbound this time, rumbled up the tracks. Axe hid behind a pillar, taking no chances. The rumble and noise bothered him less than the previous train. He didn't feel like vomiting, and he hadn't had double vision since the first train had almost run him down.

After the second train passed, Axe removed the ball cap and felt the protective inside liner.

The foam was crushed flat. The cap had done its job, taking the brunt of the impact from the deadly strike. He had survived because of a hat.

Only time, and a doctor's examination, would tell if the blow had done permanent damage.

For now, he had to stifle the remaining pain and get out of the subway.

He had a mission to finish.

112

THE COAT CLOSET

Century Apartments
Elizabeth, New Jersey

By the time Jade reached her next destination, the thrill of the morning's shooting had long worn off.

A can of iced coffee had helped. She'd stopped at a megastore for supplies after Clay's message.

But it hadn't kept her going long.

She was running on willpower alone.

And she had so much more to do.

Jade pulled into a parking space along the street just up from a large apartment complex.

Using the rearview mirror, she touched up her black lipstick.

No one would remember her facial features—only her goth-punk lips, eyeshadow, hair, and oversized men's clothes.

She couldn't risk leaving the rifle in the bass guitar case inside the vehicle. This neighborhood looked decent, but the upscale SUV would be a prime target if someone saw the case in the back and was desperate enough to smash and grab. But she could use it as a backpack. She loaded the rest of her supplies inside and prepped the lock pick set she'd brought from the safe house.

With the guitar case slung on her shoulder, Jade strolled down the sidewalk toward the apartment complex, careful to disguise her exhaustion.

Cars passed, but there were no other pedestrians. At this time of day, people were still hard at work. The residents of these modestly upscale apartments were likely lower-end white-collar workers in Manhattan or, like her potential target, logistics and other experts working at or servicing the shipping terminal a few miles away.

The lock on the side door was child's play. She had it open in seconds, and she kept her face toward the ground, avoiding the security camera mounted high on the wall in the entryway.

Jade took the stairs to the third floor, head still down, acting tired now to justify her slumped posture. If all went well, no one would think to look at the security cameras, but it made sense to be careful.

The apartment door lock was no more of a deterrent than the main door had been.

A bachelor lived in the apartment, but he wasn't a slob. A pizza box sat on the countertop next to the trash can; at least it wasn't on the coffee table in the small living room.

Against the far wall, where a large TV would normally be, Evan had a desk with a laptop computer, large external monitor, and faux-leather gaming chair.

Jade checked the bedroom to make sure Clay's wayward teammate hadn't come home early. The room had a pleasant, manly scent. She debated taking a nap on the queen-sized bed. It had been made that morning with the comforter pulled up to cover the pillows and looked incredibly inviting.

She could set her alarm and be up in time to hide before Evan came home for the scheduled video conference.

Best not to risk it. She returned to the main room. Right off the kitchen, by the front door, a coat closet was mostly empty. It held only a small upright vacuum, a mop that looked barely used, and a few jackets, including an old-fashioned, thrift store trench coat.

The bass case fit fine in the corner next to the mop. As she settled in next to it, she took out the hammer from her Soho apartment. It had a nice heft in her hand. And as pleasant as it had been to use it to pound nails into the walls to decorate, it would feel even better for a different, more satisfying project.

She next slipped the silicone dragon mask from the case and pulled it on. The cutouts for the nose and small hole for the mouth made it harder to breathe, but slipping it on once Evan was home might make too much noise.

As tired as she was, she'd sleep fine despite the mask. She could rest for a while.

With her back against the wall on the right, she was confident the main door closing would wake her, but she set an alarm on her phone—buzz only—for one minute after the start of the video call, just in case. It would be embarrassing to sleep through her next scheduled killing.

Jade leaned her body and head into the corner of the closet, closed her eyes, and slept.

113

BLAKE'S BLOG

The Blake Blog World Headquarters
Arlington, Virginia

Blogging about politics was supposed to be Blake Clinaire's path to greatness.

He had planned to go from college to the big time in less than a year.

That hadn't happened.

This afternoon, he sat at the world headquarters of the blog—a corner of his studio apartment—and proofread his latest post.

It was juicy, but not enough.

Something better would come along soon. It always did, now that he'd abandoned his ethics.

The plan had been to break stories that the larger papers couldn't, or wouldn't, cover. Blake would do hard-hitting investigative reporting. Nonpartisan. He'd have a reputation for honesty and integrity.

None of his carefully researched and well-written content went viral.

No one cared.

Advertisers stayed away in droves.

The seed money he'd cobbled together from family and friends dwindled, vanished, and was replaced with mounting credit card debt.

Blake Blog On the Verge of Closing had been the headline of his post, a desperate plea for help.

Jade Pang, a friend he'd met in college, had read the news. She reached out to suggest he switch to covering scandals.

Gossip. Dirt. Sleeze.

Which lobbyists were sleeping with politicians to gain influence.

Which junior congressmen with wives and families back home spent time at all-night "networking" parties.

Jade had an off-the-record source for him.

The next day he published "An unconfirmed rumor going around the district."

His website traffic spiked so much that his internet hosting company crashed.

After that, people reached out to him. Surely some, maybe most, were planting stories to settle scores.

But it paid.

Advertisers swarmed. Not the high-end, ethical companies he had originally dreamed of, but still. Their money spent as well as anyone else's.

This morning, a message from Jade had promised something big. She was putting it together for him.

His cell phone buzzed with a call on the secure communication app. He listed his contact information at the top of every blog post, and this had become the primary way he heard from sources.

He hit the speakerphone option. "Blake Clinaire." He clawed for a pencil and grabbed a partly used legal pad.

"Who am I speaking with?" Blake asked. Few people told him the truth, but it was a way to start. How they answered said a lot.

"I work at the SEC—the Securities and Exchange Commission," a man said. He sounded a little older than Blake, so late-twenties, maybe early-thirties. "This is deep background. That's the only way I'll talk. Agreed?"

Other reporters might not touch such conversations, but they were Blake's bread and butter. Since he didn't work for a big newspaper or mainstream media, he could print whatever he thought he could get away with. As long as he didn't think he'd get sued, it went onto the blog. He would couch the reporting with terms like, "An unconfirmed source claims that…"

Readers loved it.

"I've got it," Blake said. "No problem. What do you have for me?" He flipped to a fresh page on the yellow pad.

"This morning, a man was shot on his way to work. Twice, by a high-power weapon, in Silver Spring, Maryland." The caller hesitated, as if torn by what he was about to say or overcome with emotion.

"It's okay. Tell me the rest."

"No," the man said, the one word conveying that he'd gone into full panic mode. "Sorry, I can't do this."

"Wait!" Blade practically yelled into the phone, then held his breath, listening intently.

The caller was still there, breathing heavily, maybe crying.

"I'm not recording this," Blake said, using his most reassuring reporter voice. "No one can trace the call. I don't even need your name. Just tell me what you know. I'll take it from there. You'll never be identified."

After a deep, rattling breath that held back a sob, the caller spoke again. "The man shot was a Securities and Exchange Commission staffer. I knew him well. That's all I'll say. But he confided in me. He found some stuff…"

"What stuff?" Blake said, writing **SEC** in big letters at the top of the yellow pad.

"Listen, this is big, right? So, just… be careful. He discovered that several publicly traded companies have been cooking the books. Not illegal, but very unethical. They've been using a loophole and weren't being entirely honest in their filings. The gist of it is that there are companies that are hiding big losses from the public. Think Enron, that big energy firm in Texas that eventually declared bankruptcy. Today, my friend was going to present his report to the higher-ups, along with recommendations to close the loophole."

Blake scribbled frantically. "Okay, I got it. You're doing the right thing coming forward. This type of thing shouldn't be swept under the rug."

"Yes. Someone killed my friend to keep this quiet."

That seemed like a stretch. More than likely, the guy's friend had gotten robbed, or the shooting had been a gang initiation. Nothing to do with his job.

But it didn't matter. Publicly traded companies with shady accounting? A dead SEC guy? To Blake, this was pure gold. His conspiracy theory readers, especially, would love it.

"I can publish what you've given me, but what would help is… Did your friend write a report to give to his bosses? A slideshow presentation? Or did he have notes? A picture of the pages with your phone would be enough."

There was a long pause, though the man hadn't disconnected. "He was worried, you know?" the caller said, on the verge of tears. "He thought the higher-ups might do what you said and sweep it under the rug. But neither of us thought anyone would kill him over it."

Blake held his breath. If he pushed, he'd lose the guy.

"I…" A long pause. "He gave me a copy of his report last night." The quality of the call switched—he was on speakerphone. "I can't believe I'm doing this, but it's for Stevie. I think this is what he'd want."

Blake's app buzzed. When he opened the file the caller had sent, it looked legit. The author was Steven Marshell at the Securities and Exchange Commission.

Blake skimmed the introduction and smothered a gasp. The top two paragraphs summed up the report and listed names of companies that Blake easily recognized.

"I got it," he said. "I can work with this. You won't be named or referenced. I'll cite sources granted anonymity due to the sensitive nature of the information. And I don't know your name, or any details about you, so you're good. And, if anyone blames you, deny, deny, deny. When I publish this, they might pull people into meetings and claim they have proof it was you who talked to me or passed along the report. It's a common tactic. Act confused, angry, hurt, whatever you'd really feel if you were innocent. They won't have anything—it'll be a bluff. Got it?"

"You think that's going to happen?" The guy was back in full panic mode.

"Maybe, maybe not. It's what I tell all my sources, though. Hang tough. No one can connect us or knows that you've reached out. I'll make sure this sees the light of day. Stevie would be proud."

"Thank you for your help," the caller said, choking back another sob.

"No, thank you," Blake said, entirely serious. This was the story of a lifetime.

Finally, the guy ended the call.

Blake looked at his scribbled notes, made a few more, then flipped to a new page. With the phone leaning against his laptop, he read the full SEC report.

The headline for the story came to him easily: ***Murder, Mayhem, and Scandal on the Stock Market.***

He would publish tomorrow morning right before the markets opened.

But tonight he'd call his father and get him to sell certain stocks.

No reason Dad had to lose money when this story hit.

Greenwich Village
Manhattan

Tate ended the call and dropped the burner phone on the couch next to him. He would zap it in the microwave for a few seconds, stomp on it, and scatter the pieces in trash cans around the city later.

The acting classes had finally paid off.

The thousand dollars for the gig meant he was now a professional actor, even if he couldn't tell anyone about the role.

He wasn't an idiot. Something supremely shady was going on here. Messing with the stock market to make money was his guess. That bogus report he'd sent the reporter? Come on. He couldn't believe the guy fell for it.

Earlier this spring, a cute Asian-American woman had seen him in a school play and approached him about a potential gig this summer.

And all he had to do was act.

One thousand dollars. Not bad for some rehearsal and improv.

No one would trace it back to him.

And the money was already in his account.

He was getting dumplings tonight thanks to… Damn. He'd never gotten the woman's name.

114

THE BISTRO

Greenwich Village
Manhattan, New York

Axe climbed through the small door into the back of the van, welcoming the dark interior and plush seat. His head throbbed and he hurt from being kicked, but he'd live.

"You make it back to the van, Papa? How you doing?" Johnboy asked over the comm line.

Axe had reported the ambush, going light on the details, as soon as he'd snuck out of the Fourteenth Street subway station.

The walk south to the van, plus a bottle of water and a lot of aspirin from a bodega—had helped clear his head.

His ego hurt more than his body. He'd gotten ambushed for the second time in two days.

He had reacted better today, though, moving instinctively before he consciously realized the tango was there. Plus, he'd held his own against a younger, faster opponent, and emerged victorious.

Not bad, all things considered.

"I'm good to go," Axe told the team. "I'll check in with Blondie again. See if she has a line on the EKIA," he added, referencing the enemy killed in action. He'd sent her the dead man's picture once he had cell signal. "Anything happening?"

They would have reported immediately if there was, but it never hurt to get a situation update. It occasionally brought up a concern or detail not worth making a formal report about.

"No movement here," Tex said.

"Nothing here either," Johnboy said.

"As long as you're fine, Papa…" Mad Dog started. "I know it's not quite time for a meal, but maybe there's like a senior special for you. Old people like to eat early. Anyway, what's the budget for food? There's this little Italian bistro nearby, but it's too expensive for my pocketbook. How about Uncle Sam buys us dinner and a nice bottle of wine as a team expenditure? Takeout, I mean, obviously."

"You wouldn't know a rosé from a Riesling," JB said.

"Fine, whatever," Mad Dog came right back. "Chicken parmesan with a light lager, maybe. A lovely vintage of hops."

Axe chuckled to himself, careful not to encourage Mad Dog openly but appreciating the moment of levity.

"I'm hoping Blondie has something for us soon," Axe said. "Dinner might be the least of our concerns. Void? You out there?" Axe asked, calling out to the young hacker.

"Sorry, I didn't know if you meant me, too," came his hasty reply. "I'm here." He was still in a coffee shop down the street from Jade Pang's apartment. "No sign. But it sure is good to be out of the condo."

"Yeah, about that," Axe said. "We're not equipped for twenty-four seven work, so we're going to have to do something different soon. After the ambush in the tunnel, we have a much more solid position to take direct action, but we might have to involve the local police or the feds. I'm hoping to hit Darius's condo, Jade's, or both. Stay in place for now. We'll have new orders shortly."

He had a good feeling. Action produced results. And a dead assassin in the subway tunnel only a few blocks away should give them more to do than sit around on a stakeout all night.

115

THE THEORY

Conference Room 3
Central Analysis Group Headquarters
Arlington, Virginia

All day, Haley had worked with the rest of the team, glued to their laptops, waiting for word from Axe in Manhattan.

They checked every few minutes for another cyberattack to go along with the early morning hack of websites around the country, with its mysterious, ominous warning.

All was quiet.

So the team switched the large TV on the wall to a twenty-four-hour news network, muted the sound so the closed-captions played, and resumed their work on the potential threat from Jade Pang and the young men in New York City.

Haley hunted, right next to Marcus, Nancy, and Dave.

Thanks to the video of the coffee shop from Void's cell phone, Haley soon identified the three friends of Rami bin Raslan—Rami—the young man in the expensive maroon sweater who Mad Dog had seen meeting with Yaz bin Mishari.

None of Rami's friends had criminal records, traffic tickets, disciplinary problems at school, or anything else that would land them on the United States government's radar.

They were above average but not stellar students in their final year of college.

All came from very wealthy families, wore designer clothes, and rarely posted on social media—mostly birthdays and the occasional exceptional test score, or a picture from social gatherings with friends.

From all Haley could see, they were ordinary rich foreign students from Saudi Arabia.

"What do you have for me?" Gregory said from nearby, breaking Haley out of the zone. He pulled up a chair at the conference room table, looking as well put together as always with his longer graying hair and fashionable glasses.

Marcus cleared his throat and looked at Haley for permission. She nodded for him to go ahead.

"First, Axe got ambushed in a New York City subway tunnel!"

"We're leading like that as you said," Haley muttered.

"He's okay, I take it?" Gregory asked.

"Yes," Marcus said. "Axe pushed the guy onto the third rail, electrocuting him."

"Darius was tailing Mariana," Haley said, "or so they thought. He broke off. Axe followed him into the subway. He followed Darius onto the tracks, but the Iranian disappeared in the distance on the way to the next station. Someone jumped out as Axe walked by, hit him on the head, and they fought."

She clicked on her computer and displayed the picture of the dead man from the tunnel. "Chinese heritage. The computer is still searching—"

"Got it," Dave said from his laptop. "Lu Tantai. Business major at New York University. Second-generation American from… San Diego, California. The same as Jade Pang."

"It could be a coincidence," Marcus muttered, but he didn't sound convinced.

"There are no coincidences," Haley said.

"A second attack on Axe proves this is a serious threat," Gregory said. "Was the warning note on the websites this morning part of it, or a separate issue?"

"We're unsure," Marcus said. "Nothing else has happened on that front. There have been no further website hacks and no attacks on the country. It's nothing at all like the SystemSpike two months ago. There was the warning—those four ominous lines—then nothing. The exploit that was used to hijack the websites has been fixed now; most websites are back up and running fine."

As soon as Marcus finished, Haley spoke up. "We have information about the young men Rami bin Raslan—Rami, the field team calls him—met with."

She used the remote control to switch the monitor on the wall to mirror her computer screen. It showed the short dossier she had compiled, with passport photos of the men, and a few pictures from their limited social media postings. "They're average guys. Decent students in their final year. Not a hint of trouble. They graduate soon and will return to Saudi Arabia —or at least, their student visas expire, and they haven't applied to remain in the country. All have well-connected fathers who are very rich. It makes sense that they're friends with Rami. Nothing out of the ordinary there. But…" She nodded to Nancy sitting next to her.

"Axe managed to record their conversation," Nancy said, avoiding Void's contribution to keep his involvement to a minimum. "It's hard to understand because the phone was in Axe's jacket, which was too far away for clean audio, and the coffee shop was noisy. But they mention a new plan, plus one clear statement. This is Rami, their leader, speaking."

She played the file. Rami's voice filled the room, along with the din of a coffee shop in the background. "I will see what I can do, but I urge you to consider the opportunity here. I may—may—be able to simply ensure a return of your original capital out of my own proceeds, but that is not the smart play. We know the future. This is an opportunity of a lifetime."

It was the third time Haley had heard the segment, and it still gave her a chill. "We know these three are part of a 'new plan,'" she said. "They met immediately after Rami spoke with Yaz, so we can logically conclude that Yaz is the source of that new plan, or a participant at the minimum."

Gregory didn't have questions, so Haley continued.

"On Wednesday, thanks to Axe, we know Yaz met with Jade and the other two men Nancy originally identified." Haley clicked her screen and brought up the pictures. "Darius, the Iranian, and Kareem, the Egyptian. We'll stick with first names as they're easier."

Gregory nodded.

"Okay," Haley continued. "After the meeting with Rami, Yaz flirted with a worker at the breakfast place. She posted online several minutes later." Haley played the short video, which they had saved to the CAG server to make it easy to find again.

When it ended, Gregory spoke. "This crew is going to somehow crash the stock market in the next two days? That's what you're thinking?"

Haley looked at Nancy, Dave, and Marcus, who all nodded. "That's our working theory, yes."

"How? Why?" Gregory asked. He was concerned, not argumentative. It looked as though they had convinced him.

"We're still working on both—aside from the obvious: more money," Dave said.

Gregory didn't buy it. "These young men from wealthy Middle Eastern families need money? They wouldn't manipulate the stock market only for that. Why do it?"

The team sat silently. "Fun?" Nancy finally said.

"Because it's there?" Dave added, quoting a famous mountaineer's reason for wanting to climb Mount Everest.

"We don't have enough about their motives and intentions," Gregory said, "but they made a major tactical mistake by ambushing Axe. Before that, they were a bunch of college kids acting suspiciously. Let's discuss options."

116

THE NEXT STEP

Conference Room 3
Central Analysis Group Headquarters
Arlington, Virginia

Gregory had to hand it to his team. They had taken Nancy's original suspicion about the foreign students in New York City and run with it.

With one call to Admiral Nalen, Gregory could have an asset travel to San Diego and investigate the backgrounds of the two university students who were from there. Thomas "Bone" Marks was Nalen's latest recruit, a former SEAL turned schoolteacher who had recently become Nalen and Gregory's covert asset.

But was that necessary?

And was there time?

"What about the other one? Kareem?" Gregory asked, giving himself a moment to think. He wanted his head to catch up with his gut.

"No sign of him," Haley said.

At the beginning of his career, Gregory had been a hotshot, instinct-following intelligence analyst like Haley. His role now, though, was to manage and lead. At times, that meant playing the skeptic, though tonight, the team was clearly onto something.

They had enough to take action—but what was their next move?

"Yaz talks to the coffee shop worker about crashing the stock market,"

Gregory said, talking it out. "Shortly after that, his buddy mentions the opportunity of a lifetime and knowing the future. Could they simply have insider information about upcoming earnings reports from major companies, or economic statistics? A friend who works at a hedge fund with a prediction about the market?"

"They could," Nancy said. "Or they might know about an upcoming event in their country that would shake the world economy. Maybe OPEC is going to reduce oil output or raise prices."

"Saudi Arabia could be planning a move against an enemy," Dave suggested. "A major strike against Iran that might affect our stock market?"

"I'll take our thoughts to the president," Gregory said. "There are a number of plausible scenarios to be concerned about. The students don't seem to be the type to directly strike a site like Wall Street, and they don't have obvious hacker skills. But with their resources, they could easily access hackers for hire to do the dirty work. They could also have advance knowledge of an upcoming major event that will shake our stock market and economy. We need to know more about their motives and intentions," Gregory said. "Luring Axe into an ambush, though, means we can move on them."

The energy in the room surged. His people were ready for the next step.

"We don't know where the suspects are, except for Yaz, who the team thinks is at his brownstone," Dave said. "If they grab one to question—Yaz—the others might hear about it and run."

"Or launch their attack immediately, if that's what's happening," Marcus added.

"We talk to Rami and his friends," Gregory ordered. "Quietly. Leave Jade Pang and the three main students out of it. Get Tex and Mad Dog dressed as New York police officers again. Have them start with Rami bin Raslan. He has the closest contact with Yaz. Ask for his help with information about a crime he may have witnessed, like something at the coffee shop this morning. Tell the team to be polite. Rami and his friends aren't implicated, they've done nothing wrong, etcetera. Interview Rami at his home. After they get him settled with the coffee shop discussion, switch to questions about potential terrorists. Scare the hell out of him. Then pick up the others and take them all to the safe house in Queens if warranted. Keep me informed. I have some calls to make."

Nancy had a question. "What if they want lawyers, or refuse to cooperate?"

Gregory paused. There were rules to be followed—for good reason. "Done right, they won't think of that. They'll be frightened and, aside from being told about a scheme where they could make a lot of money on the stock market, they're innocent. But if pushed, promise everything and take them to the safe house. I'll update the president and get us additional legal cover and guidance. But remember: a calm chat only. No threats, understood?"

The four of them nodded, already turning to their laptops and phones.

"And find Jade Pang," he said as he left the conference room.

117

THE VIDEOCONFERENCE

Century Apartments
Elizabeth, New Jersey

Jade woke from a dream of Turbo the hacker falling toward her, his arms windmilling, his eyes locked on hers, face filled with shock until he hit the ground in front of her with a *splat.*

She froze as she blinked herself awake in the dark, disoriented but sensing that silence was required.

Evan's apartment.

Keys hit the counter on the other side of the closet door. Evan returning home had woken her.

Jade hid in the tiny coat closet near the apartment's entry door.

What were the odds that Evan had worn a jacket on what had been another nice spring day, and that a bachelor would bother to hang it in the coat closet when he got home?

Minutes passed without the closet door opening. Evan went into his bedroom for several minutes, returned, and started cooking dinner.

Jade's latex mask and the small space had grown uncomfortable, but she waited patiently for her cue, casually holding the hammer.

A while after Evan finished his dinner, a man's voice came through high-end speakers from the other side of the door and across the apartment's living room, right on schedule. "Welcome. Are we all here?"

Darius asked. He had the voice of authority that comes with privilege; unearned, but never in doubt or questioned.

No one else would be able to tell, but he sounded nervous.

Maybe something else had gone wrong while she napped.

She'd find out soon, after her performance.

Across the apartment, on the large monitor Evan used instead of a television, there would be ten boxes: video feeds from Evan and the rest of Clay's team of weekend warriors who believed they were going to make a difference in the world.

Darius would be wearing the Grim Reaper mask she'd picked out for him.

Her window would be blank. In New York, at the apartment with Darius, her laptop would be logged in with the camera and microphone off. It would remain dark throughout the meeting—though the gathered audience would see her soon enough.

Jade loved her green 3D latex dragon mask. It had cost a few hundred dollars, but money wasn't an object. The pointed spikes in dark green across the forehead and along the sides, plus the long, white pointed teeth at the mask's mouth, made it look angry and aggressive. Lighter green scales along the nose and the rest of the mask added to the effect. She'd purchased the masks for any disguised video chats she'd have to have with Clay's team, never dreaming she'd wear it for something more than a rallying speech to his troops.

"Um, who are you? And where's..." Clay's voice trailed off, smart enough to not say her name. His jealousy was obvious through the speakers, across the apartment, and through the closet door.

Poor guy. Another sucker.

One more unsuspecting asset she had painstakingly cultivated, just in case—and she needed him now.

Hopefully, what happened next wouldn't push him, or his team, over the edge.

If it did, she'd have more messes to clean up.

"Ah, Devil, Dragon asked me to apologize to you," Darius said. He was playing his role perfectly, deferring to Clay and treating him with respect. "She's nearby and will be along shortly. I'm the Grim Reaper— her assistant. She wanted us to get started without her. Are all your men present?"

Clay hesitated only a second before responding. "Yes, this is all of us. Are you sure we shouldn't wait for her?"

"She'll be onscreen in a moment," Darius said, his tone hinting at a secret soon to be revealed.

The words were the cue she'd been waiting for.

Jade twisted the knob and eased the closet door open, not worried about making noise. Her victim would see the movement of the door in the reflection of his monitor, if he was paying attention.

He was.

The man spun his computer chair to face her and wasted precious seconds staring at her rushing toward him, his blue eyes wide behind the latex lion mask that covered his face.

By the time he grasped what was happening, Jade was already swinging the hammer.

He raised his arms to block the blow, but he was too late.

Lion gasped in pain as the hammer slammed into his skull.

He fell back, stunned.

Jade brought the hammer down.

Again and again.

Eventually, she forced herself to step back. Lion had been slumped in the chair, dead, for the last several blows, but she had been having too much fun to stop.

Jade stifled a giggle. The fierceness of the lion mask contrasted comically with the man's blood and brains.

Lion was no longer king of the jungle.

She wiped the hammer off on Lion's light-gray hoodie, removing the blood and brain matter as best she could, taking her time to do the job properly. There was no hurry—she had the full attention of everyone watching.

When Lion's sweatshirt was a mess of gore and the hammer was mostly clean, she leaned toward the computer, waving at the small camera where the laptop's webcam broadcast the scene to the silent, stunned audience.

"Here I am," she said in a chipper voice, not even out of breath from her exertions. "Sorry I'm joining late."

Jade straightened, put her hands on Lion's shoulders, and slowly spun the chair so his body faced the webcam. His head dropped forward as he turned, revealing the mess at the top, above the mask, where his skull had been less than a minute earlier.

To the audience's credit, only a few of the men gasped, though one gagged, turned his back to the screen, pulled off his mask, and vomited into a pizza box.

Jade tugged on a relatively bloodless hunk of Lion's hair to raise his head until their masked faces were side by side.

"Lion got cold feet and was going to betray us," she announced.

The rest of them didn't need to know that Clay hadn't been completely certain of Evan's lack of commitment.

She let the revelation sink in. Without being able to see anyone's faces —Clay wore a red-and-black devil mask, and there was a scary clown, a dinosaur, a zombie, a green space alien, a werewolf, and one hockey goalie mask—it was difficult to gauge their reactions, but their silence was enough. Each would wonder if they were in danger, and what she would do to them should they falter in their mission.

"Thankfully, I learned about his imminent betrayal, and I have interceded in time," Jade continued. "He shared nothing. We are safe."

She released her grip on Lion's hair. His head flopped forward, and his lifeless body slowly tumbled to the side and fell to the floor.

"Reaper will continue the meeting on my behalf. We're nearly ready to change the world. Devil will lead you. It's a simple operation that you will accomplish easily. Now, please excuse me—I have some tidying up to do."

She clicked the mouse to disconnect from the web conference.

The blood seeping from Lion's skull mesmerized her for a moment, but time was passing, and she had a busy night.

There was work to be done.

The research she had conducted after receiving Clay's warning had been accurate. The apartment had a gas range.

A small candle she'd purchased from the superstore on the way back from Maryland went on Lion's computer desk. She lit it with a disposable lighter, which she left next to the candle.

In the kitchen, it was simple to disconnect the electronic igniter wire from the gas stove.

Jade filled a pot with water, covered it with a lid, put it on the stove, and spun one of the knobs to the highest position. Gas hissed from the burner but didn't ignite.

The gas would quickly fill the small apartment and explode when it reached the candle.

She slipped on the vintage trench coat from the closet. It was too long, but it covered the few blood splatters on her clothes.

The dragon mask and hammer went into the bass guitar case, which she slung over her shoulder as she stepped out the apartment door.

Darius would brief Clay and his men about their assignments and give them a pep talk to further their belief that what they were about to do would improve the country and the planet.

Jade walked back to the SUV, head down, just a goth punk woman on her way to a gig or band practice.

She relived the killing as she went. The *squelch* of the hammer blows on Evan's skull joined the *splat* of Turbo the hacker landing on the sidewalk in Brooklyn three nights before as her new favorite memories.

The *squelch* had been better than the *splat*, probably because it had been more immediate and visceral.

This morning's target, with his shocked expression and spilled coffee on the sidewalk, took a distant third.

Killing thousands in the SystemSpike had been its own rush, but it couldn't compare to what she'd accomplished the last few days.

And the week wasn't over yet.

118

SECOND THOUGHTS

Chilton Street Apartments
Elizabeth, New Jersey

Clay tried to pay attention to his computer screen where the Grim Reaper —Jade's assistant—gave them a pep talk.

But his mind kept returning to the rise and fall of the hammer, the sound, and the blood, and Evan's brain…

"Right, Devil?"

Clay snapped back to the present. He hadn't heard what the Reaper had said, but it had to be safe to agree, so he nodded.

"Okay, great. Devil will have more details for you shortly. Remember: you are the vanguard. You will make an incredible difference. Get inside, sabotage the port—Devil has the details—and get out. No heroics or last stands. Dragon has more plans for the summer. She needs you. You've trained as a team, but it's not about death, just destruction. Let poor Lion's fate be the only sacrifice. But don't let it be in vain."

Clay nodded along with the rest of his crew on the computer screen— down to seven now that Lion was gone and his little videochat square was dark.

"More details and exact timing to follow. Dragon will be in touch with you shortly, Devil," Grim Reaper said. He waved his hand in a kind of salute, then his screen went black.

For a long moment, his team sat in silence. Finally, one of his teammates, wearing the scary clown mask, spoke. "What the hell!"

Clay didn't know how to respond; the words summed up his feelings entirely.

"He could have exposed us all!" Werewolf said, his voice full of anger.

"It's better this way," Alien Mask agreed.

"That. Was. So. Cool," Hockey Mask said. "We saw his brain!"

Clay kept himself still as he suppressed a gag.

The others erupted into conversation about the details of Jade's assault.

I have created monsters, Clay thought.

It was impossible to know whether their words stemmed from fear they might be next or true belief, but it hardly mattered. They sounded enthusiastic.

His work colleagues had started out as upper middle-class guys from New Jersey, just like him. Over the last several months, they had trained together. Talked about the world and the injustice of it all. They had grown into warriors, ready to change the world.

Clay had thought he was ready for this, but after tonight's… He didn't have a word for it. Assault? Bloodbath? Carnage?

He had a sudden realization.

I warned Jade. I'm a co-conspirator to murder.

That was just the start. Soon, maybe tonight, he and the others would break into the shipping terminal to disable equipment.

He and his team were prepared to shoot anyone that stood in their way or prevented them from escaping.

"We have to do everything possible to pull this off—and not wind up in prison," Green Alien said when Clay tuned back into the conversation on screen.

"Or dead," Scary Clown added.

The others nodded and waited for Clay to speak.

He had a vision of Jade coming toward him with her hammer and forced himself to make a speech. "Be ready at a moment's notice. My guess is we go later tonight. Keep your phones on. Cancel plans—come up with good excuses, say you're not feeling well—and be ready. We're going to wake up this country." It didn't come out with its normal forcefulness, but they repeated their mantra anyway.

"We're going to wake up this country!"

Imitating the Grim Reaper, he saluted his troops. It felt right. They were going to war.

They saluted back, and he clicked off the video chat.

Were his beliefs worth the risk?

Was Jade?

Evan's brain matter…

Clay forced himself to think instead of pleasant memories, like Jade's soft skin against his, or her laugh…

But that reminded him of Jade's stifled giggle after she'd hammered Evan to death.

Clay ripped the Devil mask off and ran to the bathroom, praying he made it in time.

119

THE OPTIONS

The West Village
Manhattan

The situation had gone from bad to worse.

Kareem strolled east on Christopher Street in the West Village, carefully making his way back to Greenwich Village.

He had spent the rest of the afternoon north of Fourteenth Street, where the team of covert operatives was unlikely to look for him.

Jade's friend the assassin, Lou, hadn't checked in after the ambush.

Kareem hoped he was dead in the subway tunnel. Otherwise, he was in a room somewhere being interrogated by the authorities, but hopefully keeping his mouth shut.

While waiting anxiously to hear from Lou, Kareem had thought through what could happen if any of them were caught.

Lou was a wild card he could do nothing about.

Jade would never break. She was too strong, too determined.

Darius had diplomatic immunity. Realistically, if not officially. His father, and Iran's Supreme Leader, who he advised, would never allow Darius to be held for long by the Americans.

Darius would keep his mouth shut and wait for his father to save him.

Yaz was the weakest link, along with his financial patrons.

Kareem had two options and hated both.

First, he could run. He had money, a second passport, and multiple escape options.

Second, he could stay and clean house. If he killed everyone involved in the SystemSpike and peace summit scheme, he would be safe.

After that, he could flee the country and there would be no one left to compromise him.

The second option was riskier but felt like the better strategic move.

For the second plan to work, he would start with Yaz. The Saudi prince had to die first.

To do that, Kareem had to see who was watching Yaz's home—and kill them.

Kareem slowed as he turned onto Yaz's street, still several blocks from the brownstone.

Most of the city's residents were outside again tonight, enjoying this week's perfect weather. The sidewalks were busy. With Kareem's expensive black leather jacket, longish hair, and good looks, he blended in easily. He tucked in behind groups of twos or threes, pretending he was with them as he used them for cover.

At each pizzeria and coffee shop along the street, Kareem inched closer while scoping out the tables or counters, looking for the muscular soldier from the park earlier this morning, the dark-haired warrior from the coffee shop, the hairy, barrel-chested man, or the curvy woman.

He took his time. Caution was much more important than speed.

Finally, he saw her. The woman.

There, drinking coffee at the counter near the window, eyes on Yaz's building.

What he had planned was risky, bordering on reckless. But it had to be done.

The knife would be preferable, but the pistol would be quicker and less bloody. Even with the suppressor, though, the weapon would make a distinctive *pop* that people would hear and remember.

Kareem moved back a few feet until he could only see the woman's hand holding the coffee cup. She was turned away from him with eyes only for Yaz's doorstep, but now that he'd found her, he had to maintain his advantage.

At some point, she would have to leave the café and walk past a dark alley, or turn down a street temporarily empty of people. Killing her would only take a moment. Then he'd be free to enter Yaz's apartment building and proceed with the rest of the plan.

All he had to do now was wait.

Or he could be proactive and set a trap, if he trusted Yaz enough to get his help.

Kareem leaned against the wall of the next storefront, one leg kicked back, head down, attention supposedly on his phone while he watched, waited, and weighed his options.

120

THE WEAKEST LINK

Greenwich Village

"Okay, we have new orders," Axe called over the team comms. He'd been on the phone with Haley and Nancy for what seemed like forever, working out a plan plus the usual contingencies.

It was finally time to act.

He moved from the rear of the surveillance van, through the narrow access door, and slid into the driver's seat.

"Our excellent work today has produced enough intel to convince the powers that be of a realistic threat to the United States. We've been given the go-ahead to 'invite' Rami and his three buddies to discuss what they know about the situation, hopefully implicating their buddy Yaz. We approach them nice and gentle, we need their help, all that. The excuse to get in the door will be that they may have witnessed a crime this morning in the coffee shop near Washington Square Park. Tex and Mad Dog, you're up in your police uniforms again. I'll be along as a plainclothes Homeland Security officer."

Axe started the van. "Johnboy, sorry, you're stuck in Greenwich Village. Rotate to cover Yaz—he's the only one we've seen at home today, and probably the weakest link, so let's stick with him. I doubt Darius has the guts to return home after luring me into an ambush.

"Tex, break off and move west. I'll pick you up on Sixth Avenue.

"Mad Dog, we'll grab you three blocks south. You two will change into your NYPD uniforms in the van."

"Copy," Mad Dog said. "Moving now."

"Moving now," Tex answered.

"I'm a few minutes out," JB said. "Do you want Tex to hold until I get there?"

"No," Axe said. "I want to get eyes on Rami and his buddies right away. Yaz is a known commodity. If he happens to leave when we don't have coverage, we can probably find him easy enough." He put the van in gear and pulled into the street during a break in the slow-moving side street traffic.

"Copy that," Johnboy said. "I'm on my way."

"Void," Axe said, "you stay on Jade's apartment. You good there?"

"Perfect, thank you," Void called. He sounded grateful to be remembered this time. "They have ultra high-speed Wi-Fi."

"Great. Stay alert. Report if you see anything unusual."

Axe worked his way through the mid-evening traffic, hoping they were in time to catch Rami, or at least one of the other young men, at their homes.

The short, curvy woman stood in a hurry and drained her coffee cup.

She was on the move.

Kareem had barely enough time to spin away, take a few steps, and walk into a small sushi restaurant.

The woman marched her way along the sidewalk right outside the door like she had an urgent mission.

Kareem watched in the mirror above the restaurant's host stand as she hurried right by him.

He had a bad feeling. Something had changed. The woman had gone from sipping coffee, waiting and watching, to action.

She had abandoned the stakeout of Yaz's home, which meant she and her team had a new target.

It obviously couldn't be him.

Darius had checked in after the attempted ambush and said he had a place he could hide out. He probably had a safe house where he and Jade plotted and planned.

Jade was preparing to crash the stock market tomorrow so they could all make money. Out of all of them, she was the most careful and crafty. It wasn't likely to be her the surveillance team had found.

That left the weakest links, aside from Yaz. Either Kareem's own financial patrons, who he had yet to meet, though he'd sent them a brief explanation of what was coming, along with the specific investment instructions from Jade and Darius. But aside from the early morning message telling them he had to reschedule, followed by the recommendation of how to invest their money for maximum gain, he hadn't been in touch with them.

There was no way for the warrior and his team to know about Kareem's benefactors.

The Americans had watched Yaz's financial backers meet this morning in the coffee shop.

They've been identified and are about to get a visit from the authorities.

Kareem dialed Yaz. There was no time to lose.

"My friend," Yaz answered after one ring. "I'm getting ready to go to a club. Miss Number 493 awaits. Would you care to join me?"

"This is an emergency," Kareem said, his voice low and tense. "Give me the names and addresses of your patrons. Right now. There is no time for explanations. You have to trust me."

Yaz hesitated, and Kareem was ready to stomp across the street, break into the home, and beat the information out of him. Anything to get a jump on the team of American covert operators that were on their way to Yaz's people right now.

"I… I don't know where they live. We always meet at a coffee shop."

Kareem kept control and thought fast.

"You have a group message thread with all three? Or do you only contact one main person and he does the rest?"

"I have all their information, but usually I speak only with Rami. He's—"

"You will do this. Message them all now. It's an emergency. Have them meet you…" Kareem paused, thinking it through. The men might be suspicious. That wouldn't work for what he had in mind. And he couldn't send them far.

"They live near school? Not uptown?"

"No, here, I'm sure. Nearby."

"Fine. Tell them to meet you in front of the Le Petit Chérie on Mulberry Street just south of Houston. Have them take a taxi, not a ride service or their drivers, if they have them. Nothing that can be tracked. And they must hurry—it's an urgent update for getting their money back, and speed is essential. Have them leave wherever they are immediately. Don't tell them anything else. Can you do that?"

"What's going on? Are we in danger?" Yaz was losing it.

"No, no, it's fine," Kareem said, putting on his most soothing tone. "But I heard from Jade. We have to make slight changes to our plan, and there is no time to waste. It has to be tonight or we won't profit as much. Okay? And can you leave as soon as you send the message?"

"Yes, but my driver—"

"No driver. Walk outside, turn right, and go to Broadway. There will be taxis there, and it's a short ride to the restaurant. Hurry!"

Kareem hung up to prevent yet more questions.

Would the hasty plan work?

Or would he have to rent a car and drive to Canada tonight, with a flight back to Egypt in the morning?

121

THE INSTRUCTIONS

Jersey Street near Mulberry Street
Soho

Kareem had stumbled upon Jersey Street in Soho his first year in the city. A muscular tough guy had bumped into him late one night while he was walking home from a study session in a coffee shop.

Kareem had followed the man south through Greenwich Village, across Houston Street, and down Lafayette Street. When the man turned left only a few dozen meters later, Kareem had followed.

He found the man waiting with a knife in the middle of a short, dark alleyway that connected Lafayette and Mulberry—Jersey Street.

The fight didn't last long.

Kareem slit the man's throat with his own knife and left him to die on the sidewalk.

Tonight would be different. The area had gentrified in the past few years, with restaurants opening on nearby streets. It was busier than it had been, but the alley was as dark and foreboding as ever. It was perfect for what he had planned, as long as no one walked by at the wrong moment.

Le Petit Chérie
Mulberry Street
Soho

Yaz waited outside the pretentious-looking French restaurant, feeling naked without his diamond earrings. Maybe he could convince Rami to give them back tonight in exchange for whatever urgent instructions Kareem had.

The high-end restaurant was dimly lit, only half-full, and out of place in this neighborhood, which was much less busy and upscale than Greenwich Village to the north. A few pedestrians walked south farther down the street, but he was the only person on the sidewalk near the restaurant.

The trendy side of Soho was west of Broadway. While this part of the neighborhood had steadily improved over his time in the city, he rarely found himself here. It was merely a poorly lit area of older buildings he passed through in the SUV on the way to Little Italy, a few blocks farther south.

Rami showed up first, dropped off by a taxi—the first car to pass since Yaz arrived a few minutes before. He was dressed for dinner in a dark suit, dark shirt, and no tie.

Yaz's diamonds sparkled on his ears in the dim streetlight.

"Like them?" Rami asked with a grin as he touched one of the earrings. "A little ostentatious for my tastes, but we'll see what the ladies think of them tonight after our meeting. Maybe we can hit the club together?"

Yaz smiled, the picture of politeness, while he raged inside. He hadn't thought Rami this cruel.

"Perhaps," Yaz said, doing his best to sound warm and not like a man coerced into giving up his prized possessions.

"What's this about, anyway?" Rami asked. A taxi stopped, and another Saudi man his age stepped out looking equally sharp in his own dark suit.

"We have further investment recommendations," Yaz said, improvising off what Kareem had told him. "It's simpler to give you the instructions and answer questions this way."

Yaz had his doubts about the situation, but he couldn't let them show. Whatever Kareem had planned, he'd go along with it. The patrons had to be kept happy and made financially whole. A little clandestine meeting to make them feel like they were a big part of the plan, and that it was happening quickly, made complete sense.

Two other young men emerged from a taxi together a minute later.

"We're here," Rami said. "Should we go inside?"

"Let's wait here for my partner," Yaz said, hoping Kareem arrived soon. Yaz didn't like lying to these men and hated to admit he lacked knowledge about what was happening. The money they represented, and the power behind them, didn't rival his family's, but it was substantial enough to want to avoid being embarrassed in front of them. "He has the full details about tomorrow, and we should speak outside where no one can hear us."

Yaz typed a message to Kareem. A reply came immediately. "He's around the corner. It's quieter there. A safer place to give you the information."

Yaz turned south and led the way.

It was only ten meters to a narrow road that connected to Lafayette Street one block west.

Yaz turned the corner and checked behind him. Rami and the other men walked close together, whispering.

"Here," Kareem called from halfway down the short block. The street was little more than a dark alley; one lane wide, with a narrow sidewalk on either side. Kareem waited at a recessed doorway that offered a little privacy.

"Here he is," Yaz said. He slowed, forcing the young men to stop whispering, and they walked the rest of the way together.

* * *

Jersey Street
Soho

Kareem nodded at the men—the financial patrons, who he recognized from school, though he'd only had a passing interaction with the one wearing…

Were those Yaz's earrings? Interesting, but he didn't have time to dwell on it.

Kareem gestured for them to gather on the sidewalk while he moved farther away, onto the street, so he could address them together.

So far, everything was going perfectly.

"The timeline has accelerated," he said before any of them could ask stupid questions. "Tomorrow is the day, and you must take action tonight in preparation. I will give you detailed instructions. Find the voice recorder on your phones. You can make notes later. This will be faster."

All four dutifully reached into their pockets, unlocked their phones, and poked around until they found the voice recorder apps.

"You too, my friend," Kareem told Yaz with a smile. "You'll need this, as well."

The man standing next to the one with Yaz's earrings caught Kareem's eye. "We have not yet committed to this," he said. "We want our money back directly, not to risk it on another scheme."

This was news to Kareem, but it didn't bother him. Nothing any of them said now made a difference. "I understand. It's your choice, of course. But please listen to the new details before you decide."

The man frowned but held his phone up with the others, arms outstretched to better record the important information.

Kareem made a show of looking to the left and right to ensure no one was passing by at either end of the alley.

He held a finger to his lips, then his ear.

They listened together. No footsteps, no quiet laughter, no car engines.

"Good," Kareem said. It was time. "Let me check my notes." He reached toward his back pocket, but instead of his phone, he pulled the small pistol, with its long suppressor attached, from his waistband.

Pop. Pop. Pop. Pop. Pop.

Five shots, right between each man's eyes.

They crumpled straight to the ground.

Kareem checked left and right again.

The streets were empty.

No one had seen.

He risked an extra bullet in each head, just to be sure.

Pop. Pop. Pop. Pop. Pop.

Kareem tucked the pistol into his waistband and picked up the five cell phones, along with the ten shell casings, and checked the cross-streets again.

Still clear, though he heard a car engine from the next block.

Time to go.

As he walked west toward Lafayette Street, he stopped the recorders, then changed the settings on each phone, disabling the security features. He'd be able to wipe the data and factory reset them later, but for now he crammed them into his crossbody bag's Faraday cage that would block all cell phone signals.

He turned the corner and walked south along the quiet Soho street, already plotting his next moves.

His own financial patrons were next, but he had to find Darius and Jade tonight, too.

122

—————

THE BABY

Garden State Storage
Jersey City, New Jersey

Jade dialed the combination lock on the door of her self-storage unit in New Jersey.

It wasn't far from the one she had been to with Lou the previous night.

His larger garage unit would be her next stop.

According to a worried Darius, Lou's ambush had failed. Lou was likely dead, and the warrior was still alive. There was a small chance Lou was in hiding or in custody. It didn't matter. She could break into his storage garage and take all she wanted.

Jade hadn't planned for Lou to die while helping Kareem and Darius.

It was just a lucky break, and a good omen.

It made her life much simpler.

The lock clicked open, and Jade slid the narrow metal door upward. It made a harsh clanking noise in the quiet of the facility, which was deserted at this time of night. Few people needed to access their junk at eight p.m.

Jade pushed boxes aside to squeeze her way into the room.

Beijing didn't know about this secret hideaway. Unlike Lou, with his garage filled with weapons and supplies, the Ministry of State Security didn't think she needed a secret, secure facility for storage.

After all, to them, she had no need for weapons. She was only good for seducing people, becoming their best friend, or listening to them drone on and on about their stupid American lives.

Oh, and eventually working crazy long hours for years on Wall Street, then marrying an up-and-coming American man and making babies.

She moved more boxes on her way to the rear of the unit.

Across the back wall was her contingency plan.

Plugged into an electrical outlet, which she had to pay extra for, was a heavy-duty surge protector.

Jade had her burner cell phone collection plugged in, charging and ready to go.

She smiled at the thought of what they would do tonight and tomorrow.

Next to the phones, stacked neatly one atop the other, were her two special boxes.

The clear tape across the top was undisturbed. No one had gotten into the storage unit and checked inside.

Jade tore the tape off the top one. It contained a sturdy, plain black backpack. She lifted it out by the top handle, struggling with the weight despite her strength.

After double-checking behind her to make sure she was alone, Jade opened the top of the backpack and checked inside.

Her baby waited.

It had been her long-term hope to acquire it, and merely a fantasy that she'd ever use it.

Without the proper explosives, the device was dangerous but useless.

With her recent seduction of Lou, however, and the ability to access his well-equipped storage garage, her dream could become a reality.

The gray, battered steel pressure canister, about the size and shape of a small fire extinguisher, was heavy because of the lead lining on the inside to protect from radioactivity.

It had a handle welded to the top, bent and twisted in a way that suggested a worker had been in a hurry to finish the day and had welded a used, cast-off piece of metal instead of wasting money on a new piece.

There were two prominent yellow and black stickers with the universal radiation warning symbol: three wedges pointed inward, evenly spaced in a circle. The words on one were in English: **RADIOACTIVE**. The other sticker had the same but in Russia's Cyrillic letters.

The top of the canister could unscrew to access a padded space for a capsule that was about the size of a thumb or a AA battery, but doing so without protective equipment was suicide.

Can I go through with this?

Once she started down this path, there was no stopping. Unlike cyberattacks, especially by using cutouts—like she'd done with Boris Zorinov and the Russian hackers—physical evidence increased the risk of identification and capture.

As careful as she was, she might accidentally leave fingerprints on the device.

Or DNA—like a strand of hair—in or on the backpack.

If all went to plan, the C-4 plastic explosives and detonator from Lou's storage garage down the road would destroy it all.

Even then, the law enforcement personnel in the United States were exceptional. Americans had long memories and didn't stop hunting until they found, caught, and punished those who wronged them. The authorities could have ways to identify her that she didn't know about or understand.

But she had to get out of the life the MSS planned for her.

If that meant going rogue, risking capture, taking the money from the stock market crash, and fleeing to a far-off corner of the world, so be it.

It was no longer possible to prove to the men at the Ministry of State Security that she was capable of so much more than seduction and persuasion and still work for them in the capacity she wanted.

That time had passed.

But finishing the mission would be enough for her.

Ripping the tape securing the lower box, she removed two countdown timers in padded boxes, along with two large bundles of wires.

Jade added the items to the pack and closed it.

She unplugged the array of burner phones, turned each on, and added them to a small pocket on the outside of the pack.

With one arm through the backpack, she lifted it and slid her other arm in the second strap. The pack was heavy, but she could manage.

There was now nothing important—or incriminating—in the storage unit.

It was prepaid through the end of the year. By spring, when she hadn't renewed the lease and paid for another year, the unit's contents would be sold at auction.

She would be long gone.

If all went well, she'd be in the jungles of Guatemala, on a beach in

Belize, or in the forests of eastern Paraguay, all countries where China had little reach.

If she failed again, she'd be dead.

But at least she wouldn't have to commute to Wall Street every morning, work at a job she hated, and wait for Beijing to pick the next man for her to seduce and exploit.

Jade slid the door down, locked it, and left the storage unit behind forever.

123

THE C-4

Hudson Lock and Load Self Storage
Jersey City, New Jersey

Jade parked the SUV outside Lou's self-storage garage and unlocked the sturdy padlock with the keys she had pickpocketed while kissing him goodbye before dawn.

I wonder when—or if—he noticed they were gone.

She pushed aside the storage tubs and moved to the middle of the unit on the left wall, where she found the light switch.

There was a place for her heavy backpack near the rear of the unit, next to the band equipment.

The front door slid down much more smoothly and quietly than her storage unit. It would hopefully block most of the sound she was about to make, though this larger self-storage facility was deserted tonight, too, so it shouldn't matter.

The heavy-duty crowbar from a big-box home improvement store she'd stopped at moments before it closed made quick work of the wooden door guarding the weapons section of the garage.

Jade took everything she needed. Explosives. Detonators. A knife. Better weapons for Clay and his crew. Lots of ammunition. And a pistol for herself.

She'd thought she would have to convince Lou to give her whatever else she wanted, or kill him.

This way was so much better.

She sat cross-legged on the floor next to the backpack and started on the explosives.

Though her training had largely focused on her role as a seductress for China, her first year of instruction had been the same as the other spies.

The Ministry of State Security didn't expect bomb making to be a priority for any of them, but their training had been thorough.

Thanks to Lou's well-equipped garage, the bomb for the battered, lead-lined container with the poorly made handle came together quickly.

The generous amount of C-4 plastic explosives she attached wouldn't destroy a building.

With a radioactive—or "dirty" bomb—deadly invisible particles would do the actual damage.

It wouldn't be like the movies—cesium-137 wasn't the material in a nuclear bomb. No one would die immediately.

Instead, there would be a tremendous increase in the rate of cancer and thyroid disease weeks or months later.

The fear of radiation would do the most harm.

The poisoned area would have to be sealed off for years. Cleanup would take decades and cost billions.

People would abandon a large area nearby as well. Few would believe that they were far enough away and that there was little risk of a slow, agonizing death from radiation poisoning, no matter what they were told.

The social and economic effects would be devastating.

The best part, though, was that the mere threat of a dirty bomb would make the stock market plummet.

124

THE KISS

Malvern Shopping Plaza
Newark, New Jersey

Jade was pleasantly surprised when Clay parked next to her SUV in the darkest corner of the strip mall.

She had wondered if he would come, or if the sight of his friend being hammered to death would cancel out the radicalization she had encouraged and shaped while they dated.

The memory of swinging the hammer nearly caused her to smile, but she kept the lost, puppy-love look fixed in place as Clay climbed out of his car.

"My love," she said, and rushed into his arms.

After only an instant of hesitation, he returned the hug.

"I am so sorry about Evan. Lion," she said with a hitch in her voice. "It had to be done and had to be gruesome to motivate the others. I hope you understand."

"It was… a lot," Clay admitted.

Jade moved back and kissed him, putting everything she had into the perfect mix of apology, understanding, love, and lust.

"By Saturday, my love, we will be together. The rest is noise."

He sighed, and she had him back.

"Any questions?" Jade asked.

They had transferred the weapons and ammunition, packed in duffel bags, into the trunk of Clay's car.

The bombs of C-4 plastic explosives, wired to the timers and burner cell phones for backup, were in a backpack that Clay had slung over one shoulder.

Clay shook his head, and the look on his face required one more kiss to fix his resolve.

"Remember," she said after several seconds in his arms. "Do not call or text my old contact ID. Use the new one I programmed into your phone. Unless you want to blow up a bomb."

"What about the other phones on the bombs?"

"Backup. For me. I hate to think about it, but should something happen… I won't allow your efforts to be in vain."

He gulped, and she had to kiss him again. "Saturday night. A romantic dinner. We'll read the news to each other about how the shipping port is still closed, and how Americans are coming to their senses."

Did Clay believe the nonsense he had researched online that she had nurtured and shaped?

Or was he merely under her spell as so many men were?

Did it matter?

He would go through with the plan.

Or he wouldn't.

Either way, it would be a distraction and serve her purposes.

After one more kiss, they parted.

Once in the SUV driving away, she could finally relax and focus on the fun she had planned for the rest of the night.

And no matter how it worked out, she never had to see Clay again.

125

SEMPER FI

West 13th Street
North Village
Manhattan

Axe kept watch a few steps away from the modern five-story building where Rami bin Raslan had an apartment. This area of Greenwich Village was upscale—much pricier than Axe could dream of affording, even to rent—but less historic and charming than a few blocks south.

Tex and Mad Dog, dressed again in their New York Police Department uniforms, waited after pressing the buzzer for Unit 5A. It had been a minute, and so far no one had answered.

A thin, wiry Caucasian man who looked ancient, but could have been anywhere from sixty to eighty, approached along the interior hallway and swung open the building's glass front door. He sized up Tex and Mad Dog, but his eyes flicked to Axe and addressed him instead. "Who are you here for?"

Tex and Mad Dog took a step back so Axe could approach.

"Rami bin Raslan," Axe said. "5A."

The man held his gaze for a moment, still standing in the doorway and ignoring Tex and Mad Dog. "You have a warrant?" he finally asked.

"No, nothing like that. He isn't in any trouble, but he may have information about a crime this morning at a coffee shop closer to the park."

The man took a deep breath and let it out. "I'm the building superintendent, and I have clear instructions. No police without a warrant. No excuses." He leaned forward a few inches. "But I can tell you that you don't have to come in. You just missed him. Got in a taxi… I don't know. Ten, fifteen minutes ago maybe. Ran down the stairs, didn't wait for the elevator—it's slow. That's how I heard him. My apartment's in the back. The kid never takes the stairs. So something is up. That you?"

"I don't see how it could be, but maybe," Axe admitted. The guy had the air of a by-the-book veteran upholding the letter of the law—the rules he had to follow—while doing his best to help them out.

"It's a long-shot, sir," Mad Dog said, respectful, polite, and not the funny man for once. "But did you catch the taxicab company, license plate, taxi number, anything like that?"

The super's eyes switched to Mad Dog and lingered, checking him out. Mad Dog straightened under his gaze.

"1K68," the super said with a slight—sad—smile.

"How…" Tex muttered, but Axe jumped in. "Anything is easy to remember if you associate it with something you know," he said. "Can I guess?" he asked the super.

"Be my guest." There was an amused challenge in his voice.

"Going by your age and demeanor, I'd guess you're a Vietnam vet. And in 1968, it got real at Khe Sanh. 1-K-68."

The super's head dipped once in acknowledgement, and his smile grew.

Axe stuck his hand out. "Thank you for your service," he said, and shook.

"You all go and do what you need to do," the super said.

"Much respect, Marine," Axe said, making another informed guess.

"Semper Fi," the super said, and gently closed the door, which latched shut.

As they stepped away from the entrance, Tex already had her phone in hand, thumbs tapping out a message much quicker than Axe could have.

"Blondie says she'll have the taxi's destination intel for us soon," she said after a minute.

"How did Rami know we were coming?" Mad Dog asked as they made their way back to the van.

"That's an excellent question," Axe said. "And I wish I had an answer."

126

PRINCE FANCYPANTS

Corner of Mulberry Street and Houston Street
Soho

Axe steered the van closer to the flashing police and ambulance emergency lights that lit up the night. Traffic slowed to a crawl. Even jaded New Yorkers seemed interested in the many police cars on Houston Street, blocking the entrances to both Mulberry and Lafayette Street one short block apart. Yellow crime scene tape stretched between light poles, stopping foot traffic anywhere near the corners.

Axe slowed, looking for a temporary parking place.

"Probably a coincidence, right?" Mad Dog joked. "Nothing at all to do with the guy we're after, who happened to be dropped off by a taxi less than an hour ago within a few hundred feet of all that police activity."

"Yeah, right," Tex muttered.

Neither had been willing to sit in the back, which left them sharing the passenger seat like a brother and sister who refused to let the other win.

Mad Dog was crammed against the door, and it looked like Tex only had one butt cheek on the seat.

"Both of you," Axe said, "change out of the police uniforms and tuck them away. I'm calling this in."

He hit a speed-dial button on his phone as the traffic crept along. The comms app connected him to Haley in a moment.

"Lafayette and Houston Streets," he said. "Houston and Mulberry, too. Right near where the taxi dropped off Rami. There's major police activity. I'm going to stop and ask questions unless you can get a line on it before we get closer."

"Hold on," Haley said and covered the phone.

Nearly a minute later, Axe had inched closer to the mess. He pulled into a small open area between two police cars along the street. "Hey," he said into the phone. "I'm here and going mobile. Anything?"

"Sorry, it's taking time," Haley came back a moment later. "There's a lot of pushback about details, but it's a murder scene. Multiple victims. That's all we're able to get right now. Can you look into it?"

"Absolutely," Axe said, relishing the chance to get into the thick of it again. After two ambushes and a day in the van, his head was finally back in the game. "What do you think? FBI? Homeland Security?"

"Do you have an ATF badge handy?"

"Lucky I'm in the van—I've got them all."

"Use that. FBI might be on the scene soon. Alcohol, Tobacco and Firearms is legit and won't likely be there—we would have heard if there were weapons or a bomb."

"Copy." Axe called to the back. "Hey, Mad Dog. Look in the far-right drawer and grab me the ATF creds."

"Sir, yes sir!" Mad Dog snapped off from the back, sounding like a gung-ho private.

"Better you stuck with him than me," Haley said with a laugh. "You want to be in the field, this is what you get."

"Yeah, yeah," Axe muttered. Mad Dog's thick, hairy arm reached through the narrow doorway a moment later with the leather bifold wallet containing the shield-shaped gold federal badge and Axe's laminated photo ID.

"Back in a few," he told Haley and hung up. "You two are in charge," he called to the back. "If anyone asks, flash them your Homeland Security credentials, not the NYPD ones. One of you get up here to sit in the—"

"Dibs!" Tex called, followed by Mad Dog's muttered cursing.

"Shotgun," he mumbled. Tex laughed.

"You can't park there," a young, fresh-faced uniformed officer yelled from twenty feet away as Axe stepped out of the van.

"Alexson," Axe said, holding up the cred case and flipping it open. "ATF. Who's in charge? Precinct Captain? Or are the detectives on scene already?"

The young man frowned but nodded his head to the south. "Who knows? But it's all going down right outside the alley. Before you go, though, I have to check that. Let me see the ID again." He gave it a thorough inspection, comparing Axe's photo to his face and holding the ID to the light, studying the holograms and seal. "Peters," he finally called to another uniformed officer as he handed the wallet back to Axe. "ATF. Escort him back to whoever is in charge." He turned back to Axe. "Good luck. I hear it's an execution."

Axe followed Peters under the crime scene tape and down the street. It was quieter here, with uniformed officers standing back out of the way, waiting and watching to make sure no one approached.

Farther down the street, other patrol cars blocked access to the street from the south.

A rotund man in his mid-sixties, wearing a light-gray sport coat and dark slacks, his belt under a bulging belly, stood with his arms folded several feet back from the alley, watching.

"ATF, Captain," Peters said before stepping back to give them space.

The captain glanced at Axe and nodded.

Outside the alley, tall stands with glaringly bright lights stole the night from what otherwise would have been a dark alley. A crime scene tech in a white protective suit took pictures. Five bodies lay crumpled on a narrow sidewalk in the middle of the alley. There was little blood.

"I've been doing this forty-two years," the captain muttered, only loud enough for Axe to hear. "And if you're really with ATF, I'm not a police captain, I'm actually a prince—Prince Fancypants."

Axe bit back a smile and said nothing.

"Five victims," the captain said. "Young men, early twenties. Shot to the head once, then it looks like follow-up shots after they were already dead on the ground. Someone really wanted to be sure," he added. "Light-brown skin. Possibly Middle Eastern by their features, but that's profiling, so you'll have to wait until we get their IDs out—if their wallets weren't stolen."

The captain glanced at Axe, then back to the scene in the alley.

A younger man also in slacks and a sport coat—a detective—got the go-ahead from the crime scene photographer and approached wearing booties over his shoes. He knelt and felt in the first man's pocket, fishing out a thin wallet, which he opened with gloved hands, checked on the name, and called over his shoulder to the captain and another detective near the corner with a small notebook. "Yazeed bin Mishari." He moved to the next body, stepping carefully, and repeated the process. "Rami bin Raslan." He shook his head. "No robbery—you should see these huge earrings. Diamonds big as rocks. No way to miss them, and they're worth a fortune." He moved to the next body.

The captain turned to Axe. "Okay, ATF. Help a brother out. What do you know?"

Axe couldn't help but channel his inner Mad Dog. "Have a good night, Prince Fancypants." He turned and walked back up the street. The captain would have to work it out on his own, or Gregory at the Central Analysis Group could make some calls. But that was way above Axe's pay grade.

127

THE BIG PICTURE

Corner of Mulberry Street and Houston Street
Soho

Axe reclaimed the driver's seat from Tex and shut the van door on the noise and chaos of the corner. Tex nudged Mad Dog to the side to sit on half of the other seat as Axe called Haley.

"You're on speaker," he said. "Five victims. It's Yaz, Rami, and his three buddies from the café this morning."

Haley, Tex, and Mad Dog all uttered soft curses under their breath.

"We were about twenty, maybe thirty minutes too late," Axe added.

"Coincidence?" Haley asked. There was shuffling in the background—she'd put them on speaker, too.

"Maybe," Axe said. "But it's more likely that Darius, Kareem, and Jade are cleaning house after the failed ambush. They could have had eyes on us this afternoon, I guess. We're not necessarily the most invisible people. We're warriors, not spies."

"If they're tying up loose ends, who's next?" Nancy asked from Haley's end. "The remaining three turn on each other?"

"It doesn't matter," Gregory said. "This is a stronger indication that Nancy's original concerns were warranted. The possibility of a cyberattack or physical strike on Wall Street or elsewhere is much more probable, too.

I have to take this back to the president. Everyone's going to get in on it now."

"But we're here already!" Tex blurted out, then bit her lip. She mouthed, "Sorry!" to Axe.

"No one's pulling you, Rodriguez," Gregory said. "But in a few minutes, everyone on our side is going to be looking for Darius, Kareem, and Jade Pang." He paused. "We will do what we do best: big picture. Is there an actual threat? If they are working on something, which it certainly sounds like, what could it be? Taking them at their word, how could they crash the stock market? Our job is to figure it out and stop it. If an NYPD officer stumbles upon them, we welcome it. As you said, Rodriguez, we're here and up to speed. We're in a position to do what the police, FBI, and the others can't. So let's get on it. Brainstorming session next, then shake the tree. You do that very, very well."

128

THE HISTORY

Central Analysis Group Headquarters
Arlington, Virginia

Haley stood at the whiteboard, a black dry-erase marker in hand. Red, green, and blue ones were on the metal shelf below the board.

"Let's sketch it out," she said. They were all tired, but there was no time to rest. The country was in danger. "What are the most likely ways to crash the stock market?" She wrote ***Stock Market*** in the middle of the board and drew a square around it.

"The simplest would be a mass casualty event," Dave answered immediately. "Wall Street or elsewhere in the city. A small team with semi-automatic weapons or explosives. Anything to cause panic and fear."

Haley added ***Mass casualty event*** on the board, circled it, and drew a line from the main square to the circle.

"That wouldn't crash the market," Nancy argued. "The president would call a halt to trading. It would stay closed at least until the initial panic was over."

"Four days for 9/11," Dave said. "That day—Tuesday—and three days after. The US markets only opened again after the weekend."

"What if the stock market dropping is only a potential side effect, not the goal?" Haley wondered out loud.

"Then it could be anything," Dave argued. "An assassination of the president. An unsuccessful yet serious attempt might do it."

"Another attack on our oil or energy infrastructure," Nancy said. "If we hadn't stopped the attacks in Texas a while back, I shudder to think what it would have meant for the economy."

Haley added the brainstorm ideas to the board, purposefully not thinking through what it would mean to lose Uncle Jimmy—the president. She drew circles and lines to connect the ideas.

"Also," Marcus said, "the ideas we had earlier. OPEC drastically reducing oil production or raising prices would do it. A coordinated strike against Iran, or any large, sudden geopolitical move might spook the market."

Haley added Marcus's suggestions, but it didn't feel right.

"This isn't it," Haley muttered. She stared at the board, frustrated. After several seconds, she put the cap back on the marker and set it gently on the shelf.

She turned and offered an apologetic smile to Nancy and Dave.

"Haley, no, come on," Dave muttered.

Gregory entered and stopped short, closing the door behind him.

Haley stuffed her computer, charging cord, headphones, and yellow legal pad in her computer bag, shrugged to Dave, gave a little wave to Nancy, and headed across the room.

Gregory stood in her way, blocking the door, his arms crossed. His normally perfectly ironed shirt had wrinkled during the long day, and his hair, securely held in place this morning, had a few loose strands at the temples and by his ears.

Haley stopped in front of him, computer bag slung over one shoulder. "I'm not going into the field. Only Kelton's apartment." She paused. "Do you want to give me permission, or would you prefer plausible deniability?" When he didn't speak, she tried again. "With your help, Void and I can be working together on this in ninety minutes."

Gregory's eyes narrowed.

He hates the idea. But he knows the stakes.

"An attack is likely imminent," she said. "There's a chance we catch a break and stop it the normal way. But with Void, the odds are better. The two of us there, with these three, and you, here? That's a hell of a lot of brainpower."

"Haley, what he does? It's illegal."

That's it. He's going to say no.

She had one last argument. "It's computer systems. Numbers. Data. To him, it's a giant puzzle, a game. I'll be there too, I'll rein him in. Keep him focused on foreign systems, nothing in the United States. You have plausible deniability. If it goes wrong, he takes the hit. If it goes past him, it falls on me. Never you, the Central Analysis Group, or the president."

Gregory was wavering. It wasn't on his face, but Haley could sense it.

"The country has a long history of hiring former black hat hackers to use their talents for good, not evil," she said. "This is a continuation of that. Besides," she said with a chuckle. "You and I have this history. This is what we do."

Gregory leaned forward an inch to make a point.

"If he's detected, or worse, caught, he goes back to prison. I won't be able to cover for him, even if he's working for us. I doubt the president will, either. You, too, Haley. After the SystemSpike, Congress, the states, everyone is more serious about cybersecurity. They'll throw the book at him. You, too. Know that going in."

"I understand."

"Does he?"

Haley hesitated. "I'll make sure he does. But illegal, legal, Void doesn't think in those terms. And I bet he'll be ready, willing, and able to help."

Gregory stepped to the side, opening up the path to the door. "You get to Kelton's apartment, and you stay there. Do you understand me? It doesn't matter what I tell the president about how capable you are or how he should let you do your thing. It's not just your life you're risking. It's the country's security and my head if something happens to you. You read me?"

"Loud and clear." She gave it a second, not wanting to push harder so quickly, but time was passing. "Um, one more thing."

Gregory's eyebrows went up.

"I need a helicopter to take me to New York, and Tucci is too far away to get here quickly."

Gregory's eyes closed.

He's counting to ten to stay in control, I bet.

After three seconds, he opened them. "I'll make a call. Fifteen minutes in the parking lot. Take that time to continue brainstorming with Nancy, Dave, and Marcus. Figure out a way for this to work that will keep them isolated from anything… less than fully legitimate, let's call it."

"Well said, and thank you," Haley told him. She turned back to the conference table and the team, who had the decency to pretend they hadn't been listening. "I've got fifteen minutes. Let's make a list of everything we wish we knew or had access to. And I'll take it from there."

129

THE SEARCH

Unit 47A
The Summit at 57th
Manhattan

After a high-speed helicopter ride to the roof of Kelton's building, Haley had borrowed Kelton's fancy desk chair and wheeled it into Void's room, along with a small square puzzle table Kelton had stored in a closet.

She had her laptop open, and Void had reluctantly parted with one of his large monitors for her. He was relaxed, focused, and ready to work. He had clearly benefited from being away from house arrest in the condo.

The glow of the screens was the only illumination in the room.

"Before we start, you have to understand," Haley said. "Gregory is willing to look the other way and let us do this because of the possible imminent threat against the country. We are, however, unsanctioned assets. If we get caught, his hands are tied. We won't explain to the authorities that we had permission. In fact, we'll claim we were doing it on our own. We'll lie and say we were looking for system vulnerabilities that we could exploit for our own personal gain. We will be disgraced and considered criminals at best, traitors at worst. You'll go back to jail. I'll lose my career and maybe be in prison with you." She paused, needing to make sure he understood the gravity of the situation. Void looked impatient, with hands near his keyboard without quite touching it.

"You can say no," she added. "I can do most of it on my own; I've done it before. But with your access, with your help…"

"We're unstoppable," Void said with a delighted smile. "And I'm still a part of the team, right?"

"Yes—unless we get caught."

"Got it. Don't worry. I'm good at this." He turned away from her, cracked his knuckles, and placed his fingers on the keyboard. "We'll start with the idea that sooner or later, everyone makes mistakes. There has to be something."

"Let me do that part," Haley said, turning to her computer and opening a spreadsheet, a notes tab, and a series of top-secret government intelligence databases. "Gregory is seeking approval for us to do much of this by the books, but it takes time we might not have. If we get it, though, we use that access first. In the meantime, what I need from you is…"

"Highly illegal and morally ambiguous?" He grinned over at her.

Damn it, he's enjoying this too much.

"Let's stick with moderately illegal and ignore the morality for the moment. Start with finding Jade, Kareem, and Darius. If you can find their frequently contacted people, that would be outstanding, too."

"You want me to track their phones?" Void asked, already typing. "I might have to access their school files to find their contact numbers, then break into the cell phone providers… Not easy, but with the tools I have, and maybe some phone calls pretending to be a desperate IT guy needing a favor, or about to be in major trouble with his boss… I might have to talk my way inside instead of hard-core hacking, but first let's try…" He seemed to fade away. "An hour or two," he muttered, his eyes never leaving the screens. "Depending on… Never mind. You wouldn't understand. See you soon."

Haley slipped on her headphones, Void's earlier words on her mind. Everyone makes mistakes. All she had to do was find one and exploit it.

She focused on her screens and began the hunt.

130

THE MISTAKE

Unit 47A
The Summit at 57th
Manhattan

Haley stood behind Void's chair. He was focused on his computer screen, which showed a map of Manhattan. Two red dots flashed in Greenwich Village.

"Jade Pang is at her apartment on the third floor," Void said. He had hacked computer systems to get the information she should have been able to access legally—if they had more proof of a potential attack on the country.

"Or rather," he continued, "her phone is there. It hasn't moved since…" he checked the side of his screen. "Late Tuesday afternoon."

"Axe discovered her at a café with our other targets that night," Haley said.

"Okay, we'll backtrack to that timeframe in a minute. First, here's Darius's phone. No movement at all, not even a few feet to take it with him to the kitchen or bathroom. They have burner phones, obviously."

"Yes, which itself is a sign they're up to something."

"We use burner phones," Void pointed out, glancing back at her.

Haley ignored him. "What about Kareem El-Sayed Mahmoud?"

"Interesting. Same thing, almost. No movement on Tuesday night for a few hours, then movement around his home, here," Void said, pointing at a spot off Washington Square Park in Greenwich Village. He was excited by his find. "Then, Wednesday morning, it stops moving. It must be next to his bed. He switched to a burner, too."

"Wednesday morning. When the team started their surveillance. That's how they knew about us."

Had she made a mistake sending Axe and the team on this? Should she have told them to be more careful, more subtle?

Had Axe—or one of the team—been too obvious?

It wasn't time for recriminations. For now, they had to look forward and focus on the solution.

She had to protect the country.

"Look at this, though," Void said, still excited. "Yazeed bin Mishari. Yaz. Active non-stop, lots of movement until earlier tonight when it went offline. Not turned off. Poof. Someone put it into a Faraday bag is my guess. It blocks the cell signal completely."

"In Soho, where he was shot in the head. Twice."

"Yeah." The reality of the situation sobered Void. "But let's backtrack."

He clicked his mouse, and the screen changed. "This is the cell phone activity Tuesday, late afternoon, early evening. You said Axe tailed him, right? Look! He didn't switch to a burner phone! It goes from his brownstone, over to the East Village, goes in a small square of streets, and stops here." Void clicked and zoomed. "The Saffron Café. That's where they had their meeting?"

"Yes. Tell me he took it inside with him."

Void turned to her and grinned. "He took it inside with him."

"He's the weakest link," Haley muttered while Void went back to work on his keyboard. "That's why they killed him."

"I need you to get with Axe and have him tell me the exact times he saw the targets enter and exit," Void said. The excitement was gone, replaced by a commanding tone. He was in his element and on the hunt. "Also, which direction each of the others went when they left." He paused and turned back to her again, his face set. "I'm going to get all the phones that were active in that area for the timeframe involved," Void said. "Even if they were turned off, I might be able to track them. Then I'll eliminate the ones that we're not interested in. By the time I'm done, I'll have the burner phones of Kareem, Darius, and Jade—if they used them. If they left their daily phones at home and didn't bring burners, I won't get anything."

"You can do that—match phones to the location?"

Void hesitated a second. "Probably. Honestly, I don't know. It's a fun challenge. I might get all three at once or maybe one by one. It will be easier with Axe's help, if he can tell me which direction each person went. He followed Jade, right? That will make it much easier to narrow down the phones and find hers. I'll have to get a tower dump for the sector, access some historical visitation datasets, link them to anonymized device IDs, hack the…" He trailed off, fingers tapping away at the keyboard. His screens changed as he used the mouse to click on them, and Haley realized she wasn't going to get any more until he came back to this world.

She returned to her makeshift desk and sent a message to Axe with the questions Void needed answered.

Then she turned to her own system and got to work.

What was the connection between the four primary targets?

What did they want, aside from Yaz's claim to crash the stock market?

What had they already done?

And what were they up to next?

131

THE BIRD

Unit 47A
The Summit at 57th

Haley pushed back from her computer.

The implications of what she and Void had discovered in the past hour were staggering.

She'd have to report to Gregory and the team at the CAG soon, but not yet. She and Void had a little more work to do.

Haley could sense that the operation was coming together. Void sat at his workstation, lost in the data. She recognized his expression. He looked like she felt when she was in the zone.

Boris Zorinov, the man suspected of stealing polonium-210, using it to poison the Secretary of State, plus being the man who may have directed Abdul Khan Dagar in the SystemSpike attack, might be on his way to Manhattan.

It couldn't be a coincidence that he was coming exactly as Jade, Kareem, and Darius had a plan to harm the country, crash the stock market, or both.

Or rather, it might be a coincidence, but she doubted it.

And the banking data Void had hacked into...

Monumental.

Any minute now, Void would discover Jade's burner phone and be able to track it.

This was about to turn into a full-fledged field operation.

Haley needed a way to move Axe, Mad Dog, and JB around the city, and maybe the tri-state area, as quickly as possible.

The helipad on the roof of Kelton's building was available.

She hated to do it, but she had to. She couldn't use a government helicopter for an unsanctioned mission, and until they found more proof of an imminent threat, that's what this was.

Haley dialed the number.

"Tucci Helicopter Services," Robert Tucci said in a tired voice, but he didn't sound like she'd woken him. It wasn't that late yet.

"Hello, Tucci. You know who this is?"

"What, he's too scared to call himself?" Tucci asked with a chuckle. "But yes, I know who this is."

"He's had a long day and is pretty busy."

"Okay. Would it do any good to argue?"

"No, probably not."

"What if I hang up?"

"You're not hard to find."

"You prepared to buy me another new helicopter if something happens to this one?"

"Didn't I get you that one?"

"Only after you two got my last bird shot down."

"You've got me there, but come on. Nothing beats being back in action."

"Actually, you know what beats that? Everything! Peace and quiet. Boredom. Predictability. Safety."

"That's not us," she said, quiet and serious. "You or me. It never will be."

She waited him out. It was in his voice. Deep down, he was still a Night Stalker with plenty of dangerous missions under his belt.

After a few seconds of silence, Tucci cursed. The sound of the call changed—he'd put her on speakerphone. She could almost picture him pushing up from an easy chair, turning off the TV, and grabbing his shoes.

"Where do you need me?" he asked with a sigh.

"First stop is the helipad on Kelton's building," she told him, with the cross streets and what he needed to know to land. "By then, or soon after, we'll know the next step."

"Got it."

"And Tucci?"

"No," he said immediately. "Don't say it."

She wanted to chuckle, but the threat was too serious. "Sorry, I have to." She paused, waiting for him to protest, but he didn't. He knew what was coming. "Bring your shotgun."

132

THE BIG PICTURE

Unit 47A
The Summit at 57th

Haley made the next call, reluctantly prepared to both make and ruin Gregory's night.

"I have intel," she said when Gregory answered.

"Am I going to like it?" he asked.

"Yes. And no. You should put me on speaker." The sound of the call changed.

"We're all here," Nancy said. "What did you find?"

"I don't have information on everyone, and it's not comprehensive—"

"Stop hedging," Dave muttered loud enough for her to hear. They were all exhausted, and he was right. It was long past time for that.

"The Saudis: Yazeed bin Mishair, Rami bin Raslan, and Rami's three friends, all five men dead in the New York alley? These guys, with access to allowances, savings and investment accounts in their own names, even limited access to family funds… They're broke." She paused for effect, then continued. "Broke being a relative term, of course. What money they have—which is more than any of us dream of—has been added in the last few months. It looks like it's their allowances, most likely, directly deposited into accounts they can use worldwide with credit and debit cards should they need cash."

"How many months?" Nancy asked.

"Two," Haley said.

"Since the SystemSpike?" Dave asked.

"Yes," Haley said. He had to suspect where she was going with this.

"Up until two months ago, these five men spent nearly every cent of their allowances, cleaned out their primary checking, saving, and investment accounts, and borrowed more, it looks like, which they also spent, for the past three years. Not on flashy cars, vacations, jewelry, or electronics. Not drugs, either. There is no history of that, and no rumors either. There's nothing to show for the money. Just outgoing wire transfers that get rerouted so quickly I can't trace them."

She avoided mentioning Void, who had done the bulk of the work, using his incredible hacking skills to access several foreign banks and financial institutions—their records only, he had explained. He couldn't touch any money, as it was part of a different system that was much harder to hack.

Haley paused to allow for questions, but no one spoke up.

Were they seeing—and thinking—what she had?

"Haley…" Gregory muttered. "Please don't do this to me again."

She guessed he had put the entire picture together already.

"Planning for the luxury resort in Oman was started three-and-a-half years ago," Dave said.

Two months before, he had come to her with a wild theory that the building had been designed and built to collapse on demand.

Tonight, he had immediately gotten what she was hinting at.

"The funding came through a little less than three years ago—a private-public consortium that guaranteed half of the money from a shell company I haven't been able to penetrate. There were quarterly payments; the money wasn't put up all at once."

Haley abandoned all pretense. Dave was already there, and Gregory suspected what she meant. "My gut tells me that Rami and the other three, and probably other young men from wealthy Middle Eastern families that are in their circle at the university, tapped into their savings and investments, which could easily total millions…"

She paused, giving herself a moment to rethink this, to back away and continue investigating, to carefully follow the data until she was certain, to use logic instead of trusting her instincts.

But Gregory had to ask the question. "And?"

"I believe they sponsored the purposefully flawed design and construction of the resort in Oman where the Middle Eastern Peace Summit was held, which resulted in its collapse. It would have killed the most important leaders in that region, plus aides and advisors, if not for President Heringten's well-timed speech."

She'd seen a redacted report from their allies in the region. Reading between the lines, it was clear that President Heringten had used the intel Axe, Haley, Nancy, and Dave had provided to keep the entire group of leaders from entering the building for a welcome speech and opening night dinner. He had saved everyone's lives. His timing was accidental, according to the reports, though there was much suspicion about the president's so-called luck.

Dave jumped in. "And by extension, that group helped finance the SystemSpike. It's too much of a coincidence to think the two events, so close together, were unrelated."

"Someone wanted to remake the world," Nancy said, bringing it home. "The USA and Russia at war. Chaos in the Middle East."

"Who benefits?" Marcus said.

"China," Haley said. "I have no proof yet, but I believe Jade Pang is either the mastermind behind the attacks, or at least the agent in charge. It's all her. Whether she was acting under orders or went rogue, we'll have to work that out."

They paused while they considered the implications of Haley's theory, and the concern that Jade Pang was currently at large somewhere in the area.

"While you were working, we've been busy on this end, too," Nancy said after a moment. "We've discovered that Boris Zorinov traveled to New York City twice. Once a little more than three years ago, right before the Oman project ramped up. The second time was about two years ago, right before Abdul Khan Dagar, who we know was the original Malik before his brother took over, left Afghanistan, moved to Dubai, and bought a multi-million-dollar apartment. He also purchased the fourteenth and fifteenth floors of that building through a separate series of shell companies."

"This from a man who had lived an impoverished life in a small village in Western Afghanistan prior to his move to Dubai," Dave added.

"Jade, Darius, Kareem, and Yaz worked with Boris Zorinov to plan and implement the SystemSpike and the Oman resort collapse," Haley said, putting it all together.

"Your theory makes sense in a wild way," Gregory said, "but it's still circumstantial. We need to connect Boris Zorinov with the university students."

"We can work on that," Dave said.

"More pressing, however," Gregory continued, "is what Jade Pang and the remaining two men—Darius and Kareem—are doing now. Do you have any more information about that?"

"Not yet," Haley said. "I'm working on the ID and location of Jade Pang's burner phone."

"And when you do?"

"Axe and the team will be ready," she said.

"Axe and the team?" Gregory repeated.

"I'll be here coordinating—and hunting for intel."

"Exactly," Gregory said. "Theories are good," he said, addressing everyone. "Proof is better. The priority remains finding Jade Pang, Darius Valiollahi, and Kareem El-Sayed. We have 'Be on the lookout' alerts with the city and state police departments, as well as the FBI and Homeland Security. We, however, are more highly motivated, and this is the only mission on our plate. Let's throw our considerable talents at this, find those people—including Boris Zorinov, since he may be already in or on his way to the United States, and stop what they may be attempting."

After a moment, they clicked off, and Haley turned to Void. "You got all that?"

Void nodded and said nothing. He turned back to his screens and continued the hunt.

133

———————

VERMONT

Unknown Location

Boris woke confused. The pitch of a nearby engine had changed.

He checked his surroundings. He'd been sleeping on his back, covered by a blanket.

It was an airplane. A private jet.

What was happening?

He felt so tired.

He longed for a chair, a glass of wine, and the sun on his face.

He remembered a yacht, and the gentle caress of an ocean breeze.

The sound of the surf in the distance.

People on shore kicking footballs, children building sandcastles.

That is where he should be. Not going to…

Where was he going?

And why?

He sat up, throwing off the suddenly too-warm blanket.

A flight attendant hurried to him from the rear of the plane. "We'll be landing in a while, sir. Would you like to freshen up? Or can I bring you water? Wine?"

Boris wanted to know their destination, but he held back. Admitting he was lost and didn't know where he was going would show weakness.

"Oh," the flight attendant said, bending down to pick up an envelope from the floor. "You dropped this, sir."

Someone had written **Important—Read Me NOW** on an envelope in large blocky, childish letters, but he had no interest in reading anything at the moment. He had to figure out where he was, why he was here, and what he was doing.

"What's your favorite thing to do there?" he asked her, mustering some of his old charm.

"New York?" she said. "We don't get much time to sightsee. We'll stay overnight near Teterboro and fly home tomorrow. Will you be returning with us, sir?"

New York City. It rang a bell. He was flying from Monaco? Or France?

The information slipped away.

And why?

He was angry about something.

Or at someone.

He stuffed the envelope into his pocket and settled into the now upright seat. "I haven't decided yet," he said in answer to the flight attendant's question. "But I will take some water, please. And freshen up before we land, as you suggested, thank you."

* * *

Teterboro Airport
Teterboro, New Jersey

Boris had enjoyed watching the lights of New York City from the plane, but he was no closer to knowing why he'd taken a private jet to the United States from… wherever he'd been. He hadn't thought of a clever way to ask the flight attendant without sounding addled.

After an easy trip through customs and immigration at the private jet terminal—his passport had his name as Boris Yarko, which didn't sound right, but he'd kept quiet—he emerged into a crisp spring night to find a chauffeur waiting. "Right this way Mr. Yarkov," the man said. They walked to a luxury sedan. The chauffeur said nothing about his lack of luggage.

Boris assumed he would be taken somewhere. Someone had obviously arranged the trip for him. If he waited long enough, all would be revealed, or his memory would return. He had an inkling that there had been episodes like this before. His gut told him that riding them out was key.

He settled into the plush rear passenger seat and looked forward to the trip into Manhattan. He had a feeling that he knew and liked New York, though he had no memories to confirm it.

After several seconds of waiting for his passenger to speak, Oleksandr turned slightly to catch his eye. His latest passenger was a perfectly ordinary man in his mid-sixties, with a round face, blue eyes, short gray hair, and gray stubble from not shaving for a few days. "Sir? Where would you like me to take you?"

The man looked tired, with deep bags under his eyes. Not surprising, considering he'd landed at ten p.m. and had possibly flown all day. He had to be jetlagged. But he also seemed confused. He reminded Oleksandr of his grandfather in the last months of his life, when his body had been fine, but his memory had gradually slipped away.

"Manhattan?" the man asked.

It came out as a question, but Oleksandr took it as an order. He'd had stranger passengers than this.

"Of course, sir."

Depending on traffic, it would take a while to get through New Jersey and into the city. The man would likely have more specific directions then.

Oleksandr had driven this route so many times that the traffic occupied only part of his mind. The rest was free to enjoy the city's architecture in the distance, and to daydream about his eventual retirement to a small house in Vermont.

But he kept returning to his sad, confused passenger, so much like his grandfather back in Ukraine. Oleksandr adjusted the mirror enough to see the passenger's face. The man sat placidly, watching the New Jersey streets slide by.

The car passed under a light, and the man's profile dropped the final piece into place.

It was him. Boris Zorinov, though the man had answered to Yarkov, the name on the reservation. But the car service had issued a company-wide alert... what? Two days ago? Three? Everyone was asked to be on the lookout for a man resembling his backseat passenger. There was no picture, but the description was right on.

Oleksandr focused on the traffic and refused to think about the cash reward offered by the company for information about Boris Zorinov. He waited until a stoplight, then leaned forward to casually take his cell phone from the holder clipped to the A/C vent. It took only a few seconds to type the message to the company dispatcher.

Zorinov with me. Going 2 Manhtn. Instructions?

He hit send and set the phone on his lap.

A reply came back within seconds.

Report final destination and keep him in sight if possible. $$$$$$ for success.

The dream of a small house in the woods of Vermont suddenly seemed much closer to reality.

134

THE BETRAYAL

Teterboro, New Jersey

The driver had betrayed him. Boris didn't understand how he knew or when it had happened, but he did. He trusted his gut. It had always kept him safe. He knew it in his soul.

The energy in the sedan had changed. One moment, the man had been driving. Relaxed. Doing his job.

The next, after a glance back at him, he had tensed.

Boris couldn't remember where he'd been the previous day or why he had flown to New York.

But he recalled his childhood. Fighting for his life, for a scrap of food to keep going another day.

He had developed excellent instincts, and he trusted them now.

"I…" Boris said, leaning forward. "I'm so sorry, I think I'm going to be sick." He put his hand over his mouth. "Please! Pull over. There, behind that service station." A well-lit, multi-pump fueling station took up the entire corner ahead. "Hurry!"

The driver changed lanes, cutting off a car behind them, and charged into the service station. "The back—I don't want people to see me sick," Boris said, feigning dry heaves.

As soon as the car stopped, Boris opened the door, jumped out, and knelt. He pretended to vomit, loudly, his back to the side mirror.

After a moment, he stood, waved his hand to the driver without looking, and moved to the rear of the car. He leaned against it, the picture of a man who had been ill taking a moment to recover.

Boris slipped the belt from around his waist, wrapped one end around his left hand, and returned to the backseat of the vehicle.

"My apologies," Boris said, acting embarrassed as he closed the door.

"Are you okay?" the driver asked. He seemed genuinely concerned, but Boris didn't second-guess his original intuition.

"Yes, yes. Can we just sit here a moment please? And maybe turn the air conditioning lower? Perhaps I'm overheated."

The moment the driver looked forward to adjust the temperature, Boris lunged.

He hooked the belt around the driver's throat, looped it a second time, and yanked with all his strength. Boris planted his feet against the seat in front of him and pushed back. The man's body, trapped by the front seat, had no place to go.

The driver flailed and tried to dig his fingers under the belt at his neck, but it was too late.

Had he been smarter, he might have unlatched the seat belt and launched himself into the backseat, or put the car into gear and driven into a wall hoping the impact would harm Boris enough to loosen the improvised noose.

The driver only struggled, wasting precious time and oxygen.

He lost consciousness after twenty seconds.

Boris held strong. A part of him knew the man wouldn't be dead for at least three minutes. Five would be better, but he didn't need to wait that long.

After two minutes, Boris released the pressure, slipped the belt from around the man's neck, and moved to the front passenger door, threading the belt into his pants.

No one watched, though twenty meters away, cars passed on the road and others came and went at the service station.

Boris grabbed the driver's arm and pulled, dragging the man centimeter by centimeter to the passenger seat. The driver was still breathing, as planned. If anyone came along, his friend had had too much to drink, and Boris had convinced him to switch drivers, thank goodness.

After much effort, Boris settled the man into the seat and buckled his seat belt, then returned to the driver's seat.

Boris had to sit for several seconds until the dome light went off.

Then, with a last check around to ensure no one had taken an interest in his activities, he turned to the driver, took his head in hand, and twisted, snapping his neck.

Boris felt like himself for the first time in… well, he didn't remember, but it had been a while.

He grinned as he adjusted the rearview mirror.

He was a predator.

A wolf.

He suppressed a gasp as the memories returned.

Jade Pang.

He was in New York to kill her.

135

THE BIKE PATH

Kareem waited just inside the tall bushes that lined the jogging and bike path along the East River.

Cars rumbled across the Williamsburg Bridge a few hundred meters to the north. Nearby, an unused two-story brick building made an excellent landmark for a clandestine meeting.

There were still people out. Joggers, bike riders, and walkers, with and without pets.

A young man wearing black running shorts and a bright-white T-shirt approached from the north, slowing to look around.

"Here," Kareem called softly as he stepped from the bushes. "Hurry!" He kept his right side—and the hand with the knife—turned away from his so-called friend.

The first financial backer had arrived.

"What are you doing hiding there?" the man asked as he approached. He looked around, as did Kareem. The path bent to skirt around the fenced-off old building. They were alone for the moment.

"Come," Kareem said, gesturing. "I have important news."

"In the bushes?" the man said, distrust heavy in his voice.

Kareem whipped his hand up, slashing from the side.

The knife sliced his friend's throat. Not as deeply as Kareem would have preferred, but he had to seize the moment.

The man's hands flew to his throat. Blood spurted. Kareem stayed out of the way and stepped behind the man, stabbing the knife into his upper back, angling toward the heart and lungs.

Precision didn't matter much, but the faster the man died, the better.

The other two financial backers would be along shortly, a few minutes apart.

"I'm sorry," Kareem said as he pushed the man deep into the thick bushes.

He wasn't really, but it seemed like the right thing to say, given the circumstances.

East Village

"It's me," Kareem said into the phone.

This was going to be a tricky call to pull off.

He hurried through the East Village, away from the park by the river where he'd left three dead bodies deep in the tangle of bushes off the bike path. They had been too bloody to drag into the water.

"We have to meet," Kareem said to Darius. "It's an emergency. I have my friends with me, the ones who have been helping us out?" Darius would understand he meant his financial patrons. "They…" Kareem wanted to imply 'demand' without saying the word and hope that Darius caught on. "They're requesting a meeting. They've positioned their money as instructed but have… concerns and want to hear more details from you two directly."

The mention of the benefactors had the desired effect. Darius would be torn between wanting to keep them happy, a preference to remain anonymous to the patrons, and his natural suspicion about a last-minute meeting at night.

"It's too late," Darius said. "Everything is in motion. Tell them not to worry, that by this time tomorrow, they'll be rich, as long as they did what we suggested."

"I tried." He lowered his voice and cupped the phone for privacy, sure that Darius would hear the difference. "We have to meet them. They're on edge. Please. Trust me. Fifteen minutes."

"It's only me at the moment, and it's getting late. I—"

Kareem held the phone away from his mouth and spoke to his patrons, as if they weren't lying with their throats slit in the bushes. "He says he can meet in an hour, but only for a few minutes."

"That's not—" Darius was saying when Kareem pretended to return to the call.

"They say that's fine. The same place as last time? It's open late. Is that close to you?"

Kareem would prefer to meet at the safe house where Darius had been hiding, but Darius wouldn't risk that. But the public café? He'd feel safe there.

"Fine. I'll meet you there in an hour."

"Thank you. See you soon." A few minutes before the meet, Kareem would send a message changing the location to a small park off Cooper Square, only a few blocks from the café. It might be secluded enough for his purposes without arousing too much suspicion from Darius.

The nearby traffic noise on Third Avenue would cover the quiet *pop* of his pistol.

136

THE REQUEST

North Fifth Avenue
Manhattan

Vasily lay on his narrow cot in the walk-in closet. The ornate primary bedroom, where the staff believed he slept, was on the other side of the wall.

Each night, he locked and bolted the door to the large, gaudy room and left it behind for his sanctuary, and biggest secret: the cot in the walk-in closet.

He had converted it himself years before, one item at a time. First, he had ordered the narrow cot and a thin, futon-like mattress for it, forbidding the staff from opening the package when it had been delivered. Plain sheets followed, and a simple wool blanket. He added a small, inexpensive light with a gooseneck arm to aim at the books he read before falling asleep. He chose thrillers, classics, or whatever he heard about online. From time to time, he discussed books with one of the staff. When they traded recommendations, he felt normal; the most himself ever. Like the wealth vanished, and he was a regular person, not a multi-billionaire.

He stacked the books on the shelves where another man would have row after row of clothes.

In here, he had two sets of plain cotton pajamas, an old pair of slippers, and a tired robe.

In here, he felt like his true self. Real.

Petrov knew about the room, for security, as did the housekeeper who did his laundry, but only one of the servants had access. He had sworn them all to secrecy.

He was about to slip a bookmark into the latest novel and turn off the light when a distant, firm knock came at the real bedroom door.

"One moment," he called. It had to be important for someone to bother him this late.

He slipped on the old robe then made his way into the bedroom and across the thick carpet to the door.

He checked the security screen mounted to the wall.

"It's me," Petrov, his right-hand man, called. He stared up at the camera in the hallway outside the bedroom. "It's Boris Zorinov. He's been found—in New York."

Vasily turned the key in the deadbolt and undid both latches.

One could never be too careful.

He opened the door to hear the rest of the news face to face.

"The word we spread to be on the lookout for someone matching Boris's description has paid off. A car service driver identified him and reported they were going to Manhattan; that's all the driver said. Nothing since then."

This was the break Vasily needed. "Pay whoever you need to, and track down that car. And do you have Mariana Rodriguez's phone number?"

Petrov shook his head. "I'm sorry, no. But I have Kelton Kellison's cell phone."

"That will do."

"Kelton," Vasily said. He stood in his office, down the hall from the bedroom. He had traded his comfortable, plain robe for the thick one hanging near the bedroom door, and the old slippers for expensive ones that didn't feel nearly as good.

"I'm sorry for the late call. This is Vasily Chekov. Did I wake you?"

"Vasily, hello. No, I'm up," Kelton said, and to his credit, Vasily couldn't tell if he was telling the truth. Lying was a useful skill.

"I need a favor," Vasily said. He continued without giving Kelton time to respond. "It's unusual, but I believe it's in everyone's best interests."

He paused. Kelton's curiosity would get the better of him. "Okay… What can I do for you?"

The man was suspicious now, but that might work in Vasily's favor. He'd done many deals, but never one quite like this. "I need Mariana's cell phone number. Or, at least, for you to get a message to her immediately. Can you help me, Kelton?"

A normal rich businessman getting a call from a richer businessman late at night, asking to speak to his girlfriend, would elicit anger, jealousy, or disbelief.

But Vasily believed Kelton's girlfriend was more than his security guard and the love of his life.

"I can have her call you," Kelton said after a short pause.

There. No questions, no outrage, merely a quiet acceptance. It was confirmation of what Vasily had suspected, but Petrov couldn't confirm. The woman worked for the government—or some organization—as a spy or covert operator.

"Thank you. Immediately, please. It's an emergency. Goodnight."

Vasily disconnected halfway through Kelton's own "Goodnight."

137

SIXTH AVENUE

Greenwich Village

Mariana sat in the back of the van with Mad Dog. They had agreed that instead of fighting over the passenger seat, Johnboy should have it for the trip back to Kelton's condo.

After completing a surveillance detection route, Axe drove north on Sixth Avenue.

They were all exhausted from the long day, and they needed to eat, nap, and regroup.

The mood in the van, front and back, was grim.

They had done their best, but their hunt was over until they had new intel to pursue. The four of them would stand down and rest for a few hours at Kelton's instead of making the trek to the safe house in Queens. They'd be centrally located and ready to go whatever direction was needed when the next intel hit came.

Mariana's phone rang with a cellular call, not one on the secure comms app.

It was Kelton.

Mariana had been gone for hours, but she was working with Axe and the team. Kelton knew better than to bother her.

Something had to be wrong.

"It's Kelton," she said, holding the phone.

"Answer it," Mad Dog said. He was like a brother to her, and while he often got on Axe's nerves, she thought he was fun and funny—most of the time.

"I… I don't want to," she whispered. Whatever the call was would change her life. She could feel it.

"Answer it," Axe called from the front. He had latched open the narrow door between the front and the back. "It has to be important."

She tapped the green button. "What's wrong?"

"Nothing," Kelton said, even and reassuring. "Well… No, not nothing. Vasily Chekov just called. He needs to speak with you. It's an emergency, he said."

"Chekov wants to speak to me," she said to Axe, Johnboy, and Mad Dog.

"Are you… are you all okay?" Kelton asked.

"Yes, we're fine."

She didn't mention that Axe had almost died in a subway tunnel ambush and that they had spent hours pointlessly cruising around Greenwich Village in the surveillance van tonight hoping to luck into seeing one of their targets that was possibly planning a terrorist attack on Manhattan.

"I texted you the number so you don't have to write it down," Kelton said. He was thoughtful, rich, smart, and caring.

For some reason, he had picked her over the many supermodels or the wealthy women he could have had.

"Thank you," she said, hoping her voice conveyed not only her appreciation but also her love for him. "I'll call him. We'll be home soon, just for a break. Clean up, take a nap. We're…"

"You're working. I get it."

He understood. He'd been on a few adventures with Axe.

"See you soon. Be careful."

"I will."

They hung up, leaving the mushy stuff for another time.

"What the hell does Vasily Chekov want with you after eleven at night?" Mad Dog asked. "A glass of warm milk? Someone to tuck him into bed? Or maybe he didn't get enough of you threatening to kill him?" Mad Dog said with a huge grin.

"Boris Zorinov," Axe muttered. "That's my guess. As if we don't have enough on our plate right now."

Axe accelerated, driving much faster than normal. "Hold on," Axe said. "We're going to Chekov's. He's not going to say much over the phone, no matter what he wants to talk about."

Mariana clicked to Kelton's message, highlighted the number, and called Chekov. She put the call on speakerphone and turned up the volume.

"Mariana, thank you for calling," Vasily said in his smooth, businessman tone, then hesitated. "Am I on speakerphone?"

"Yes, but don't worry," she said, enjoying his sudden discomfort. "We don't have to talk on the phone."

"Oh? But... I have some news I—"

"We'll be at your place on Fifth Avenue in fifteen minutes," Mad Dog called with a chuckle.

The van surged ahead. "Ten," Axe muttered.

"We'll be there in ten minutes," Mariana said.

"And some food would be great, please and thank you!" Mad Dog said.

"Ignore him. He missed dinner," Mariana explained.

"Three of you are coming?" He must have heard Axe.

Axe shook his head.

"Just the two of us," Mariana said.

"But I'm super hungry," Mad Dog added.

After a pause, Vasily rallied. "Then I'll see you soon. I'll have the staff put together something for you and your friend to eat while we... chat."

She ended the call as Mad Dog rubbed his hands together in excitement. "Oh, this is going to be great," he said. "It'll be fun to watch you shoot him."

"I'm not going to shoot him."

"We'll see."

138

THE CHEESE

North Fifth Avenue

Vasily barely had time to brush his teeth and dress properly.

Petrov put the on-duty kitchen staff to work.

By the time the guests arrived at the building's front door, the staff was placing a spread of cut fresh fruit, a tray of cheeses and cold cuts, plus a variety of breads and condiments on the round kitchen table.

His last confrontation with Mariana had been in Kelton's kitchen.

He would return the favor in his. This time, he was much more aware of her capabilities and planned to act accordingly.

A few minutes later, Petrov escorted Mariana Rodriguez and a short, burly man with thick arms and a mess of brown hair and a beard into the room.

"Welcome," Vasily said, putting warmth into the greeting.

"Finally," the hairy man muttered. He marched past Vasily to the food and began assembling a sandwich. The man looked like a large bear cub Vasily had seen at a traveling circus when he was a boy.

"Don't mind him," Mariana said. The two were dressed in a similar fashion: black pants, black shirts, and black jackets.

A nod from Petrov, standing near the door next to one of the kitchen staff, told Vasily all he needed. As expected, his guests were both armed and had refused to turn over their weapons.

No matter. The security staff had flooded the area outside each entrance to the kitchen the moment his guests had entered.

"Given your rapid response to my call, you must be quite busy, so I'll get to the point," Vasily said.

"This is great," the bear said with his mouth full, interrupting on purpose, Vasily suspected. "What is this cheese? Gruyère?"

He had to give the man credit. Vasily often used the tactics of interruption and distraction to get under the skin of business opponents.

He was rarely on the other side of the equation, however.

It had become a pattern in his dealings with Mariana. She had put him on his back foot from the start during their last encounter.

Vasily glanced at the kitchen staff member near the door. "Sir, it's Gruyère d'Alpage, Réserve, aged two years," she said. "From a mountain cave near Fribourg, Switzerland."

"Yummy," the bear said. He swallowed. "Sorry I interrupted. What were you saying?"

Vasily got right to the point. "You haven't said it, but you must suspect me of the theft of polonium-210 from Russia that was used to assassinate Secretary of State Wilson a few months ago." He paused, expecting one or the other to deny, confirm, or at least say something, but neither did.

Mariana pulled a stool from under the kitchen island and sat.

The bear took the thick sandwich he'd assembled and joined her, trailing crumbs. He took another large bite. More crumbs fell.

"I would very much like to clear my name," Vasily added.

"Not sure how you're going to do that," the bear said, again with his mouth full. Vasily could read people, though he'd failed spectacularly with Mariana in her kitchen a few nights before. This man, however, he could see through. He was pretending to be a slob and a joker. Beneath the shaggy hair and beard, and hidden behind the muscles and the acting, was an exceptionally intelligent man.

"I have information you need that would help us both," Vasily said. "I believe it will help you realize I am not guilty."

"Okay, so give," the bear said.

Mariana glanced at him. He shrugged but returned to his sandwich.

"You want to negotiate," Mariana said, finally speaking again.

He nodded.

"How'd it work out for you the last time you negotiated with her?" the bear muttered with a bright grin.

Vasily couldn't help but laugh. "Not well!"

"There you go," the bear said and took another bite.

"Your friend is right, of course," Vasily said. This wasn't going as he'd expected, but it was surprisingly enjoyable. He was more convinced that the path he'd decided on was the correct one. "If the information clears my name, I should be happy to offer it freely, without condition. Yet still, I have one request."

He raised his eyebrows at them both, seeking permission to continue without interruption this time. When neither spoke, he hesitated, glanced at the staff by the door, then asked Mariana his question. "How happy are you with Kelton?"

He realized it sounded wrong the moment it left his mouth.

Faster than he could react, the bear had put his sandwich on the granite island, stood, and had squared off to him.

Mariana stood as well.

Vasily held up his hands, but the damage had been done.

"Are you seriously asking me to leave him? For you?" Mariana asked, her voice cold and dangerous.

"Dude," the bear said. "Money don't buy people."

Vasily closed his eyes. How could he be so successful at business matters and absolutely horrible at this? "I'm sorry, it came out differently than I meant."

"I hope so," the bear said, "because it sounded like you were offering to buy my friend from Kelton, or bribe her into leaving him and 'working' for you."

"No, no…" With a wave of his hand, the staff cleared the room—including a reluctant Petrov—leaving the three of them alone together.

"I'm sorry," Vasily said. He was flustered and hated it. But this was exactly the reason he was extremely wealthy yet unmarried. Business discussions and deals were so much easier to handle than casual or romantic interactions..

"May I be completely frank, Miss Rodriquez? And…"

The bear ignored the polite request. "I'll refer to you as Mr. Bear," Vasily said.

The man shrugged. "Works for me. Hit us with your best shot."

Mariana nodded as well. "Say what you have to say."

Vasily hesitated, glanced around the room, shifted his weight, and felt his face flush.

"I will give you the information, but I would very much appreciate if you, Miss Rodriquez, would promise to help me find a wife. To act as a matchmaker. To help me find the woman of my dreams, the way you and Kelton seem to have found each other."

Vasily stood before his guests, his soul bared.

"I have everything money can buy except love. And I want to do all I can to be sure that, when I find love, it is real and not based on my wealth. For the life of me, I cannot figure out how to do that. If anyone can, perhaps it is you—with Kelton's help, if you think it's needed."

He was beyond embarrassed and regretted the whole discussion, but it was out there now, for better or worse.

The bear sat on the stool and took another large bite of his sandwich.

Neither offered the derisive comments Vasily had expected or laughed at his predicament.

Mariana stepped toward him and offered her hand. "I don't know how I can help with your situation, but I'm willing to try."

They shook hands. Vasily wondered if he was doing the right thing, but it was too late now to back out.

"So what do you have?" the bear said around the sandwich.

Vasily smiled. He was going to enjoy this part. "Boris Zorinov arrived in New Jersey at ten p.m. He was most recently reported in a car approaching New York City."

There, the expression on both of their faces, that's what he had been hoping for. Hunger. They wanted Boris Zorinov badly. He was already on their radar.

"I can see you know the name. Boris is the one you want, not me. He is the likely thief of the polonium-210. I'm waiting for his precise location," Vasily said. "Please join me. It shouldn't be long."

The bear made another sandwich, smaller than the previous one, tore a paper towel from the rack near the sink, and wrapped it. "Midnight snack," he said with a thumbs-up to Vasily.

Mariana made herself a small sandwich and stood by the table eating it. "Okay, so what are you looking for in a woman?"

"Someone like you," he said, and raised a hand immediately to stop her. "But age appropriate for me. Late-sixties to mid-seventies. Intelligent. Someone who has more inside than might appear from the outside. Most importantly, someone for whom all of this," he said with a motion to the condo outside the kitchen door, "means little."

"Someone who loves you for you, not the money," Mariana said.

"Exactly. Like what you and Kelton seem to have. If you don't mind me asking, how did you two—"

A knock came from the kitchen door, and Petrov poked his head in.

"Tell us what you know," Vasily said.

"Boris arrived on a plane from France. The car service hadn't heard from the driver, but they have a tracking system on each vehicle. We persuaded them to allow our people to investigate. The sedan was found parked in a garage in the West Village. Unfortunately, the driver was in the trunk, strangled to death."

"When was this?" the bear asked.

"We found the car moments ago," Petrov said. "We have Mr. Chekov's considerable resources looking for Zorinov. He's using a Maltese passport in the name of Yarko."

Mariana and the bear rushed by Vasily, their earlier discussion clearly forgotten for now.

"I will pass along whatever else I find," Vasily called to their backs as they hurried through the kitchen doorway.

139

THE WIFE

Times Square
Manhattan

The lights of Times Square shone brightly despite the hour. The streets were busy, though not with wall-to-wall traffic as there would be in the daytime.

Pedestrians strolled, though their numbers would dwindle soon. The city might never sleep, but the residents and tourists had to.

It had been a very long day for Ekaterina. Dmitry had driven her to a small airstrip in Finland, just over the Russian border, where a private jet had been waiting.

From there, it had been a long flight to the United States. She had finally landed north of New York City in a place called Westchester. A car service ride into Manhattan completed the journey.

She'd had a restful nap on the plane. Now at the start of her seventh decade, she needed less sleep than ever. And with the time difference between New York and Russia, it was morning for her. She was awake and ready to find Boris Zorinov.

Outside the well-lit entrance to a large hotel just off Times Square, Ekaterina adopted the role expected of her based on her looks. She slowed her steps and shuffled her feet, changing her gait from the normal smooth, silent steps of a trained assassin with the grace of a ballerina. With her shoulders hunched upward a few centimeters, and by leaning forward at the waist, she transformed from a nearly invisible ghost who slipped through crowds unnoticed into a woman at least ten years older. She would seem small, tired, and frail.

Ekat entered the touristy, impersonal hotel. It was the kind Boris Zorinov wouldn't normally stay in, but he would avoid the top hotels. They were too obvious. After a life of high-level crime, he was wealthy; not quite an oligarch, but rich enough to have a yacht the Western authorities had confiscated.

If he was here in the city to hide out, or to stay while he bought a suitable apartment, he would find a busy hotel where he could blend in. A place nice enough to provide the luxury he demanded, but not where the staff would pay close attention to him.

With so many hotels in the city, Ekaterina's job was nearly impossible, but until her government produced a lead on Boris's whereabouts, which was unlikely, or Blondie contacted her with information, she would do what she could on her own.

Ekaterina shuffled to the front desk. A young woman looked up from her phone and forced a fake, tired smile.

"Welcome. Checking in?"

Ekaterina shook her head slowly. "I… My husband…" She composed herself and purposefully made her English rougher than usual. "He has addiction issue. And, from time to time, violent tendencies. I am looking for to bring him home. Before there is trouble." She held up a picture of Boris that Dmitry had supplied. "You have rules, yes. I know this. But if he is here, you call room. Tell him wife is in lobby. For to help. I wait. You have seen him?"

Ekat's tired look and the mention of her husband's potential violent nature sold her story.

The young woman looked closely at the picture but shook her head. "I haven't seen him, but I only work overnight, so…"

"I leave number. Day people can call. You take photo of Boris's face with phone. Share with them, yes? I thank you. You are a wife yet? No. Someday, maybe. You will understand a wife's love for her husband."

After providing the local number of the phone Dmitry had provided her for the mission, the clerk took a picture of Boris with her phone and promised to share it with the daytime staff.

Ekaterina shuffled outside and mentally checked off the hotel from her list. There were two others in the busy area. She would then go east, then uptown, and finally across Central Park to the Upper West Side.

Boris had to stay somewhere.

It was boring yet important work. As the Russian saying went, "Without effort, you won't pull even a little fish out of the pond."

And Boris Zorinov was far from a little fish.

140

THE WATCHERS

The West Village

Boris had left the car in a twenty-four-hour parking garage near the Hudson River, with instructions to the attendant that he wouldn't need it for several days.

No one would find the driver's body in the trunk until it started to decompose.

The walk through the cool evening invigorated him.

He was minutes away from Jade Pang's apartment.

The look on her face when he knocked on the door, forced his way in, and beat her to death would be exquisite.

After eleven p.m. on a weeknight, the city was quiet. Most people on the street looked like they were going home.

Boris was exhausted, but killing Jade was worth staying awake for.

As he approached the West Village address his Russian hackers had provided him at the start of this mission, he slowed. No sense bumping into the woman coming home from a late night of studying or her boyfriend's home and losing the element of surprise.

A man in his late-thirties with very short hair leaned against the wall of a closed shop at the end of Jade's block, enjoying the evening, killing time.

Ahead, near a fire hydrant, an older four-door sedan with tinted windows looked out of place among the more upscale cars of the neighborhood. It had cheap tires, several dents, and no bumper stickers.

From Moscow to Paris to Barcelona, undercover police cars all looked the same.

Boris wouldn't have worried had he seen only the car or the man leaning against the shop. But both? No. The authorities were on surveillance.

But were they watching for Jade Pang, someone else… or waiting for him?

They had to be on the lookout for Jade. The man hadn't given Boris a second glance when he walked by.

Boris jaywalked across the street, moving to the far side, away from Jade's apartment building and the waiting police car.

He passed by at a steady pace, eyes on the closed restaurants and stores on his side of the street.

No one called out or followed him.

What had Jade done to bring the attention of the police?

Or was it a coincidence? Perhaps a drug dealer lived in Jade's building, or a suspect drank in the bar down the street.

Boris's hackers had identified Jade's boyfriend as a student from Iran who lived several blocks away, in Greenwich Village, near Washington Square Park.

Boris walked on, going north one block, continuing east, then south to check his tail, but no one followed.

He had to stop and ask for directions twice, but everyone knew where Washington Square Park was and happily pointed the way.

Boris neared the boyfriend's north-south street, slowing as he reached the intersection. A white-and-blue electric company panel van waited near the corner.

Halfway down the block, a few doors away from the Iranian's address, a tall young man with short cropped blond hair poked at his phone, killing time.

Boris kept walking, puzzling out the situation.

Both homes under surveillance?

Jade wouldn't know for sure he had discovered the location of her apartment, but she could guess. She understood how resourceful he was— or she wouldn't have hired him to manage the terrorist attack of the century.

But would she suspect he could also learn about her boyfriend—and find his address?

Possible, but not likely.

The two police officers loitering near the apartments weren't bored from days on end of fruitless watching. They were alert. Ready.

Tonight was their first shift.

They weren't after him.

The authorities knew about Jade Pang.

But why? And how?

She was an extremely capable woman. Brilliant, even. Her plans for the attacks on the United States and the idea of having the resort in Oman built so it could be destroyed on demand were ingenious.

Jade Pang was too smart to be caught by the New York Police Department. It had to be something else. Bigger, like the FBI.

Boris reached Broadway and turned north. With the chance to kill Jade tonight lost, his exhaustion intensified. He needed to rest, regroup, and decide what to do.

Should he continue his quest for retribution?

Or give up, return to the New Jersey airport, and fly to Europe on the same airplane that had brought him to New York?

With only the credit cards in his pocket, he could purchase a small boat. Not a luxury yacht, but a vessel big enough for a captain, a few crew members, and him.

With the memory issues he'd had lately, that made the most sense.

But first, he had to sleep.

The dead chauffer was a problem. Who had he reported to? And what resources did they have?

The driver had picked Boris up under his new name, so his new passport could already be flagged.

The credit card he'd used to pay for the flight and car service had to be suspect, as well. He had a second card, in the name of a shell company, but he had to save it for whatever the next step was.

Boris walked up Broadway, weighing his choices, and hoping he remembered his decisions in the morning.

141

THE UPDATE

Union Square
Manhattan

Boris slowed as he walked north, looking for a place to sleep. The nap on the plane hadn't been enough. He was close to collapsing. Only the thrill of the hunt had kept him going. He had to sleep soon.

A group of tourists, middle-aged men and a few women, loitered near the entrance to a large hotel on Broadway at the edge of Greenwich Village. They laughed and chatted, finishing a pleasant spring night in New York City.

It was the perfect situation. Boris could stay safe while checking whether his identity and credit card were flagged.

The check-in process went smoothly, though it was not the level of service and deference he preferred.

Boris reached his room on the fourteenth floor, found the ice bucket, and returned to the door to wait.

It didn't take long. Down the hall, the elevator dinged softly.

Any footsteps were muffled by the carpet, but the door's fisheye security lens showed one of the middle-aged men from the front of the hotel walking toward Boris's room.

Boris opened the door and stepped out. "Excuse me," he said. The man slowed but didn't stop. "Did you notice where the ice machine was?"

"No, sorry," the man said, continuing on, his room key already in hand. He stopped one door down and across the hall from Boris, who stood looking left and right as if uncertain.

When the man placed his key on the scanner, Boris swung the metal ice bucket by the handle. It clocked the man in the back of the head, making him fall into the door with a thud.

Boris rushed forward, turned the handle to open the door, and dragged the stunned man into the room.

The dazed man put up only a token fight as Boris snapped his neck.

The body wouldn't smell until long after Boris was gone.

The man fit nicely in the bathtub. Boris slid the shower curtain closed after taking his wallet, cash, and cell phone, which instantly unlocked when Boris had held it to the dead man's face.

Boris removed its security login to make it easy on himself later, should he need a phone and want to risk carrying something so easily traced.

Boris washed up in the sink and dressed in clean clothes from the man's suitcase. There was an envelope in the back of his pants—the one the flight attendant had handed him. He remembered now. It was a note to himself explaining his situation. Too late tonight, but it would be valuable in the morning if he woke up to another memory issue.

He found a cheap pen on the hotel desk and added to the letter, drawing a bold line with an arrow to the new section.

UPDATE—Wednesday night, around midnight.

Jade Pang is wanted by the authorities.

Her apartment has police outside. So does her boyfriend's.

Do not approach.

If he had trouble in the morning, what would he need to know immediately to keep himself safe?

The time for a decision was here.

After a few seconds, he had it.

He had gotten from Europe to New York and didn't remember how.

Older memories were intact, but the past few weeks were hazy at best.

If he continued on this path, eventually he would make a mistake.

The American and Russian authorities might still be hunting for him.

There was no reason to make it easier for them by wandering around with memory problems.

He refused to be caught. All his life, he had avoided capture and prosecution. The details were gone, lost to his memory trouble, but he remembered bribing and killing many people to remain free.

It had been worth it.

He had his decision.

Return to Teterboro Airport in New Jersey immediately.

Charter a private plane to Miami, Florida.

Use the GOLD credit card.

The authorities may be aware of the PLATINUM card.

Find a small boat for sale.

Buy it and hire a small crew. Try to hire a nurse as well.

Tell them you have memory trouble but want to enjoy your last days in peace and quiet. It will be an easy job for them. Promise them anything.

Stock up on wine. And vodka.

Tour the Caribbean.

If your memory is deteriorating as fast as I believe it to be, the crew will eventually desert you or dump you somewhere. By then, though, it won't matter.

He had to ensure his future self understood what he had done. It was essential.

Be proud. You have accomplished so much in your life.

Most recently, you had your biggest achievement. You orchestrated the cyberattacks on the United States.

You coordinated the construction of the resort in Oman that was built to collapse—and it worked.

He left out the part about no one dying in Oman the way they should have. Future Boris didn't need that detail.

You deserve to relax now. Find a boat and go. Enjoy the time you have remaining.

Boris returned the page to the envelope and slipped it into his back pocket.

He added a large note to the palm of each hand: *Read the note in your pocket! IMMEDIATELY!*

Finally, he moved the sheets, pillows, and duvet next to the door. He'd hear a swarm of police officers if they descended on his room across the hall.

Boris could barely stay awake. He turned off the light, lay on the sheet, his head next to the door, and slept.

142

THE TOURIST

The East Village

Kareem waited inside a pizzeria down the block from the Saffron Café, watching for Darius.

The café was in the middle of the block.

Darius would most likely approach from the Third Avenue side, only meters away from the pizzeria.

Darius would walk right past him.

Kareem would wait until he passed, slip around the corner, and make the call announcing the change in meeting place to the small park one block to the south before Darius reached the café.

Within the next fifteen minutes, Kareem would have only Jade left to kill.

Darius walked by on the other side of the street. His reluctance for the meeting was clear by the way he moved.

Kareem raised his phone and held his finger over it, ready to call.

Before he could press the button, Darius stopped and checked his phone.

Kareem glanced down, but he hadn't placed the call.

Darius read a message, turned, and hurried back the way he had come, toward Third Avenue.

Kareem called. What text had the man received to be warned off the meeting?

Darius glanced at his phone but ignored the call.

At the corner, he stepped to the curb, raised his hand, and hailed a cab.

Kareem's plan was going wrong.

Darius slid into the taxi. "Thank you for stopping," he said in careful English, playing the role of a foreigner. The driver glanced back but said nothing. "I am a tourist. I am jetlagged. I want to see the city. Will you drive me? A tour? I will tell you where to go."

"Expensive," the driver said. He didn't look like he cared either way. He only wanted to be paid.

"Yes. I have money." Darius removed a credit card and a wad of the emergency cash he had taken from the safe house. "Cash? Card?"

The driver shrugged. "Either. Where to first?"

Jade needed him at Times Square. She hadn't given him a reason, which was worrisome. But her message had the correct code phrase proving it was from her and that she wasn't under duress, so he had to go.

Kareem was at the café down the street, but the team from Greenwich Village would still be hunting them both.

It was time, as always, for precautions.

"Flatiron building? On Broadway?"

The driver didn't respond, but he pulled into traffic for the first leg of Darius's surveillance detection route.

Kareem had to time it perfectly.

He memorized the license plate and taxi ID, and waited until Darius's cab was a block away, slowing for a red light.

Walking deliberately, hoping not to draw Darius's eye, he left the pizza place and strolled to the corner.

There were plenty of cabs. One stopped immediately, and Kareem got in. He had two one-hundred-dollar bills ready. He showed the driver both and slid one through a slot in the plastic barrier separating the front and back seats. "I think my girlfriend is cheating on me with a man in a taxi up the street. I have to see where he goes. Can we follow him?"

The driver took the money. "You pay, I drive. I don't care where we go."

He pulled into traffic. "Two blocks ahead," Kareem said, and told the driver the license plate number. "You ever watch spy movies?"

The driver shrugged. Kareem pulled out another hundred-dollar bill. He held one up. "For the fare." Then the other. "Another tip, but only if the guy in the cab doesn't realize we're following. Understand?"

The driver nodded and changed lanes. "No problem."

Kareem sent Darius a message.

We're here waiting. Where are you?

It didn't take long for Darius to respond.

Can't make it. Sorry. Something came up.

Kareem had an imaginary conversation with his dead benefactors before replying.

My friends aren't happy. Can you meet in the morning instead, before the market opens?

"That it?" the driver asked.

Kareem checked the license plate. "Yes." The driver changed lanes and backed off before Kareem had to explain what to do.

This might work, Kareem thought.

Darius's response came through.

Tomorrow morning maybe. Message me then. Tell them not to worry. J. says plan is going well. $$$$$

Kareem imagined what his patrons would say and decided not to write anything. He clicked on the last message and sent a thumbs-up emoji. That would be enough.

He leaned forward to help the driver watch for Darius's taxi and wondered whether the Iranian was on his way to meet Jade.

Maybe Kareem would be able to kill them both tonight after all.

143

THE BURN

Unit 47A
The Summit at 57th

Axe gathered the team in the kitchen, except for Void, who was busy with his computer.

Mad Dog made coffee while Johnboy raided the refrigerator. It was going to be a long night.

"No," Mad Dog said, in the middle of describing the life-changing sandwich he'd had at Vasily Chekov's home. "It was Gruyère cheese, but some extra-special fancy kind that only the super-rich people buy. I thought about pocketing—"

"Okay," Axe interrupted. "Let's get this show on the road." He didn't want to be in charge, but it was on him to step up.

"Void is working on tracking Jade, along with Darius and Kareem. When he has something for us, we go. In the meantime, thanks to our buddy Vasily Chekov—"

"And his new Director of Romantic Relations," Mad Dog interrupted, sweeping both hands toward Mariana, who rubbed her eye with her middle finger. Mariana had told them all about her negotiation with Chekov.

"Thanks to Tex," Axe continued, "we know Boris Zorinov, suspected of coordinating the SystemSpike attacks, is in New York. Void is looking into that, as well. So are Nancy, Dave, and the entire night staff at the Central Analysis Group."

Axe accepted a tall mug of black coffee from Haley and sipped before continuing. "Tex, you're on Boris Zorinov duty. Work with Ekaterina." The Russian had messaged Haley that she was in New York and searching for Boris. "Make sure she doesn't do anything we wouldn't."

"That's pretty vague," Mad Dog muttered.

"Use your best judgement," Axe added.

Mariana nodded, but had something on her mind. "Spit it out," Axe ordered.

"The Boris mission is important, but I was hoping to go with you guys. Stop whatever is happening."

"You want to run and gun," Mad Dog said.

"Well, yeah, I guess."

"I know you do," Axe said. "But not this time. Mad Dog, Johnboy, and I have specialized training, and we're a solid team in a firefight. As good as you are, it's a hard no this time. I'm sorry."

"I liked you better when you weren't Admiral Nalen," Mariana muttered.

"Oh, burn!" Mad Dog said.

"Sorry," Mariana said. "That came out harsher than I intended."

Axe refused to let it bother him, though for a second, the words had kicked him in the gut. "No problem. I deserve it. Maybe we'll get Nalen back in the field with us someday, but until then, it is what it is."

"It is what it is," Mad Dog, Johnboy, and Haley repeated, with Mariana stumbling along as well, a little late.

"But he'd say the same thing, Tex," Axe said. "Boris is a huge target. We need him. Alive, preferably. There are many people who would like to chat with him. But if Haley and the team at the CAG are correct, he has the blood of thousands of Americans on his hands. Whatever happens, happens. Justice must be done. Copy?"

"Copy," Mariana replied.

Axe tossed her the keys to the surveillance van. "Don't destroy the van —it's a loaner. And keep Ekaterina in line. Watch your back. She saved my life, so she's trustworthy to an extent. She was an enemy, then became an ally, but she and I agreed that was temporary. If the mission changes and it's a decision of Russia versus the USA—or her against you—she's going to choose her country and herself, not us. I don't want to find your cold, lifeless body somewhere and regret this decision, you hear me?"

"I hear you, Papa."

"Go. Find Boris Zorinov. Handle the situation. And thank Ekaterina for saving my life."

Mariana nodded, fist-bumped them all, and headed out to meet America's enemy-turned-temporary-ally.

144

THE GEAR

Haley set her coffee mug on the counter and moved to the pantry on the far side of the kitchen. She entered an eight-digit code onto a keypad nearby that blended in with the cabinets, and the door popped open. "If you're going on a real mission, you better have more than pistols and light body armor," she said. With a flourish, she opened the cabinet door to reveal its contents.

"Score!" Mad Dog said, hopping down from his stool and rushing over. "This is like Christmas morning!"

"Help yourself," Haley said, stepping out of the way.

Johnboy and Mad Dog dug through the closet, gearing up with carbines—the term for short-barreled rifles, which were often better for close-quarters combat—along with ammo and military-grade plate carriers.

"Night vision! Nice!" Mad Dog said, pulling out enough of the gear for each of them.

"Kelton, Mariana, and I went on a little shopping spree while you were recovering," Haley explained to Axe.

"Little?" Axe asked.

Haley shrugged. "Kelton is rich. It beats fancy china."

"Kelton should buy some of the cheese that Chekov had. See, it had this nutty flavor not found in all Gruyère…"

Haley leaned close to Axe and whispered while Mad Dog went on and on. "You sure you don't want to stay in the chopper on overwatch and send me along with Mad Dog instead?"

"Don't tempt me," Axe muttered, and made his way to the pantry to pick out his gear.

Axe had to admit it felt good to be geared up with the team. Maybe that had been his problem—he'd been off on his own for too many missions. The SEALs were team-based. Team members relied on each other. It was smarter and safer. No one could do it all. The Team was always much more than the sum of its parts.

This time around, they would go to battle as a group.

But right now, they were missing a crucial member.

Axe pulled out his phone and dialed from memory.

"Tucci Helicopter Services," the man said, sounding more awake and alert than Axe had expected.

Good, maybe that will make this easier.

"Hello, brother," Axe said, smiling. He could guess what came next.

"No. N.O. Absolutely not. Last time you had to buy me a new helicopter!" Tucci really sounded pissed off, like he wasn't joking at all.

It put Axe back on his heels. Wanting to be talked into going on the mission was one thing. This sounded serious. Tucci's help was crucial. They needed to be mobile, and in the New York area, with its 24/7 traffic, a helicopter would get them where they needed to go quickly and easily— though conspicuously.

"You were trained to put yourself in harm's way," Axe told Tucci. "There's no escaping who you are."

"No. Not this time. I'm serious. I'm hanging up now."

The line went dead.

"He hung up on me," Axe muttered.

He glanced around the room, disappointed, confused, and embarrassed that the rest of the team had witnessed Tucci turning him down cold.

After all they'd been through, Axe never figured Tucci as a man who would walk away from a battle.

"You should see your face," a voice called from the doorway. Tucci stood there with a huge grin.

It clicked into place. "Haley already called."

Tucci nodded. "Yep. Nice to see you again, brother. You thought I'd sit this out? No way. Army is here to save the day as usual."

Axe had only one concern. "Did you—"

"Yes," Tucci said with a laugh. "I brought the shotgun."

145

THE VOTE

Unit 47A
The Summit at 57th
Manhattan

Haley moved to the storage cabinet while Axe and Tucci caught up. She removed a long gun—a sniper rifle. Only the front side windows of Tucci's helicopter could be opened, so she would have a limited field of fire, but at least they could fight back from the air if necessary.

Haley also selected a carbine like the ones the boys had, along with a plate carrier, and extra ammunition.

She took her time slipping on the plate carrier and slinging the carbine.

"Haley?" Axe said from behind her.

There it is.

Haley turned, smiling.

"Oh no you don't," Axe said. He sounded like he meant it, but she hadn't gone to work on him yet.

"I can't stay in the condo," she said. "That's out. But don't worry, I'm not going into battle. This," she gestured to the weapons, "is just in case. You never know. The three of you are a fire team. Tucci flies the bird. I'll stay with him as command and control. I can also offer limited overwatch through the small side windows with the long gun. Or medivac and, in a dire emergency, a quick reaction force. You guys can't fight and coordinate a response with Void, the CAG, and Tex at the same time. I'll be more effective if I'm nearby—without getting my hands dirty, of course."

Axe thought it over, staring at her as if he were searching her soul. She meant every word. This was the only logical way to do it. They had no idea where they were going next or what they'd encounter. She had to be brought along to help.

"You can only go if you stay in the bird," Axe said. It wasn't up for discussion. Axe had assumed Admiral Nalen's role—and he sounded the part.

"Copy that," Haley said. "This isn't a roundabout way to sneak into the field. But you may need eyes on. I can look at the big picture and coordinate."

"I'm happy to have you along," Mad Dog said. "You've got my vote."

"It's not a democracy," Axe said, but gave her a nod. "Happy for you to watch our backs, Blondie."

146

THE REUNION

Broadway and 52ndStreet
Manhattan

Ekaterina stood in the shadows across the street from where Blondie had told her to wait. Simple tradecraft: do not be where expected.

The tall work van arrived.

Ekat stepped from the darkness, met the eyes of the young woman driving, and walked across the street.

The passenger side door was unlocked, and she slid inside.

"Ah. You," Ekaterina said to the curvy, dark-haired young woman. She looked wary. "From Los Angeles."

The woman had been with Alex and the large, muscular man who had abducted her when Ekat had tried to kill Alex in a coffee shop.

"Mariana," the woman said with a slight nod. "Tex, if you prefer."

"Mariana," Ekat repeated, buckling her seatbelt as the van pulled away from the curb. "I am Ekaterina. Kat or Ekat for short."

"Axe said to thank you for saving his life," Mariana said. She oozed distrust, which was understandable. She had another quality Ekat could sense but couldn't identify.

"Ah, Alex. You call him Axe. Call sign, yes? Good. He is well? Recovered?"

"Yes." There had been the slightest hesitation before she spoke.

Perhaps he is not fully recovered from his injuries.

There was a story there to hear if time allowed. Or maybe Ekat and Alex would meet soon under quieter circumstances than Los Angeles, Dubai, and Oman.

Mariana turned the van left, south on Eighth Avenue.

"You have location of Boris Zorinov?" Ekat asked. "Blondie is smart, she finds him, yes?"

"Not yet," Mariana admitted. "We have people working on it. For now, we head south toward Greenwich Village. He may be targeting another person we are looking for. The mastermind of the operation."

"You know this? Certain?"

"It's Blondie's working theory, but we have no proof. This other suspect—her name is Jade Pang, she's a university student here—may be planning another attack on our country. And now Boris Zorinov appears in New York. It can't be a coincidence."

Ekaterina checked the passenger mirror, noted the cars to the left and front, and memorized the license plate numbers, keeping track of the vehicles surrounding them.

How much of what she knew from Dmitry should she divulge?

She was in a van with an enemy-turned-temporary-ally. Mariana had to be trusted. There might come a time when they had to rely on each other to survive.

"I tell you the truth, yes?" Ekaterina said. "You tell few people if you can. We must trust each other."

Mariana glanced her way, eyes narrowed, but nodded, conceding the situation.

"Russia Foreign Intelligence Service think Boris took polonium-210 used to kill your Secretary of State," Ekaterina said. They were making good time with the light traffic, catching most traffic lights green. "They send special forces team to his yacht. He vanished. Perhaps Boris believe the mastermind of operation—Jade—attacked him, not Russia."

"He is retaliating—and cleaning house."

"Cleaning… ah, yes. In Russia we say *zachistka*. But no matter, yes? We find Boris Zorinov, ask him many questions."

Mariana glanced over at her again, a look in her eyes.

"No torture," Ekaterina said. "I ask. You look mean. Or other way: you ask, I stand smiling. He will understand and answer questions."

"And then?"

Ekaterina checked the cars out the window, but none of them concerned her.

"Then we decide what next."

147

THE TRACKER

Level B3
The Ministry of State Security
Beijing, China

Level B3 of the Ministry of State Security building housed the men and women of China's elite computer hacking division. All younger than twenty-five years old.

The deputy bureau chief checked his shirt again. He had misbuttoned it earlier in his haste to return to the office for his briefing with the bureau chief, only discovering the error after the meeting.

He must have looked like a fool.

The door in front of him buzzed and clicked open.

A thin, pale young woman waited inside the door.

The young woman, a stern mid-level manager of the hackers, escorted him into a small, glass-fronted conference room, gestured for him to sit at the round table, and moved to stand in front of a computer screen attached to the side wall.

"Greetings," she began. "My team has the information you requested." She used a small remote control to turn on the screen, revealing a slideshow presentation. "The subject known as Jade is not currently using her assigned cell phone. It has been stationary at her registered residence in New York City for several days. She is using a burner phone."

"How long until you can locate her?"

The woman's expression didn't change, but he could sense her annoyance. "She is leaving New Jersey on her way to Manhattan."

"How did you manage to find her so quickly?"

The woman's lips twitched in the slightest smile. "She is in an SUV provided to another asset in New York. It contains a very well-hidden tracker that we can activate on demand. From this, and the vehicle's movement, we were able to identify her burner phone. You have several options. We can remotely disable the vehicle. We can call or send a message of your choosing to the burner phone. If you'd like, we could also, or instead, send an exploit. It will turn on the phone's camera or microphone, so you would be able to watch and eavesdrop on what she is doing. This would also enable us to read all messages, including any she sends or receives via a secure communications app. However, sending the exploit is not invisible. It would appear as a spam message. She would not have to click or open it, but she would likely suspect she has been pinged by an adversary and abandon the phone."

While the deputy bureau chief was sure the bureau chief would prefer to have full access to Jade's phone, including the microphone, keeping the asset unaware that she was being tracked was paramount.

"We only need real-time tracking of Jade's location for now," he said. "I would like to remain in this room and direct the ongoing operation, with your assistance if possible." It was half request, half command. On this floor, despite his higher rank, the computer experts were in charge.

The woman nodded. "I will display the location data on this monitor and return with a technician to assist us. Do you need anything else?"

"A secure terminal to communicate with a field team. And tea. This may take some time."

"It will be done."

The manager left the room, leaving him to consider what had to be done. The first step was vectoring in the covert operations team.

What happened next would be up to them—and Jade.

148

THE BLUE DOT

Unit 47A
The Summit at 57th
Manhattan

Void didn't mind the dark room after being in coffee shops all day. Escaping the confines of his bedroom, and the terrifying heights of the forty-seventh floor, had done wonders for his mood.

As long as it wasn't windy, which made the building sway, he could pretend he wasn't so high above Manhattan.

Accessing the cellular backbone switch network hadn't been easy, but with software tools he'd bought on the black market before combining and turbocharging them, he had discovered a way in through a third-party vendor exploit.

The majority of his time had been taken exploring and learning the system.

He was in the database with the phone numbers, SIM IDs, and device IDs.

After comparing the data with the information Axe had provided about the meeting at the café and Jade's movements afterwards, Void ran a simple search query...

He pinged Haley.

I think I have her! Can you come in?

In the large condo, it was easier and quicker to send a message than to go find people.

Void debated leaving his main screen fully displayed; he was proud of his work. But the less Haley knew about what he'd had to do to get her the information she needed, the better. Accessing these systems was a big risk. His priority was finding the data Haley needed to protect the country. But a close second was keeping himself safe. As terrifying as the forty-seventh floor was, he lived in a luxury condo with staff to cook and clean, along with Mariana and Kelton, who were fun to hang out with from time to time.

He also felt responsible for Haley. She couldn't know how much risk he was taking. If things went wrong, he couldn't take her down with him.

Void checked his connection for the tenth time in an hour, making sure his efforts to hide his location and identity were solid. Everything looked good, but he added another relay to be sure—one extra hoop for anyone looking for him to jump through. In a few minutes, he would add more, drop the old ones, and keep that going until he'd done all that Haley and Axe needed.

If anyone tracked and caught him, maybe they would only see a fraction of what he'd been up to tonight instead of all the hacking he'd done.

At a knock on the door, Void pressed a single button to hide the main screen, which showed the inner workings of the cellular networks and databases he had wormed his way into.

"Come in," he called, and zoomed in on a map of New Jersey. A blue dot blinked at The Essex Exchange Lofts in Newark, New Jersey.

"She's by the Newark Airport," Void said as Haley entered, followed by Axe. "Do you think she knows we are onto her and is getting ready to leave the country?"

Haley stopped next to his desk, and Axe stood behind him. He and Axe were now on the same side, but the guy still made Void nervous.

"There—that blue dot? That's her?" Axe asked.

"Yes. Or that's her phone, at least. A prepaid phone—a burner," Void said. "The one she had with her—but turned off—at the Saffron café Tuesday night."

"Calls? Texts? Messages?" Axe asked.

"I haven't had time to find that part of the system," Void explained. "I can work on that next, though that's trickier. See, accessing location data, or viewing bank records like we did earlier, is merely extremely hard. But making changes, or in this case, viewing private messages, that's a much tougher level of security."

"She's not moving?" Haley asked. "Just hanging out at an apartment?"

"Looks like it," Void said. "But understand, I don't have full access to the phone. Give me some time—hours, maybe a day. I might be able to send a phony text. If she clicks on it, I could gain access to the camera and microphone, but that's state-level hacking. I need to buy some expensive tools from shady people on the dark web, and—"

"This will all be over by morning," Axe muttered. "My prediction, at least. She's either running or hitting something nearby."

"Like the airport," Haley said. "A plane? How? Security is tight these days."

"A seduced TSA worker. A baggage handler. Or she could try to blow up a cargo plane. It wouldn't be as spectacular as a passenger plane, but if she has access to the right material, she could try to ship a bomb."

"Or..." Void mumbled, then shut up. These two didn't need him adding his stupid ideas.

"What?" Axe asked.

"No, nothing."

"Tell us," Haley said. She was serious.

"Well, look. Right next to the airport," Void said and used his mouse to move the map and zoom in more. "As soon as you said, 'shipping a bomb,' my eye caught this." He jiggled the mouse so the cursor moved over the waterfront. "This whole area is the major hub for container shipments in and out of the Northeastern United States. Security is tight at the airport, and I'm sure it must be at the shipping terminals, too, but as tight? Passenger airplanes versus container ships?"

"Not likely," Haley said.

Void took her words as encouragement. "Maybe, I don't know, they try to steal one of those big ships? Ram it into something. Try to take out a bridge?" He moved the cursor south to hover over the Verrazzano Bridge.

"Even sinking a boat in a channel would wreak havoc for days or weeks until it could be cleared," Axe said.

"So, can't we, like, have the police go over there to check it out first?" Void asked.

"We don't know what she's capable of," Haley said. "Or, really, if she's up to something at all. We only have our suspicions."

"She tried to kill Axe," Void said.

"No proof," Haley said. "Axe didn't see her do it, and we didn't find any security camera footage."

"What about the ambush in the subway tunnel?"

"Jade wasn't anywhere near that. Only Darius. Her boyfriend, yes, but again, it's at least one step removed. No, we have to do it our way."

"And we're fine with that," Axe said. He turned to go. "Keep on it. Let us know if she moves. Do you know where Darius and Kareem are?"

Void shook his head. "Still working on it. It's harder than you think. They didn't bring phones to the meeting Tuesday night. So I have to—"

Axe cut him off. "First, check for phones near Jade. See if she's with other people. We'll be on comms." He moved toward the door and spoke to Haley. "Come on, Blondie. You want to be on overwatch? It's time to go."

Axe hurried from the room, but Haley held back. "Well done, Void," she said. "Ping me or call with whatever you find."

"He knows it's not simple, right? Only a few other people in the world could do what I've done tonight." Void called as she left at a jog. "It's..." He trailed off. They didn't understand the amount of work it was. But at least he was in this system now. As long as the system administrators and cybersecurity team didn't discover what he was doing, he could do it.

"Figure out where Darius and Kareem are," Void muttered, imitating Axe's commanding voice. "Who is Jade with? Hey, don't forget about Boris Zorinov. Oh, and whatever you do, don't get caught."

At least he was on the team and doing his part.

The risks were worth it.

149

THE BACKPACK

Near the Port Newark-Elizabeth Marine Terminal
Newark, New Jersey

"We get in, sabotage the cranes, and get out," Clay told his team in the back of a beat-up white panel van. One of the guys had an elderly neighbor who went to bed early, was three-quarters deaf, and left his back door unlocked like it was the 1950s. The key to the van was on a hook near the door. If all went according to plan, they'd have the van back before dawn with no one looking for it—or them.

Everyone wore latex gloves, long sleeve black shirts, black pants, and, of course, their masks. They would leave as few traces as possible. No fingerprints, nothing on security cameras to identify them, no DNA.

"From now on, no names, just our masks," he added.

Clay's dark-red Devil mask, complete with small black horns, made him feel anonymous—but hot.

The rest of the men fidgeted as they crouched, adjusting their masks and checking the upgraded weapons Jade had provided.

Scary Clown, who Clay had worked with for three years, had the biggest, best bolt cutters money could buy. He would cut the chain-link fence.

"Everybody ready?" Clay asked.

Nods all around.

"This is different from our usual paintball tournament, but we've trained for it. Don't shoot unless you have to. The workers here aren't our enemies. They're guys putting in the hours and living paycheck to paycheck. If you can, aim for a leg. Drop 'em, disarm 'em, wrap 'em up, and move on." They all had zip cuffs—industrial strength zip ties pre-shaped into two circles to make it easy to secure people.

"But if it's us or them," one of his crew wearing the Zombie mask said, "We light them up. Plenty of ammo, just like in paintball. This goes south, we fire. Tactical retreat to the van. No one left behind, including a body. Too easy to tie us together. Agreed?"

Zombie had wanted to be the leader for a while now. Clay didn't mind him being bossy. He had good ideas.

"Agreed," Clay said, along with the others.

He was getting out of this alive, even if he had to shoot his way to freedom.

Jade would be waiting.

"Okay," Clay said. "Let's knock this place out."

Tomorrow, the United States would understand how horrible cheap products from other countries were. The people would finally start to wake up.

Scary Clown led the way out the back of the van, which they'd parked near a vulnerable section of the port's miles-long security fence. Because of the sprawling size of the East Coast's largest container terminal, there were soft spots. The port police couldn't be everywhere, and the men sitting in the security office weren't able to monitor every camera all the time.

With stealth and speed, they could cut the fence, run inside, and blow up as many of the fourteen gantry cranes as they could, choking off the supply of everything from food to clothes and toys to machinery coming in, waste paper, scrap metal, even bulk chemicals going out.

He followed the last man out—Werewolf—and gently shut the van's back door. It made a soft click in the dark.

None of the men had asked how he'd acquired the bombs in his backpack. They didn't want to know anything more about Dragon than they already did.

150

THE ALARM

Unit 47A
The Summit at 57th
Manhattan

Void was closing in on more of the intel Axe and Haley needed when his computer went crazy. The speakers blared the *honk honk honk* of a car alarm.

It took him a frantic second to lower the volume, and another to remember what that alarm meant.

He clicked a button on his mouse to display an overview of the dozens of windows littering his screens.

One flashed red.

Void silenced the alarm, then navigated to the window.

A man named Boris Yarkov—Boris Zorinov's fake name—had used his credit card to check into a hotel on Broadway near Union Square, on the edge of Greenwich Village.

Void opened a group chat on the comms software. He included Haley and Mariana. Axe would be too busy fighting off bad guys at the container port to deal with messages.

Boris Yarkov (Zorinov) checked into The Grand Ambassador Hotel earlier tonight. Room number to come.

He hit send. A moment later, both Mariana and Haley acknowledged receipt.

Void navigated to the hotel's website.

Let's see how good your security is.

Greenwich Village

"We found Boris," Mariana announced. She and Ekaterina had been driving the narrow side streets of Greenwich Village, hoping for lightning to strike. Was it too much to ask for Boris to cross the street in front of them, Jade to stroll along the block on her way home, Darius to leave a bodega, or Kareem to need a midnight snack?

Mariana made a quick calculation and turned onto Sixth Avenue, where she'd been riding in the van with Axe only two hours before.

"He's in a hotel nearby," Mariana told her new temporary partner. Ekaterina didn't talk much, but Mariana enjoyed her company and was growing to trust the Russian woman.

"Let us go see him, yes?"

"Absolutely," Mariana said.

151

THE GATHERING

Times Square
Manhattan

Crane had his team of operators spread out over a two-block area of the bright lights and touristy glitz of Times Square to better follow Jade Pang.

All four were dressed in black jeans and long sleeve black T-shirts against the chill of the morning, but their military training had conditioned them to ignore minor issues like cold, hunger, and tiredness, all of which they felt tonight but suppressed.

They were on a critical mission, one they'd hoped for and dreamed of, but never thought they'd experience. Discomfort didn't matter.

Black earbuds allowed them to communicate via an encrypted group phone chat. They looked like nearly every other New Yorker or tourist listening to music as they strolled through the city late at night.

They had secured pistols and zip ties from a small twenty-four-hour storage locker in Chinatown, both options if Jade Pang refused to accompany them willingly.

A few minutes earlier, Crane had picked up Pang's tail when she had walked through a small public area in the middle of Times Square before doubling back.

Exactly as expected. It's what they would have done in her situation to ensure they weren't being followed—and they were ready for the move.

Crane had ducked into a glass-enclosed building housing a modern subway entrance when Vulture had reported Pang was coming his way. They had three objectives from the Ministry of State Security: find out what the undercover asset was doing, stop it, and bring her in—alive.

"I've got her," Crane said. He stood well back from the building's windows, partly hidden behind a kiosk that displayed a huge subway map. "She turned east onto Forty-second Street and is... Wait. Target has entered the building. The one under construction. There's a service entrance with signs that say *Restricted*." Crane hesitated, torn between keeping Pang in sight and getting caught by her if she was performing yet another surveillance detection route. "Cover the other three sides of the building," he ordered. "Quickly! We need to learn if this is her destination, if she's going to reappear any moment to see if she's being followed, or if there's another exit she can use to lose any tails."

"I have the west side covered from across the street," Vulture reported.

"North side partly covered," Sparrow said. "Moving to a position to see the entire area. Fifteen seconds."

"Northeast corner is secure," Owl said. "And... yes, I have the east side in view. No sign of her."

"Well done," Crane said. "She couldn't have made it through the building fast enough to lose us, so she's still inside. It's either her target building, or she's holding back for a few minutes."

There was a subway entrance next to the construction door to the building, but any interior connector door would be locked this late at night. Not that Jade couldn't pick a lock, but it would take a lot of planning and luck to slip into the building only to use it to access the subway. It was a chance he was willing to take.

"Did she notice us?" Owl asked. He was the most careful of them.

"I don't think so," Crane said after a moment. "No change in body language or speed. After five SDR moves, she would have felt in the clear."

They'd tailed her from a parking garage, where they had been concerned they would lose her, but she emerged from the single entrance a few moments after they had spread out in the area.

They'd been waiting on a side street in Midtown in a car available specifically for this type of emergency when the message came in via secure comms: Pang, in a trackable SUV, was on her way from New Jersey to Manhattan. The MSS had vectored them to a parking garage near

Times Square quickly enough to cover the area in time to see their target emerge.

Unfortunately, the local asset they'd been told to expect—a covert assassin based in New York—had gone dark. They were on their own.

"The backpack looked excessively heavy," Owl muttered, voicing the thought that was on all their minds.

"Too heavy for weapons," Sparrow said.

"What weighs so much? Not C-4," Sparrow said. They were familiar with the plastic explosive.

"If she has gone rogue, the building would make an excellent sniper position," Owl said. "A long gun wouldn't fit in that short of a pack, but at these distances, a carbine would be enough to kill many people. The bag would hold a lot of ammunition."

"We'll find out what it is shortly," Crane said with more confidence than he felt. Pang's behavior meant she was definitely in mission mode. Her actions weren't those of an about-to-graduate American college student moving onto a job on Wall Street.

Aurelia Tower
Times Square
Manhattan

The punk-goth outfit worked for Jade after midnight in Times Square. Most tourists were in their hotels, except the ones who were jet-lagged and not scared of walking around New York City late at night. Otherwise, only workers, partiers, and weirdos were out on a Wednesday night into Thursday morning.

The backpack partly ruined the ensemble of black clothes, short spiked black hair, and goth makeup, but there was nothing she could do about that. Her baby was inside. It was her whole purpose for being here, and the surest way for her plan to work, no matter what Clay and his band of idiots managed.

With the bomb, and the emergency alert she'd send once back at the safe house in Soho, the stock market would plummet.

She would make millions, and the financial patrons of the past attack would be appeased. They might be happy and greedy enough to support her future missions.

"I'm here for the rave?" Jade said to a sleepy guy about her age sitting on a wooden stool near the side door of the building she'd picked out. She had originally planned on using one of the hotels in the area, but the skyscraper undergoing renovation had been on her newsfeed and was much better. It was twenty-two stories tall—though she didn't need to go that high to accomplish her goal—and empty at night. There would be no prying eyes or people questioning her moves, except for one tired guard at the construction entrance.

"Rave?" he asked, eyeing her outfit and lingering on her backpack. "Like a late-night dance?"

Sleepy and not the brightest bulb, she thought.

"Yeah, this is the place, right?" She held her latest burner phone in her left hand, screen toward the guard.

He leaned forward to see it.

Jade jabbed him in the throat with a razor-sharp tactical knife from Lou's storage garage.

The sounds he made were extraordinary. A *gurgle* from the blade in his throat combined with a *gasp* and a choking noise as he struggled to breathe. His eyes were wide with shock as he searched her face for an answer she didn't have for him.

Jade lost track of time, but it couldn't have been more than several seconds before she refocused and yanked the knife from the now-dead guard's throat.

She dragged the guard's body farther into the building and set him in a corner with his head slumped forward, hiding the worst of the gore. He looked like a young man who had snuck away to take a nap.

Jade opened the comms app on the burner phone and carefully selected a speed dial number. It wouldn't do to blow up one of the bombs she'd given to Clay.

At least, not yet.

And it would be worse to send a signal to the one in her backpack. She would be far away when it blew.

Darius answered. "I'm almost there. Where are you? And what's going on?"

"I told you, I'll explain everything. I'm inside—look for a wooden stool by the door and come straight in."

Tonight, Darius would prove his worth—and his commitment to her.

Or she would leave him behind.

She wondered what noises he would make as he died? Gurgles and gasps if she killed him like she'd done the guard? Or could she take her time and make him beg? That might be fun.

Either way, the C-4 explosives would demolish his body.

One more loose end eliminated.

———

42nd Street
Times Square

"I'm going to enter the building," Crane said on the comms. "Owl, shift south to cover the door and as much of the west side as you can keep in view. There's a small subway entrance immediately to the east of it. If she slips past me, I don't want her to duck around the corner and vanish into the subway system."

"Copy. Give me twenty seconds."

Crane moved to the exit, never taking his eyes off the building across the street…

And the young man hurrying toward it.

"Hold," Crane said. "I have the target's boyfriend nearing the construction entrance."

Darius was an asset who Pang had recruited on orders from the MSS, according to the briefing material they had sent Crane for this mission.

"He's gone in," Crane said, hurrying to leave his stakeout position. He had to get inside the other building. If he lost them, they would have to search level by level until they found the target and her asset-turned-boyfriend.

But should he go alone or bring all the men in?

"Give me sixty seconds, then converge on this entrance," he ordered. His gut told him this was the moment. It all fit: the strange punk-rock outfit, so different from what he'd been told to expect. The heavy backpack. The boyfriend. All in the middle of the night in Times Square, New York City's premier tourist area?

Nothing good could come of waiting. They had to intercept Pang now, confront her, and convince her to come with them.

Or take her by force.

Aurelia Tower
Times Square

Jade stared at the body of the dead guard, committing the scene to memory, until her boyfriend—for at least the next half hour—slipped through the doorway and stopped short next to her, in front of the guard.

Darius looked at the dead body, then turned away, ignoring it. "Will you please tell me what's going on? This wasn't part of the plan."

"I had to make some changes," Jade said. She would have liked to give him the backpack to carry but didn't want to risk it. He would eventually question the heavy pack, but the longer she could put it off, the better.

"Come on, we have to get to a higher floor," she said. "I'll explain there."

The freight elevator call button lit up when she pressed it, and she smiled. She wouldn't have to lug the bomb—and deal with Darius—up several flights of stairs.

See, everything's working out perfectly.

42nd Street
Times Square

Kareem slowed on his way to the doorway Darius had entered a few moments earlier. It could be a surveillance detection move, though he doubted it. Darius had taken a roundabout route here in the taxi, passing several of New York's top tourist locations.

Darius likely felt he'd put in plenty of effort to disguise his destination. But he had just gotten out of the taxi, so Kareem removed his phone and leaned against a gray wall of the building next door, a short half block east of the construction entrance door Darius had entered. He was partly hidden by a series of construction support poles holding up an extensive awning, and this stretch of Forty-second Street, just around the corner from Times Square, was as dark as New York City got. Enough for him not to stand out.

I'll give him sixty seconds. That would be enough time for Darius to feel secure and leave the building if it wasn't his actual destination.

A building under construction would be the perfect place for him to eliminate Darius, especially if he could throw the man out of a window or down a flight of stairs. Anything to raise a doubt about whether Darius had killed himself, had an unfortunate accident, or had been murdered.

But why would the Iranian leave the Greenwich Village area and come to Times Square this late at night?

It made no sense. There were other buildings under construction closer to school and their homes.

Kareem was about to push off the wall and continue when a man jaywalked across the street directly toward the construction entrance door. He had Asian features and was dressed in black pants and a long-sleeved shirt. He moved with too much focus for this late at night. Not hurrying, exactly, but… intent.

As casually as possible, Kareem turned, looking at his phone, and crossed the street to the opposite side.

He has to be an operator—but why is he after Darius?

Unless Jade had brought friends on board, like the one who had tried to ambush the warrior in the subway.

Kareem found another subway entrance along the street and went down the steps just enough to disappear from view but still see the street and bottom part of the door to the building.

The operator went directly through the construction entrance.

Not long after, three other men, all short with fine black hair, dressed in black, entered as well.

A team of operators.

Following Darius.

Darius is meeting Jade here for some reason. And she has friends.

If Kareem's theory was correct, it would be him against four trained operators, Jade, and Darius.

He could take Darius. No problem there.

Jade? She had an inner rage and bitterness, carefully hidden, but he had caught glimpses over the past few years. She was also quite strong, though she didn't have the combat training he had.

The operators were the problem.

After giving the men a minute, Kareem hurried up the stairs, across the street, and along the sidewalk.

Surprise was on his side.

152

HOUSEKEEPING

The Grand Ambassador Hotel
Union Square
Manhattan

Mariana still didn't understand how they were going to access Boris Zorinov's hotel room or get him into the van parked in the hotel's loading zone.

Ekaterina had breezed past two security guards, waving a beige keycard at them—from a different hotel—with a little-old-lady smile. She and Mariana waltzed across the hotel lobby and into the elevator without any questions.

Mariana followed Ekaterina along the long, quiet hotel corridor. The carpet was a typical abstract design in dark purple, gray, black, and beige.

Ekaterina slowed as they neared the door to room 1421 and gestured for Mariana to stay back. She used the keycard she had flashed in the lobby to knock on Zorinov's door.

"Housekeeping," she called, her accent more pronounced than usual. "Is water leak from floor fifteen. We must check your room. Apologies. Open please."

She waited ten seconds, then knocked again. The plastic key pierced the early morning quiet of the floor. Surely any nearby guests were waking up, too. "Housekeeping. Water leak from floor above. We check. Open now please. Sorry to wake you."

She stepped back, angling her body so Boris could look out and see a harmless-looking little old lady.

This was the opposite of the subtle, stealth approach Mariana preferred, or the semi-official plan she'd presented to Ekaterina: go to hotel security, flash Mariana's Homeland Security badge, explain about a potential witness to a terrorist attack, and demand they unlock the room.

Ekat hadn't bothered to respond. She'd merely smiled slightly and shook her head, discounting the idea from the start.

Mariana watched carefully, part of her wondering at what point Ekaterina would knife her in the back, or grab her by the head and twist. From all Axe and Haley had said, the "little old lady" was a stone-cold killer and a force to be reckoned with. When Axe had related his trip to Dubai, where the woman had approached him and suggested they work together, he'd spoken of her with respect and wariness.

Ekaterina caught Mariana's eye while they waited after the second knock. A barely perceptible move with her eyes, along with an expression that Mariana took as, "Don't look now."

Then she heard it. The smallest noise from the door across the hall.

Ekaterina turned slowly to face room 1423 while Mariana eased across to that side of the hall.

Ekaterina spoke in Russian. All Mariana caught was "Boris."

Boris had woken to a sense of danger, but mostly confusion.

Why was he sleeping on the floor with his head against a door?

And where was he?

The door had a peep hole for security.

Boris had stumbled to his feet, cast off the sheet and blanket, which he'd gotten wrapped up in as he slept, and checked the hallway.

A short woman with thinning, obviously dyed hair cut short, stood in the hallway holding a keycard.

Was she a maid?

She had used the keycard to knock on the door across the hall.

That's what had woken him—the knocking.

None of this made sense. He was…

He frowned.

He was…

Boris.

Boris… something. He was rich. He was sure of it. But the rest was lost. His memory had been giving him trouble lately. He remembered that.

This was obviously a hotel room. The ugly hallway carpet and the door with the peep hole proved that. And he had the sense it wasn't as nice as the hotels he preferred.

He had left the door behind and gone to the bathroom, lit by a nightlight, relieved himself, and washed his hands.

There had been a time in his life when such luxuries were out of reach.

The pleasure of a clean, nearby bathroom accessible when needed.

Running water to wash up with.

His memory might not be what it had been, but he'd come a long way since his childhood.

He had returned to the door to observe the drama in the hallway.

The little old lady stepped close, looking directly at him. "Boris, open the door," she said. "We must talk."

Before, she had knocked and called out in English. She spoke to him in Russian.

What did that mean? The entire situation raised alarm bells.

He didn't want to open the door, but what choice did he have?

He kicked aside the bedding on the floor and checked the bedroom area.

No clues.

Could he escape?

There was no other door. Pulling the curtains aside showed a view of a city he wasn't familiar with, and he was on too high of a floor to escape out the window.

A knock came from the door, soft this time. The woman hadn't used the keycard.

He didn't hear what she said, so he moved closer and looked out again. The woman was right there, separated only by the width of the door. Her head came to just below the peephole, and her gray roots were visible.

"Boris," she said again, still in Russian. With them so close together, it felt strangely intimate despite the door. "It is late. We are all tired. You have my word—no harm will come to you tonight."

He was out of options.

Maybe talking to this woman would jog his memory.

He opened the door.

153

THE TIMER

Container Storage Area
South Dock
The Port Newark-Elizabeth Marine Terminal
Newark, New Jersey

The shipping terminal was far bigger than Clay had expected. He helped with logistics for shipping companies, and conceptually understood the size, but the sheer magnitude of the facility came as a shock to them all.

"This sucks," Scary Clown muttered. They were all gasping for breath. In paintball tournaments, they ran hard, but for twenty or thirty yards. They focused on frequent, short sprints, not this ridiculous run down a long dock.

The cranes loomed in the distance. They'd already been running for what seemed like forever, and they had a long way to go.

"You wimps," Zombie said. He was their fitness freak, often going for jogs during their lunch break and eating healthy—a salad at the Italian restaurant after a tournament win instead of pizza.

He was also the most gung-ho about tonight.

"Give me one of the bombs," Zombie said.

They cut between two huge shipping containers, sheltering in the shadows. So far, they had run undetected through the night. There were lights on tall poles reaching into the night sky, but there were plenty of shadows near the shipping containers, especially this far from the cranes where the lights were fewer and less bright.

Clay unslung the backpack and removed one of the small packets. It looked like two chunks of light-gray modeling clay with cling-wrap surrounding them. Wires connected a phone strapped to one side to something inserted most of the way into the C-4 explosives. There was a small black timer on the other side of the packet. Jade had shown Clay how to turn it on, set the time, and start the countdown. "Ten minutes?" he asked.

"It's going to take me ten minutes just to run to that first damn crane," Scary Clown said. He was bent at the waist, still gasping from the first part of the run.

"It's not that far," Clay said. It would only take another minute or two to run the distance. "But I'll set it to fifteen." Clay clicked the button until *15:00* flashed on the screen. "Zombie—run to the farthest crane. We'll take out the ones closest. We'll use the explosions as cover to get out of here."

"Gimme," Zombie said, though he waited for Clay to gently place the explosives in his hand. He held the C-4 and looked around the group, like he was making up his mind—or finding his courage.

"That makes sense," Zombie said. "I'll run to the first crane of the far grouping. Each group of cranes handles one ship, right? The plan was to take out as many groupings as we could, but it's too far. We'll never reach them all." His voice had a tinge of regret—though there was fear, too. The reality and magnitude of what they were doing was hitting home for them all.

"We could turn back…" Scary Clown said. He had caught his breath.

"No," Clay said, while the rest nodded—some more enthusiastically than others. "We're committed. We have C-4 plastic explosives! We were going to rip wires out or shoot up the engine of the cranes or something. But with bombs, man, we are set. This place is ours. Ready?" Everyone straightened up and prepared to run again.

Zombie held up the bomb. With a flourish, he held his finger over the timer, hesitated for a second, and pressed the start button. The counter changed to *14:59*. They all watched, mesmerized.

There was no turning back now. The bomb might be easy to disarm, but Clay hadn't bothered to ask Jade about it.

He checked his watch and figured out the time he had to set the next ones so they'd all go off together.

"Let's go!" Clay said to the guys.

Zombie took off down the long row of shipping containers toward the far cranes to the northeast. They would handle the closer ones along the southern edge of the terminal.

The brief chance to catch their breath had helped. They were ready.

154

THE FLIGHT

Upper New York Bay
New York/New Jersey Border

The helicopter skimmed the surface of the water. Off to the right, the Statue of Liberty flashed by—above them.

Haley wasn't comfortable with the helicopter flying at such low levels, but she said nothing. Axe, Johnboy, and Mad Dog looked focused but relaxed, and they had a lot more experience with this than she did. If they weren't worried, she wouldn't be, either.

"Void says the phone is moving again," she said through the headsets Tucci had provided. The luxury helicopter for ferrying wealthy people around the tri-state area, especially to the ritzy parts of Long Island, was relatively quiet, but the headsets made communication much easier. "Right across the street from where it stopped for a few minutes. It's definitely the shipping port. Southwest side."

"Where do you want me to set you down?" Tucci asked.

Haley's phone pinged with another message from Void, which she read twice, then again.

"Haley?" Axe asked. "Where can we land? And can we get in touch with the Port Police so they know we're coming to help, and not part of the attack?"

"Sorry," Haley said. "Another message from Void. While the group was stationary, probably parked along the road, Void finished working his magic. There are seven phones active in the group."

"Seven guys?" Mad Dog asked. "So much for us not being outnumbered this time."

"That's just it," Haley said. "The phones are right on top of each other." She looked up at Axe. "The phones aren't necessarily the number of tangos. I think they're connected to bombs."

The team in the chopper soaked that in for a second until Tucci interrupted. "We're going to be there very soon unless you want me to circle around. I need to know where you want me to drop you."

"What would you want to blow up at a shipping port?" Axe asked.

"The cranes," Johnboy said immediately. "They're huge, expensive, and the heart of the place. Knock them out and it shuts down a ton of capacity."

Haley zoomed in on the map. "There are four in a row at the south end, and another four along the dock running mostly north-south. That's eight close together."

"Or they could take out one or two in each set and move on to others," Axe said.

"Guys," Tucci said. "Now or never."

"Southeast corner," Haley told him. "There should be space there. Come in from the south, over the bay."

The helicopter banked left, the seatbelt holding her in place as she slipped the headset off one ear and placed a call. "911, what is your emergency?"

"This is Holly Schoharie from Alcohol, Tobacco, and Firearms," she said, using her fake name. "Alert the port police at the Port Elizabeth Terminal that they have intruders. Unknown number, entering from the southwest corner. This is not a drill. This is real-world. Time now. Also, I'm inbound in a commercial helicopter with ATF officers to help repel or apprehend the intruders. Make the port police aware that my guys are not hostiles."

"Ma'am, you're saying that—"

Haley didn't hear the rest. She clicked off the call and used the comms app to speed dial Nancy. As soon as she answered, Haley spoke. There was no time for pleasantries. "It's definitely the container port. I called 911, but contact the Port Police directly."

"I have them on the line," Nancy said. "I told them it was a drill."

"It's not a drill. Let them know the tangos, number unknown, are moving along the south dock toward the east. We're guessing they'll go after the cranes—and they most likely have multiple bombs and semi-automatic weapons."

Nancy repeated the information for the police on the line of another phone. "And tell them not to shoot at the helicopter, or Axe and the guys."

"Thirty seconds," Tucci said.

"I already told them about that," Nancy said. "They're opening up their armory now for plate carriers and heavier weapons than they usually carry."

"Smart. Tell them to let us take point. Have them finish gearing up and hang back until we assess the situation. We're only seconds away from landing. I don't want them to take shots at us in the excitement."

Haley's phone buzzed with a secure call from Void. She must have missed a message.

"Gotta go," she told Nancy, and clicked over to Void.

The helicopter flared. Mad Dog crouched at the right-side door with Johnboy stacked behind him, waiting for the signal to go. Axe did the same near Haley, on the left.

"We're a little busy here, Void," Haley said.

"There's another phone!" Void yelled, forcing Haley to hold hers away from her ear. "Jade Pang. She has those burner phones, right? The bombs, maybe. But she also has another phone. Same lot, bought from the same store, on the same day. And it's not there in New Jersey. It's near Times Square in Manhattan!"

155

THE INTERRUPTION

The Kremlin
Moscow, Russia

Dmitry slowed from a run to a very brisk walk as he approached the door to President Nikitin's office. The two guards, stationed on either side of the door, usually ignored him. As the Foreign Intelligence Service's chief spy, he had clearance to come and go at will, and reported to President Nikitin several times a week. But the guards had never seen him run before.

Both shifted, raising their weapons slightly. They looked past him down the hall, ready for trouble. "Is everything okay, comrade?" one asked.

"There's no threat," Dmitry said, forcing himself to sound reassuring.

Not from the hallway, at least, he thought.

The door didn't slow him down. He knocked twice as he opened it, not waiting for permission to enter.

President Nikitin looked up sharply from across the room. A powerful businessman sat in one of the guest chairs across from the president. He turned and scowled at Dmitry, clearly annoyed that his time with the president was being disturbed.

Dmitry glanced at one of the guards posted against the wall and nodded his head toward the guest.

The guard moved immediately toward the man in the chair.

"Mr. President," Dmitry called as he strolled across the thick carpet. "Please pardon the interruption, but I need your time for an urgent matter."

"Mr. President, I must request—"

The businessman quieted when the guard grasped his upper arm, squeezed hard, and escorted him from the room.

With a flick of Dmitry's hand, the two other guards in the room exited through the hidden doors near them.

It was the firmest and most decisive Dmitry had acted in his life, and the president noticed. He stood at his desk, concern on his face. "What is it? What happened?"

President Nikitin had the looks of a college economics professor. He seemed smart but harmless, like he would corner you at a cocktail reception and bore you to death with facts, figures, and statistics.

The well-trimmed beard and plain suit hid the sharp mind and ruthless character of a man committed to restoring his country to its former glory. Nikitin had come into power—and learned an important lesson—when his predecessor had been killed on the eve of the attempted invasion of Ukraine, Latvia, and Estonia. The invasion that would have been disastrous given the state of the army, which Dmitry helped Nikitin discover after he had assumed leadership of the country.

"What do you have that has you acting so imperious, Dmitry?" President Nikitin asked.

Dmitry had rehearsed a calm and measured presentation on the way, but it fled his mind as he reached the president's desk.

Dmitry hesitated, at a loss for words.

"Spit it out. Whatever it is, we will deal with it."

"Yes, sir." Dmitry cleared his throat. "Upon your orders, we conducted a review of Boris Zorinov's activities and connections to see if he stole anything in addition to the polonium-210 he acquired and used to kill America's Secretary of State."

The president had to prompt him again. "And?"

"We uncovered a concerning issue. Mr. President," Dmitry began, then faltered. Saying it would make it real, and he desperately didn't want it to be real. "Our investigation turned up a distant connection between Boris Zorinov and individuals at the Ministry of Health. Following up on this, my team discovered that a radiotherapy unit decommissioned in Novosibirsk shows an active cesium-137 source in its records. The paperwork claims the cesium-137 was removed for disposal, but my audit team found no confirmation of it arriving at the disposal site. We are digging deeper. There is a chance it is simply a clerical error. We hope."

The president looked confused, which wasn't a surprise. Dmitry's people had to ask questions and learn more when the inventory made the director of the Ministry of Health turn deathly white at the news of missing cesium-137.

"Sir, cesium-137, in this case, was used for cancer treatment. It is a concentrated source of cesium. Its containment canister is lead-lined. It is about the size of a small fire extinguisher with a handle on top. It is heavy because of the lead shielding. The actual core is quite small, a short metal cylinder that is no larger than a household battery. It looks like a bolt for a piece of machinery."

Nikitin still hadn't grasped the ramifications.

"Mr. President, cesium-137 is highly radioactive. It is what makes a 'dirty bomb' dirty. If someone were to attach explosives and blow it up, this small amount of material would be devastating. If detonated in a city, it would turn entire neighborhoods into poisoned ground—not with fire and rubble, but with invisible, radioactive dust that would cling to everything. There would be mass panic. Neighborhoods and possibly the entire city would empty. There would be chaos in the streets. People would die from the panic. Within months, and continuing for years, we would have a humanitarian health crisis. Depending on concentration, proximity, and length of exposure, there would be a cancer epidemic of catastrophic proportions."

President Nikitin sat, finally understanding the news.

"How easy would it be for someone to ship or smuggle the canister out of the country?" the president finally asked.

"Very easy, sir. With the protective lead lining, it would go undetected by radiation sensors. Only a visual inspection would cause an alert or alarm. There are always radiation warning signs attached to such devices, but these could be removed, of course. Then it would look like a heavy thermos with a welded handle, or a short fire extinguisher. Most people would not understand what it was."

"So it could be anywhere, whether Boris Zorinov is involved or not."

"Yes, Mr. President."

"Assuming Zorinov is involved, is there any news from Ekaterina, our assassin?"

"Nothing sir, but with your permission, I will contact her immediately and direct her to only apprehend Zorinov, not kill him, unless the cesium-137 container is also secured."

The president nodded before Dmitry finished. "Yes, do so immediately. And find the container."

"Yes, sir. Thank you, Mr. President."

Dmitry turned and hurried from the room. He had to get a message to Ekaterina before she carried out her original orders.

156

THE UNCLE

The Grand Ambassador Hotel
Union Square
Manhattan

Mariana had recognized the look on Boris Zorinov's face the moment he had opened the door to Ekaterina's quiet, almost intimate words in Russian.

The half-smile on his round face hid an attentive search for clues and context, along with a look in his blue eyes that showed a desperation to hide the truth: he didn't know what was going on.

She'd seen it on her uncle's face often enough in his last year as dementia changed him from sharp-witted with a great sense of humor to a quiet man who rarely spoke. His passions switched from devouring books, both non-fiction and novels, to spending all day in his easy chair, dozing and watching birds at his backyard feeder.

Zorinov stood in the doorway, searched Ekaterina's face, then turned to her when he came up short.

"We've been worried about you, Uncle Boris," Mariana blurted out, cutting off Ekaterina as she was about to say something. If she were guessing wrong, she'd look foolish, but it wouldn't change the situation. "We've come to bring you home. The food is so much better there," she said before turning to her temporary partner. "Kat, it's late. Can we take Uncle Boris home now?"

Ekaterina said nothing. For a moment, Mariana thought the assassin would kill the man in the doorway and be done with it, but after a second, she went along with the improvised plan.

"You're right," Ekat said. "Let's get home and have some tea…" She winked at Boris. "Or maybe vodka. That would be nice."

Boris had been uncertain until Ekat mentioned the vodka. "I would enjoy that," he said. He hesitated, looking away for a moment as if chasing a thought. "Are we going to the yacht?"

Mariana took him by the hand. She hadn't thought of that until now, but it would work perfectly. "Exactly," she said. "The yacht awaits."

"It's peaceful there. And safe, right?"

"Yes," Mariana said. "It's the safest place for us now."

Mariana gently guided Boris down the hall, saying nothing, with Ekaterina following behind. With her uncle, the smallest thing could sometimes set him off, especially toward the end.

Other times, an offhand remark between people nearby would restore small parts of his memory, and he'd be back to his old self for a few precious moments.

All they had to do was get him to the van. If necessary, they could tie him up there.

157

THE COMMITMENT

South Berth
Shipping Dock
Port Elizabeth Terminal
Newark, New Jersey

The helicopter touched down with surprising grace for such a fast ride in. Haley processed Void's words. Jade Pang had another phone, and it was headed toward Times Square.

Axe swung the door open beside her.

"Axe, hold!" Haley yelled. "Mad Dog and JB, go! Take care of this!" Mad Dog was already out of the door on the far side with Johnboy right on his tail, closing the door behind him.

Next to her, Axe stopped, one arm holding the door open, leaning out, ready to continue but waiting for her.

"Get back in here," Haley said. He followed her instructions, closing the door, but his body language showed how much he wanted to burst outside and get in the fight.

"Tucci, get us to Manhattan right now!" Haley yelled. Whether he heard her over the headset, through the door to the cockpit, or just wanted to get off the dock, she didn't care. The helicopter lifted, spinning away from the bright-blue cranes ahead of them.

"What's going on?" Axe asked. "They need me out there."

"I need you in here," Haley said. "We're going to Manhattan. Void found another phone connected to Jade Pang. It's in Times Square."

Haley juggled her phone, switching to the group chat with Mad Dog and JB. When she had them, she kept it short. "There's another possible threat in the city. Can you two handle the docks?"

Mad Dog answered first. "Sure, the two of us against an unknown number of tangos with bombs? No problem."

"Never mind him," JB said. "We're good. Go take care of the new threat. We created a stir coming in like that, but there's no contact yet."

The helicopter rushed straight toward Manhattan, skimming building rooftops instead of following the bay as they'd flown in.

Axe joined the discussion. "You two handle this. Kick ass. Don't die. Don't get blown up. Kill all the tangos you need to, but be careful of friendly fire."

"Copy that, Papa," Johnboy said.

"We got this, Papa," Mad Dog said. "Go save the city from a bomb or whatever."

"Copy," Axe said. "We're out. Switching channels. Good luck."

Haley slipped on the headset. "Times Square, Tucci. We have a lead on Jade."

"Copy. It won't be long. I'll need a place to land—a building, ideally, unless you want me to drop you in the middle of Forty-second Street and Broadway."

"It might come to that, but we'll figure it out."

"Work fast. We're less than four minutes out."

Haley's phone buzzed with a message from Void, along with a map. "The phone—Jade—has stopped at a building right at the heart of Times Square. It's been completely gutted for remodel."

"I bet it's a bomb," Axe said with his headset on so all three of them could communicate easier. "The attack in New Jersey could be a distraction."

"Oh, great, a bomb," Tucci muttered from the cockpit. "And we're flying right toward it."

"How close can you get me that won't give away we're coming for her?" Axe asked Tucci.

"It depends on the building. Modern windows will block most of the sound."

"Void says several floors of the building are nearly finished. New windows were put in earlier this spring," Haley said.

"Can you land there? Or is this a drop me off and go sort of night?"

"Better drop and go," Tucci said. "I've got plenty of fuel and can set down on a helipad in the vicinity if needed, or return to New Jersey to support and exfil the guys."

"Let's plan on that, then," Axe said. "If there's a break in traffic, can you set me down in the middle of an intersection?"

"A big one, yes. It's iffy for a smaller street."

"Wherever looks good."

"Copy that. What is it about terrorists and Times Square?" Tucci muttered.

Axe loved these moments. The calm before the storm. Riding into battle on a helicopter. Chatting with fellow warriors. Doing what he did best.

"Aside from the former Twin Towers," he said, "it's the symbol of Manhattan, of New York, of America."

"Hang on. We'll be there soon."

Axe didn't bother to hide his smile. He was finally completely back in action.

The Grand Ambassador Hotel
Union Square

Ekaterina had been surprised for a moment when Mariana spoke with Boris as if he was a frail old man instead of a rich master criminal, but it had worked.

The white envelope jutting from Boris's pocket as they walked to the elevator called to her. She expertly pickpocketed it and slipped it into her own pocket for later.

While they waited for the elevator, her burner mission cell phone gave the faintest buzz, felt but unheard in the hallway.

Ekat checked the screen without Boris noticing. It was Dmitry from Russia with an urgent update.

Only her years of experience kept her from cursing aloud.

Instead, she wrote a short message to Blondie and hit send, right as the elevator doors opened.

She stepped inside with Mariana and Boris, hoping that Blondie and Alex would survive the night.

Times Square

Axe had his hand on the doorknob, ready for the word from Tucci as the helicopter flared.

Haley's phone buzzed. "It's Ekaterina," she said, and read the message.

She locked eyes with Axe. After everything they'd been through together, all the missions, the danger, he'd never seen her look so scared.

As Mad Dog would say, "That can't be good."

"Void found Boris," Haley said. "Tex and Ekat have him, but Ekat received an urgent update from her people. Boris may have stolen the materials for a dirty bomb. He could have given it to Jade Pang."

The helicopter hovered twenty feet off the ground, waiting while a taxi zipped by underneath them.

The helicopter finally touched down. Axe nodded at Haley. "Copy that." He opened the door and stepped into Times Square, its neon and LED lights making it more like midday than the middle of the night.

He turned to close the door and nearly collided with Haley.

"No!" he yelled over the noise of the rotors, but she only glared at him, closed the door, and pounded twice on the helicopter before grabbing his hand and dragging him toward the target building up the road.

"This is bigger than me and my safety!"

When the helicopter was higher and they could hear each other easier, Axe opened his mouth to speak, but she cut him off. "Papa, I'm not going in with you. I'm doing my best to honor my commitment to Gregory, the president, you, and myself. Pang is just one person. She may be a spy, she may have training, but you're Alex Southmark. You've got this—no problem. You're back. I can feel it. But if for whatever reason you don't get the job done…" She trailed off.

"Someone else has to," he finished.

"I'll bring reinforcements, but I think stealth is the way to go at first. We don't want an obvious presence here for her to see. If she's cornered, she might blow the bomb and herself with it. You find Jade and the bomb, take her out, and be done with it. We'll be ready here just in case."

"My thoughts exactly. Nothing matters as much as preventing the bomb from going off."

"Yes." They bumped fists. "I'll be here, coordinating the cavalry. Get in, do the job, and get out."

There was nothing more to say.

Axe turned and ran toward the building, hoping they were in time.

THE STAIRS

2nd Floor Landing
Aurelia Tower
Times Square

Crane swore he'd heard the sound of a nearby helicopter coming up the stairwell. Maybe he was simply being paranoid. But a helicopter at low level in the middle of the night while they were hunting Jade Pang because the Ministry of State Security believed she had gone rogue?

It couldn't be good.

"Return to the ground floor and guard the hallway," Crane ordered Sparrow in a voice so low no one else would hear. Though their target had taken the service elevator to the sixth floor, it paid to be careful—always.

"If we're compromised, buy us time," Crane said. The already challenging operation to convince the rogue Pang to return to Beijing would be exponentially more difficult if she was being chased by the authorities.

He didn't know the protocol for that but would find out. Sparrow turned to descend the stairs. Crane gestured for Owl to lead the way upstairs, while he sent a terse secure message to Beijing for more instructions…

He didn't have cellular service. The concrete staircase blocked the signal. He would have to exit the stairs to get a signal. Until then, he would follow his previous orders and continue the hunt for Pang.

Crane hurried up the stairs after Owl. They had to get to the sixth floor.

1st Floor
Aurelia Tower

The sleeping guard in the corner didn't fool Kareem for a moment. The blood dripping down his shirt made what had happened obvious.

Jade had definitely come this way. And if she was killing building guards, whatever she was doing was bigger than she and Darius had outlined to him for crashing the stock market.

With Jade's persuasive power, though, she could have sweet-talked her way into the building.

Maybe the four operators who had followed Darius had killed the guard?

But where is Jade—and Darius, and the operators?

The logical assumption was that Jade and Darius were meeting here.

And that the four operators—all with Asian features—were working with Jade.

The building was twenty-some stories tall. He didn't want to wander from floor to floor searching for Jade, but he preferred not to wait for her and Darius to leave, either.

On impulse, he pressed the elevator call button. As he'd hoped, the small display to the upper right of the door lit up with a *6* and a down arrow.

The elevator had last stopped on the sixth floor.

He'd take the elevator to the fourth floor to avoid being obvious and make his way up.

Sparrow barely reached the ground floor in time. The stairwell door had a glass window, reinforced with wire mesh. He had an angle to most of the hallway.

A man in a black leather jacket and longish black hair had entered the hallway and pressed the button for the elevator.

He sent a message to Crane, hoping it went through. The cellular signal cut in and out, blocked by the concrete walls and fireproof doors, but near the door to the hallway he had a weak signal.

One man coming up elevator. Black jacket. Long black hair. No visible weapon. One of Jade's accomplices?

Axe sprinted toward the building that Void said Jade's phone was in. There weren't many pedestrians, but plenty of vehicles traveled on the major east-west street across the city. They slowed as the drivers gawked at him as he ran with a black carbine, night-vision goggles over a black watch cap, wearing a plate carrier with extra magazines in the front pockets.

Axe slowed as he neared the building's service entrance. He had a Department of Homeland Security badge in one pocket, FBI credentials in another, and the ATF identity he'd used earlier that night, which seemed like forever ago. Any of them would get him free access to the building.

He slipped inside.

The dead guard didn't need to see his ID.

I'm definitely in the right place.

The indicator light on the freight elevator showed it had recently stopped at the fourth floor, but Axe didn't want to be stuck in an elevator and blunder into a dangerous situation when the doors opened.

He'd take the stairs at the end of the hall.

Sparrow waited for Crane to confirm his message and debated stepping into the hallway to get a better signal.

He caught movement on the other side of the door. A warrior, fully outfitted for combat with armor and a carbine, moved purposefully toward the stairs.

His phone pinged. Crane acknowledged the message and passed on new orders, which Sparrow only had a second to speed-read before preparing to deal with the warrior.

New orders. Capture OR KILL subject. Prevent her from falling into hands of Americans. Weapons free. Scorched earth.

They could now use any methods to accomplish their mission and return to China. They could burn their identities and kill as necessary.

It sealed the warrior's fate. He was in a big hurry to get to the action above, and it would cost him.

Sparrow moved to a small alcove created by a column to the right of the doorway, barely wide enough for his body to fit into. It would keep him out of sight as the warrior opened the door. He slipped the long, narrow chef's knife purchased earlier in the day from its sheath, controlled his breathing, and waited. It wouldn't be long.

Axe reached the metal door to the stairs.

He was charging into the unknown, and he wouldn't have it any other way.

Axe pulled the door open…

And stopped.

His combat sense, which had been returning much too slowly after the injuries he'd sustained, screamed that he was in danger.

Axe spun to his right—his blind side—bringing the carbine to bear.

Someone flew at him, but Axe focused on the long, gleaming knife in the man's hand.

If Axe had been caught off guard, or a moment slower, he would have taken the knife in the back or across his neck, whichever his attacker preferred.

But not today. Axe pulled the trigger as he dodged to the side.

His assailant grunted in pain and adjusted course, but Axe fired again, and again. The man's body jerked with each shot, his eyes went wide with surprise, and he tottered for a moment, arm still out, knife in hand, but not moving toward Axe any longer.

A moment later, the man dropped to the ground.

Axe kicked the knife out of the man's hand, put a bullet into his head, and trained the carbine up the stairs.

The suppressor on the end of the weapon kept the noise to a tolerable level in the confines of the ground-floor stairwell, but if anyone was within a floor or two, and knew what a suppressed gun sounded like, they would know there had been a fight.

There was no movement.

No sound.

The tango had a black earbud, but his phone was locked with a passcode, not his face or fingerprint. Axe pocketed it anyway.

The tango looked like a young warrior: very fit, everything in its place. The kitchen knife suggested a spy or covert operator more than a soldier. Axe had taken kitchen knives from the fourteenth floor of Malik's home two months before and used them in place of a traditional combat knife.

"Blondie," Axe whispered, hoping they were still connected.

He had no signal.

Once again, he was on his own.

159

THE CONTAINERS

South Dock
The Port Newark-Elizabeth Marine Terminal
Newark, New Jersey

The port facility was lit up like a gigantic football stadium. Lights on poles at least one-hundred feet tall made it seem like daytime.

Johnboy had led the way to cover behind long shipping containers in a row north to south at a slight eastern angle. A gap of about six feet, probably wide enough to get a forklift or other machinery through, then another column of containers started. From the air, it looked like the row of shipping containers went on forever, though some of the columns only had a few containers each.

And this is when a ship isn't docked.

Johnboy couldn't imagine how hectic it would be with a huge container ship being unloaded.

At least it was quiet. With no ships in this area, there were no personnel, and hopefully Haley's message through Nancy would keep the good guys at a distance while Johnboy and Mad Dog scoped out the situation.

"Nice night for an ambush?" Mad Dog asked.

"Would be if we knew where they were going," he said, "and they hadn't seen us fly in on a helicopter. The cranes have to be their targets, though, right?"

"Let me see. Big, expensive machinery? Check. But beefy, too. What, they're going to take out a bunch of cranes with a few bombs?" Each crane had four girders that looked difficult to destroy.

"The bigger they are, the harder they fall?"

"Could be. Or maybe it's enough to damage them. Inspections, insurance adjusters, OSHA, the unions, everyone wanting to make sure nothing bad's going to happen if they get back to work. Slows everything down. That enough for these guys?"

"Hard saying, not knowing," Johnboy said, quoting a line he'd heard Axe use.

"What's that even mean, anyway? Axe says it all the time."

"It means what it says. It's hard—" He stopped. "Movement. One hundred meters, along the containers. Someone stuck his head around, then popped back."

"Port police?"

"Too furtive," JB said.

"Work toward them or let them come to us?"

They exchanged glances. "Yep, got it," Mad Dog said. They had to split up, and they both knew it. Mad Dog turned and stepped a few feet away. "Comms check," he said. Johnboy heard him mostly through the earbuds.

"I've got you. Let's do this."

Mad Dog sprinted down the gap between the containers to make sure they weren't getting flanked. Johnboy took a knee and slowly eased his head around the corner of the shipping container hiding him.

No one there.

"All clear," he muttered to Mad Dog.

"Copy. Almost to the corner."

The first of four giant blue cranes loomed above Johnboy. He'd have a clear shot at anyone running across the open traffic lanes.

They'd wait a few minutes. See if the tangos found their guts, or if the Port Police came by. Either way, no amateur weekend warriors were getting past him and Mad Dog.

160

THE INSURANCE

Aurelia Tower
Times Square
Manhattan

Jade was having second thoughts about picking this building. She could have rented a room for the night at one of several hotels in the Times Square area instead and prepped the bomb in comfort and security. It would have meant burning her identity as Jade Pang and her picture from security cameras would have been everywhere after the explosion, but it might have been better than wandering around this building looking for a safe place to hide the bomb.

The sixth floor had been her first choice. It was high enough to disperse the cesium-137 across a large area, but low enough that every pedestrian nearby would receive an incredibly high dose of the radioactive material.

Unfortunately, the sixth floor had been wide open with no walls or other places to hide the bomb.

The seventh had been further along, but actively under construction. It had some interior walls, but nothing near the exterior of the building.

Jade had to plant the bomb near the windows for full disbursement—plus the shattering glass would likely harm or kill people below—a bonus.

The eighth floor was perfect. It had plenty of walls up, and an entire row of offices already constructed along the west wall, closest to central Times Square.

After going from office to office, she'd selected the one at the corner. It appealed to her sense of irony. The Ministry of State Security had hoped she would one day occupy such an office farther south, on Wall Street, as she clawed her way up the corporate ladder before they married her off.

This spacious office had its own washroom and, more importantly, a small walk-in closet. Even in the daytime, the closet would be dim; it would take a work light or flashlight to notice the backpack, and then it might be ignored as a worker's bag.

It was a chance she had to take.

She should have come to the eighth floor first. Eight was a lucky number in China. It is associated with success and, more importantly in this case, financial prosperity.

Jade would take all the help she could get with this mission.

"Here," Jade said, handing Darius her phone after opening the camera app and selecting the video function. "Get me unpacking this but keep my face out of it. I don't want to have to edit the video, so if you mess it up, tell me and we'll start over. Understand?"

She had ignored his initial questions and asked for his help to pick the right floor, telling him she'd explain everything when they found the right spot.

He listened and did as asked, though she'd used none of her many persuasive techniques.

Darius was the one man who seemed to respect her and treat her as an equal.

Maybe she wouldn't have to kill him tonight, after all.

Jade ducked out of the office and paced off the distance to the windows, checking one final time to make sure this was the place.

Everything was fine. With the amount of C-4 explosives surrounding the fire-extinguisher-size canister, the entire office—and the windows— would easily be destroyed.

The corner of the building would be blown open and look great on the television and internet news, and social media feeds.

The blast would disperse the cesium-137 across Times Square. The nearby buildings' ventilation systems would suck in the particles and spread them across every floor, office, and hotel room.

The wind would blow it along the streets, funneling it to more areas of the city.

Thousands would eventually suffer and die from exposure to the radiation.

The thriving area would be rendered uninhabitable for years. The cost of cleanup combined with the loss of revenue would be mind-numbingly high.

In other words, this was perfect.

New York City would suffer.

The stock market would plummet.

She couldn't wait.

"A close-up of the backpack as I open it, okay?" Jade said. "And no talking. They could identify us from that."

"Wait," Darius said. "What's going on? What is all this? You promised to explain."

"Later. Trust me. This is the best way to ensure the stock market crashes. Now, record."

Darius looked near the end of his rope, but he complied, pointed the phone downward, and hit the red button to record. The phone's small but bright light cut through the darkness of the office closet, making it easier for Jade to unlatch the top of the backpack.

As she pulled back the top, she caught Darius's eye and put her finger over her lips in the universal sign to be quiet.

She didn't need him to gasp or start asking questions when…

Jade widened the top of the backpack and grasped the poorly welded small handle on the bomb to lift it out of the bag, while also using her foot to push down the fabric of the pack.

Darius barely kept himself quiet despite her warning a few seconds before.

Jade set the canister on the bare concrete floor, producing a metallic ringing that echoed around them.

Darius was doing a decent job of keeping the canister in the frame— and her out of it. On his own, he moved closer to show the yellow and black radioactive warning stickers in English and Russian.

She gestured to the timer on the side closest to her. The black numbers on the small gray screen ticked down the hours, minutes, and seconds.

8:47:09

8:47:08

8:47:07

The timer would reach zero after the stock market opened. Hidden in this far closet of the nearly finished floor, the bomb was unlikely to be discovered, but if it was, that wouldn't be a problem.

On the other side of the bomb, her final burner phone waited for a call that would trigger detonation sooner, if needed. She would keep an eye on the news. The minute Times Square was evacuated, or the news reported an unidentified police buildup in the area, she would dial the number.

But ultimately, none of it mattered.

Panic was the goal here.

If the authorities found the bomb and evacuated the area, it would serve her purpose almost as well as the actual explosion.

From a financial perspective, at least.

As long as the market opened, she would win.

After a few seconds more of Darius filming, Jade touched his arm and nodded at the red button. He pushed it, and the recording stopped.

She took the phone back. If Darius clicked on the wrong icon on the home screen, the phone would dial a number and the bomb in front of them would explode.

"It's insurance," Jade told him once she double-checked the phone was no longer recording and the video he'd taken was usable. With a few clicks, she uploaded the video to an encrypted cloud server. If something happened to the phone, she'd still be able to access the recording.

Jade hefted the bomb back into the pack and clipped it closed. The black bag in the back corner of a dark closet would go unnoticed. She was positive. It felt right.

She ushered a stunned Darius out of the closet and took both his hands in hers.

He spoke before she could reassure him.

"Jade, that… that's a dirty bomb," Darius said. In the glow from all the neon and LED lights outside, advertising everything from soda to Broadway plays, his face looked pale, and his eyes were wide.

"After what we've done, this bothers you?" she asked. She may have a way with men, but at times they were so hard to understand.

"It's too much," Darius said. He'd found his resolve. "I can't explain why, but it is. You've gone too far. Disconnect it."

"It's probably not even real," Jade said, glancing at the closet. "I doubt there's cesium-137—the radioactive core—inside. A year ago, I negotiated with Boris for the material—sorry I didn't tell you until now. He claimed he couldn't get it, but near the end, he said a source of his had come through. He charged me extra—nearly the entire amount we had left in our operating account. He shipped it to me, but it didn't arrive in time for the main event two months ago. So I held onto it with this day in mind."

Darius dropped her hands and made a move toward the closet door, but Jade stepped in between it and him. "No."

They glared at each other in the dim light from the giant signs outside, both ready to fight for what they wanted…

Until the distinct sound of a piece of metal scraping against the bare concrete came from somewhere outside the office.

161

THE COVERING FIRE

Container Storage Area
South Dock
The Port Newark-Elizabeth Marine Terminal
Newark, New Jersey

The helicopter changed everything.

The two heavily armed men had come because Clay's team was at the port. There was no other explanation.

But Zombie was gone. Clay didn't know where Zombie had run before the helicopter arrived, but he needed him back. It was time to leave. They had to abandon the mission immediately.

The rest of the guys felt the same. He could feel it.

The two well-armed men who moved... Well, they moved exactly like Clay and the rest of the guys wanted to move, hoped they moved, but knew in their hearts they didn't.

The tall, muscular guy and the short, barrel-chested one with the bushy beard were trained and seasoned warriors. Both men had seen combat. Clay had no doubt. Not stupid paintball tournaments. They were the real deal.

"We can't just sit here," Scary Clown whispered. He—and the rest of the team, except for Zombie, who had run off to the far side—crouched behind a container. "We have to bail. Police are one thing. Half of them that work here are overweight and cowards. The other half probably haven't been to a shooting range in a year. We can handle them. But the guys from the helicopter? No way am I going head-to-head with them."

They couldn't wait here much longer. If the guys from the helicopter knew about them, the police would be coming, too. At least it was an enormous facility, and they had all gotten to cover as soon as the helicopter had come close. They were safely hidden—for the moment.

"With Zombie out there, don't we have to continue?" Clay asked the guys. "If something happens to him, the FBI or whoever will eventually come to the office and ask around. The people at the office will say, 'Oh, sure, he plays paintball with some other guys nearly every weekend. They're quite good.' And the FBI will go, 'Huh, a group of guys that train together for paintball combat? Which guys? We should ask them where they were the night the terminal got blown up.'"

Clay stuck his head around the corner again, trying to see… anything. Where the two guys had gone when they ran away from the fancy helicopter that dropped them off and flew away fast.

"Let's play this as if were a tournament," Hockey Mask said from the back of their line. "Half of us flank, the other half up the middle. Catch them from both sides. Find Zombie, then retreat."

Clay checked his watch. The timer on Zombie's bomb had several minutes before it blew, unless Zombie figured out a way to turn it off or add time. It shouldn't be that hard—just hit the plus sign, he figured. But would he do it, or think they were going ahead as planned? If Zombie had acted fast enough, he could have gotten down the long row of containers, across the lanes for truck traffic, and into the next group of containers.

He could be closing in on one of the far cranes by now.

"No," Clay said, slipping easily into combat mode—or the equivalent from their time as paintball warriors. He removed the bombs from the backpack and lined them up on the ground. One by one, he set the timers, getting the minutes and seconds pretty close so they'd all go off at more or less the same time. "We each take a bomb. We're going to blow shit up, whether it's the cranes or not. Anything will buy us publicity for the cause. And we'll all have a good shot at doing something big we're proud of. You two," he said to Space Alien and Werewolf, who were best friends at work. "Flanking maneuver along the far end of this row." He gave them each a ticking bomb. "Go. The rest of us," he said as they ran down the narrow row between containers, "we head for the cranes but stick close to the containers for cover. Leapfrog. Covering fire. Grab a bomb. Plant it somewhere important. Cranes first, containers next. Anything could be in these," he said, tapping the container next to them. "Incoming means cheap televisions and toys. Outgoing ones have toxic chemicals, medical waste, anything going to poorer countries. Blowing these is a solid fallback if we encounter too much resistance."

He took stock of the guys. It was hard to tell with the stupid masks they wore, but they seemed to be with him. They'd all grabbed a bomb and stuffed it gingerly into the waistband of their pants.

"I'll lead. Clown—you provide covering fire. Ready?"

Nods all around. "Let's do this."

Clown leaned around the corner, leading with the carbine Jade had generously provided them, and started firing.

Clay stepped from behind cover, head down, ready to sprint to the next opening between the rows of containers.

A feeling hit him hard—of danger, or maybe fear—an emotion so overwhelming he slammed to a stop.

Clown fired, the noise of the weapon loud in the relative quiet of this part of the facility.

A bullet skimmed by Clay's arm, so close he could feel the disturbance of the air.

He fell back around the corner. Scary Clown followed an instant later.

"What the hell? Are you hit?" Scary Clown asked.

"No. He missed," Clay said. The guy had been ready for him—and was an excellent shot.

"Damn," Johnboy said. "I think I missed. He stopped short. That'll give them something to think about, at least. Their covering fire was off target. Definitely not pros."

"Copy," Mad Dog said. "Contact left." A flurry of shots came from the other side of the container and up the lane. The tangos had split up to flank them, as Johnboy and Mad Dog had expected.

"Might have hit the covering fire tango, not sure," Mad Dog said. "No movement. Looks like we have them pinned. I'd say advance, but it's impossible to cover, fire, and move up with only two of us, and separated like this."

"True. Police help would be nice."

"Red and blue lights in the distance, coming down the road—or lanes, whatever you call the place where the trucks drive," Mad Dog said. "Wait for them?"

"Yeah." Johnboy didn't like his options. Moving ahead without covering fire would be dangerous. One lucky shot from the tangos and it was lights out. But he also didn't want to put the police in danger if he could help it.

"Heavy hangs the head that wears the crown," Mad Dog said.

"You still smarting over Axe putting me in charge?"

Mad Dog laughed. "No, I was just busting Axe's chops earlier. I'd follow you anywhere."

"Good to know," JB said. "Okay. The current plan is to wait for the police to help. That will split the tangos' focus so we can advance on them."

"After we make sure the police know we're not the bad guys."

"Well, yes, that goes without saying."

"How are we going to do that?"

"I haven't figured it out yet, but all will be revealed in good time."

"Copy that," Mad Dog said. "Good times."

162

———

THE LIE

8th Floor
Aurelia Tower
Times Square
Manhattan

Crane froze as they neared the office where he'd heard the voices.

Owl had kicked a nail or drywall screw, sending it skittering across the concrete floor.

In the office a few paces ahead, a fierce, whispered conversation stopped. It had been too quiet for Crane to clearly make out the words.

He and Owl were near the offices on the side of the floor's large open middle area where someday desks or cubicles would go. Colored lights from Times Square's many signs, screens, and advertisements gave them enough illumination to see.

The voices had come from the corner office.

There was nowhere to hide.

Crane's new orders were clear but left him plenty of discretion.

He had to attempt to convince Pang to return to China with him.

If she refused, she lost all remaining trust and support from the Ministry of State Security. Crane had to detain her and force her to accompany him.

If she resisted and apprehending her proved impossible, Pang was too far gone. At that point, she was expendable.

And if anyone stood in their way of accomplishing the mission, they had to be dealt with.

Permanently.

Vulture covered them from near the door to the stairs, waiting and watching for the man Sparrow had messaged him about. At a glance from Crane, Vulture raised his hand, pointed to the stairs, and indicated he was going to check the stairwell.

Crane nodded, communicated his own part of the plan, and rushed the rest of the way toward the office, Owl beside him, ready to deal with Pang.

Kareem had gotten off the elevator at the fourth floor and snuck up the nearby stairs, lit only by dim emergency exit lights, knife out and ready, checking each floor briefly along the way.

As much as he would have preferred the pistol, he was more experienced with the knife. Gunshots would bring a faster response from the rest of the four-man team, should they have a man behind as a guard.

When he reached the sixth-floor landing, however, there was no one there. A red exit sign glowed dimly, providing enough illumination to confirm no guard hid in the corner or waited halfway up the next flight of stairs.

Whoever had used the elevator before him—Jade or Darius, he assumed, because no soldier would—had gotten off and moved upward as he had. Smart. Probably Jade.

Kareem moved to the seventh-floor landing and heard nothing from the other side of the door.

Eight was a lucky number in China. Maybe that's where Jade had gone?

He climbed another flight of stairs, his unease growing. Had he missed them on six? Or seven?

He edged closer to the door on the eighth floor. If he didn't hear them here, he would go back and clear the other levels.

The tall, narrow window would give him a chance to—

A quiet sound of the door bar being pushed open alerted him to the enemy and gave him the second of warning he needed.

A dark figure with a pistol in a two-handed grip eased the door open with his hip.

There was no time for questions or discussions. Kareem's gut told him the man was an enemy. If he was another of Jade's friends, he'd apologize, but right now, the man was a threat to him until proven otherwise.

Kareem grabbed the weapon with his left hand, catching the man by surprise, and slashed at his exposed throat.

The man reacted instantly, turning away from the attack, attempting to reclaim control of his pistol.

Kareem's knife sliced into the man's shoulder instead, far from the deadly cut Kareem had planned.

They tangled on the landing as the door swung shut behind them. Kareem kept hold of the man's gun hand and thrust the knife into the man's lower back, but again the man twisted at the last moment. Instead of plunging into the spine, Kareem stabbed him in the kidney.

His opponent grunted in pain but paid Kareem back with an elbow to the head. Kareem staggered, stunned but coherent enough to twist the knife as he pulled back, making the man gasp in pain and drop to a knee.

Kareem charged forward, acting on instinct. He couldn't allow the man a moment to bring the gun around and shoot him. He stabbed with the knife but missed, still too disoriented from the sharp blow to focus well. But his momentum took the man to the ground.

The gun clattered away, as did Kareem's knife.

The man was shorter than Kareem, but more muscular. Better trained, too, which was obvious immediately as they grappled on the floor.

Kareem's punch to the kidney brought a *squelch* of blood and a gasp of pain from the man, followed by a grunt of resolution as he grabbed onto Kareem's jacket and rolled them down the stairs, locked together.

A battle raged on the landing above Axe.

Who the hell is fighting?

Jade and a security guard? The grunts of effort and a sharp gasp of pain sounded like men.

Then the fighters tumbled down the stairs, slamming to a stop on the dimly lit landing half a floor above him.

Jade stood in front of the closet, shielding it with her body, but it wouldn't be enough. Whoever was coming across the eighth floor toward them couldn't find her baby.

With Darius looking over his shoulder to identify the sound, Jade stepped toward him, swung him around, and pushed him away from the closet. She nudged the door closed with her hip as she drew the pistol she had taken from Lou's storage garage.

She snuck her left hand around Darius's side and pressed close to his back, shielding herself from whoever approached. "Trust me," she whispered, then put the gun to his temple, and walked them both away from the closet, toward the center of the room.

Crane took one side of the open doorway to the office. Without a word, Owl stopped at the other.

Crane inched his head around the corner for a peek.

Pang and the boyfriend stood in the middle of the room, the constantly changing lights in Times Square behind her creating a kaleidoscope of colors and patterns on them—or the boyfriend and Pang's pistol, which is all Crane could see of her.

With his head still barely around the corner, he spoke in Chinese, offering the first part of the identity code-in from a well-known poem every child learns in school. "In spring I sleep, not knowing dawn has come."

Any other Chinese person would automatically reply with the rest of the line: Everywhere, I hear birds singing.

Pang's response should be from a different, yet equally famous poem.

After a second of hesitation, a woman's voice came from behind the Iranian. "At sunrise, river flowers are redder than fire."

It was the correct response, confirming that she was Pang, and he was a contact from the Ministry of State Security.

Crane lowered his weapon and eased several centimeters to the side, into the open doorway. Enough to show himself, but not enough to present a good target.

"Does your hostage speak Chinese?" Crane asked in Mandarin.

"We can speak openly," Jade answered in English.

"Good. I am 'Crane.' They're pulling you from the field," he said, doing his best to soften the blow. He still had hopes that Pang would come quietly. "I don't have the details," he lied, "but they need you back at headquarters. An urgent assignment. A promotion, I was told. Planning and coordination. We leave immediately. They've sent a private jet for us."

He didn't order her to drop her weapon or come along. It would be interesting to see whether she believed the lie. If she had gone as rogue as Beijing thought, she would see right through it.

"What about him?" Jade asked, lowering her pistol.

Crane shrugged. "He's not in my brief. Whatever you think is best."

"He goes free. Back to his life at the university. One day, he's going to be the president of Iran."

"Fine. Shall we go?" Crane asked. He didn't trust her. There was no explanation of why she had killed the guard at the entrance or why they were in this building. He hoped to get that information out of her on the elevator before they left the building.

"Yes," she said. She lowered her weapon and stepped slightly aside, revealing herself. Testing him, perhaps? When he made no move to shoot or close to grab her, she spoke to the boyfriend. "I'm going with them. You know it's been my dream to return to Beijing for another position. Now that I've completed my studies, they're calling me home."

"I understand," the boyfriend said. He turned to her, and they kissed briefly.

"Okay, let's go," Pang said. They walked toward Crane, the boyfriend leading the way.

Crane watched her come, the picture of compliance, and marveled. She was either coming with them or an incredible actor, which he'd been warned she was.

If I were in her place, however, I would wait until I had a clear shot—and kill everyone.

Did he dare continue with the story the Ministry of State Security had told him to use—a promotion to headquarters in Beijing? Or abandon the ruse, confiscate the pistol and any other weapons, use zip ties on her wrists, and stuff her in the back of the car for the trip to the executive airport?

The lie seemed to be working—or at least she was pretending well. He let it go for now. Owl would be right behind her as they walked. Nothing would happen.

They also still had to ask Jade about the heavy backpack that had disappeared, but that could wait until the elevator. In the light, he'd be better able to watch her eyes, her body language, and judge her truthfulness.

Crane glanced at Owl, and a silent agreement passed between them. They wouldn't let their guard down.

163

THE SIX

8th Floor
Aurelia Tower
Times Square

Jade didn't believe Crane, but she had to lead him out of the office and away from the bomb.

She could get out of this. Every man had a weakness, and she had an innate ability to discover and exploit it.

Somehow, before she got on the airplane, Crane—and the men he'd brought along—would be under her control.

Failing that, she would find a way to kill them and seduce the pilot instead.

A private jet at her disposal for a fast getaway would be perfect.

She slipped the pistol into the concealed carry holder in her pants as she passed through the doorway. It would go a long way to reassuring Crane that she was prepared to return to China.

Did he really think she was stupid enough to believe the Ministry of State Security would activate a covert ops team to find her, deliver a message, and escort her home?

Unless…

Her MSS-assigned phone was sitting at her small apartment in

Greenwich Village. She hadn't been near it in days. Had she missed a coded message from headquarters?

Was there actually a promotion waiting for her, and the MSS needed her badly enough to send a team?

A chill came over her. Had her request for a different assignment finally filtered through student-advisor Zhao and been granted?

It couldn't be…

And yet the thought enticed her.

She had to play this carefully. Go along with Crane, while still ensuring the stock market crashed, so no matter what happened in the next few hours, her future would be assured.

Pain spiked up Vulture's leg. It had to be broken. But the man who had jumped him as he came through the door of the landing above had taken as much punishment when they rolled down the stairs. He groaned under Vulture's weight and fought to sit up.

The movement shifted Vulture's leg, making him gasp.

This fight wasn't over.

Vulture punched the man, not as hard as he wanted, but enough to gain a second to push himself away.

He drew the backup pistol from the ankle of his broken leg. It took only a second, and the attacker was still groggily coming around, pushing himself up from prone with one arm.

Vulture would shoot him and not risk a further scuffle. Crane had to have confronted Pang by now. The noise wouldn't be a problem.

The tiniest movement caught Vulture's eye from the stairs below the seventh-floor landing.

A man with night vision goggles worn over a watch cap had a carbine and a military-grade armor plate carrier with an excessive number of extra magazines.

An enemy.

Vulture raised the pistol and aimed for a headshot to remove the man's armor from the equation.

Axe had raised his gun, aiming toward the next landing as he poked his head around the corner of the seventh-floor landing.

Both of the men on the landing between floors seven and eight were injured, but one had clearly come out on top...

And was aiming a gun at him.

Axe pulled the trigger. The noise of his suppressed carbine was drowned out by the tango's pistol firing at the same time.

***

As Jade walked across the barely lit floor toward the elevator, she waited for her chance. Crane led Darius and her, while the second Chinese man followed behind.

All she needed was a chance. A distraction, like Darius doing something brilliant—or stupid.

Anything to make a move.

The undeniable sound of a muffled pistol shot from the stairwell bought her the instant of distraction she needed.

Jade gasped as she stopped walking, and ducked low, as if she were worried about being shot at.

An entirely normal reaction for a civilian. Or a spy, really.

As she ducked, Jade whipped her pistol out of its holster, turned, and shot the short Chinese man in the head from below, blowing off his face.

She fell into Darius, aimed between his legs, and shot Crane, who was already turning.

Her shot missed.

Crane fired.

Darius cried out and crumpled, falling onto her.

Jade got her arm out from under him and fired in the general direction of where Crane had been.

Darius twitched as more bullets slammed into his body.

The noise from the gunshots was deafening despite the openness of the floor.

Out of the corner of her eye, she caught the movement of a shadow. She put her pistol against Darius's stomach and fired her last rounds.

She felt more than heard the *thud* of what she hoped was Crane's dead body hitting the concrete floor near her, but she had no time for that.

Jade pulled herself away from Darius, lying on his side, but continued to use him as a shield. Lying on her back, pressed up against his unmoving body, she reloaded faster than she ever had in training.

There was no movement from where Crane had fallen.

She pushed against the floor and scooted forward enough to see around Darius's head, his hair as perfect as always, smelling of the hair product she'd bought for his birthday.

Crane lay sprawled on the floor, eyes toward her but seeing nothing.

Six, Jade thought.

The number of men she'd killed in person this week popped into her mind. Turbo, the SEC worker on the street, Evan the lion, the guard downstairs, Crane, and the other Chinese operator.

And—almost—the black-haired warrior she had pushed into the bus on Broadway, but she couldn't count that.

Technically, she hadn't killed Darius. Jade was pretty sure he'd been dead when she unloaded on Crane through his stomach.

She'd have to consider whether she could take credit for him or not.

Had Darius believed she would get him out of the building and away safely?

Or did he die thinking about her betrayal with the bomb in the closet?

She felt the tiniest amount of regret, but smothered it.

There would be time later to mourn the only man she might have loved.

Jade sprinted across the floor. The gunfire from the stairs that had distracted the operators for an instant meant there was someone out there who could stop her.

There had to be another set of emergency stairs on the far side of the building she could use to escape.

And a window she could stand near to make some phone calls before she fled to the safety of the safe house in Soho.

164

THE TIMERS

Container Storage Area
South Dock
The Port Newark-Elizabeth Marine Terminal
Newark, New Jersey

Clay rested with his back against the container, several feet from the corner, his pulse still pounding from the near-death experience of the bullet zipping past his arm.

He didn't dare make another attempt at sprinting ahead. The covering fire should have worked to protect him. Who maintains their focus while getting shot at like that—and does it well enough to shoot so accurately? If Clay hadn't had the overwhelming feeling of—what, dread? Terror?—the moment he stepped out from behind cover, he'd be dead right now.

The guys from the far end of the row of containers, Space Alien and Werewolf, were back. They'd run into accurate fire when they made their move, too. Werewolf had nearly gotten his head shot off.

The soldiers had them dialed in.

"We're trapped. What are we going to do?" Scary Clown asked, his voice more frustrated now than afraid like it had been before.

"We reset the timers on the bombs," Clay said, the idea coming to him in one glorious vision. "We can toss them as far toward the soldiers as we can, like grenades."

"Those guys are too far away," Scary Clown said.

"Yes, but when the bombs blow, we'll have a few seconds while they keep their heads down. We use that for a tactical retreat. Get the hell out of here and hope Zombie is smart enough to do the same."

Not bringing their cell phones had seemed like a good idea at the time —even burner phones—but he regretted it now. He wanted to talk to Zombie, who always had good ideas, or call Jade and ask for help. She'd know what to do.

"How long?" Scary Clown asked. He and the rest of the guys had their bombs in hand.

"Thirty seconds. But spread out," Clay ordered. "We want a big field of destruction. One container per person has the best chance of hitting something essential inside that could explode or burn. That will make the news for sure. I'll count to three, we'll start the timers, and throw the bombs. Then we all meet here at the corner and get ready to run."

They turned their attention to the timers. The narrow space filled with high-pitched *beeps* as each of them pressed the plus button thirty times.

"We'll get out of here and think of a new target," Clay said with what he hoped sounded more confident than he felt. "Kick ass then."

There were murmurs of agreement, but Clay couldn't shake the feeling that if he could see the faces of his friends, they would tell a different story.

They spread out along the row. Though destroying shipping containers wouldn't have the same impact as incapacitating the giant cranes, the explosions would hopefully be enough for them to get away.

165

THE TOWER

8th Floor
Aurelia Tower
Times Square

The bullet from the tango on the stair landing had pinged off the railing next to Axe's head before bouncing around the confines of the concrete and embedding into the block wall somewhere.

Axe's ears were ringing from the gunshot in the stairwell, but he heard well enough to catch the pounding on the stairs above him.

At least one of the two men from the landing was still alive. In the brief glimpse Axe had before firing, he thought it could have been the long-haired Kareem.

Leading with the carbine, Axe poked around the stairs and immediately drew back.

No shots. Just the body of a man who looked like the one Axe had killed on the ground-floor stairwell.

Axe had aimed well. The man was dead.

I've still got it.

Axe climbed the stairs and slowed as he reached the landing.

The pounding had stopped.

Someone was waiting for him.

Jade had her phone in hand and unlocked by the time she found the other staircase.

She backed into an alcove where a row of file cabinets would go, or perhaps a copy machine, close enough to the windows to have decent cell reception but hidden from the far stairwell all the way across the building.

The authorities may have tracked her via the burner cell phone. She had to ditch it, but first…

Had Clay placed the bombs already and set the timers?

Or had he been caught?

Killed?

She couldn't risk it. The bombs had to be blown up now to do whatever damage they could.

In fact, it might be better for Clay to die without knowing she had never cared for him, that he was yet another one of her pawns, men—and a few women—desperately searching for validation, attention, friendship, or love.

They were all easily manipulated fools who saw what they wanted to see and heard what they wanted to hear.

Jade pressed a button to speed dial the first of the burner phones attached to bombs in New Jersey.

166

THE BOOM

Container Storage Area
South Dock
The Port Newark-Elizabeth Marine Terminal
Newark, New Jersey

Boom

From somewhere to Clay's left, close to the second set of cranes, a bomb exploded, the sound unmistakable.

Clay looked at Scary Clown, ignoring the ridiculous mask and focusing on his friend's eyes.

"Zombie changed the timer?" Scary Clown asked.

The bomb had gone off too early.

"He must have," Clay said, wanting to believe it.

"Do you think he made it? Or…"

"Did he go out with a bang? Take one for the team? I don't know." Clay also wasn't sure which he preferred. If his friend was blown to pieces, the rest of them running away wasn't nearly so bad as leaving him behind to fend for himself.

Plus, Zombie wouldn't be alive to question—and there might be no pieces to identify.

"I hope he's okay," Clay said, wondering if it sounded as phony to Scary Clown as it did to him.

8th Floor
Aurelia Tower
Times Square

Jade realized how ridiculous it was to dial the numbers one after another. She didn't have time for this; she had to escape.

A text to each phone would trigger the bombs the same as a phone call.

With the speed of someone who had used a cell phone since long before she could type complete sentences, she added the remaining numbers to a group chat, typed *bye*, and hit send.

Container Storage Area
South Dock
The Port Newark-Elizabeth Marine Terminal

"Eyes on?" Johnboy called over the comms. The explosion to their right had been impressive, but wasn't close enough to him or Mad Dog to be an issue.

"Negative," Mad Dog responded. "It came from the next section of containers, on the other side of the lanes, but not near a crane. Maybe—"

A hundred yards ahead, right where the tango had opened fire while another had attempted an advance, an entire row of shipping containers exploded.

The sound hit an instant later, an impressive *kaboom* that reminded Johnboy fondly of his time downrange.

"You good?" JB called.

"I'm good. What do you think?"

"Gotta be careful when you play with your toys," Johnboy said. "I think they just blew themselves up."

"On purpose, or accidentally?"

"Does it matter?"

"No, not really. See, this is why amateurs can't have nice things. Do we need to go mop up?"

The shipping containers—or rather, their contents—burned, sending dark smoke into the sky.

"Pretty sure I breathed enough dust, sand, and toxic fumes while on active duty," JB said. "Think anyone's still alive there?"

"No way. That many containers—the whole row? Had to be six bombs, easy. Plus the one to our right? That's all of them."

Johnboy agreed. Their mission was over. "Maybe we sit this part out. We can cover from here for a bit, just in case, while the police move in. Let me get on comms with Haley. See if she wants us to liaise with the good guys, confirm all the bad guys are bits and pieces, or slip away."

"If we can help it," Mad Dog said, "I'd rather not go through the rigmarole of being identified, questioned, photographed, and all that. I'm more of the strong, silent type. Not all heroes wear capes."

JB had to chuckle at that one.

"And it's a nice night for a swim," Mad Dog added.

The water, a Navy SEALs best friend, waited only fifty yards away. Their gear would weigh them down, but they could work around that.

They'd done it before.

167

THE EIGHTH FLOOR

9th Floor
Aurelia Tower
Times Square

Kareem neared the ninth-floor fire door, limping up the stairs as quickly and quietly as his badly sprained ankle allowed.

At least two of his ribs were cracked. Maybe broken. His wrist hurt—his first shot might be fine, but after that, with the recoil, he didn't know. He certainly wouldn't be able to shoot as well as he normally could.

He also had a concussion from hitting his head as he rolled down the stairs. His vision doubled for a moment, but he grasped the fire door's handle on the second try, pressed down the latch, and slipped through the door, easing it shut behind him. It latched with a *click* that, even with his hearing damaged from the proximity of the operator's pistol firing near his head, sounded much too loud.

He backed across the floor. It was empty—a wide-open, bare concrete floor from the windows on one side to the other, and brighter than the stairwell; lights from the many signs in Times Square splashed the room with color.

He would crouch along the wall by the door, wait for the warrior to appear, and fire before the man could shoot him.

It wasn't much of a plan, but aside from hobbling down the stairs and confronting the soldier directly, or lurching across this level to another set of stairs and using them to escape—slowly and painfully—this was the only way.

Kareem had recognized the warrior the instant he had stuck his head around the corner and shot Kareem's opponent.

How had the man come to this building? Had he tracked Jade? Darius? It didn't make any sense, but Kareem wouldn't take any chances. He would ambush him and end the fight here.

The warrior had to follow, no matter the risk. It was a basic tactical principle: don't leave an enemy alive behind you.

Kareem found a spot close enough for him to hit his target but far enough that he would have a second before the warrior spotted him, took a knee to steady himself—and relieve some of the throbbing from his ankle, which was swelling like a balloon inflating—raised the pistol, and prepared for the shot of his life.

———

8th Floor
Aurelia Tower

Axe crept up the dark stairs toward the eighth floor, straining to hear the scuff of a shoe against the concrete stairs or any other indication of where Kareem was waiting for him.

There had been a click, and the sound of the door on floor nine closing, but that could be a ruse. It's what he might do: make a noise on purpose to fool the enemy into thinking one thing, then do the other.

Axe stopped one stair from the landing, centered himself, and poked his head around for a quick look up the stairs, yanking his head back an instant later.

No shots followed.

Kareem wasn't on the landing halfway to the ninth floor, where the stairs turned 180 degrees before continuing up.

But Kareem could be positioned as a mirror image to Axe, just around the corner, one step up, ready to fire as soon as Axe moved into the open.

This could take all night.

A moment after Axe had killed the tango on the landing below, there had been gunfire from floor eight.

Two pistols exchanged fire.

Since then, nothing, which meant one of the shooters was dead.

Or both.

Was Jade alive and doing whatever she'd come here for?

Or was she lying in a pool of blood?

Whoever shot her could be in the middle of their own mission—like stealing the dirty bomb to use themselves.

The answer was on the other side of the door to floor eight.

Not up the stairs, pursuing Kareem.

Axe used all his skill to step silently up the last stair.

Slow is smooth and smooth is fast.

He eased his body across the landing, weapon aimed up the stairs in case Kareem poked his head around for a shot.

With his left hand, Axe grasped the handle, pressed the latch down, and threw open the fire door, praying he wasn't about to be shot at from the stairs in front of him and the survivor of the shootout on floor eight behind him.

He threw himself through the doorway, twisting in the air, ready to fire, and landed on his feet as the door *clanged* shut behind him.

Three bodies lay in a large pool of blood halfway across the room, closer to the elevators than the stairs.

Two of the men were dressed in black, holding pistols. They had to be more foreign operators.

The third was Darius, lying on his side, bleeding from several bullet wounds, the small pompadour undisturbed.

And Jade wasn't there.

168

THE SWITCH

9th Floor
Aurelia Tower
Times Square

The faint but distinct *clang* of the eighth-floor door slamming gave Kareem a chance to relax his aching wrist. He lowered the weapon for a moment.

If the warrior was being sneaky, he'd allowed the door to make noise so Kareem would have a false sense of security. Meanwhile, the warrior would creep up the stairs, hoping to catch Kareem by surprise, but walking right into an ambush.

Kareem's wrist felt better after resting it. He raised the weapon again, aimed, and gained control of his breathing as his father's top trainers had taught him.

He was ready.

8th Floor
Aurelia Tower

Axe swept the large open room as he moved toward the windows, acutely aware of the potential threat behind him from Kareem. The man could sneak down the stairs at any moment.

Axe included a pivot to cover the stairwell door every few seconds as he continued with his primary mission.

His comms with Haley had disconnected, but he was close enough to the windows now to fix that. He stopped with a wall against his back, checked the area to make sure he was safe for the moment, and pulled his phone out. With a click of an icon, the call connected.

"Go," Haley said.

"One EKIA on the main floor," Axe said, referencing the enemy killed in action at the first stairwell. "Three more near or on floor eight. Foreign operators, Asian heritage, possibly Chinese. No wallets, IDs, or identifying information. Pistols—and kitchen knives, probably bought locally before they could secure weapons.

"Darius is dead. Looks like he got shot in the crossfire of a fierce firefight while I was otherwise occupied. I think Kareem is injured and on the ninth floor, right above me. Jade isn't here. Can Void track her?"

"Wait one. I'll patch him in."

Three seconds later, Haley was back. "Axe, you there?"

"Here."

"Void?"

"Here."

"Hey Void," Axe said. "Jade is gone—or at least, I don't see her. I'm on the eighth level of the target building. The whole place is being renovated—no occupants. This floor is finished except for paint and carpet, so there are walls, doors, some offices and conference rooms along the south, north, and northwest.

"I'd rather not clear each one single-handedly, and if she has hidden the bomb, I don't want to be searching when it blows up."

"On it. Looking for her phones now. She was pretty sneaky, buying so many burners to discard when they got hot. But she messed up when she got them all at the same store..." He trailed off. "This isn't an exact science," he said, his voice softer. "But there's one phone active near you. Within 150 feet—to your northwest. There's no telling if it's on one of the floors above or below you. Any chance of that?"

Axe said nothing. He was already moving.

"Good work, Void," Haley said in Axe's ear as he advanced northwest. There were large offices along the far wall for executives to look down on the tourists in Times Square.

"If there's a corner office…" Haley said, but Axe had already made the connection. He clicked his tongue once, a sound that would only carry over the connection to Haley and Void.

The door to the corner office was open.

Axe swung inside, clearing the room, refusing to be distracted by the view of Times Square below or the lights and colors of the many signs outside the windows.

There was nowhere to hide—except the attached executive bathroom or the walk-in closet.

It was dark in the bathroom. The night vision goggles made it easy to check.

Nothing.

The thin drywall wouldn't offer protection if Jade was waiting to ambush him, so he flowed immediately toward the closet, fully expecting to get shot.

Instead, a black backpack sat in the corner.

"I have a backpack here," Axe said.

"Copy," Haley replied.

"You're right on top of the phone," Void said.

Axe slung his weapon and squatted. He did a quick check for wires but felt nothing.

Despite the risk, he had to know. Booby trapping a backpack would be challenging, and likely too much for a spy. Or that's what he told himself.

He delicately flipped up the flap covering the top and expanded the opening, then slid the sides of the pack down enough to reveal a canister about the size of a silver fire extinguisher.

It was ringed with C-4 explosives that had a mess of at least a dozen thin wires leading to a timer on one side and a small, cheap cell phone on the other.

A crude carrying handle made of bent and twisted metal had been welded to the top of the device. It looked utilitarian, like it had an industrial use in a foreign country—not a nice, American-made, professional standard container.

There were radiation warning labels in Russian and English on the sides.

"I found the bomb," Axe said, with no worry or panic in his voice. Calm was contagious.

"Is it something you can handle, or should I send the bomb squad up?" Haley asked, equally professional and in control.

Axe flipped up the night vision goggles, checked his back for Kareem, and bent forward with his pocket flashlight. "The timer is set for…" He did a rough calculation. "Between 9:30 and 10:00. But there's a secondary trigger: a cell phone. Blondie, call in the bomb squad. I'll send you pictures." He quickly took two photos and sent them to Haley. If something happened to him in the next few moments, at least she would have some idea what he'd seen.

"Got them," Haley said.

"Good. Void, can you turn off the cell phone coverage for this area? Like, right now?"

"Um, that's not really how it works. There are towers from all three of the major carriers. It's one of the best-covered areas of—"

"Blondie?"

"Even with the advanced notice of the potential threat, it's going to take at least a few minutes to go through the proper channels," she said, sounding distracted. "It's not one master switch to flip." She was probably sending a flash message to Gregory.

"Void, how long will it take you?"

"I don't know, I've never done anything like this before. It's different than just looking up the location of cell phones."

"As soon as Jade is clear, she'll call the number and blow it," Axe said.

"Hold on," Void and Haley said at almost the same time.

Not at all what I want to hear right now.

169

THREE, TWO, ONE

1st Floor
Aurelia Tower
Times Square

Jade's quads burned from sprinting down the stairs, but she'd finally reached the first floor. She emerged from the stairwell after checking through the door's glass panel. The back service corridor had no guards. Only a padlocked door halfway down that looked unused and another— the main one—at the end. The unused door had to lead to the subway station.

There was no cellular reception in the stairwell.

It would be much better for the bomb in the closet to explode via the timer after the stock market opened.

But could she risk it staying hidden until then?

The safe play was to find cell reception and call the burner phone attached to the bomb.

Blow it up now.

Get it over with.

Create total chaos, slip into the safety of a subway tunnel, away to the safe house, change her look again, pick up her spare passport, and slip out of the country.

The stock market might still crash, though the authorities would likely halt trading before it opened when a dirty bomb exploded above Times Square.

She controlled her anger and eased through the door into the hall.

Through no fault of her own, another mission had once again gone sideways. She had done everything right.

Now, her new priority had to be staying alive.

She would live to fight another day.

But first, she would get out of this damn country.

She held the phone high in one hand, searching for a signal, and her pistol in the other.

Still no cellular coverage. She had to get farther away from the concrete of the stairwell and the metal of the building's frame.

Jade had left the lock pick set in the SUV. She wasn't sure it would work, but she stepped back several meters, aimed at the padlock holding the side door closed, and fired, hoping the bullet wouldn't ricochet and kill her.

Though, she couldn't help but think, it would be a fitting ending to the day, another failed mission, and her life.

The lock jumped before settling, partly destroyed.

Jade hurried to remove it from the clasp.

She double-checked that she had the proper screen ready on the phone. The speed-dial icon for the phone attached to the bomb upstairs was ready.

Jade yanked the door open, pistol up. She would get clear, trigger the bomb, and disappear into the subway tunnels while chaos reigned in Times Square.

—

9th Floor
Aurelia Tower

Kareem had spent a year training with his father's best men: spies, soldiers, and killers.

But as the minutes had passed, his ankle swelled, his wrist tired, and every breath hurt because of the broken ribs.

And his doubts grew.

Perhaps the warrior was stalking him.

Or the authorities were going from floor to floor, clearing the building of potential threats.

As his anxiety increased, he changed his strategy.

Waiting only put him at a disadvantage.

He had to go on offense and eliminate the warrior—or escape.

The decision was easy. He was in no shape for a head-to-head fight.

He could retreat instead. Take the subway straight to the Bronx. Find a taxi to take him to White Plains and the commuter train station. Ride that to the end of the line: Poughkeepsie. Switch to an Amtrak train to Canada.

It was one of his pre-planned emergency escape routes, researched at the start of his relationship with Jade Pang.

Maybe all along he'd known his association with her would be his downfall.

He had a spare passport. Plenty of cash.

It was time.

The elevator would be faster and easier, but if the authorities had been alerted, he would be trapped.

The stairs weren't much better. The warrior might be waiting. But time had passed. Would the man be that patient?

The soldier had to be hunting Jade and Darius.

Looking into the shootout on the eighth floor.

It explained why he hadn't fallen for Kareem's ambush.

Kareem hobbled to the stairs, ready to fire if the warrior decided to make an appearance after all.

The stairwell was as dark and deserted as before. Kareem took it slow, both for stealth and his damaged body.

This felt right.

There was no movement or sound from below.

The building was quiet.

He stepped down, stair by stair, to the landing between floors.

With a quick movement, he stuck his head around the corner, low, next to the railing, and pulled back.

There were no shots, and he hadn't seen the warrior at the eighth-floor landing.

Kareem led with the pistol, finger on the trigger, ready to fire, as he moved around the corner.

Three steps lower, he froze.

Was that… talking?

He hurried now, as quietly as possible, until he was at the fire door.

There was definitely a faint noise from somewhere on the other side. It sounded like someone had yelled or cursed.

This was his chance. If the warrior was distracted, Kareem could kill him and whoever he was with.

If the warrior, Jade, and Darius were talking, either because the warrior had taken them into custody or they were negotiating their surrender, Kareem could eliminate them all.

He pressed the latch on the door, cursing the noise, and eased his way onto the eighth floor, lit by the signs of Times Square outside the windows.

8th Floor
Aurelia Tower

"Void, shut down the cell coverage right now," Axe had said, his voice louder and more forceful. Haley reacted well to calm. Void needed stronger, more forceful orders.

Jade could be near a window on the far side of the floor, or already onto the street below, moving far enough away to send the pulse that would blow the bomb.

"It's not that easy. I can't limit it to—"

"It's my call," Axe interrupted. "I'll take the heat. Shut down the whole city if you have to."

"Working," Void said. The loud clicks from his end of the call sounded like he was destroying his keyboard with the effort. "Almost there. Haley, Jade will head downtown. I believe she has a safe house south of Houston Street and east of Broadway. East Soho and Little Italy. I tracked her original burner phone from Tuesday night to that area."

"I'll go after her," Haley said.

"Void," Axe said, "the police already have Jade's picture, but work with Nancy and Dave to get Jade's description and pictures to every fire department, sanitation worker, and every city employee, but not the general public."

"On it," Void said.

Unit 47A
The Summit at 57th

Void was almost there. The cellular networks' internal systems weren't the least intuitive designs he'd seen, but they were close. Legacy systems had been cobbled together with updated technology into a labyrinth of dispersed subroutines and obscure commands.

"Very close now," he muttered. "Five seconds."

"One down." Void shut down one of the three systems for the entire midtown region and switched screens.

The next was simpler. "Two down. Last one coming."

42nd Street/Times Square Subway

Jade had finally picked up one bar of cellular signal.

She was in a wide subway system corridor, halfway between the stairs to trains on her left and the exit to the street on her right.

No one was around.

She pressed the speed-dial button.

The display changed:

Calling…

Unit 47A
The Summit at 57th

Void switched screens again, bringing up the system for the final cellular network.

There. This one was easy. A few confirmation clicks and he was done.

"Three, two, one—"

He was about to click his mouse when Axe said, "Don't move."

That was for someone else, not me.

There was nothing Void could do except follow Axe's original order and keep the bomb from being remotely detonated.

Void pressed the button on his mouse, shutting down the last of the midtown New York cellular coverage, and the call cut off.

"Good luck, Axe," he whispered.

170

THE DEAD

Axe's hearing wasn't perfect, but it didn't have to be.

Kareem had fallen for the trap. Axe's louder than necessary call with Haley and Void had brought Kareem out of hiding, and Axe knew what to listen for.

And at least one of Kareem's feet or ankles was damaged.

There was a hitch to his step, and the slightest drag of a shoe on the bare concrete floor outside the office.

He wasn't as silent as he thought.

Axe crouched inside the office doorway.

It would be preferable to take Kareem alive. The guy would be a treasure trove of information, and Axe had a lot of questions.

Who was the mastermind behind the dirty bomb plot?

Were they trying to crash the stock market, wreak havoc on the United States, or something else?

Who had put them up to it? Their home countries? Or were they acting on their own?

After that, there were plenty of questions about who had organized, directed, and paid for the SystemSpike attack.

And who had orchestrated the operation in Oman to kill the region's leaders.

Axe would give the kid a chance—but he wouldn't put his own life in jeopardy for it.

When Axe's gut told him it was time, he eased a few inches into the doorway, only enough to see and bring his gun to bear.

"Don't move," Axe said. Commanding. Calm. Professional. He didn't need Kareem startled and overreacting if the kid was willing to surrender.

Kareem froze fifteen feet away. His pistol was pointed at the middle of the door opening.

Chest high.

Not low where Axe crouched.

Kareem froze.

He had badly miscalculated.

Which would dishonor his father's name less?

Surrender?

Or being shot to death in a Times Square building undergoing renovation?

When the kid's pistol twitched lower, Axe fired three times, putting two rounds in Kareem's chest and one in his forehead.

The young man fell backward, dead.

"Void? Haley?" Axe called.

No one answered. Void had done his job well.

Jade was still on the loose, with possibly more threats at hand.

But Axe and the team had at least prevented a dirty bomb from being exploded above Times Square.

For the moment.

The timer continued to tick down, and there was a mess of wires to contend with.

Some skilled bomb makers intentionally disguise which wires are connected to the blasting caps. Dummy or hidden wires, parallel circuits, concealed splices and loops, even booby-trapped lines with secondary triggers.

Axe wasn't an Explosive Ordnance Disposal technician, but he'd spent a night buying one beers after his mission with his former SEAL Team to Mexico a while back. The guy had been full of stories, and confirmed Axe's belief that the door kickers and shooters had an easier, safer, less stressful job than the EOD techs.

Axe would leave the bomb to whoever the NYPD sent up.

In the meantime, he dragged Kareem's body to the middle of the floor, next to the other dead guys, collected the weapons, and returned to the office.

The wall next to the doorway was a great place to wait, ready to ambush anyone else—like Jade—who thought they could drop by and mess with the bomb.

42nd Street/Times Square Subway

Jade's screen hadn't changed.

Calling…

The three periods marched on and off, showing the phone was still trying to connect the call.

She cancelled it and tried a text. It might go through when there was one bar of coverage…

The display at the top of her phone had changed.

There were no bars.

Only a line with a circle.

No connection.

She had to get farther away.

Jade chose the stairs to the subway entrance. It might take longer to get cellular coverage, though some train platforms had relatively good signal. If not, she would escape via the tunnels, then make the detonation call.

The entire area was deserted. No police, no sanitation workers, no late Wednesday or early Thursday morning commuters. The lights were on, but no one was around.

It looked like the station had been evacuated.

They know about the bomb, Jade realized.

It couldn't be the Ministry of State Security. If they had known, the four special forces operators would have demanded information about it immediately.

Then they would have shot her once they had the bomb.

There was probably a ring of police on every street corner keeping people away—and watching for her to exit the building.

By exiting through the far stairwell, she'd reached a lesser-used part of the building with the locked access door to the subway entrance. When the renovations were complete, the doorway she had taken would offer direct access from one of New York's busiest subway stations into the city's premier Times Square building.

In the chaos of evacuating the area with the threat of a dirty bomb, this corridor had slipped through the cracks, or the authorities didn't have the manpower for complete coverage so early in the morning.

Jade hopped the subway entry turnstile and ran along the platform.

The plan could still work.

If the authorities didn't know what type of bomb it was, the stock market might still open. And if they found and defused the bomb, trading would definitely start.

All she had to do was watch the news and wait until 9:30. If the stock exchange started trading as normal, she could detonate the bomb remotely, wait for it to explode via the timer, or...

She could bluff.

The video Darius had recorded would cause mass hysteria. She could claim the device on it was a second bomb hidden elsewhere in the city.

If there had been an early morning evacuation of Times Square as she thought, it would make the claim more credible.

The entire city would panic. People would try to flee, creating more problems.

She smiled as she jogged through the subway tunnel as best she could with the dirty, uneven floor, the oversized men's clothes that made up her punk look, and the cheap high-top sneakers.

She was alive, free, had a safe place to hide, and the rest of the plan was still in play.

The stock market limits, or circuit breakers, were disabled.

She had access to the country's emergency broadcast system via Oliver at FEMA and could easily send the warning about a new bomb with an order to evacuate Manhattan.

All was not lost.

In fact, things were looking good.

This setback would not define her.

In the end, she would win and prove to everyone how capable she was.

171

THE LETTER

Interstate 495—The Long Island Expressway
Long Island, New York

Ekaterina sat in the back of the surveillance van with Boris, waiting for him to abandon his ridiculous game.

But, as he snored, tipped back in the plush seat next to her that faced a long row of high-tech equipment, she became convinced his act was real.

The criminal had become a shell of his former self.

His history as a fixer was legendary. He was a man most people feared. Rumors said he had helped one of Russia's former presidents with criminal matters. The president had been as power hungry as any of the old czars, and his time in office had been full of bribes, shady deals, and corruption. What Zorinov had helped with would have been incredibly large, complicated, and lucrative for the president to use him instead of his usual enforcers and facilitators.

Oligarchs, too, had supposedly enlisted Boris's special services for money laundering, the theft of priceless art, and—always a booming industry—the elimination of rivals.

Ekaterina had read the letter she had pickpocketed from Boris, then read it again. It rang true. The letter had his voice and explained everything.

The envelope had childlike printing on it in Russian.

Important! Read Me NOW!

With glances at Boris every few seconds, Ekaterina read the letter a third time. The inside was neatly written.

You are Boris Zorinov. You have memory loss.

Don't worry. This note contains all you need to know.

There was a bold line with an arrow to a section lower on the page.

UPDATE—Wednesday night, around midnight.

Jade Pang is wanted by the authorities.

Her apartment has police outside. So does her boyfriend's.

Do not approach.

It went on to order his future self to buy a boat and live the rest of his life drinking in the Caribbean.

After the update, the letter was a windfall of intel. It reminded Boris of much of what he had accomplished.

The rumors were correct. He had orchestrated assassinations she would have been proud to have managed.

He had planned operations that had stolen millions—perhaps billions, if the letter wasn't exaggerating—and earned piles of money for his efforts.

The third section went into great detail about what the Americans called the SystemSpike, along with the attempt to kill the world leaders at the peace summit in Oman, where Ekaterina had rescued Alex.

Boris was clearly proud of his role and what he had accomplished, though he gave grudging credit to Jade Pang for much of the original idea, plans, and funding.

The last part was less legible. Ekaterina suspected he had grown tired.

You are Boris Zorinov. You came from nothing. An orphan living on the streets of Moscow. You stole, fought, and killed to stay alive. You rose to become one of the greatest criminal minds in Russia and never went to prison. You have had a great life. Use the time you have left to relax. Drink vodka and wine. Sit in the sun. Slip away. Or, while it doesn't appeal to me in this moment, take the other path. It will be your choice, my future self. Good luck. A toast to us: "To what has been and will never return."

Ekaterina folded the letter. The last line was a common Russian toast for reminiscing about the past. The letter, Boris's upbringing, and the toast struck her surprisingly hard. It some ways, Boris's life matched her own.

"To what has been, and will never return," she whispered to the snoring man next to her.

172

MINE ALL MINE

Onboard *Mine, All Mine*
Manhasset Bay Water Club and Marine Center
Port Washington, New York

Mariana led a groggy Boris onto the luxury yacht, using her thumb to open the lock securing the main lounge doors. She escorted him to the starboard cabin—the smallest onboard, designed for a staff member, with its own bathroom but only one tiny window. Mariana got him settled on the bed and closed the door behind her. There was no lock. One of them would have to be on guard duty at all times, sitting where they could watch the door.

"Alex owns yacht?" Ekaterina asked in a low voice. Boris had landed on the bed and had been asleep by the time Mariana had closed the door. Her uncle had slept more and more toward the end, too.

"What? No." Mariana hesitated. She had agreed to tell the truth to Ekaterina, and while it was a small thing, she would continue. "Well, sort of. It's a long story."

Ekaterina accepted the answer. "Well done in hotel. Your uncle is real? Dementia?"

"He was, yes. He died."

Ekaterina nodded and spoke Russian, which Mariana didn't understand but suspected it was something like, "My condolences."

"Now what?" Mariana asked. Haley hadn't answered comms, and she was reluctant to reach out to Axe, Gregory, Nancy, or Dave. And as much as she appreciated Void, he wasn't someone she could turn to for direction with this. Neither was Kelton.

It was her and Ekaterina for better or worse.

"You can drive boat, yes?" Ekaterina asked, standing and inspecting the ship's bridge. She didn't wait for an answer. "We leave here now. Bay to ocean. Safe from prying eyes. Impossible for Boris to escape. You drive, yes?"

Kelton was an expert boater, and she had learned a lot from him on the trip helping Axe near Venezuela.

It was as good of a plan as any.

Mariana got busy prepping the boat. It would be dawn in a while, and the weather was calm. It was a nice night for a cruise.

173

———

MARA

Onboard *Mine, All Mine*
Long Island Sound

Mariana sat at the helm, guiding the boat through the night and the calm, deserted water. She throttled back to a slow cruising speed. They had nowhere they needed to be.

Ekaterina sat nearby at the yacht's main table, sipping tea, on guard duty, ready should Boris wake as his old self.

Her uncle had been at his best in the mornings.

They were far from shore, though with the clear weather, she could make out faint lights to the north and south, about ten miles away in each direction. It wasn't like being in the middle of the ocean, but it was close.

They were far from prying eyes, especially before dawn, this early in the season.

"What are you required to do?" Ekaterina asked. As they had left the dock behind, she had read Mariana the letter found in Boris's pocket.

Twice.

And gave her time to ponder the implications, along with telling her what her contact in Moscow had said about the dirty bomb components Boris might have given to Jade Pang.

"You are police first, yes?" Ekaterina asked, surprising her.

Was her background and how she carried herself that obvious?

"A trial for him, perhaps?" Ekat continued. "Your fine American justice system?"

Mariana couldn't tell if the Russian was mocking the country's legal system or admiring it.

"I'm…" Mariana started, but immediately faltered.

What was she, really?

A former police officer, yes.

But now, she was a covert operator with Axe, Haley, and the team.

She answered to Haley. Or Axe. The hierarchy wasn't exactly spelled out.

They reported to Gregory Addison at the Central Analysis Group, who met with the President of the United States a few times a week.

There were laws, rules, and guidelines.

And while it seemed like the team did whatever it wanted, however it wanted, whenever it wanted, the guiding principle seemed to be to always do the right thing.

No matter the cost.

When Mariana didn't answer, Ekaterina continued. "Now perhaps working together is problem, yes? I have mission from my country. Boris is Russian. Our responsibility. But he is in America. Is complicated situation."

"What are your orders? Your mission?"

Ekaterina tilted her head. "For me to decide. Much lee.. Lee…"

"Leeway."

"Yes, leeway. With this?" she held Boris's letter up. "Is clear what to do."

Mariana glanced at her before returning her focus to piloting the yacht. This was so far beyond what she had expected to be doing a year ago. She was way out of her depth.

"He doesn't know what he did," Mariana said, hating to defend Boris. His inadvertent confession letter sat on the table.

"That is dilemma. If had fought in hotel, he would be dead now, yes?"

Mariana nodded. That's what she had expected. Confront career criminal Boris Zorinov, have him deny his involvement in the SystemSpike and the rest of it. Or maybe he'd admit it. Either way, he would pull out a pistol or physically attack them.

He'd go out in a blaze of glory like the criminal—and terrorist—he was. She would have gladly killed him.

But the man sleeping in the starboard cabin had no memory of his heinous acts.

The man on the boat was, essentially, innocent.

Ekaterina seemed to read her mind. "Do not say he is innocent. He killed your truly innocent countrymen. Tried to make Russia and the United States go to war. He is monster—whether he remembers or not." She paused. "First," Ekaterina said, "you must decide who you are."

When Mariana looked back at her, a small pistol sat on the table.

"Twenty-two caliber. Headshot, close. Little blood. No mess in pretty boat." Ekaterina paused. "*Nosce te ipsum.* You know this? Latin."

"Know thyself?" she asked, pulling it out of long-term storage that had recently been refreshed with the discussion of her uncle. It had been one of his sayings.

"Inside you is…" Ekaterina trailed off. "Not anger. Not rage." She muttered a word in Russian. "Same as lion. Tiger. Bear. Like savage, but not same."

"Fierce? I have a ferocity in me?" It rang true even as she asked.

"Yes. Fierce. You must soon choose. Tonight, maybe." She stood and moved next to Mariana, leaving her tea but bringing the pistol. She set it near the helm. "You are police? Covert operator? Spy? Or…"

"Or?

"Killer. Silent, secretive. An assassin."

Mariana wanted to laugh it off but couldn't. She contemplated the Russian's words, the scene on the Los Angeles rooftop hotel coming to mind. How she had attacked, running into battle to kill her enemies.

And earlier this week, her desire to rip off the arm of the man in the lobby of the condo building when he'd thought she was a delivery person.

"Do not think so hard," Ekat said. "Is easy. You are a killer, yes. Best is to be who you are. Morana." She said the name with the emphasis on the second syllable.

"Mariana," Tex corrected absently, her mind running with the momentous decision. Was she a cold-blooded killer? Could she embrace that side of herself?

"No," Ekat said, interrupting her thoughts. "Not Mariana, your name. Morana," she said again. "Americans. Ignorant of other cultures. Morana. Mythical goddess of death—Eastern, Central Europe. Poland, Slovakia, Russia. There, name is short: 'Mara.' A female spirit who prays on living. She is cold and pale—you are not. But she is ruthless. Cold-blooded. These describe you, yes?"

"Mara." It felt right as Mariana said it.

"Yes. Mara." Ekaterina nodded at the pistol. "You must be close to use." Ekat brought her empty hand up in the shape of a gun and pointed it at Mariana's head, stepping forward until her finger was two feet away. "Bullet goes into head, scrambles brain, person dies. Quick. Painless. No exit wound. A weapon for a killer. For Mara."

All Mariana had to do was pick up the pistol.

"We are who we are," Ekat said with a sad smile. "Mara."

She left Mariana at the helm, curled up on the table's long cushion, and went to sleep.

174

THE EOD

8th Floor
Aurelia Tower
Times Square

For Charlie Hofmen, leaving the Navy had been a tough call. His lifelong goal was to be an EOD tech—an Explosive Ordnance Disposal technician.

But the war on terror had mostly wound down. Bombs and improvised explosive devices were less and less common. He spent his days in training, training, and more training.

Boring.

He retired and immediately scored a job on the New York City Bomb Squad for a lot more money than he'd been making.

Not as much as he could have working for a private company or a billionaire worried about pipe bombs and exploding packages, but working with a unit to protect America's premier city suited him.

And days like this, with a real bomb?

Priceless.

The heavy bomb suit was hot as hell, restrictive, and heavy, but at least he hadn't had to put it on until he stepped over the dead guy on the seventh-floor landing.

Charlie entered the eighth floor on his way to the corner office and an operator who was guarding the device.

"On floor eight," Charlie said over the radio to his partner outside and around the corner in the safe zone.

Better him than me, Charlie thought.

The idea of being a Number Two—waiting, listening, providing support—no thanks. The stress would eat him up inside. Aaron—his buddy—might be outside the hot zone, but Charlie had the better job. At least he was in control of his fate.

Charlie looked into the closet. The bomb was right where it was supposed to be.

"I've got it," he told the forty-something guy with dark hair in full combat kit standing outside in the office who had found the device. Charlie had seen enough SEALs to know the look. "Did you touch it?"

"I unclipped the backpack cover and pulled it down and away," the warrior said. "That's it."

"Copy. I've got it. You should get out of here."

"I'll stay if you don't mind. The person who planted it is still at large. I doubt she's coming back, but…"

Charlies shrugged, or as much as he could in the suit. "Your call, but I welcome the guard—thanks."

"I'll be outside the office," the warrior said. "Yell if you need something."

Charlie waved.

It was time to earn his money.

First, Charlie used his flashlight to inspect the door frame, floor, walls, and ceiling for triggers, trip wires, or other booby traps.

The operator had been in and out of here, but intel got mixed up. People both exaggerated and underplayed their stories.

Charlie took no chances. He'd left home this morning before his kids were awake, and he had every intention of picking them up from school this afternoon. Maybe going out for pizza with them and his wife.

"No obvious traps," he told Aaron. "X-ray time. You ready?"

"All set on our end, though we're likely out of range."

The wireless system, state-of-the-art thanks to plenty of money in every city's budget post 9/11, sent a signal over secure radio link to the command van.

In this building, however, this high up, the distance might be too far.

Charlie unslung the backpack with the portable X-ray. He stepped into the closet sideways, the only way to get through in the bulky bomb suit, and carefully placed the X-ray generator box on one side of device. On the opposite side, he set the detector panel, about the size of a large laptop or extra thick tablet.

Finally, he stepped out of the closet and used the control unit to trigger the shot.

A few seconds later, a grainy image, black and white, high contrast, popped up. It wasn't like the X-ray at the doctors when his daughter had broken her ankle playing soccer; there were no fine details. But he'd had plenty of experience deciphering the bright-white metal and the other, more subtle shadings of plastic, cloth, wood, and the faint lines of wires, depending on the device.

"You seeing this?" Charlie asked Aaron. "The core is shielded with the lead lining, but the bomb itself is pretty basic. What do you think?"

"Hold on." Several seconds passed. "We've got nothing," Aaron said. "Too far away."

"Want to come on up? You all are welcome." The brass was safe in the van, probably looking over Aaron's shoulder, literally breathing down his neck. Everyone who was anyone wanted to be on the scene—as long as it wasn't dangerous, and the van was as safe as it got while still being close to the action.

"Let me check," Aaron said, both of them playing it straight but the idea of any one of the big shots climbing eight flights of stairs without having a coronary was something they'd laugh about later over coffee, assuming Charlie lived through the morning.

"Please provide more detail," Aaron said.

Guess that was a no-go on a trip to the hot zone.

"Looks like a medical-use canister, Russian. The outside has radiation warning signs in Russian—Cyrillic—and English." Charlie took his time to inspect the canister, going over it inch by inch. "Interesting… There are visible marks that look relatively recent. My guess is it's been opened within the past six months. Could be the core was inserted, replaced, or removed. No way to know."

Charlie double-checked the rest of the device via the X-ray, using the control panel to zoom in, just to be sure.

"The C-4 is real," Charlie said, "as are the detonators, timer, and cell phone. It's definitely a bomb, but there's no way to know if it's an RDD— a radiological dispersal device. A dirty bomb. No matter what, I recommend not—repeat not—blowing it in place. I can disarm it. No problem. Someone knew enough about bombs to make it look complicated, but it's not. Give me the green light, and I can take the explosives out of the equation. We can bring it down—safe—contain it, and let the experts sort out the radioactivity without fear of it exploding."

"Confidence level?" Aaron asked, surely repeating the question of one of their superiors.

"Very high."

"If you're wrong about the complexity…"

"Times Square is ruined for years, panic in the streets, New York City empties out, yada yada yada. I get it."

"Give us a minute," Aaron said, professional, of course, but with a tinge of exasperation for the situation they found themselves in.

Once Charlie was promoted—a year or two at most if he didn't die before then—he wouldn't be like the bosses. Questioning. Debating. He'd man up. Listen to the advice of the experts and let them do their jobs.

"We have the word from on high," Aaron finally said. "It's your call."

Charlie stifled a cynical chuckle. After all that, they were passing the buck back to him. If he was right, they'd take credit for trusting him.

If he blew himself up and ruined New York City for decades, it was his fault for being wrong.

"Copy," Charlie said. He unclipped wire cutters from his suit and held them ready as he carefully dropped to his knees in front of the device.

In the bright-white beam of the flashlight, he traced the tangle of wires from the cell phone to the detonators. Once, then again. It looked like a mess, but there was only one wire that mattered.

If he got this right, he'd repeat the process on the other side for the timer.

At least the powers that be could turn on the cell phones again; they'd be thrilled with that.

But one potential boom at a time, that was his approach.

Charlie closed his eyes and took a breath, picturing his wife and kids. If he was wrong and about to blow himself up, he wanted their images on his mind and their love filling his heart.

"Please don't let me mess this up," he prayed, and cut the black wire.

175

THE RAGE

At Sea

Boris woke to the calming motion of the boat cutting through the water, the light throb of the engines, and the smell of the sea.

He was home on the yacht.

The memories returned slowly as he stretched in bed and got up to use the bathroom. He had to scrub at his hands—there was blue ink smeared on both his palms.

The ink triggered the memory. He had written on his hands to remember to read the note in his pocket.

He checked his pants. There was no note.

The letter had been about… what? A warning not to go to a part of New York City because of the police.

The police were hunting him?

Or—no. Not him.

It tumbled together in his mind, rushing in like a sudden ocean squall. There were gaps and many missing details, but he had the gist of it. He had accomplished an important—illegal—mission.

Had helped to kill hundreds.

No, thousands.

And was on the run from the authorities.

But he was safe on the boat. He had a captain—the name escaped him, but he could picture thick, hairy arms, deeply tanned by a lifetime at sea. And staff in white shorts and striped shirts.

They would have breakfast for him. Something delicious, like caviar with toast and butter.

Later, in the afternoon sunshine, they would anchor off the coast. He would enjoy a glass of wine. Or some vodka.

Vodka.

The word triggered memories of the past night. A hotel. Murdering the middle-aged man so he could hide in the man's room.

And the small woman who spoke Russian to him, plus her dark-haired friend with the hard eyes who had called him Uncle Boris.

He stared out the small window at the dark sea and the hint of dawn in the sky, and a sinking feeling settled upon him.

He had been captured.

Mariana prepared more tea for Ekaterina.

A few minutes later, the cabin door opened.

Ekaterina now held another pistol. She rested it on the table and sipped her tea with the other hand.

"Good morning," Boris said. He sounded different. Self-assured. Stronger. Smarter. And meaner. He was hiding that part, but Mariana could sense it in him.

He glanced at Mariana at the helm, Ekaterina's gun, and moved slowly to sit across from the Russian at the table.

"You talk now, yes?" Ekaterina said to Boris. "Tell us what you know. Who you worked with. All involved. How you did it. Everything."

"That is the problem," Boris said. His English was better than Ekaterina's, nearly as good as a native speaker, without much accent. "I don't... I don't remember everything."

That was a confession of sorts.

"We'll take what you know and go from there," Mariana said, splitting her focus between steering the yacht and backing up Ekaterina.

The small gun tucked into her waist at the small of her back seemed much heavier than it should be.

"And in exchange?" Boris asked.

"We will see," Ekaterina said.

"I had a note. Can I read that?"

"Later."

"My memory. It's getting worse, I think. I have information you want. Not all, I am sorry to say, but some. Most, perhaps, once I start remembering. And you have something I want."

He paused, but neither Mariana nor Ekaterina spoke.

"I want to live my final days in peace. On a boat. This one will do. The ocean breeze. Wine. Vodka." He was referencing their conversation from the hotel. "Let me…" He swallowed hard and composed himself. "Let me fade away here or on my yacht. Not in a prison."

Ekaterina's face was stone. "We will see," she repeated.

Boris glanced at the pistol in Ekat's hands. "Or, I tell you all I can, and you…" He looked from Ekaterina to Mariana, seeking an answer.

Finally, he shrugged. "I will trust you to do what is right. But not prison. Not prison."

He stared out the window at the coming dawn. "What do you want to know first?"

"Dirty bomb," Ekat said. "You give to Jade Pang?"

Boris looked horrified and shook his head immediately. "No. Never. I…" He paused for an instant before continuing. "I would never provide a weapon like that to her."

Mariana let Ekat continue to take the lead, and throttled back the boat to its slowest speed. She needed to watch and be a part of this.

"You like the warmth, yes?" Ekaterina said. "Spain. The Mediterranean. The Caribbean Sunshine. Wine. Vodka. Not cold, like dark, wet cell in basement in Russia? Or Polar Wolf—you know this prison, yes? Beyond Arctic Circle. Very cold. American prisons much more comfortable, but, maybe worse in some ways, too, yes?"

Mariana shrugged. She didn't think American prisons would be half as bad as anything in Russia, but whatever it took to scare Boris into the truth was fine with her.

"I… I don't remember," Boris said. "There is a thought of shipping a canister, but the memory feels like…" He smiled then, a twisted look that revealed who the man had been once upon a time. "It feels like I received a lot of money for nothing." He looked first at Ekaterina, then Mariana. "I have a feeling I sent her a fake. I betrayed her."

Mariana believed him.

Mariana grabbed her phone and sent a text to everyone on the team. They had to know that Boris believed he hadn't supplied a true dirty bomb to Jade.

"Very good," Ekaterina said. "Now we continue."

Boris drank tea and ate a packaged breakfast bar the American woman offered.

He answered their questions truthfully. It was the only way he saw to get what he wanted.

He was as lucid as he'd been in a while, and he remembered much of what the letter to himself said. He was a criminal, but his time was coming to an end. The memory episodes were worse and more frequent.

He was fine with it all until the American blurted out a question. "Why did you do it? You told us about money transfers. Malik. Jade Pang. But nothing about why. Did Pang work for China? Did your government tell you to do it?" She paused though her eyes bored into his. "Why?"

Just beneath the surface, Boris's rage bubbled like a covered pot about to overflow. He attempted to defuse the feelings threatening to spill over and answered flippantly.

"Why do people climb mountains? Why work twelve-hour days when you are already a multi-millionaire? To make life interesting."

"That's it?" the woman asked. Her face stilled, and her eyes seemed to darken. This woman was as dangerous—perhaps more so—than the Russian sitting across from him who, the more he spoke with her, seemed like the Grim Reaper incarnate.

"You killed so many innocent people," the American said. "For money? For fun? What is wrong with you?"

He couldn't hold back the rage. It rose in him, and he had a moment of crystal clarity. All his memories snapped back. All he'd been through—and all he'd accomplished in this life.

"You think I am crazy? A sociopath? I am not. You have a home? A safe place to sleep at night? I never had that growing up. I lost my family young. Ran away from an orphanage because the streets were better than that place. I then stayed awake all night defending myself and searching for morsels, literal crumbs, to eat so I could survive. I hid in the daytime. It was warmer. There was less chance I'd freeze to death when I fell asleep. And there were people moving around to keep the vermin away. I am not talking about animals, these vermin. They were adults who sought the young like me and the others..." Boris trailed off. "Some adults were horrible, evil human beings..."

He shook off the thoughts. He liked it better when he didn't have those memories. "In the daytime, it was more difficult for them to prey on me and the other street kids. To me and the others back then—the wealth you have? Luxuries we never dreamt of. Even now, children like me are in America, Russia, nearly every country. To them, the average person is like a billionaire. Such riches. Fresh water. A bathroom. Toilet paper. I came from nothing! I had nothing. What I have done, I did because of people like you," he said to the American. "And you as well," he added in Russian to the little old lady who, he had realized was so much more than that. "You expect me to forgive? Never. Jade had a plan to harm your country and mine. To disrupt the power-hungry in the Middle East and replace them with younger leaders who might treat their people better. I had the skills and the ability. And I had the drive to do what no one else could have!" He paused, trying to get control of himself. He used the back of his hand to wipe his lips. "I spit on you all."

He had revealed himself to these women. He hadn't meant to, but the rage had taken over.

His outburst had left him exhausted. Boris closed his eyes. "I am done for now. I have told you much. Consider my request. We will talk again soon."

Boris stood, slowly, to not to alarm them, and returned to the cabin.

He had given them what they wanted.

Would they honor his request?

He refused to go to prison. He'd successfully avoided it his entire career. Whether he'd had to bribe or eliminate people, the charges never stuck, or the cases were tossed out of court.

Boris wasn't about to waste away, his memory fading day by day, in a cold, lifeless cell.

He hadn't worked so hard, overcome so much, for it to end as a prisoner in a cage.

He would be under house arrest on a yacht, enjoying his remaining time—or he would be dead.

176

———————

THE CHOICE

Onboard Mine, *All Mine*
Long Island Sound

Mariana had allowed Boris a chance to compose himself after the outburst.

His time was up.

Ekaterina sat at the helm, keeping them on course.

She was giving Mariana the space she needed to make her decision.

Mariana couldn't decide if it was a test, a choice, or a step into a new life.

Or a lesson, perhaps.

Mariana stared at the cabin door, willing Boris to step out and resume talking.

If the same man as before emerged, it would be easy to do what Ekaterina thought had to be done.

Well, not easy. But easier than if the confused old man appeared.

Maybe bad Boris was waiting for them to come get him. It could be like what she had pictured would happen in the hotel room. An attack. A response.

Over.

Simple. Not messy, like this.

She wanted more details from him, especially whether Jade Pang had acted alone or on behalf of her government.

Boris had said he wasn't sure, but thought it was possible she had planned it all herself with financial help from people in New York. Still, Mariana wanted to ask again if China had been responsible.

If she negotiated with Boris, and gave him what he wanted, would he tell her? Was he holding out for that?

Axe had said to handle the situation.

Did he mean this? Was she expected to negotiate with a criminal and admitted terrorist?

She couldn't give bad Boris a life of luxury on a yacht after the lives the monster was responsible for taking. No way.

But it wouldn't really be that man she was allowing to fade away, would it?

Did it matter?

Mariana had the distinct impression that Ekaterina had made up her mind already, and this was going to end exactly how she wanted.

The only question seemed to be whether Mariana was going to embrace the fierceness within her or not.

Mariana dreaded having to deal with the confused Boris who acted so much like her uncle at the end that it made her sick to her stomach.

Years ago, she had been in a similar situation.

The memories still haunted her.

The sun was coming up. Ready or not, it was time.

She stood, prepared herself, and went to the cabin door.

She knocked—and raised the pistol from Ekaterina. If Boris attacked, this would end the way that probably all of them wanted.

When she opened the door, the room was empty.

So was the small bathroom.

The bed was still made. The wrinkles from Boris sleeping on top of the sheets when they'd first arrived had been smoothed.

Boris's pants and shirt were folded neatly at the foot of the bed. His shoes were placed side by side out of the way.

The cold air through the open window chilled the room.

Mariana slid the window closed.

For a long moment she stared out at the ocean. The swell had picked up. They were miles from shore. The water was cold. There were no boats around.

She left the cabin with mixed emotions.

"He's gone," she told Ekaterina.

The Russian didn't look surprised.

Mariana took the helm.

She turned the boat in a wide arc and pushed the throttles forward.

It was time to return to the marina.

But first, she had to call this in.

177

THE WATER

Long Island Sound

Boris shivered as he swam.

He loved the ocean, but this water was different from the Mediterranean.

The water was colder, the currents stronger, and the swells bigger, even on this calm morning.

The farthest he'd ever swum was two miles in a quiet bay off the coast of Spain.

He had been exhausted at the end, and he'd had a yacht to climb aboard, a full crew to bring him towels, drinks, and food, plus a comfortable bed to slip into for a nap.

Here, he had nothing.

If he somehow made it to shore, he had no money. No wallet. No passport. No phone.

Only a memory that could fail him at any moment and leave him wandering until he died of malnutrition or exposure.

Or he might be picked up and housed somewhere, waking up from time to time with the realization of all he had lost.

The water was ice cold, but the dawn was bright.

He stopped swimming and floated on his back, reliving his memories, relishing them like a fine wine.

Already he felt them slipping away again as a cold drowsiness overtook him.

He didn't fight it.

His life was always going to end before he wanted it to. He'd known that the moment he had embraced the life of a criminal.

From his first day on the streets, he had refused to let others determine his destiny.

He wouldn't let anyone dictate his demise, either.

As the sun hit his face, he let out his breath and sank.

PART 6

THURSDAY

178

THE EXHAUSTION

254 Lafayette Street
Soho

For the average New Yorker, it was just another Thursday morning.

For Jade, it was the start of a new life that would be completely different from everything she had prepared for.

She was exhausted. In the past forty-eight hours, the only rest she'd had was a nap wedged into the small corner of the closet in Evan's apartment—right before she'd hammered him to death.

The memory perked her up. She was almost at the security of the safe house. The sun was coming up. There were a few things to do, but she would be fine.

In fact, there was probably time for another quick nap. It would be smart to face the day rested, with a clear head. She'd be able to better enjoy the coming success.

Jade had decided not to send the signal to the bomb. She had to wait until the stock market opened. There was a good chance her bomb wouldn't be found, but if it was, that would only work in her favor.

Her new plan would work better, anyway.

Two and a half miles away, Times Square was likely evacuated and shut down because of her dirty bomb, but without a radio, television, or cell phone—she'd left hers behind in the subway tunnels—you wouldn't know it here.

Early risers jogged, walked their dogs, or hurried to school and work.

The bagel place around the corner from the safe house smelled delicious.

The firehouse across the street had its big red roll-up doors open. Two firefighters stood outside chatting.

Jade slowed, going up the three flights of stairs to the apartment. After running down eight flights at the building in Times Square, jogging through the subway tunnels until she reached a station she could slip out of unnoticed, and speed walking the rest of the way—punk-goth girls don't jog along the streets of New York at dawn—her strong legs were done.

She and Darius had stocked the small apartment with a month's worth of food; it might make sense to crash the stock market, make millions of dollars, and hole up for a few weeks until the country went back to normal.

As she unlocked the apartment door, the thought of Darius brought a twinge of sadness. The place smelled like him.

Jade opened the window in the back of the apartment, ignoring the tiny fire escape where the two of them had sat in the middle of the night, whispering their plans for the future.

She passed through the kitchen, small living room, and into the bedroom to open the front window. The morning cross breeze would air the place out, eliminate his scent, and cool it down, which would help her focus.

First things first: her laptop and breakfast. She ate a container of yogurt at the small, round table in the middle of the kitchen, computer open to a news site.

The headlines warmed her heart.

Times Square Trouble

Terror in Times Square

Cell Phone Network Out in Midtown

I Can't Hear You Now: Cellular Networks Shut Down in Midtown Manhattan

Subways in and through the area had been stopped—she'd seen that. Traffic and pedestrians had been rerouted. An evacuation was ongoing.

The authorities had shut down the cellular networks from Fifty-seventh Street to Twenty-third Street and from the Hudson River to the

East River. The rest of the island was fine, but people near Midtown were annoyed, confused, and frightened.

There was nothing yet, but the authorities must have found her baby. The police were keeping it quiet. Perhaps the mess of wires and her attempt at making the device confusing to all but an experienced bomb technician had worked.

It didn't matter. The chaos was divine.

Half-dressed tourists had stumbled out of hotels and had been rushed away down side streets.

Dozens—maybe hundreds—of police and firefighters guarded corners, keeping people from entering the normally busy area.

One news site showed live streaming video with a ***Breaking News!*** bulletin. A large, boxy truck with ***NYPD BOMB SQUAD*** in dark-blue letters on the side filled the screen.

Jade turned up the volume.

"The bomb squad sent a single man into the building earlier this morning, but so far there is no official report from the authorities. Sources nearby who were in the area when police arrived to begin evacuation, however, claim that they were told there was a potential RDD—radiological dispersal device. In layman's terms, a radioactive or 'dirty' bomb."

Jade muted the computer but left the live report streaming to watch more later.

It was too early to check on Oliver, her blackmail asset who worked at FEMA, the Federal Emergency Management Agency, where he maintained the Integrated Public Alert and Warning System—IPAWS.

Jade had to give credit to her handlers at the Ministry of State Security in Beijing. They were forward thinkers. Targeting Oliver and men like him throughout the United States government was a brilliant move. Not at all sexy—Oliver would never be in a position of management or power—but the everyday people keeping the country running were often easy prey.

How many could resist the offer of some extra money in exchange for information on the internal workings of their network, a password for twenty-four hours of access, or "accidentally" plugging a flash drive into their work computer?

There were so many who had been overlooked for promotion, denied their preferred week for a vacation, or dumped on by their manager.

Which employees were easily flattered and ready to do a small favor for a relationship with the person of their dreams?

Beijing didn't want war with the United States, but when and if it came, they would be ready.

Not merely with planes, missiles, and bullets. They were expensive.

Men and women like Jade were cheap, effective, and destructive.

And many Americans were soft and gullible.

The food hitting Jade's stomach made her eyes droop with fatigue. But she couldn't wash off the stupid black makeup, strip off the ridiculous punk costume, and drop onto the futon on the bedroom floor until she checked on Clay at the port in New Jersey.

There was only one short news report.

Explosions at Port Elizabeth

Firefighters were called to the Port Elizabeth container offloading and storage area early this morning after several explosions were heard. Authorities say no one was injured, though several shipping containers were destroyed. An investigation is ongoing.

Jade slumped in her chair, more exhausted. After all her planning, this was the result? One paragraph online?

No expensive cranes tumbling into the water or crushing a container ship?

Or shipping containers filled with chemicals spewing thick black toxic smoke into the air?

How about mass casualties?

The capture of a group of domestic terrorists armed with automatic weapons and C-4 explosives?

Anything to make the news and spark panic would have been acceptable.

The researchers at the Ministry of State Security had identified Clay as a target and the specific buttons to push for her to seduce him.

She had made contact. Flirted with him. Endured his fumbling romantic encounters. The late-night political lectures. Shaped his confused extremist urges into real-life action.

All for nothing. For it to fizzle away like her time—her body—was nothing. Worthless.

Jade had a fake Canadian passport from the MSS and money in her investment account.

No matter what happened today in the stock market, she could take an Amtrack train to Florida, fly to South America, and disappear.

The MSS would attempt to track her, but with her money and skills, it would be easy to hide.

Maybe giving all of this up was the best idea. Not bother with the rest of the plan.

Nothing seemed worth it anymore, though that had to be the exhaustion talking.

She'd sleep on it.

The video from her phone that Darius had recorded was ready on a cloud server. With a few clicks, it would go directly online, plus be sent to the top New York news agencies.

She'd do that at 9:31, right after the stock market opened—assuming it would. With the threat in Times Square eliminated, the authorities weren't likely to stop trading for the day.

She'd use Oliver's credentials to log into his system, prep the alert, and send it out around 9:45 or 10:00 when the news started reporting about her video and the threat of another bomb in Times Square.

The stock market would plummet.

Seth's circuit breaker hack would kick in.

The lack of the expected halt in trading after a seven percent loss would fuel a further panicked selloff.

If she found the will to go through with it.

The idea of causing so much fear would normally excite her, but she was too tired for that.

She'd feel more herself after a two-hour nap. She was safe here.

During her espionage training, a top special forces soldier had lectured them on the best ways to stay as sharp as possible through sleep deprivation.

Then he had kept them awake for twenty-four hours, when they'd taken a challenging cognitive test. At thirty-six hours, the man had administered a similar test, and again after forty-eight hours of no rest. After sixty hours, they'd taken the final test and been allowed to sleep.

When they had recovered, the test scores had surprised no one.

The same soldier returned to explain the importance of naps, even in the middle of a mission. Their minds, they saw clearly, had greatly diminished function as early as twenty-four hours into an operation.

"As long as you aren't on guard duty or in imminent danger, a nap is one of the greatest tactical tools you can employ," he had told the class.

She would put the lesson to work now.

Without a phone, she set an alarm on the laptop, and a second to be sure.

Jade had no energy to take off the makeup or change clothes. She stumbled into the bedroom and dropped to the futon, forcing herself to ignore the smell of Darius on her pillow.

They had a simple, old-fashioned clock radio on the floor next to the bed, which she set for eight a.m. A redundancy to the redundancy, as she had been trained.

Sunlight streamed in from the window, so she rolled onto her other side, closed her eyes, and slept.

THE PERCEPTION

The President's Exercise Room
The White House
Washington, D.C.

Gregory arrived five minutes early to his morning workout session, but President Heringten was already dripping with sweat.

"Good morning, Gregory," the president said. He finished sliding a weight plate on the side of the bar at the bench press. "You're just in time to spot me."

"Yes, sir."

The president lay on the bench, planted his feet, and arched his back. "I've already done my warmup."

"Yes, Mr. President," Gregory said. He stood at the head of the bench and prepared. He wasn't usually needed until the last few reps of the third set, but the president was in a mood this morning and had added more weight to the bar than usual.

"And then you can tell me what the hell is going on in New York," he muttered before shaking his head, taking two deep breaths, and lifting the weight off the J-hooks.

On the fourth rep, the president grunted and strained to push the bar up. Gregory leaned forward to help but got an annoyed grunt from the president. Inch by inch, the president raised the bar. Gregory kept his hands ready underneath but not touching.

With an explosive exhalation, the president dropped the bar onto the J-hooks, took a second, then sat up. He turned to Gregory.

"What do you have for me?"

As sometimes happened, Gregory would have to get his workout in at the CAG office. This morning would be all business.

"Thanks to my team, and Alex Southmark in particular, a suspected radiological dispersal device—a dirty bomb—was found and defused in a building under renovation in Times Square. New York's bomb squad is investigating more fully now."

The president waved him on with the universal hand signal to speed things up. "I heard that before coming down here. Who did it and why?"

"We're working on that, sir, but my team's current theory is that the same people who were responsible for the SystemSpike—and the incident at the resort in Oman—are behind this."

Gregory let that sink in for a moment before continuing. "I'll have a full report for you later this morning, or as news comes in, but the person we believe is the mastermind is still on the loose. Jade Pang, an American from California going to school in New York City, has been on our radar for the past few days. As I reported yesterday, she attempted to kill Alex Southmark by pushing him in front of a bus. As of a half hour ago, we have confirmation in the form of a confession from her co-conspirator, a high-level Russian criminal named Boris Zorinov, that Pang was indeed responsible for the SystemSpike, and for planning the Oman incident, but he had no information on the latest threat. Or threats."

The president frowned.

"I'm sorry, sir. I know it's a lot to throw at you, but this is a fluid situation."

President Heringten nodded and mopped sweat off his face with a hand towel that had the presidential seal embroidered on the corner.

"Threats, plural?"

Gregory took a breath and nodded. This was going to suck.

"Yes, sir. We believe there is a strong possibility of another attack this morning. "

"What kind of attack, and what are we doing to prevent it?"

"The target, we believe, is the stock exchange, with the goal being to somehow crash the stock market. But whether that is another infrastructure attack with more bombs, or cyberattacks as we saw two months ago, we don't know."

"That's not a phrase I love hearing."

"I understand, Mr. President. Believe me, I hate saying it."

"An unknown threat? A terrorist at large? What can we do to stop this?"

"I recommend you coordinate with the Securities and Exchange Commission to strongly request that the stock exchanges not open today, that trading be suspended until tomorrow."

"And you'll have this all resolved by then?"

Gregory had anticipated the question. "We hope to, sir, but there's no guarantee."

The president stood, abandoning his workout, and paced the small room. "The threat in Times Square has been neutralized. That's a win. If you had a specific threat…" He trailed off, eyebrows raised.

Gregory shook his head.

"And if I order the exchanges closed today, open them tomorrow, and that's when they'll strike?"

Gregory remained silent, recognizing a rhetorical question when he heard it.

"The problem is perception. If I halt trading or delay the opening of the markets, people will think New York City is about to go up in flames or have radiation rain down on it. Plus, we don't want our enemies, whether individual extremists or other countries, to feel like they can manipulate us, mess with our economy, get us to shut down trading every time they threaten us."

"Yes, Mr. President." It had been a tough sell from the beginning, but Gregory had to try.

"I'll reach out to the SEC and the exchanges and put everyone on alert. If something happens, we'll shut trading down quickly. But not until then." The president checked his rugged, black-and-silver-dive watch. "You have a little over three hours. Happy hunting."

"Yes, Mr. President." He'd been dismissed, but as he turned and walked the few steps toward the door, the president spoke again. "Gregory. What about Haley? Is she safely at the Central Analysis Group office as I've repeatedly requested from both you and her? Or is she… being Haley?"

Gregory turned. He didn't have to say a word.

"Ah," the president said. "I see." He didn't sound as angry as Gregory expected. More disappointed—and unsurprised. "You're doing everything in your power to ensure her safety?"

"When I left the office thirty minutes ago, she was in a reinforced command trailer with the New York Bomb Squad in the safe zone."

Technically, he wasn't lying. Gregory doubted Haley was still there, but he didn't have to say that.

President Heringten seemed to see through the ruse. He offered a wry grin. "I understand the predicament she puts you in. But keep her safe, okay?"

"I'll do what I can, Mr. President."

THE FIREHOUSE

Lafayette Firehouse
Lafayette Street Between Prince and Spring
Soho

"One last thing," the lieutenant said as he finished the roll call. The firefighters coming on duty stood in a semicircle around him in the apparatus bay. "You've probably all heard about the mess in Times Square. Thankfully, there was no damage and no loss of life. But there's a suspect wanted for questioning." He held up a sheet of paper. "This is a printout of a woman to be on the lookout for. Check it out and keep your eyes open. And stay sharp today."

"Hey Lieutenant," one of the guys called. "Let's see the pictures. Nathan is always on the lookout for a woman."

The man accepted the piece of paper. "Cute. Look at those dimples."

The firefighters gathered around, peering over his shoulder at the black and white printout showing two pictures. In one, a young woman with long, straight fine hair and dimples stared directly at the camera, as in a passport photo. The picture on the right was of poorer quality, probably from a surveillance camera at what looked like a coffee shop.

"Hey," one of the men said. "She looks kind of familiar. Right?"

The joking simmered down as the group took the situation seriously.

Someone else spoke. "Nathan? You're the expert," he said, to much laughter.

Nathan took the paper with a flourish and peered at it. He stepped closer to the open roller door to get some natural light, followed by the others, but he shooed them back.

"I think that's the woman who lives across the street," Nathan whispered.

"The jogger! That's where I recognize her. You're right. Third floor, I think."

"Hey Lieutenant," Nathan called, and hurried over. "Who are we supposed to call with information? I think this is the woman who visits her boyfriend from time to time across the street."

THE SECOND WARNING

Broadway and Houston Street
Soho

Between Haley's fake Homeland Security credentials and being the one to identify the bomb threat in Times Square, she'd had no trouble requisitioning three NYPD officers—and one of their personal cars.

She sat in the passenger seat, out of place still wearing her full military gear: extra magazines of ammunition filling the front pockets of her black plate carrier, short-barrel carbine, and a pistol at her hip.

At least she had her long blond hair up in a tight, sensible bun.

They were back at the starting point of their grid search.

"The same streets again?" the plainclothes officer driving his car asked. He was a few years older than her—mid- to late-twenties—and he was having a great time driving around Manhattan with her and two of his buddies.

They were in a ridiculous car for Manhattan—a black, low-slung muscle car with a loud, rumbling engine.

At least she was in the front. The two other guys were crammed into the small backseats, their knees practically pressed against their chests.

"We've covered every street?" Haley asked. She'd had a slow-speed cruise of every block from Houston Street to Canal Street, Broadway to Bowery, focusing on Soho and Little Italy as Void had suggested.

No sightings of Jade.

Hours wasted.

It had been a long shot, but it beat standing around a command center drinking horrible coffee with police officers hitting on her.

"Yes," the officer in the back said. "Three times." He wasn't having as much fun stuck back there. It had probably sounded a lot more exciting when she'd requested help driving around lower New York, hoping to luck into catching a suspected terrorist.

"We could expand the zone," the driver said. "Farther east?"

She didn't want to join Axe investigating Jade's apartment, as well as Darius's, Kareem's, and Yaz's. There was intel to be found, and she was the intel queen, but with the NYPD, FBI, and everyone else swarming the area, interviewing neighbors, and looking into how Jade had acquired C-4 plastic explosives, a fake dirty bomb, and weapons, and where she had stored them, Haley would be a small fish in a huge pond.

Axe had to direct the searches and be on hand in case Jade's safe house was closer to her apartment or Darius's.

He was continuing in Admiral Nalen's role, which gave her the freedom for this fruitless search based on one hacker's wild theory, but Void was that hacker—and wild theories were the unsanctioned asset team's bread and butter. Void had previously been able to track Jade's phone to the general vicinity but hadn't been able to pinpoint her location because of the area's cellular tower makeup and coverage.

"Once more through the streets," she told the driver. "Maybe we'll get lucky this—"

"Haley," Nancy said over their comm chat in her earbud. The cellular network in Midtown had been restored, and this part of the city had never been cut off, which made communicating with the Central Analysis Group headquarters, Axe, and Void easy.

Haley held up a finger to the guys in the car and pointed at her ear as she unmuted her line. "Go ahead."

"You're in Soho? How far are you from Lafayette Street between Prince and Spring?"

"Yes. We're two blocks west and one block north."

"Perfect. We've got a hit from the expanded BOLO notice Axe had us send out. Firefighters at a ladder company near you recognized Jade as a woman who stays in an apartment across the street from their firehouse. She comes and goes—she isn't there all the time."

"That sounds right. Have they seen her this morning?"

"No, this is coming from the day shift. They came on duty a few minutes ago and saw the pictures at their shift change meeting. But the window at the front of the apartment is open."

"East or west side of the street?"

After a few seconds, Nancy came back. "The apartment is on the west side of the street. Third floor walkup."

"Get me to the southwest corner of Lafayette and Spring—quietly," she told the driver. He eased forward, south on Broadway, the beast of a car rumbling.

"Get one or two of the firefighters washing their truck or something to keep an eye on the apartment window and the front door. Something subtle. Wait—can firefighters do subtle?"

The cops in the car chuckled and shook their heads.

"I'll make sure they get it," Nancy said.

"Also, I'm going to need their help."

"Breeching the door?"

"You got it. Maybe we should get you into the field next time?"

Haley could picture the woman, wild hair flying in the breeze as she ran down a street, pistol in hand.

Nancy chuckled. "Hell no."

"Have one of the fire department trucks go out on a call and meet us at the corner of Prince and Spring with breaching gear ready. Seriously—two of their biggest, fastest guys who can get a door open quickly."

"We've already discussed it. They're ready. Do you want me to roll the NYPD to the location, too?"

"No," Haley said, looking at the guys in the car. "I'm all set. Let's make this a surprise visit."

254 Lafayette Street
Soho

Jade woke to the *beep beep beep* of the alarm on the floor next to the futon. She shut it off and went to the kitchen table, where she stopped the two alarms on the computer.

Coffee, a quick shower, and a different outfit.

She got the coffee pot working, stripped in the bathroom, cleaned up, and put on black leggings, a sports bra, and a long, loose gray sweatshirt that hid the shape of her body.

The short haircut felt weird, but it was certainly easier to wash, dry, and maintain. She smoothed her hair down and added product to hold it in place, going for a more normal look than the spiked hair. The goth-punk girl had seen a lot of action yesterday. She'd avoid going out, but until her hair grew back, this would be her new look. Different from her previous styles: conservative student, the frumpy, pimply girl disguise, and the killer punk girl with the backpack that was probably on security footage near Times Square.

If it wasn't on the news yet, it would be soon.

With coffee in hand, she sat at the kitchen table. The nap had done wonders for her attitude and focus.

The news showed Times Square largely back to normal.

The cellular network had been shut down for a large part of the city but was now back on.

A bomb had been discovered, deactivated, and while the scare was all over the news and social media, life in New York City went on.

There was no danger of the stock exchanges closing.

She was once again ready to fight for what should be hers.

It started now.

Using Turbo's original secondary hack, which was easy to manage with the log in details he had so generously provided before his flight off the edge of the building, Jade navigated to an online portal and uploaded the next warning message she and Darius had worked out.

By the time she'd finished her first cup of coffee, it had hit websites across the country.

You think you're safe?

You're not. Far from it.

Your world is about to crumble around you.

Again.

Only this time, it will be worse.

Prepare yourselves for the end.

There weren't as many vulnerable websites compared to the ones she had hijacked yesterday, but it would be enough.

Five minutes after that, the social media site SPOT named it a trending story.

Her school friend Lauren would be richly rewarded later today when the stock market plummeted.

Circlebuzzz was next—they copied everything SPOT did.

By nine a.m., Xavier at the wire service must have done his work. The warning hit the news sites.

Paying off ten thousand dollars of his student loans had been money well spent.

From the firehouse across the street, one of the ladder trucks thundered out of the garage—a common sound most days. At least they didn't turn on their siren—normally, they waited until they were on Broadway or needed to clear traffic, shielding the neighborhood from the noise.

After Jade's second cup of coffee, she was thinking fast and ready for the rest of the plan. She filled the coffee mug one last time and prepared the rest of what she needed.

It was going to be an excellent day of chaos—and profit.

182

THE PREPARATION

Lafayette and Spring
Soho

All three police officers and both of the firefighters she'd picked were taller and beefier than Haley, but she had no trouble holding their attention.

They were gathered well back from the corner of Lafayette. The firehouse—and Jade's potential safe house—were ninety yards up the block. Less than a football field.

"Everybody understand the plan?" Haley asked.

"Why does he get to go up the stairs and I have to watch the fire escape?" the driver of the car asked. He was tough about it, challenging her.

Haley had her reasons. The guy in the backseat, who she'd picked to back her up, had long legs and moved well—she'd seen it near Times Square earlier that morning. It might come in handy once they breached the apartment door.

The driver had mentioned hunting as a kid while they drove around. If Jade jumped out the back window and down the fire escape, he'd have the best chance at a long-range shot before she closed on him.

And the third guy had slightly darker skin than the others, whether from being outdoors in the sunshine or his heritage. That would come in handy for the distraction she had planned.

But if she stopped to explain herself, used logic to justify her actions, took them step by step through why they needed to do what she wanted, it wouldn't stop. Her every move would be second guessed.

Whether he was questioning her because she was young, a woman, an outsider from the NYPD, or because he desperately wanted to be one of the door kickers and not have to wait in the alley, didn't matter.

She'd have lost before the operation had begun.

So Haley turned to the police officer with the question and gave him the look. She had learned it initially from Axe, but had made it her own over the past missions. It revealed what she'd been through, the people she'd killed, and how tiny the man was in the grand scheme of what she had done.

The poor guy withered in less than a second. "I've got the back," he said.

Haley didn't bother to respond. "Close in," she said to the five men. They leaned in, locked on her words.

"We suspect this woman of being the mastermind of the SystemSpike attacks. She orchestrated the killing of more than three thousand Americans. We have solid evidence of that, along with her involvement in this morning's suspected dirty bomb scare in Times Square. And we believe she is in the middle of another attack on the country today. She is an imminent threat, so she ends up in custody—or dead."

Haley turned to the officer who would cover the fire escape. "She doesn't get by you. Do you understand me? Whatever you have to do. Her escape is not an option."

He nodded.

Haley looked at the long-legged cop. "If she takes me out, you shoot to kill. No warnings."

Lastly, she focused on the two beefy firefighters, who were several years older than her. "You two will be in the hallway. She's armed and dangerous. If the officer and I are down, you're up. You're trained to save lives. Can you take one if you have to?"

Both hesitated half a second before nodding.

"Excellent. Let's do this." She clicked her earbud. "Nancy, we're starting. I'll let you know when to flood the zone with the NYPD."

"We're ready," Nancy said.

Haley looked at the men gathered around her. "Let's go."

183

THE START

Conference Room 3
Central Analysis Group Headquarters
Arlington, Virginia

Marcus felt like the odd man out.

He'd helped after the container port attack, tracking down the suspected attackers who had either blown themselves up or had their explosives triggered by Jade.

But otherwise, he had little to do. He adjusted his bow tie, making sure it was on straight, and prepared. This was likely the calm before the storm.

Nancy had her noise-cancelling headphones covering one ear so she could be in touch with Haley on comms. She held one of the conference table phones to her other ear, on the line with someone high in the NYPD chain of command who knew how to make things happen, though the top dog was surely listening in and approving every move.

"Haley is moving," Nancy reported. "She'll sneak up the block to the apartment building, pick the exterior door, then have to quietly climb the stairs to the third floor before breaching Jade's apartment."

Dave monitored the stock market pre-trading.

"Only a few minutes until market open," Dave said. "Already, trading is down three percent due to the dirty bomb scare."

Gregory leaned against the wall near the door, arms folded, looking tired but calm and in control, though a few strands of his hair had escaped the hold of whatever product he used to keep it in place.

Marcus's laptop pinged with an alert. He was finally getting into the game.

"It's started," he said. "A second warning has taken over websites across the country. Not as many as the other day. Sounds like the same author's voice."

He read the warning aloud to the others.

You think you're safe?

You're not. Far from it.

Your world is about to crumble around you.

Again.

Only this time, it will be worse.

Prepare yourselves for the end.

"The market has it," Dave said a few seconds later. "Another one-quarter percent drop in pre-market trading. Now a half. Three and a half down and holding."

"That's not enough for her," Gregory said from his spot. "There's more coming."

Marcus received another alert. "Whoa," he muttered. "There's a Washington, DC blog that's known for its deep background but often accurate scoops. This one is a biggie. The headline is, *Murder, Mayhem, and Scandal on the Stock Market.*"

Marcus skimmed the story, speed-reading to catch the high points. "This claims a man shot yesterday in Maryland was an SEC insider with information about accounting irregularities at fifteen big, publicly traded firms. 'Like Enron, only worse.'"

"I have half of these stocks in my brokerage account," Marcus said. He read the names of the biggest ones and Dave typed them in.

"The first one is down ten percent, pre-market open," Dave said. "Eighteen for the second. The index is down four percent, but the first few stocks on your list, Marcus, are plummeting."

"Jade is going to make money," Gregory said. "At least half of the trades are going to be run by algorithms, automatically executed if the price of a stock—or the index—goes to a certain level. It's going to get worse, but so far, we can weather this." He moved to a spare laptop, sat down, and started typing.

"The report has to be fake," Marcus said, clicking into an investment database.

"A man was shot with a high-powered rifle on his way to work yesterday in Maryland, outside of DC," Gregory said. "Dave, dig into him. Sending you the info now." He clicked the trackpad. "Seconds count here, people. Make it fast."

184

CEASE AND DESIST

The Blake Blog World Headquarters
Arlington, Virginia

Blake had his feet up on his desk, his computer open on his lap, and the TV on the wall of his studio apartment tuned to the financial news channel.

"DC-based blogger Blake Clinaire with a scoop this morning," the host said. Blake's picture—the one from the home page of his site—appeared in a box over the man's shoulder. "He has a report that, if confirmed, will rock the financial world."

Blake was famous.

Tomorrow, he'd have his pick of which morning shows to appear on.

He was about to hit the big time.

The first thing he'd do was get a real office. No more working out of his tiny apartment.

He'd hire other reporters, and a secretary—or executive assistant. That sounded better. More professional.

Even better, he had not only convinced his dad to dump his positions in the fifteen companies who were lying and cheating, but to short them—bet on their drop in price—as well. The more the stocks' values dropped, the more money Dad would make.

Blake's cell phone seemed to explode with notifications, both pings from conventional texts and buzzes from the secure comms app.

On his computer, the email screen went from a nearly empty inbox to one hundred unread emails. The next time it refreshed, there were more. Several had similar headlines:

Cease and Desist: retract your story immediately

Notice of impending legal action unless you retract your false statements

URGENT: Immediate retraction required

Inaccurate information and false claims in your blog

All had email addresses from the legal departments of the companies he'd named.

That was fast.

Of course they'd be ready for a report like his. They were crooks and knew they'd eventually get caught.

You can threaten me all you want, but the truth is out now.

There was no way the SEC could bury this. Stevie—the SEC employee who had been killed for discovering the scandal—could rest in peace.

Blake's cell phone rang, but he hit the red button to send it to voicemail.

Less than a second later, it rang again.

He tuned in to the TV as the financial news host cut to a red-faced man glaring into the camera. "We're lucky enough to have with us in studio the CEO of one of the companies named in the blog story, who was previously scheduled to appear on our show in the second hour. Mr. Kaslucas, thank you for moving up your interview. What can you—"

"Sorry to interrupt, but I have to state in the strongest terms that this report is completely false. I don't know how Mr. Clinaire came upon this information, and I'll note that he doesn't name his source, or reference more than one person who provided the information, which is a common professional journalistic standard, but our legal department has already reached out to him about a retraction of the false claims."

"As we speak, as we're about to start the trading day, your company stock is down… thirty-four percent. How do you—"

"We will be suing Mr. Blake Clinaire personally for libel, and we encourage the SEC to conduct their own thorough investigation. Our legal department has confirmed that a SEC staffer was murdered yesterday morning on his way to work, and his friends and family have our condolences. But the supposed report cited in Mr. Clinaire's story is, we believe, entirely made up."

"Your company is suing Mr. Clinaire for libel? That quickly?"

"Absolutely. I cannot stress that—"

Blake muted the TV and turned to his laptop to take a closer look at the emails.

Across the room, the door shook in the frame as someone knocked with what sounded like their fist. "Mr. Clinaire? Please open the door. We need to speak with you."

Blake's stomach dropped.

He had the feeling that he'd made a horrible mistake.

185

THE TARGETING

Conference Room 3
Central Analysis Group Headquarters
Arlington, Virginia

"Give me what you have right now," Gregory ordered. His team had their heads down, focused on their laptops. "Perfection is the enemy of done. Better to get out what we know already than wait for an in-depth report later."

Marcus looked up. He had been researching the murder of the Securities and Exchange Commission staffer. "Not to speak ill of the dead," Marcus said, "but the man who was shot on the sidewalk—by who we assume was Jade—had no enforcement or reporting responsibilities. He worked at the SEC, but he must have been targeted for the hit because he was easy to find and kill. His professional profile on a career-focused social media site has a clear picture of him, identifies him as an employee of the Securities and Exchange Commission, and lists the city where he lived. He was a prolific social media poster on other sites as well, all set to public view, not private or friends only. Look at this." Marcus didn't bother mirroring his screen to the monitor on the wall—he merely turned his computer toward Gregory and pointed. "He recently moved into a new apartment." The man stood in front of a sign showing the name of the apartment complex. "He even mentioned the two trains he could take to make it to work in time—and how close the train station was. If someone wanted to target an employee of the SEC, he made it easy.”

“Compile that intel, clean up the presentation, show how someone unscrupulous likely targeted the poor guy, and get it to me. I’ll send it to the SEC for their investigation—and to a reporter I know.” Gregory turned to Dave and raised an eyebrow.

“The market is going to open shortly for trading,” Dave said. “The fifteen stocks on the list are way, way down, but the market index is hovering at only a five percent loss so far.”

“I hope it holds,” Gregory said.

“Haley is in the Soho apartment building,” Nancy said. “The police officer is going to start the distraction. Sixty seconds.”

“Be safe, Haley,” Gregory muttered.

186

THE DEMAND

254 Lafayette Street
Soho

Jade's coffee was long gone, but she was in the zone and feeling fine.

She could sleep more this afternoon when the market closed and she was rich.

Stock trading had started down, but not enough to trigger the circuit breakers yet—the circuit breakers Seth had disabled.

But in a few minutes, when Jade executed the two scripts she'd written —short computer programs that, in this case, would do a number of different tasks at once—the market would plummet.

On one side of her computer screen, she had emails ready to send to every news organization in the city and tri-state area.

The authorities got lucky with the bomb in Times Square, but they missed the second device. It is safely hidden somewhere in Manhattan.

The video (see links) was taken this morning.

Yes, that is another dirty bomb. :)

In less than thirty minutes… boom!

Bye-bye New York!

Once she pressed the button, the video she'd already uploaded to five public streaming sites, including one overseas, would go live.

The drama would begin, but would truly ramp up when she moved the cursor to the right side of her screen.

Oliver's login credentials had worked. She had full control of the Federal Emergency Management System's Integrated Public Alert and Warning System—IPAWS.

The alert was composed and ready to send. With one click, the message would go to every phone, radio, and television in the area.

ALERT. WARNING. This is not a drill. A credible threat of a nuclear device has been reported in New York City. Evacuate Manhattan immediately. If unable to evacuate, shelter in place. Suspend all air conditioning and ventilation. Seal all windows and doors. Repeat. Evacuate Manhattan immediately.

This was going to be fun—if it worked.

The entire scheme now relied on a bluff.

The vague second threat of doom.

The fake SEC report about stocks that were hiding the truth about their businesses. Fifteen Enrons.

A fictitious second dirty bomb in the city and a real FEMA evacuation warning.

It had to work.

The mission would be a success, she would be rich, and though she could never return to China, she would have already proven the men there wrong. She was more than a seductress, and much more than a future wife and mother.

"Darius!" a voice called from the street out front. "I know you're in there somewhere! I want my money, you bastard. Get out here!"

Jade's head whipped around, and she was up, through the narrow living room and into the bedroom, though she slowed as she neared the window, hanging back out of sight.

The thin white curtains fluttered in a light breeze, giving her a glimpse of a man standing in front of the firehouse across the street, glaring at the apartment building.

"Darius! Darius Al-Nafisi. I. Want. My. Money. Show yourself!"

Jade couldn't place the man, but they had intentionally kept the patrons that Yaz and Kareem had recruited at arm's length for security—and to avoid exactly this type of scenario.

How had the man found the apartment?

The loud *clang* of metal hitting the front door and frame in the kitchen came as a total surprise.

The follow-up *crunch* of the door being forcefully wedged open didn't.

Jade rushed toward the kitchen, to grab her laptop, continue to the bathroom at the back of the apartment, and down the fire escape to freedom.

187

THE COMMAND

254 Lafayette Street
Soho

Haley had to hand it to the firefighters. They were focused, strong, and fast.

One slammed the Halligan fork—a tool with a wedge-shaped blade, a two-pronged head, like the back of a jumbo hammer, and a pick—into the door frame with a force that nearly blew out part of the wall.

The other took an axe and helped the first man pop the door open.

Haley moved through the doorway an instant after the door opened but slammed to a stop just inside the apartment.

Jade stood before her in the kitchen, lifting an open laptop with her left hand.

The fingers of her right moved toward the trackpad.

Haley had her speech planned. She would convince Jade to confess, to tell her who had helped her plan and execute the SystemSpike and the other attacks two months before, in addition to the plots of last night and today.

Mariana's report from Boris Zorinov was inconclusive. The Russian hadn't known if Jade was taking orders from others or if the operations had been her idea.

Haley needed to know if Jade had acted on her own or if China's Ministry of State Security had ordered an attack on the United States.

But the standoff changed the situation.

Did Haley dare take the shot not knowing who was to blame for the SystemSpike—and what else Jade had prepared?

It could be another dirty bomb set to explode at the press of a button.

Or a SystemSpike-type hack that could shut down the electrical grid, short-circuit the Air Traffic Control System, or damage the support system of one of the country's nuclear reactors, increasing the risk of a catastrophe.

How much damage could Jade do with the press of a computer key?

They locked eyes.

They weren't all that different. Two young women in what was predominantly still a career—and world—for men.

Haley had the angle. At this range, as long as Jade stayed still, the bullet would enter Jade's forehead slightly above the nose bridge, between her eyebrows.

It would go straight to the woman's brainstem—a human being's anatomic off switch.

Her body would instantly shut down.

No twitching fingers.

If Haley didn't miss—and had the guts to take the shot.

Jade faced down the blond woman dressed in tactical gear.

The woman's weapon didn't waver.

The police and two firefighters behind her wouldn't be a problem. Jade wouldn't go free. It was much too late for that. But she could bend the men to her will enough to sweet talk them into giving her the second she needed to drop her finger to the trackpad of the laptop computer and click twice. The emails would be sent. The video of the "second bomb" would go live. And the emergency alert would be sent.

Jade could bargain from there. Negotiate from a position of strength.

Or at least she would have the satisfaction of knowing she had crashed the stock market and caused a mass exodus from New York.

All Jade had to do was use her considerable persuasive talents on the young blond in front of her.

"Don't shoot," Jade said in a tone that compelled obedience.

Haley sensed the effect Jade could have on people. The woman had a gift.

The words and tone might have worked on Mad Dog.

Johnboy? Also maybe.

Axe? Tough call.

But it didn't work on her.

"You don't have to do this," Haley said. She tightened her finger on the trigger, an instant away from shooting.

Jade tried to read the woman's face. Had it worked? Had Jade created the tiny seed of hesitation she needed to be arrested after clicking the trackpad instead of being shot beforehand?

She wasn't certain, but if the woman kept talking, Jade could use that against her. Most people wouldn't interrupt themselves, especially to shoot someone holding nothing more dangerous than a laptop computer.

Haley sensed the change. Maybe it was a micro expression on Jade's face, or her slightest shift of weight.

"You don't have to do this," Haley repeated. "Tell us who—"

Jade's eyes flicked to the computer screen and her right hand twitched lower.

Haley pulled the trigger.

The shot boomed in the confines of the kitchen.

The bullet slammed through Jade's lower brainstem, at the base of the skull, where the brain meets the spinal cord.

Her eyes glazed and mouth opened, slack jawed as her head fell forward.

With no motor signals, her body dropped straight down.

The laptop hit the cheap gray linoleum floor an instant later.

"Clear," Haley yelled, hoping the tall police officer in the hall behind her wasn't coming in with his gun blazing.

The officer stood at the door, fingers clenched white on his pistol, which he at least had pointed at the floor.

Behind him, the firefighters crowded close, ready with the axe and Halligan fork.

"Target down," Haley said. "Clear the rest of the rooms."

Haley pivoted to the bathroom a step behind her. It was empty.

A few seconds later, the officer returned from the front of the apartment looking much less stressed. "Clear," he said, staying out of the kitchen.

Haley holstered her weapon, picked up the computer, and checked the screen, which had cracked but was still functional.

There were two windows. On the left, the cursor rested on a button to send an email blast to a long list of New York media outlets and publish a video to several streaming websites. The thumbnail of the video showed a canister surrounded by C-4 explosives and a timer. It looked like the device Axe had found.

Haley pulled out her phone and found the pictures Axe had sent.

She had to be sure.

The unique, twisted and bent metal handle on the canister Axe found was the same as the one in the video.

It was the same device.

The NYPD had already uncovered security camera footage tracking Jade's trip from New Jersey to New York City, her drive to a parking garage, and the walk from there to the building in Times Square. The entire time, she'd had only the backpack large enough for a single canister.

There were no bombs in her SUV.

She had no accomplices—aside from Darius, who they found footage of arriving at the building with nothing in his hands, and no backpack.

This video had to have been recorded by Darius in the Times Square building. It was the bomb Axe had discovered in the closet.

The emails and video—the entire threat—was a last-ditch bluff designed to scare people and crash the market.

The right half of the screen showed an internal federal alert computer system, with a warning to evacuate Manhattan typed into a box and ready to send.

Haley inched the cursor into the upper right corner of the screen and placed the computer on the kitchen table next to an empty coffee mug. She'd have a tech expert handle it, just in case.

The police officer stared at Jade's body. She had landed on her side, one arm trapped beneath her, looking like she had decided to lie down on the kitchen floor for a quick nap—except for wide-open, unseeing eyes.

Haley tapped her earbud to unmute her line. "Threat neutralized," she said. "One EKIA. No friendly casualties. Get me an expert computer tech and send up the rest of the NYPD. There's evidence to collect."

PART 7

FRIDAY

188

THE REPORT

The President's Exercise Room
The White House
Washington, D.C.

Gregory jogged on the treadmill to warm up for the weightlifting session.

Next to him, President Heringten did the same.

As always, Gregory waited for the president to speak and direct the meeting.

The president tapped a button on the treadmill repeatedly to change the speed and slow to a walk. Gregory matched the move.

"I'll read the full report in the office, but sum it up for me," the president said.

"Yes, sir. Jade Pang, a college student in New York, was killed yesterday while attempting to crash the stock market by bluffing about a second radiological dispersal device—a dirty bomb." He rushed forward, not giving the president a second to ask who had killed Pang. "She likely orchestrated an ill-fated attack on a container shipping port in New Jersey and was responsible for the earlier, defused and what ultimately turned out to be a fake dirty bomb in Times Square. My team is digging right now, but we suspect Pang is not who she claimed to be. We'll have more in a day or two, but it's probable she was a foreign agent."

"Chinese?"

"That is her heritage, but who she may have been working for is unknown. There were, however, four covert operators killed in the Times Square building where Axe found the bomb. They also have Asian features but no identification. We're tracing them. So far, they come back merely as wealthy Chinese tourists."

The president toweled off his face and took a sip of water.

Gregory gave him a moment, then continued. "We have independent confirmation that Pang was the ultimate contact for Boris Zorinov, the wealthy Russian criminal fixer who we now know was responsible for recruiting and directing Abdul Khan Dagari—Malik, who..." Gregory hesitated. He suspected the president had somehow killed or had ordered the killing of Malik in Oman, but there was no proof—just his hunch. "Who died when the resort collapsed in Oman, along with his brother Gogol, who Axe eliminated in Dubai."

"Zorinov? Did he act alone, or at the behest of Russia? Are we going to get more out of him?"

Gregory shook his head and stepped off the treadmill. It was time to lift weights. It was leg day. "He is dead. Unfortunately, he escaped from custody while on a break during his interrogation. He slipped through a very small window of a yacht and drowned. We called in the coastguard for help, and they found his body. We believe he acted without knowledge of the Russian government. And while being questioned, he said he believed Pang might have been acting on her own, with the financial support of people recruited from the university she was attending."

The president moved to a squat rack and added enough weights for a warm-up set.

He was about to ask the obvious question when Gregory spoke first. "These financial patrons, along with three of Pang's suspected conspirators, are dead, as are three other university students from the Middle East who were found in a park near the East River with their throats slashed. We believe they were also financial backers of the operation."

The president gave Gregory a look, but Gregory shook his head again. "Axe killed one of the conspirators—Kareem—who was attempting to shoot him in the Times Square building. Another—Darius—was killed in a shootout with the four covert operators. It looks like they got into a shootout with Pang for some reason, and the man was caught in the crossfire. The rest, we believe, were killed earlier in the evening by the

Kareem, the man Axe shot. Kareem carried both the gun and knife used on the victims."

"Kareem was cleaning house."

"Yes, Mr. President. That is the most likely explanation. And with the men who likely provided funding for the operation, that suggests Jade Pang acted alone without her government's knowledge."

They paused while the president did a warm-up squat set, followed by Gregory taking his turn. The president added weights—far more than Gregory would use—and squatted four reps while processing the report.

Once he finished, he took the extra weights off one side while Gregory did the other.

"Bottom line. Did China plan, execute, order, and or finance in any way the SystemSpike, the assassination of Secretary of State Wilson, or the events in Oman?"

Gregory took the question in, but focused on his squat form. If he didn't nail it, the president would call him on it and "suggest" he do the set again correctly.

Gregory backed up, reracked the weights, and added the president's plates to one side so he could do set two.

"Mr. President, that is a top priority to uncover. But right now, my gut and a few of the clues point to Jade Pang going rogue and doing it on her own. Was she a Chinese deep cover asset? Likely. Did China attack us through her?" Gregory hesitated.

"It's just us here. Tell me what you think, not what you'll write in the report to cover your team's ass."

Gregory held back a smile. "Yes, Mr. President. I believe she acted alone, but we'll do our best to confirm or deny that theory."

"Thank you, Gregory. So we've finally gotten to the truth of the SystemSpike and the rest? Besides that bullshit story we sold the public, I mean?"

"Yes, sir. We may get further eventually, but at least—for now—we can identify Jade Pang as the mastermind and Boris Zorinov as the person who implemented her plans."

"And they, along with Pang's accomplices and the financial supporters, are all dead?"

"Yes, sir."

The president nodded and backed up to the squat rack for his second set. "That's good enough for me. Well done, as always. And for once, we won't discuss Haley's participation, if that's okay with you."

"Thank you, sir."

"I look forward to the full report—and the results of the digging you'll do—but as far as I'm concerned, it's over for now."

He shook Gregory's hand, a more formal gesture than usual. "Thank you—and my thanks to your team. Justice has been served."

189

THE ASSETS

Empire Bagels and Coffee Brewery
Greenwich Village
Manhattan

Tabitha touched up her bright red lipstick for the short video. People loved the color on her, and consistency was key to attracting followers.

She scooted the chair around to frame out the grimy light switch on the back wall of the kitchen. "Recording," she called, not that it would keep people from making normal noise while they worked, but they'd keep the yelling to a minimum.

She wet her lips, checked her face and hair one last time, and hit the record button on her phone.

"Well, friends, news flash. Did the stock market 'crash'?" she asked, making air quotes with the hand not holding the phone. "Down five percent yesterday. It doesn't seem like much because… it's not! No big surprise. And the guy who predicted the future and promised ten thousand dollars to my favorite charity, and a yummy vegan tasting meal? You guessed it. Vanished. Probably went home to his mommy. That's no big surprise to some of you who called it Wednesday."

Tabitha didn't mean to let her disappointment show, but when she realized it did, she went with it. "Yeah, okay, I'm disappointed. He was cute. So sue me—no, not really. Come on. But it would have been nice to donate to my favorite charity, and a cute single guy who wants to have fun and maybe—I'm just saying maybe, if the timing and the chemistry and all that is right—maybe more than that? If you're out there, hit me up."

She blew a kiss, winked, and cut off the recording.

Another viral video. No doubt.

"Tabitha?" the manager yelled. He'd been much less lenient since she posted Wednesday's video about the rich guy who had now ghosted her. "We need you out here on the tables."

"Coming, coming, jeez."

The fun never stopped in the big city.

The Federal Emergency Management Agency
Washington, D.C.

When Oliver Renolds returned to work on Friday, only his manager asked if he was feeling better.

No one had missed him.

The day before, he had logged in for work as ordered by the mystery woman, left the laptop on the kitchen table, and gone back to bed. He binged a streaming series, but barely saw it. His mind was on the laptop, his job, and what he would say when the shit hit the fan after his laptop was "hacked."

He kept waiting for the shoe to drop, for the manager to call him into his office, for someone to mention the Integrated Public Alert and Warning System—IPAWS—system getting hacked or taken offline or something. No one had said a thing, but it had only been one day. He wasn't out of the woods yet.

But most of all, he waited for a message from her, his… well, not exactly girlfriend, he'd never call her that in one of their message exchanges, but really, was there any reason not to think of her that way? No. And not that anyone ever asked, but if they did, he might let drop that, oh yeah, he had a girlfriend.

But as the day passed without word from her—not that it was unusual, they'd go a week or two without exchanging messages—he had a weird feeling that he'd done something wrong that made her mad, and he was never going to hear from her again.

16th Floor
Stock Exchange Annex
Wall Street
Manhattan

Sean Finelan had expected police cars at his apartment on Long Island when he went outside to catch the train into the city, but the area was clear.

There were no men in suits and dark glasses in SUVs with government license plates outside the offices on Wall Street, either.

When his manager arrived almost an hour after him, Sean was greeted warmly as always by the overeager idiot.

At the workstation to his right, his colleague logged in using the same password as always and started work, keeping the stock exchange running smoothly.

The day before, the market index had dropped slightly more than five percent.

Sean's program never kicked in.

Jade's plan had failed.

His code had erased itself by now. It had only been set up for yesterday.

He was in the clear, except for the hundred-thousand-dollar home equity line of credit on his house for a remodel that hadn't happened.

Jade had that money somewhere.

He felt like a complete idiot.

She had conned him.

The daydreams about where they would go together when they were rich were fake.

All that talk about ten times, twenty times, thirty times returns.

The late nights figuring out how to write the code in such a way that prevented the circuit breakers from kicking in when the market dropped were an elaborate ruse.

All along, it had been so much simpler than that.

He thought he was being recruited by a foreign government asset? A honey trap?

No, Jade was a simple con artist out to get his hundred grand.

How naive could he be?

What a moron.

There was a small chance he was wrong, that the grand plan had failed for some reason. If so, Jade would contact him. But he wasn't holding his breath.

Jade and his money were probably long gone.

———

SPOT Headquarters
Austin, Texas

Lauren Canisey leaned to the side to see past several other cubes for a glimpse of the Austin sunshine.

Her phone sat silent on her desk. She'd already rebooted it twice, and sent a message on the comms app to a colleague who used it to ensure it was functioning.

There was no word from Jade.

Not only had the stock market not tanked yesterday like she had hoped, it was up the five percent it had lost plus another three.

She was losing money with every point it ticked upward.

Lauren sent another message. The last one for today, she promised herself.

Everything okay???? Text me. Worried.

Nothing.

This was pathetic. She was acting like a spurned lover.

Lauren checked her online brokerage account.

The number hurt so much she had to click away from the site.

There was a delay. Jade would turn this around. She was too brilliant not to.

All Lauren had to do was trust and ride this out.

She buried herself in her work, acutely aware of the financial ruin she faced if the stock market didn't drop a bunch by the end of the day.

———

The Source Wire Service
Lower Manhattan

Stories about a dirty bomb defused in a Times Square building Thursday kept Xavier busy.

The hackers from the previous day had managed another ominous warning on a smaller number of websites the day before, too.

Xavier had dutifully moved those up the priority distribution list without a reminder from Jade. She had paid off ten thousand dollars of his student loans; he'd do anything she wanted, within reason, no explanation needed.

He only hoped she'd keep her promise and pay off the rest of his loans for the admittedly easy job he'd done for her.

All he had to do was give her a little time.

190

THE RETRACTION

The Blake Blog World Headquarters
Arlington, Virginia

Five lawyers in expensive suits—and one pantsuit—stood in a semicircle around Blake.

He typed a more detailed retraction of the one he'd already posted yesterday by lunchtime when the calls, messages, emails, and people knocking on the door had convinced him that he'd been lied to.

"That should be a semicolon," one of them said.

Blake wanted to argue, but he kept his mouth shut, backspaced, and changed the long dash to a semicolon.

It has always been my practice to take sources at their word; I am a trusting individual who believes people and has always wanted to give voice to those who need it.

"Run-on sentence," a different lawyer said.

"There should at least be a comma between 'people' and 'and,'" a third said.

Blake waited them out. They were getting paid hundreds of dollars an hour each. Of course they would nitpick.

"Just keep typing," the fourth one—the woman—said. "We can clean it up later if necessary."

Blake typed.

Yesterday's post was accurate reporting, but I was lied to.

"No," all of them said at once.

He erased the line and tried again.

Yesterday, I shared a blog post that was 100% wrong. An anonymous source lied to me about everything. I believed them and, without following common journalistic practices, shared the information as if it were fact. Though I prefaced the reporting with disclaimers, it simply wasn't clear enough that the information was unverified and possibly a total lie, which in fact it turned out to be.

I am terribly sorry my poor journalistic standards caused such damage to the fine corporations slighted in my erroneous reporting.

This had to be the first time he'd ever used the word 'erroneous' on the blog. He hoped his regular readers would see it as the lawyer-driven BS it was.

Henceforth—another lawyer word—*the blog is on indefinite hiatus as I work with the attorneys for the corporations harmed by my actions to reach a settlement whereby I may return to reporting with a much higher ethical, moral, and journalistic standard. Until then, thank you for reading.*

Blake took his hands off the keyboard and waited. It had taken two hours to get this far. His first several attempts had been non-starters, but he'd finally caved and had written what he figured the lawyers wanted. Anything to get them off his back and out of his tiny apartment.

When they left, he would have to figure out a way to help his dad make back the money he lost betting against the fifteen stocks. All of them had since come roaring back to erase the original losses before going higher.

Their increased value was the only reason the lawyers were letting him off so "lightly."

As if shutting down his blog and taking away his livelihood was a light punishment.

Though it beat being sued for millions of dollars he didn't have.

"That'll do," the semicolon lawyer said. The other agreed. They could live with it.

Blake pushed the button to publish the story, and it went live immediately.

"Change a word and we'll sue you to the ends of the earth," run-on sentence lawyer muttered in his ear.

Not that there was much to take. The laptop, a cell phone, an old desk, his futon couch in the corner, some pots and pans, and some money in the bank.

At least he had his freedom. He hadn't been arrested for anything.

Blake would let this mess die down. Get a job at a big-box home store or the coffee chain with good employee benefits.

Eventually, he'd pick up a burner phone, install the secure comms app, and reach out to Jade, his friend from college who had originally suggested he switch to scandal reporting and had given him so many tips.

She's the one who had told him a big story was on the way right before the call that had caused this disaster.

Maybe she could explain what had happened and help him get back on his feet like she had done before.

After all, this entire mess was her fault. She owed him.

191

THE BILLIONAIRE

North Fifth Avenue
The Upper East Side
Manhattan

The elevator ride to the penthouse floor was tense. Mariana felt guilty, but this was the only way to be free of her obligation.

"We owe Vasily," she told Ekaterina, whispering in case the elevator was bugged. "He confirmed Boris was in New York City and gave us a starting point."

"Yes," was all Ekaterina said. She stood straight and proud, dressed in dark, loose pants and a simple black blouse. She would disappear in a crowd—the perfect assassin.

"It's just lunch," Mariana said. "Quick. In and out."

Ekat muttered something in Russian.

"What does that mean?"

"I am lamb to slaughter," Ekat translated. "This is terrible idea." For an instant, her discomfort showed before she locked it down.

"You can go," Mariana said as the elevator pinged their arrival. "I'll find someone else."

"No. We are here. We finish it." She leaned toward Mariana to whisper. "I am not angry. I am nervous."

Penthouse Level

Vasily greeted his guests at the elevator personally.

The act had seemed charming when Kelton and Mariana had done it, but felt awkward now. It had been years since he'd waited for someone.

The elevator door chimed—had it always done that?—and opened. Mariana stood on the left. A short woman of about his age stood on the right. She had thin, wispy short hair, dyed a light brown, a narrow, lined face, and a dancer's grace.

"My most sincere welcome," Vasily said. "It is a pleasure to see you again, Miss Rodriguez."

"Call me Mariana, please. The pleasure is mine, Mr. Chekov. May I present Ekaterina."

Vasily nodded to her and greeted her in Russian. *"Dobro pozhalovat."*

She replied in kind, her voice neither cold nor very welcoming.

"And I am Vasily. Please, come with me." Petrov had suggested a short tour, but at the moment that felt foolish.

This had been a terrible idea.

But no matter what happened this afternoon, Mariana had done what she'd promised.

The rest was up to him.

"Thank you for arranging this meeting," he said to her as he led the two ladies toward the sitting room. "Consider your obligation fulfilled."

"Don't thank me yet," Mariana said. "You have to live through the meal."

Vasily chuckled appreciatively at her joke, wondering if, in fact, that's what it was.

Ekaterina stopped at the entrance to the sitting room, all glitz and glamour. "One moment with my friend, please," she said in Russian to Vasily. He nodded and walked across the large room to give them privacy.

"You go," Ekaterina told Mariana. "I am fine. He is nice Russian man. We have lunch, I laugh at jokes, play nice, and leave. No worries. You have plans tonight, yes? Meeting with Alex. Someday, perhaps, you and I work together. I teach you."

"You teach me?" Mariana asked.

"When you decide who you are. Mara. If need help, I am here. You go now. I do this, then go home." She didn't tell Mariana, but she was looking forward to getting back to her cabin in Russia and learning how to garden from Dmitry's mother, who had been tending the plants. "Hello to Alex and Blondie for me, yes?"

Mariana shrugged, offered a short wave to Chekov, a last worried glance at her, and left.

Ekaterina turned to Vasily and glided across the floor, honing in on him.

"So, we are alone together," she said in Russian. "At last." It was meant as a joke, and he took it as one.

"At last. Alone and both uncomfortable, but we will make the best of it, yes?"

She nodded once to him, giving him credit. It had been an honest, straightforward reply. "Mariana says we owe you for your help. I am here. We pay our debts."

Vasily smiled. He seemed to be enjoying her candor. "Please consider your debt paid in full. I will not hold that over your head. If you hurry, you may catch your friend and ride down together. I'm afraid the elevator is old and slow. It happens to the best of us."

Ekatarina wondered if he was still being honest and decided he was. "I will stay," she said, surprising herself.

"Good. Let us sit and chat," he said, and they moved to a couch, which looked like an antique but turned out to be very comfortable.

"You are a billionaire." Ekat raised her hand at the ornate room's wallpaper, chandeliers, antique furniture, and vases with fresh flowers. "Money means little to me. I sleep on a cot with a thin mattress. My cabin has no heater, only a woodstove. It is far smaller than this room, barely larger than the elevator."

Vasily's eyebrows rose. "What is important to you?"

She shook her head dismissively.

Vasily waited. He seemed earnest in his interest, and Ekaterina didn't know what to say.

Her garden? The tiny plants she had started from seeds in the box at her cabin window as winter faded? They were hopefully growing better under the care of Dmitry's mother.

Was the quiet of her little town near the border of Finland important?

Clear winter nights with the air so cold she could barely breathe, and stars that seemed so close she could almost touch them?

Killing certainly no longer mattered to her. While she was very good at it, she longed to leave that world behind—though she had quickly agreed to both of the missions that had recently come her way.

What is important to me?

Fire burned in her stomach, and she crossed her arms tightly, but why was she so angry?

The truth was like a blow to her soul.

It is not anger, she thought. *It is defensiveness. Uncertainty. Fear.*

She didn't know how to do this… dance. It would have been easier to kill the man than to have this conversation with him.

"Books," she blurted out, simply to answer the question and end the uncomfortable silence. "I like to read."

It seemed like such a lame response. To sit and read the day away? Pitiful.

"Could I please show you something?" Vasily asked.

What could this be?

Most likely, this pompous billionaire wanted to impress her with a tour of this vast home or show her his wine collection. Or, worse, an extensive library filled with rare, first-edition books he hadn't read.

"Perhaps I shall go," she said. There was no need to suffer any longer, including through a long, uncomfortable lunch, though she had to admit the aroma from the kitchen made her salivate. Simple, classic Russian food. Fish—herring, perhaps, which had been her favorite when she was young. Black bread. Cabbage soup. Potatoes with meat patties.

It smelled like her home growing up, before her parents had been killed in a car crash and she'd been moved to a state-run orphanage to train as an assassin.

No, as good as the food might be, she had fulfilled her duty and paid Vasily back. He'd said so himself.

Vasily stood up from the couch. He looked uncomfortable and nervous —like her.

She stood also, torn between turning toward the elevator without another word or continuing with this… this… torture.

"Please," Vasily said in such a heartfelt way that she had to agree.

I am getting soft in my old age.

Vasily led her through kilometers of corridors until they reached a door which he unlocked with his fingerprint and opened to reveal an ornate bedroom.

"You bring me here?" she asked, amused.

Vasily shook his head. He waved his hand in a way that conveyed he had no such intentions, that this wasn't what he wanted to show her. He led her across the thick carpet toward the far corner and a closed door to what she guessed was a walk-in closet.

At this point, she had to go along. She had come this far, and her natural curiosity had gotten the better of her.

Besides, she could kill the man in seconds if he tried something.

Ekaterina joined Vasily at the door, where he had stopped, once again nervous but forging ahead, like she was doing.

Vasily gestured to the plush, gold comforter on the enormous bed, the thick pillows, the gold and silver striped wallpaper, the thick off-white carpet, elaborate drapes covering the windows, the large, stately furniture, the huge television attached to the wall across from the bed. "This," he said, voice low though they had yet to pass a single servant in the home. "All of it. It's… for show. Expected of me because of my wealth. Some things, I will admit, are enjoyable. But I've never cared about most of it. This," he nodded at the door. "This is the real me." Vasily opened the door.

Inside was a revelation. A walk-in closet, as she had guessed. But more than that.

The cot with the wool blanket was similar enough to her own that it made her pause. Vasily had nearly unlimited resources. Could he have found her cabin, sent a person there, taken pictures, and duplicated it, all guessing it would lead to this moment?

Preposterous. She kept part of her attention on Vasily as she stepped inside, however, in case he made a move.

There were several books on the shelves she had read in the past few months. Others she wanted to. Some she had never heard of. Most in English, though many were in Russian. She read both languages as well.

A simple, threadbare robe hung above a pair of worn wool slippers.

"I see from your reaction that, perhaps, we are not so dissimilar after all," Vasily said. "Will you stay for lunch? We can discuss books."

She turned to face him. "Yes," she said, and returned to browsing the books on the shelf. "I will stay for lunch."

The garden at her home in Russia could wait.

192

THE CABIN

Axe's Cabin
Rural Virginia

Axe stood on the porch to welcome the team as the sun went down. The air was crisp with a late-spring cold snap.

"Need me to vacuum again?" Mad Dog asked as he climbed the stairs to the front porch. He was first to arrive, as usual, often coming early to help Axe finish cleaning up.

"No, but you can check the oven. Special treat for you."

"No. You didn't."

"I did. Chicken parmesan and a few bottles of better beer than you normally drink. A light lager. It's not an Italian bistro in Greenwich Village, but it's the least I can do."

Mad Dog made an exaggerated show of wiping tears from his eyes before giving Axe a bear hug, nearly crushing him. "I love you, man."

He headed inside as Johnboy drove up.

"Thanks for taking charge for a while the last few days," Axe told the man, who stopped a few steps down so the two of them could be eye to eye. "Well done as usual."

"Anytime."

"Better go supervise Mad Dog in the kitchen," Axe said, and they shared a chuckle.

A large SUV pulled up. Gregory, Nancy, Dave, Marcus, and, surprisingly, Dawson "Void" Reite climbed out.

"Welcome," Axe said. "Go on in, grab a drink."

Haley's SUV was last. She had Tucci riding shotgun, and Tex in the back. Tucci had flown Tex down from New York and landed in a field down the road; Axe had set it up and gotten approval from his neighbor, who owned the land. Haley picked them up on the way in.

Axe shook their hands as Tucci and Tex headed inside. Haley stopped to stand on the porch and watch the sun going down with him.

"Ready to do this?" he asked. "Tex has a story to tell."

"It'll be interesting. She's got a lot going on inside her."

"Let's talk privately later."

"You got it, partner."

193

THE EMPLOYEE

Axe's Cabin
Rural Virginia

Gregory sat near the kitchen with Axe, the unofficial seats for the "officers," a step removed from the rest of the team.

The others were scattered around the room in chairs and on the large, worn sofa near the fireplace, which Axe had lit with a small fire against the colder weather that had crept in that day.

The group was quiet as they polished off pizzas, salad, and the chicken parm, which Mad Dog reluctantly agreed to share with everyone.

Gregory looked at Axe and got the go-ahead.

"I have some news," Gregory said. Void, sitting close to the fire, swallowed a bite of pizza and blushed.

"Dawson—excuse me, Void—was unfortunately caught clearly violating his parole agreement by using computers for hacking. Starting tomorrow morning, he'll be back in prison."

A silence filled the room.

"Correct me if I'm wrong," Mad Dog said around a mouthful of pizza before he swallowed. "But from what I heard, if he hadn't zapped the cell towers in Times Square—"

"The entire midtown area of Manhattan, from 57th Street to 23rd, and the Hudson to the East River," Dave corrected. He was always a stickler for details.

"Yeah, Times Square, Midtown, whatever. If he hadn't zapped them when he did, Axe might not be here now. Jade would have connected to the bomb and… Boom. No more Axe."

Gregory nodded. "That is quite likely. Going through official channels to coordinate with three separate cellular companies was taking too much time. He managed it much quicker."

"And he's going to prison? That's not right."

There were nods and grumbles all around.

"I agree," Gregory said, "but my hands are tied. Fortunately, though, I was able to pull some strings. Void will be staying at a minimum-security prison near Arlington, Virginia. He'll have a room on the ground floor."

"I looked it up online," Void said. "It's nice."

Gregory had a sinking feeling. "You looked it up… Tell me you didn't already hack their security and internal systems."

Void looked guilty as hell and refused to answer, while Mad Dog chuckled. "Right on, dude!" he whispered to Void.

"Moving on," Gregory said. "As part of his rehabilitation, Void will be allowed to leave the facility for up to nine hours a day for work, as long as he is shuttled back and forth." Gregory paused for effect. "Ladies and gentlemen, I'd like to introduce you to the Central Analysis Group's newest hire, Dawson Reite."

"Hot damn!" Mad Dog said while the others clapped.

"Dawson's security clearance will be quite limited, but I'm sure we'll put him to good work."

"Weren't you dating an IT woman from the office?" Haley asked.

Void blushed. "It might be easier now that we're not so far apart," he said.

"In addition, Haley heard from Ekaterina…"

"She heard from her government," Haley said, taking up the story. "The missing cesium-137 was found. It had been transferred to a different container. Someone had spared the old container from destruction and, apparently, provided it to Boris, who sold it to Jade Pang. The paperwork was 'misfiled.' There is no ongoing threat."

"I'm so relieved," Mad Dog said around another bite of pizza.

The others chuckled at his banter, but Gregory offered words that only Axe could have heard. "Me, too, my friend. Me, too."

194

THE STORY

Axe's Cabin
Rural Virginia

Mariana joined the others in congratulating Void, then helped clean up.

When the leftovers were put away and everyone had fresh drinks, they returned to their seats.

The kitchen lights had been turned off, which made the cabin darker. Only a few of the lamps in the living room were on. Between them and the glow from the fire, there was plenty of light to see, but not enough to feel like anyone was in the spotlight.

The perfect setting for stories.

People sipped their beers, stared at the fire, and waited for someone to go first.

Mariana had been holding the story in for only thirty-six hours, but in another way, it had been years coming. She had to get it out.

"So no shit, there I was," she said, her voice choked with emotion. She stopped, cleared her throat, took a sip of beer, and continued. "On a boat with two people who had each killed more people than I had."

"After what I saw in Los Angeles?" Mad Dog said. "That's saying something. Just sayin'."

She glared at Mad Dog and continued. Most of this had been left out of the bare-bones report she'd provided yesterday.

"On the yacht, Ekaterina and I put Boris to bed like a sleepy child," Mariana said. "And all I could think about was my uncle. When his mind started going, I was in my early twenties, working at a boring job in the dead-end southwest Texas town where Axe found me." She raised her bottle to toast him before returning to the memories of her uncle.

"'I'm forgetting stuff, kiddo,' my uncle said one day," Mariana said, imitating his voice. "He always called me kiddo. 'Not normal old-age-y things, either. I have an appointment with the doctors in the city next week. They'll do tests and tell me what I already know. I'm losing it.'

"I told him he'd be fine, that things would work out. He let me ramble on, saying what you say in a time like that.

"We were at the picnic table in his back yard. My mom—his sister—was inside making sandwiches for lunch. Every few days, Mom had been stopping by to help out, and she had demanded I come along that day. Uncle John had something to tell me.

"My uncle leaned in so my mom couldn't overhear. 'If it gets bad, I need you to do me a big favor.'

"I got what he was saying—or not saying. I was always a tomboy, despite these curves, and knew my way around weapons. Uncle John didn't have one, but at home, Dad had a gun safe with a hunting rifle, an old 9mm pistol, and a 22-caliber plunker pistol for shooting cans and targets in the desert.

"'I can't do that,' I told Uncle John.

"'You can. If it gets bad, I'm telling you: it's what I want. By then, I won't be able to do it—or even ask. I won't have the capacity. And right now, it's too early. That's why I'm asking now, while I still can. Planning ahead.'

"'I'd get arrested,' I said, and I had him there.

"But after a few seconds, he shook his head. 'Yes, you'll probably get arrested, but no jury will convict you. It would obviously be an act of mercy. And I'll write it out, give it to you. Hell, have it notarized. But you have to promise me you'll do it.'

"'You always said you have to play the hand you're dealt in life,' I said. It was like his mantra or code, the man never shut up about it. Anytime someone complained, it'd be, 'You gotta play the hand that's dealt ya.'

"Mom came out carrying a tray. Uncle John patted my arm and whispered to me before she got close. 'I'm trusting you to do the right thing when the time comes, kiddo. I know it's a lot to ask. But you can do it. When you see me in a month or two, you'll know that's the truth of it.'

"Later, when we were ready to go, he didn't say anything else. Just, 'Goodbye, kiddo,' with a wink and a smile.

"It was the last time I saw him—the real him, I mean. The man I'd known and loved. He went downhill fast, but his body hung on a while. I guess that's pretty common. He died six months after our talk."

Mad Dog raised his eyebrows at her, sincere and serious, not making a joke of it.

"He died of natural causes," she added. "He fell asleep holding my mom's hand… and slipped away.

"What Boris said during his tirade made my skin crawl. He admitted the horrible things he'd done. What happened to him when he was a child doesn't make up for what he did. But when we were waiting for him to come back out of the cabin afterward, I went over the conversation with my uncle. Maybe I should have…"

She paused, and no one said anything for a minute.

"What did you decide to do—on the boat?" Mad Dog asked. "Did it depend on which Boris you found?"

She looked over at him. "I walked to the cabin door, knocked, and went in. The window was open. His clothes were on the bed. Neatly folded. He must have stripped to wiggle through the window. He was gone."

Mariana hadn't answered Mad Dog, because she didn't know the answer herself.

"The way Ekaterina and I handled it," she said after they'd sipped their beer for a minute. "Giving Boris that time. And him squeezing through that little window, going into the cold water miles from shore. Drowning. He had to have been himself to crawl out the window and try to escape. The docile guy with dementia wouldn't have done that, right?"

No one spoke. "Ask the real question," Axe eventually prodded.

Mariana hesitated, then got it out. "Should I have… Was giving him that chance…" She looked around the room. "What we did… Was it mercy? Or revenge for all the people he killed?"

It took a while for anyone to answer, but Axe finally spoke. "A bit of both, I think."

195

THE SEVEN

Axe's Cabin
Rural Virginia

It was late. Axe stood on the front porch admiring the stars and ignoring the cold.

Inside, the others bustled around, prepping sleeping bags, pillows, and blankets for those who wanted to sleep over. Void, Gregory, Nancy, and Dave would head home. Tucci and Mariana were debating, but Axe figured Tucci loved his helicopter too much to let it sit in a field overnight.

Haley joined him on the porch. "Well," she said. The word summed up so much. The mission. Void's new job. The weight Mariana carried from her younger days—and the day before.

"Yeah."

"Another one in the books."

"A good team." Axe counted them out on his fingers. "Back at headquarters: Gregory, Nancy, Dave, Marcus. You, for a while. Everyone was absolutely essential. Nancy had the original suspicions—we wouldn't have had anything without that. Plus Void in the apartment hacking the hell out of everything, but only getting caught for a little of it, luckily. And we have to give credit to whoever Ekaterina relied on for intel."

He looked at Haley, then the stars, and continued. "In the field: You, at the end, running and gunning despite your best efforts. Me, Mad Dog,

Johnboy, Tex, Ekaterina, and Tucci in the bird. Seven in all. And it wouldn't have happened without every single one of us."

"Don't get used to me helping you out in the field. I'm proud of my restraint this time and hope to get better. The office is the place for me. I'm sure of it."

Axe stared at the sky, not bothering to hide his smile—but not arguing with her, either.

"There are still a lot of questions about Jade Pang and the others," Haley said. "We might not ever find the answers."

Axe chuckled. "Not exactly my department."

Haley turned to him. "Are you back in the groove? You know who you are and what you're supposed to be doing?"

"Thanks to your help, yes. I'm back. All in, all the time. And ready for whatever comes next."

196

AUTHOR'S NOTE

Thank you so much for reading.

If you've finished all the books in the Unsanctioned Asset series (learn more at https://geni.us/UA-Series), the excitement continues with the Covert Asset series.

Check out ***Target: Redacted***, featuring a new hero along with several of your favorite characters from the Unsanctioned Asset Series.

Target: Redacted

Someone is killing Americans.
The suspect is connected at the highest levels.
Confronting him is impossible.
Still, justice must be served…

Long-retired Navy SEAL Thomas "T-Bone" Marks left the warrior business behind years ago. He's now a happy, small-town teacher—until the wheels come off his world.

A clandestine intelligence agency offers to help Thomas reclaim his life—in exchange for a few days of his time.

More attacks may be coming. Someone must find out the truth before it's too late.

Someone completely off the radar.

Someone expendable—and with nothing to lose.

Someone like Thomas.

He's now a man with a mission and back in the warrior business—whether he's ready for it or not.

Read the pulse-pounding, action-packed thriller!

Type this short link into your browser for more details and to order your copy. https://geni.us/Target-Redacted

(You can also order it from your favorite local bookstore.)

- Get a free prequel short story about Axe's first mission (along with my newsletter). Go to: https://www.authorbradlee.com/operationrapidrevenge
- If you enjoyed the book, please leave a five-star ranking or a written review. It helps new readers discover the book and makes it possible for me to continue bringing you stories.
- I'm active on social media, sharing photos (like Axe would take) and writing progress updates. I also occasionally ask for input on character names, plot points, or reader preferences as I'm writing, so please follow me and help out. Find me here:
- Facebook: https://www.facebook.com/AuthorBradLee
- Instagram: https://www.instagram.com/bradleeauthor/
- Note: in *A Team of Seven*, I used the names of some real places but fictionalize many details. I also take inspiration from areas but change names and some features to improve the story. My apologies if you live in or are acquainted with one of the areas and think, "Wait, that's not right." You're correct. License was taken in describing places as well as technology, equipment, weapons, tactics, and military capabilities. Where location details, distances, or technical issues conflicted with the story, I prioritized the story.
- Finally, please join me in thanking Beth, Sue, and Crystal for their help. The book is far better because of them.